continued . . .

"An unforgettable romance for anyone who has ever wondered what it would be like to love and then lose the world's sexiest rock star. *Perfect Timing* takes the reader on a vicarious thrill ride into world of fame, fortune, and family secrets, and stays with you like your favorite rock ballad. *Perfect Timing* deserves a standing ovation." —Karin Gillespie, author of the *Bottom Dollar Girl* series

"In *Beautiful Disaster*, Laura Spinella weaves the past into the present with a sure hand as she tests the boundary between love and obsession. With its evocative Southern setting and finely drawn characters, *Beautiful Disaster* confronts the reader head-on with this question: What would you risk for a love you know is right and true?" —Diane Chamberlain, author of *Necessary Lies*

"*Beautiful Disaster* is a beautifully crafted romance set against a Southern backdrop. A powerful tale about the power of love. A wonderful read."
—Wendy Wax, author of *While We Were Watching Downton Abbey*

"*Beautiful Disaster* is a lovely, sexy, soulful debut."
—Jean Reynolds Page, author of *Safe Within*

"A wonderfully intense romance that is sure to please fans of relationship fiction . . . *Beautiful Disaster* will keep you turning pages until you reach the end and find all the answers."
—Susan McBride, author of *The Truth About Love and Lightning*

Berkley Books by Laura Spinella

BEAUTIFUL DISASTER

PERFECT TIMING

Perfect Timing

LAURA SPINELLA

BERKLEY BOOKS, NEW YORK

THE BERKLEY PUBLISHING GROUP
Published by the Penguin Group
Penguin Group (USA) LLC
375 Hudson Street, New York, New York 10014

USA • Canada • UK • Ireland • Australia • New Zealand • India • South Africa • China

penguin.com

A Penguin Random House Company

This book is an original publication of The Berkley Publishing Group.

Library of Congress Cataloging-in-Publication Data

Spinella, Laura.
Perfect timing / Laura Spinella.—Berkley trade paperback edition.
pages cm.
ISBN 978-0-425-26730-1 (pbk.)
1. Women radio producers and directors—Fiction. I. Title.
PS3619.P5635P47 2013
813'.6—dc23
2013025889

PUBLISHING HISTORY
Berkley trade paperback edition / November 2013

PRINTED IN THE UNITED STATES OF AMERICA

10 9 8 7 6 5 4 3 2 1

Cover photo © Ilina Simeonova/Trevillion Images.
Cover design by Rita Frangie.
Interior text design by Kristin del Rosario.

For Megan

ACKNOWLEDGMENTS

Thank you to Susan Ginsburg for continuing to champion my work. Her insight is singular and her suggestions always on point. I love to write for her. Much appreciation to Stacy Testa as well; it's an honor to be counted among the authors at Writers House.

I have a gem of an editor in Leis Pederson. She is patient and smart, and always willing to listen; working with her is an absolute pleasure. My thanks to the entire team at Berkley, everyone who helped move this book from wishful draft to finished product.

There are first readers, in-between readers, and last-pass readers. With the assistance of Kimberly Hixson, Christine Lemp, Marianne Lonati, Jamie Spinella, and Megan Spinella, I was fortunate to have these valuable readers at each milestone. A special thank-you to author Maria Geraci; she's an incredible writer and an incisive reader. Much appreciation to AuthorBytes founder Steve Bennett, my charming, patient part-time boss and kind friend. Without Melisa Holmes, life, books, and wine wouldn't be nearly as much fun. She continues to be my thirty-year tether to good sense and the sublime.

Thank you to the professional folks who generously lent their expert advice: Jennifer Lehman, Deputy District Attorney, Schuylkill County, Pennsylvania; author and attorney David Ellis;

Walt Sosnowski, retired Sergeant, NYPD; and Melisa Holmes, who willingly donned her doctor hat to oversee my medical facts.

As always, much appreciation to the home team: Matt and Megan, Jamie and Grant. They are the real people in this house, who generously make room for the fictional ones. And those people always take up far more space than I intended.

CHAPTER ONE

Providence, Rhode Island

THERE WAS NOTHING ENTICING ABOUT WAKING UP TO A THREE-hundred-pound man who smelled faintly of cheese—even if he was a silver-tongued veteran. Worse, he'd managed to utter the name *Aidan Royce* before Isabel could untangle mascara-laced lashes, prying open an eye. Her hand groped for the volume as radio DJ Chip Wrangle wrapped things up, Isabel hearing a velvet-timbre mention of the Grammy-winning, mega-selling music icon. But that couldn't be right, she wagered, sitting upright. "Hey, did he just say—"

Rico ignored her, responding to the DJ's voice as he always did, lazily stretching and vacating the bed. Isabel cocked her head at the radio. As the content manager for *98.6—The Normal FM for Easy Listening,* she'd put a firm moratorium on celebrity gossip. But the aromatic Chip made no other reference, moving on to their Monday-morning salute to the '60s. "Just a dream," she said, flopping back onto the pillow. A hazy gaze floated upward, Frankie Valli and the Four Seasons crooning "Walk Like a Man" as Rico and his virile gait disappeared into the kitchen. He insisted on his breakfast and she rolled into reality, yelling, "I'm coming!" The two had met while Isabel was vacationing in Key West, Rico a refugee she'd picked up near the Hemingway House. He was the definition of *machismo*, excessive manliness an inbred trait. Dangling her noticeably more feminine legs over the side, Isabel tucked a thick thatch of hair behind her ear. She did a fast double take at the radio before rising. On her way out of the bedroom she grabbed a robe and a glance in the mirror. "Oh, good gosh! Seriously?" She wet her fingertips, only managing to smear a smudge of mascara, doubly relieved that it was just Rico.

Following the sounds of his disgruntled demand, before daring to fill a coffee cup, Isabel set about preparing his breakfast. But she did turn on the television as she passed through the living room. There she picked up a telltale trail: necktie, camisole, sport coat, flouncy skirt, undershirt, one black high heel. She brushed by an empty wine bottle, a mediocre merlot that had instigated last night. Rico called again, squashing an amorous visual. "Enough already!" There was a death stare in the kitchen where two sets of cat-green eyes pulsed. The TV blared. Just to make her point she smiled and hesitated. "Say again? Matt Lauer is drowning you out!" But it was smell, not sound, that dominated as odor penetrated from beneath a popped tin top. She couldn't deny him, even as she gagged, Rico's cries morphing into a loud purr, rubbing lovingly against her leg. She set the bowl of stinky fish on the floor, scratching a tufted ear as he gobbled hunks of vacuum-packed sardine. "*Bueno, Rico? Sí, bueno,*" Isabel said, having mastered a couple of words in what she assumed to be his native dialect.

From her squatted position Isabel listened. She waited for national media to repeat local radio news and confirm that Aidan Royce was, in fact, dead. It was the only fathomable reason for it to have made the 98.6 morning-host chat. Not dead, as it turned out. Just under arrest. Rico wriggled out from ardent strokes as Isabel absorbed Lauer's words about Aidan Royce and a high-speed chase, driving drunk, and assaulting an officer. She flipped him off, stalking back to the bedroom.

The ride to work was work, Isabel listening for another 98.6 update, mentally composing a strongly worded email to Chip Wrangle. But the seven-fifteen chat slot was filled with their bimonthly visit from Eleanor Papp, who ran the Providence Humane Society. She only talked about adoptable pets and donations the shelter needed. While 98.6 listeners were old school, conventional to the point of mundane, they were not without a heart. Isabel found the radio station offices quiet, beating Tanya and Mary Louise to work. The sound system wasn't on and she made no effort to correct the matter. Whether it came from Chip Wrangle, CNN, or two soup cans tied to a string, Aidan Royce would dominate the airwaves and Isabel wasn't interested. Before shifting gears she crafted an email to Chip where she bolded the words *miscreant media blight.* A Sunday-night ratings dilemma would dominate Isabel's morning, though she did take time to call Nate. He'd bounded out of her bed at an ungodly three a.m. leaving most of his belongings behind. "Hey, sorry you had to run away to the hospital. I'm guessing you found your shirt. I, um . . . I had a really great time, Nate. Despite some *miscreant* radio business," she said, brusquely hitting Send, "I've been thinking about what you asked." Isabel paused into the empty air of voicemail. "We'll definitely talk about it later." She hung up, smiling, feeling less peeved at Chip as Tanya breezed through the door. She was an impish gust of human energy. With doughnut in mouth, she waved a free hand, a double, whipped cream mochaccino in the other, immediately turning on the TV.

"Hey, Isabel. Mornin', sweetie." She sat, adjusting a leopard-print scarf as she arranged herself behind her desk.

"Morning, Tanya."

"Look at you," she said, an overly tweezed eyebrow arching. "Is that a little Monday-morning afterglow I see?" Isabel didn't

answer. Tanya was always on the lookout for a love connection—
Isabel's, her own, or anyone else's. They exchanged a smile, Isabel's
fading as Tanya raised the volume, though she couldn't really
argue. Working in the promotions/scheduling/content department
of a sizable radio station made current events relevant and real
news important. Aidan Royce was neither in Isabel's opinion, just
another self-absorbed celebrity, acting contrite for the cameras and
aghast when the world paused to gawk.

Aside from monitoring real news, it was their job to make the
yesteryear station go, dream up the giveaways, and organize
reunion concerts. An anomaly, the *98.6—The Normal FM* audience thrived on AM classics and an occasional tribute-to-soft-rock
weekend, a dash of country before country went mainstream. Of
course, she did wonder what might happen when their baby-
boomer listeners died off. That or satellite radio squeezed them
out. Isabel was a few years younger than her co-workers, although
she supervised the three-prong department. While their jobs were
important, they didn't translate into talent, meaning they didn't
rate separate offices like the DJs. It was fine. They were a great
team and good friends. Isabel liked sharing with Tanya and Mary
Louise most days. Maybe, just not so much today.

Gliding in as silently as a librarian, Mary Louise would give
anyone the first impression of prim and proper. But after three
years at the radio station Isabel was still peeling back layers. A
kale and flaxseed smoothie was in one hand, while clutched in
Mary Louise's other was last week's *In Touch* magazine. She got
it for free, i.e., swiped it from the recycle bin at the convenience
store on Madison. Her polar-opposite co-workers filled each other's gaps. The reckless squall that described one complemented the
other's curious albeit structured life. Tanya was a three-time divorcée that polite company might refer to as overly social. Tanya had
been to church, been to bars, and been to bed in hopes of meeting

Mr. Right there. But she was also adept at repurposing that well of emotion, making up as a mother what she lacked in man sense. She had plenty of practice with a child from each marriage. Mary Louise, on the other hand, was a serial monogamist, married and childless for seven years. She'd married a man named Joe Bland. No kidding. They'd met while stocking up at the Dollar Tree in Woonsocket, though frugality had come at a price. Last month Isabel rushed to meet an unusually frazzled Mary Louise in the emergency room. In an attempt to tap in to *mature audience* movies via an overhead cable wire, Joe took a tumble off the roof and broke a number of bones. Like standard radio and last week's gossip, Joe's wife felt certain avenues of entertainment should be free. But as those layers revealed, Mary Louise's naughty habits ran deep, quickly joining Tanya's tabloid-television vigil.

"Have you seen this? The drunk-driving thing, you'd expect that from somebody like him," she said, crossing to her neat-as-a-pin desk. "But a high-speed chase and assaulting an officer? That's bad behavior even for a known bad boy!" Her arm flailed so fervently it was look or be struck. Isabel recognized old news footage, a nightclub brawl that had involved the rock god years before.

"Aidan Royce tied to the whipping post of fame—go figure." Isabel rolled her eyes, saved from further comment as an email from Nate popped up. *Definitely did not want to run away. An unavoidable hazard of that medical oath. I was looking forward to a sleepy you. More important, I was looking forward to an answer. You know how to keep a guy in suspense.* She smiled, wondering how she might have discreetly engineered a six a.m. makeover. Admiring the email for a second longer Isabel went back to work, but not before seeing Aidan Royce hustled past frothing media and into a police station. It was only the half of it, a boisterous swell of female fans having assembled in his defense. Isabel guessed they let him tweet the urgent call to action from the cruiser.

"When I heard Chip say his name," Tanya said, coming around to stand beside Mary Louise, "I thought for sure he was dead."

"I thought the same thing!" she gasped, grasping her arm. "Couldn't you just see it? Sheer California cliffs, a drug-induced sex-capade, maybe an encounter with a deranged fan . . ." She paused, finishing her smoothie. "What did you think, Isabel?"

"I thought it was a fatal fall off his ego."

"Well, there's no excuse for driving like a maniac and endangering other people or punching a cop. I wouldn't be surprised if he got real time."

Reopening the email from Nate, Isabel debated a reply. She glanced up, half listening. "You really think he'll go to jail?"

"Maybe." Her slim shoulders shrugged, clearly intrigued.

Isabel looked between her co-workers at the TV. Media outlets were already on the scene, catching a probing glance of Aidan Royce's backside at a booking desk, his hands cuffed. She sucked in a breath, wondering how many times people needed to see a scene like that. How many times did she? "Confined reflection might do him good." She wanted to type *YES! YES! YES!* in reply to Nate but opted for a winking smiley instead. Big moments were better in person.

"He won't do a day in jail," Tanya said. "Maybe some cushy community service."

"That's true. Celebrity like his is so above the law," Mary Louise lamented, more disappointed than miffed. She filled the coffeemaker, her peripheral glance on the TV. "But that's what happens when you wear the triple crown of fame—talent, looks, and filthy rich. With this," she said, gesturing, "you can add the fantasy element of wickedly untamed."

"A scandalous lifestyle suits him, that's for sure." Tanya remained one with the TV, absently brushing doughnut crumbs from a fuzzy fuchsia sweater. It was a fitting complement to her bright red hair. "Aidan Royce is a textbook man-crush and all women find him irresistible."

"Not all," Isabel insisted, teeth sinking into the eraser tip of her pencil.

"Your average movie or pop star, it wouldn't be such a big deal. But when it's someone like Aidan Royce, it's way . . . way more . . ."

"Titillating?" Mary Louise suggested, Tanya nodding. "Barring an international crisis or freak weather phenomenon, it's all we'll hear for days."

"Super," Isabel muttered, studying the segments for *Sunday Evening with Country's Best.*

"Who knows what else will turn up? I heard they strip-searched him and his car. There could be drugs, maybe a sex tape. Camera equipment is so discreet nowadays and user friendly."

While *"You work in radio, you would know that how?"* ticked through Isabel's head, she prudently stayed on task.

"Wouldn't surprise me," Tanya said. "Did you see the woman he was with? Last October's Miss October."

"I saw the dress she was wearing. I own dish towels made of more fabric," Mary Louise said, mashing the remote only to come up with the same loop on channel four. "His publicist said she wasn't anybody, that Aidan was just *'giving her a ride.'* But Fox News reported that he kidnapped her!"

Tanya's head cocked. "He's Aidan Royce. Why would he have to kidnap her?"

Riding the tidal wave of sensationalism, Mary Louise paused. "Good point."

"And his publicist can spin it however she likes. Nobody's going to believe the *'giving her a ride'* story," Tanya said, punctuating the air with quotation marks. "Certainly not his current girlfriend."

"Oh that's right. I forgot about her."

"So did he, apparently," Isabel said, a hand gripping around her neck, vigorously erasing segments for *Sunday Evening with Country's Best.*

"And she's no centerfold—a lawyer from New York, I think."

Isabel glanced up, though the eraser kept moving.

"No way," said Mary Louise. "Centerfold is much more believable."

"It's true. Actually, I read they were engaged."

The back-and-forth motion of the eraser stopped, Isabel eyeing them. "Really?" she said, a droll smile curving over her mouth. "Engaged?"

"It was all over the tabloids a couple of months back."

Isabel returned to her work and penciled in *Delilah,* thinking listeners might tune in to the syndicated melodrama.

"Triple crown or not, good luck to the woman who ends up with him. Married to a rock star, it's glamorous but fatal." Mary Louise poured herself coffee, smirking at the TV. "Seriously, when does that ever work out?"

"And don't you mean *women*? Celebrity marriages are more disposable than mine," Tanya said. "There'll be three or four wives between stints in rehab."

"Maybe he'll do a reality-TV show, *Polygamy and the Rock God.* Heaven knows, I'd tune in," she said. "It would draw huge ratings when two or three end up pregnant."

On her words, the point to Isabel's pencil snapped, piercing her paperwork.

"Some women are so blind," Tanya lamented. "Clearly, he's a womanizing scoundrel."

Clearly, Tanya didn't recognize her own lack of foresight when it came to this particular character trait. Shifting restlessly, Isabel admonished the unkind thought.

"You said it," Mary Louise agreed, swirling Splenda and skim milk.

"I mean, just look at that tattoo on his neck. It only emphasizes his twisted boundaries."

The comment drew Isabel's attention, her gaze veering from Tanya's squint onto Aidan Royce's latest mug shot, his blond *GQ* looks forever marred by a coiled snake. It traveled from the base of his collarbone upward, its sharp tongue splitting at the edge of a Boeing-inspired jaw.

"Reminds me of a Japanese bondage rope," Mary Louise said, tipping her head at the screen. "And not a very realistic one. He probably dabbles in the basics, thinks he knows something."

"And if he was really into it?" Tanya queried.

Mary Louise sipped her coffee, shrugging. "Had he wanted to make a real S&M statement, he could have gone with a nipple clamp, combo riding crop—maybe a slave collar."

There was a hum of wonder from Tanya, Isabel murmuring, "Please make it stop." Abandoning Sunday night's ratings she moved onto next month's teasers, which led up to their big summer giveaway, Fruit of the Month Club for a year.

"Though I will say, whatever his motivation, a tattoo like that took nerve." Popping on her glasses, she peered harder. "I bet his record label made him do it."

"No way," Tanya said. "Everybody knows the tattoo was a symbol of Aidan's commitment to Fiona Free, the British blonde with the sitcom."

"Oh, that's right. How long were they together?"

"Until her show got canceled and she moved back to London. Two episodes in, I think."

Instead of just snapping the point, Isabel snapped the pencil right in two. "That's not true."

"What's not true?" Mary Louise said, her steaming coffee cup frozen midair.

"That's not how he got the tattoo."

She smiled, bemused. "And how would you know that?"

"I . . . I read it somewhere."

"No you didn't. You hate gossip magazines. More to the point, you don't know the first thing about celebrity lifestyles, particularly someone like Aidan Royce."

"I might know more than you think, Mary Louise." She meant to end there, but found herself caught between two intent stares, her mouth moving ahead of her brain. "Maybe he wasn't always what you see. Maybe *miscreant media blight* didn't always define him. Maybe once, a lifetime ago, there was some substance to Aidan Royce." She rose as she spoke, her co-workers looking as if, maybe, Isabel had lost her mind. "Anyway," she said, sitting, grasping at self-possession and a defense theory that would have made his publicist proud. "I can't speak for high-speed chases, drunk driving, or punching a cop. But you're wrong about the tattoo."

"Have you been watching *Access Hollywood*, maybe sneaking some after-hours *TMZ*? It's okay to admit you're susceptible, Isabel."

"Don't be ridiculous. I wouldn't waste my time."

"So how is it you know something like that?"

"I just do."

"But how?" Mary Louise pressed, skepticism bearing down.

"It's irrelevant. Can't you just take my word for it?"

"Not really. Besides, you brought it up. So how do you know?"

"Because . . ."

"Because how? Just tell me."

"It doesn't matter."

"Oh, but I think it does."

"I know," she said, swallowing hard, grabbing up the pieces of the broken pencil, "because I was there when he got it."

CHAPTER TWO

Catswallow, Alabama
Seven Years Earlier

A IDAN ROYCROFT, I WAS UNDER THE IMPRESSION THIS RELA-
tionship meant something to you!" Shanna O'Rourke's
gooey drawl dropped a decibel, but every patron seated outside
Higher Grounds heard—including Otis Dibbs who washed dishes
in the back and was deaf in one ear. "You've lived up to your god-
awful reputation and then some!" Sitting with an iced coffee in
one hand, an Austen novel in the other, Isabel pretended to be
engrossed in a tragic love scene. Really, she was glued to this one.

"Shanna, it's a date, not a lifetime commitment. Jesus, what's the
big deal? You leave for your stuck-up Sour Bush in a few weeks
anyway," Aidan said, leaning against a fiery-red convertible. It was
a close match to the current color of Shanna's burning cheeks.

"Sweet Briar . . . it's Sweet Briar College," she corrected, as though
his error was less than intentional. "So is that your excuse? Are you
saying if I were staying here, in Catswallow, you wouldn't have
cheated?"

Aidan's mouth opened and closed, his arms grazing through
empty air before coming to rest on the car frame. "I didn't cheat,"
he said, his gaze darting toward the crowd. "You and me, we

weren't *a thing*. Look, not that it matters, but Ashley Warren was a family friend, nothing more. I showed her Catswallow. That's it."

"Showed her plenty more than that from what I heard," she said, standing between Aidan and the open car door.

"Seriously, look around," he said gesturing toward a downtown trimmed in old elms, vintage storefronts, and a palpable 1950s vibe. "Highlights include the old lynching post and the site of the 1936 molasses factory flood."

"Does it also include a moonlight view of the lake? I understand there was serious horizontal stargazing." Her knowledge of the likely fact caught Aidan off guard, long enough for Shanna to slam the car door, nearly catching his fingers in it. "Tell me, is it part of the standard Roycroft tour? Because if it is, we missed that stop on my excursion."

He narrowed his eyes. "Actually, Shanna, you got the standard tour. The lake is part of the VIP package—reserved for a select few."

Her finely boned jaw dropped, her delicate hands balling into tight fists. "I . . . I just can't believe you'd humiliate me like this! I thought we had something special! After I . . . after we . . ."

Isabel sucked hard through a straw, down to the icy bottom of her drink. She rolled her eyes, catching Aidan doing the same thing. Since she'd arrived in Catswallow, middle school through high school this was the pattern: Girls saw any relationship with Aidan as too real. And Aidan? Well, he didn't see it at all. It amazed her how not one of them could figure this out. The debutante blonde, who a few generations prior would have arrived in crinoline with her mammy in tow, continued to lob accusations. Isabel suspected the busy location was a purposeful choice on Shanna's part. Unlike crinoline and mammies, high drama had not gone out of style. Mutual friends sat mesmerized, abandoning lesser gossip and french fries as they turned to gawk. Higher Grounds waitstaff and strangers did the same. Shanna's performance on a steamy Lovett Street escalated as Aidan calmly reiterated his point. They were each other's date for the town's time-honored gala, a stunning send-off for Catswallow High's newest alumni. Anything more, Aidan insisted, was all in her head. Shanna was undeterred. When her voice hit a shrill that couldn't strike a higher pitch, not without rupturing a vocal cord, the moment seemed to climax. Isabel assumed that was it. She guessed Aidan thought the same thing as he stood up straight and stepped onto the curb. It was an ill-fated error as Shanna made use of the target, Aidan taking the full brunt of her flailing hand across his face.

Everything stopped. Isabel stiffened harder than her wrought-iron chair. Her own hand gripped her cheek, feeling the sting twenty feet away. There was an echo of gasps, Jake Summerfield, a fellow Catswallow graduate, offering his input, "Damn, Roycroft, you sure can piss 'em off." The commotion sputtered and rumbled, finally settling until it was only Aidan standing center stage. Isabel was sure that his face burned hotter than the August pavement, but his casual manner never faltered. Everyone, including Shanna, watched in arrested amazement. And because Aidan was at his best under pressure, in the limelight, he never missed a beat.

He looked back, smiling. It was such an electric smile; Birmingham could draw kilowatts off it. "Nice shot," he said, his tone never vacillating. "Let's consider that closure. Forget any plan we had for Catswallow's grand finale." The haughty look on Shanna's face evaporated, realizing she'd taken the drama one step too far. Her arctic-blue eyes peeled wide, but it was too late. A week before one tiny town's mega event, a tradition survived and celebrated by generations, she'd lost the most sought-after date in decades. Aidan didn't look her way again as he reached into the backseat of her car and retrieved a guitar case. Salacious whispers stuck eagerly to humid air as onlookers pretended to go about their business. Isabel refocused, returning to Mr. Darcy and Elizabeth. But as she half expected, Aidan hesitated near the edge of her table. It was just long enough to say, "The farmhouse, Isabel, okay?"

An "uh huh" rumbled from her throat. She didn't look as he continued, alone, down Lovett Street.

IT WASN'T WHAT PEOPLE ASSUMED. NOT THAT PEOPLE ASSUMED ANY-thing about Aidan and Isabel. Their relationship flew under the radar of Catswallow gossip, but it wasn't the fare or *affair* the secluded setting of a dilapidated farmhouse might suggest. It was more like home base. The friendship meant everything to Isabel, a girl transplanted into a tin can container on a rural swatch of Alabama. Aidan lived in the next lot over, although most people assumed he lived in a McMansion near the country club. Aidan didn't wear poor very well.

His father, John Roycroft, abandoned his common-law wife before his son turned two. Rumor said he was an incredible musician, having missed his window by living in Catswallow. Aidan claimed no memory of him or his talent, but anyone who could hear saw the proof. His absence hadn't made much difference. Aidan did all right by his mother, though the scene on Lovett Street wasn't the best example of that. But Isabel also didn't see it as entirely his fault. Popularity was a dubious honor that befell him like the demands of royal lineage. Isabel, on the other hand, was all commoner, if not carpetbagger, having moved to the tiny Southern town from New Jersey six years before. It was an awkward time for both, Aidan adjusting to being a singular object of interest while Isabel made a bumpy entry into adolescence. Aside from a Jersey drawl, vastly different from the soft twang of her new peers, it was clear that Isabel was no Southern belle. Nothing was right: her clothes, her attitude, her name, which this deep-rooted culture insisted on shortening to Bella. A week after arriving, Bella, alternately known as *"that Yankee girl,"* slipped getting off the bus and fell face-first into a red puddle of sludge. If being the new Northerner in a school full of grits-eating, *y'all*-dripping Southerners was bad, doing it covered in mud sealed her fate. Things went from bad to worse, Isabel teased to the point where she was ready to run away back to New Jersey and her father, who had incited the adventure south with their mother.

Most of that was your standard story of betrayal. Isabel's father had an affair. She could say that now and without any therapy. Of course, who he had the affair with was the truly stunning part, and the part Isabel couldn't forgive. Initially, Eric Lang and his new money made grand gestures and a lot of noise about joint custody. It was almost believable. Before his affair, life felt pretty perfect. He destroyed it. Years removed, any fatherly feelings had faded, though he still wrote letters, likely spurred by his analyst's advice. They went unopened, Isabel taking them and a lighter to the farmhouse. Aidan would watch as envelopes and anger smoldered, Isabel reducing it all to a pile of glowing ash. The ritual drove him crazy, but he'd learned to keep his opinion to himself. Isabel was certain that if Aidan got a letter from his father, it would be an irresistible temptation.

Inadvertently, fatefully, Aidan diverted her from thoughts of her father and the Catswallow hell in which she was living. Isabel had discovered an abandoned farmhouse a few miles from the trailer park, often going there straight from the bus. While she was sitting on the floor in one of the upstairs bedrooms, that day, a rock flew through the window. By then Isabel had her fill of Southern hospitality and decided to show them what a Jersey girl was all about. She hurled the rock back. It missed Aidan's face by an inch. It turned out he wasn't throwing the rock at her. He didn't even know she was inside. Stella Roycroft, Aidan's mother, was a sweet woman who had the world's worst luck at keeping a job, or so Isabel learned as the years went on. Aidan was blowing off steam over her most recent trip to the unemployment line, winging the rock out of frustration. He returned the smooth but sizable stone to her, Isabel sure the incident would result in her exile from Folsom Middle School. Instead, he said he was sorry she'd missed. He liked the idea of an edgy scar marring his looks. It sparked something inside Isabel, a merger of gratitude and realization, a bond that felt as solid as the rock. Not everyone was what he or she appeared. Not even this beautiful boy who stood before her. There was a rift in his voice; a sincerity that said he was more than Catswallow's matinee idol. In him, she saw the person everyone else had missed, capturing Isabel in a way that Aidan's image never could.

The two commiserated for hours, not going home until after dark, when they were both promptly grounded. And because they were banished to the trailer park they ended up spending more time together. Isabel made Aidan Roycroft laugh, taught him how to play poker and how to cook something besides boxed macaroni-and-cheese. Over the years they did homework and took turns reading aloud novels for English class. Most important, Isabel took the time to listen. This quiet act was a basic necessity for Aidan, something like food, shelter, clothing, and a finely tuned ear—though, to this day, she wasn't sure if that was the right order. He was not needy, but he did need her. Back then, Aidan's acceptance of Isabel was all it took for the kids at school to leave her in peace. She did make friends, though neither she nor Aidan connected to outsiders the way they did to each other.

Initially, the relationship moved to the rhythm of any adolescent tryst, the unlikely swap of a watermelon Jolly Rancher leading to Isabel's first kiss, though Aidan never admitted the same to her. It was sugary-sour, sticky-sweet, and the only kiss the two had ever shared. After the fact, after Aidan crunched down on his prize piece of candy, friendship slid into a tailspin. And because he was incapable, Isabel had to choose for him. Did she want Aidan to be her boyfriend or her friend? It didn't take much to deduce that being Aidan's girlfriend would only lead to being Aidan's ex-girlfriend—even at thirteen. Subsequent years and a laundry list of girls like Shanna proved that theory like a surefire mathematical equation. And it wasn't to say that she didn't lose out by choosing not to be Aidan's girlfriend. Isabel simply had more to gain by being his friend, their finger-slice, blood-swearing status wholly suiting Catswallow's much sought-after prize.

It was the privacy that Isabel coveted most, an intimate friendship that crushed any physical moment Aidan might share with another girl. She also didn't mind the boundaries that protected her from becoming *one of them*, an Aidan Roycroft casualty. He'd been there in more important ways. Aidan listened to Isabel worry about how she might pay for college and assisted with simpler matters, like memorizing the conjugations for the French verb *faire*. He was a whiz with foreign languages—even singing in Spanish if the mood struck him. While he finessed her through three years of Madame Lameroux's French class, he couldn't help much with college. That came down to hard finances, which landed Isabel at her fourth choice, a mediocre satellite campus to a larger university. Over the summer she'd tried to find the positives. It was still higher education, even if it wasn't on the scale she'd envisioned.

As the start of classes approached, other changes entered Isabel's mind. The farmhouse, a condemnable structure with fortress-like walls, no longer seemed able to keep the future at bay. Time that ran on an hourglass was about to run out. Isabel would miss that, the louder reasons for being there, like today's Lovett Street debacle, and the tiniest of routines, like their tutorial swap of irregular verbs. With Aidan's gift for languages and a sharp head for numbers—which he generally ignored—the hourglass could have easily flipped, at least for a while. But college didn't interest Aidan. This place, the farmhouse or Catswallow, was not the beat of his heart. Music was Aidan's passion, making his departure imminent. The only unknown was how long it would take until he'd saved enough nerve and money to go. One thing was certain; he'd have no trouble walking away from Fountainhead.

Catswallow's premier mobile-home community was where they slept, though both felt more at home in the farmhouse. While it served as Aidan's music studio, lately, for Isabel, its purpose had expanded. Her mother's boyfriend, Rick Stanton, was the local-boy-makes-good story and Carrie was crazy about him. It added a third person to the now familiar mother-daughter life. And for reasons Isabel couldn't identify, she was unable to get comfortable with that. At first she thought it was jealousy, but it didn't seem to match the awkward emotions in her head. She was truly happy for her mother, pleased she found someone successful, charismatic, and driven. Isabel didn't like to stereotype, but considering the choices in a trailer park dating pool . . . well, Rick Stanton exceeded the odds. Strapped to his rocket to fame were the half-dozen car dealerships he owned, though it went farther back, having something to do with his years as a football god. Rick was a Catswallow state champion and an all-American linebacker for the University of Alabama. After college he'd parlayed his popularity into a showroom bonanza, making car dealerships look like corporate success. But Rick had loftier ambitions than cornering the Heart of Dixie's motor vehicle market. Recently, he'd announced his bid for the state senate. He definitely had the following. You couldn't drive through town without encountering dozens of Stanton Motors car emblems. But even with his success, despite his friendly demeanor, Rick's increasing presence rattled her. And

Isabel didn't rattle. Only yesterday, while waiting for Carrie, he'd offered Isabel a beer. He smiled as her eyes widened. Then he laughed, saying he'd forgotten she wasn't quite of age. She brushed it off, excusing herself to run an errand that didn't exist. She'd gone to the farmhouse, pierced by late-afternoon sun and devoid of Aidan's presence. Normally, she didn't spend time there alone. But in that moment, the farmhouse felt different, more like a refuge. Hours later, with no one to confide in, she walked home, glad to find her mother and Rick out. Isabel climbed into bed, where rattled thoughts led to a night of odd dreams, a cast of characters from Rick to Eric Lang to Aidan.

Today she decided that disrupted sleep was reason enough to swipe the beer Rick offered, which she brought to the farmhouse. Isabel would have been fine with a cooler of Diet Coke, but Aidan's mood would require a stronger pick-me-up than a carbonated beverage. As he came through the door, Isabel saw that she was right. He slammed the warped slab so hard it actually shut, walls wavering as old floorboards creaked. Steam he'd been suppressing since Shanna slapped him hissed from his pores. Sprawled across an old sofa, Isabel kept silent, the tattered piece of furniture having initiated their customary housekeeping. She remained prone in what the two recognized as her spot. She didn't make room. There was no need. Aidan never sat next to her.

"Give," he grunted, holding out his hand.

She opened the beer and he guzzled it. Isabel's eyes trailed over shaggy blond hair. The shade tended to fluctuate, framing a face that had hit the genetic lottery. There was no getting away from it. All of him was veiled in a satiny complexion, a blemish never having the audacity to show up on Aidan Roycroft's face. His eyes were more cornflower in September than sky in winter. She saw right through them, past the image, beyond his character flaws— which, on occasion, included lazy, indulgent, and slightly self-centered. Aidan didn't resemble his mother much, except for the hair, making Isabel wonder what his father looked like. Unlike Eric Lang, whom Isabel could see in a mirror, Aidan said he'd never even seen a picture of John Roycroft. Isabel envied that. He'd stood a solid six feet since he turned sixteen, Isabel perceiving his growth as an overnight event. One minute they were of similar heights, swapping spit and a watermelon Jolly Rancher; the next Aidan towered over her. There was a warm April day a couple of years before that when Aidan showed up to the farmhouse in shorts. He had hair on his legs that wasn't there the summer before. After the hair and height came shoulders. Aidan went from a bean-pole stature to having a widest point that balanced his absurdly stunning head, tapering down to . . . Isabel bit her lower lip, picking up her gaze and moving it to the cracked windowpanes. He chugged the beer and belched, the sound echoing through vacant rooms. And from beanpole to the T-shape act of God that was the Aidan she hung out with.

"You should have done that last week when Shanna trotted you out to the family country club," Isabel said, matching an indifferent tone to her glance. "That way, she could have pitched her fit in front of Catswallow's better half."

"Shut up, Isabel." She crossed her arms, narrowing her eyes. "Sorry, I'm sorry. You know I didn't mean that." Everything quieted and Isabel could see, if only from his peripheral glance, that her ruffled feelings were overriding his bruised ego. "So why didn't you stop me? You knew it was a train wreck."

"Ha! You flatter yourself, Aidan. Worrying about *your* love life isn't on my to-do list." She slumped farther down, flinging a thick wave of auburn hair over the sofa's arm. It was her crowning glory, prettier than his. "So, are you really *not* going to take her to Catswallow's main event?" she asked, curious if things were as doomed as the scene indicated.

"You're kidding, right? I wouldn't take her across Lovett Street—not unless there was a whole lot of traffic."

"That's what I thought." Along with his reputation for attracting girls, discarding them before they could spell *novelty*, he tended not to rekindle these relationships. In all probability, Aidan Roycroft would forever treat girls like a stick of gum—once the flavor was gone, out it went.

"It won't be too big a deal, not for me, since I'm working it." For the second straight year, Aidan handily beat out bands from as far away as Tuscaloosa, earning him single billing at the gala.

"Shanna would have hated it, Aidan, having to share you all night with the stage."

"Hell, I'm not worried about her either way. If she turns up stag, I'll see to it that she gets a spotlight dance all to herself."

"That she'd probably love." They both laughed, Aidan opening another beer. She watched but didn't comment.

"Listen, Isabel, it, um . . . it does leave me with one problem."

"What's that?" She rolled onto her stomach and stretched over the sofa arm, reaching for the cooler. Glancing back, maybe unexpectedly, she caught Aidan's eyes in a radar lock with her butt. Faster than a flapjack, she flipped back over. She didn't look at him. Her gaze was trained on dark-painted toenails, inching up denim-covered legs, bumping past a hole that revealed a blistery mosquito bite. With her stare stuck on the hem of her shirt, she tugged it past her waist. She'd imagined it. The same way she'd imagined Rick's innuendo. Isabel coaxed herself to look, ignoring an achy pause that only she heard. Aidan was oblivious. He stood on the other side of the room, fiddling with a guitar. "Get a clue, Isabel," she mumbled.

"What?" he said, absorbed in a chronically flat E string.

"Nothing. So what's the problem?" Sitting up straight, she tucked her legs tight and stretched sideways. Isabel grabbed for a bottle, but the wet beer slipped from her grip, toppling back into the cooler. She snatched it up and popped the top, the beer gushing like an icy geyser. "Damn it!" Jumping to her feet, Isabel looked toward Aidan, only seeing the guitar. Seconds later he reappeared with a handful of paper towels. It was a natural reaction, Aidan blotting the drenched cotton shirt. A moment into that it became apparent *what* he was blotting, the simple but soaked garment looking primed for a wet T-shirt contest. And instead of an achy pause, there was an alarming stare, Isabel thrusting his hands away.

"Sorry!" he yelled as she grabbed at the soggy paper towels and her breasts. "I didn't see . . . I was just trying to help."

There was a wicked arc to his smooth voice and Isabel just wanted it to go away. But because calm was what she did best, she kept talking as if the last few seconds hadn't happened. "Uh, you didn't say. What, exactly, is your problem?"

"You're my f— Oh, right, yeah. It doesn't matter." There was a hissing sigh, Aidan pursing his lips. "Why do you always do that?"

"Do what?" Beer dripped from the waded paper towels, Isabel deftly ignoring it.

From the crates that served as a coffee table, Aidan picked up his beer and downed a long mouthful. Cornflower eyes creased into something she couldn't put a name to, his gaze veering out the dirty windows. "Be so fucking in control—all the damn time." He glanced back. "Anyway, it's not important. Forget it."

"Will you just tell me the problem?" Solving Aidan's problems was as familiar as tying her shoes, and Isabel stayed the course. "Did you hire a limo, pay for two gala tickets? Rent a hotel room?"

He looked back, Isabel amazed that his eyes could narrow even more. "I'm the entertainment. I don't need a ticket."

"Right." She discarded the paper towels and sat, pinching the bridge of her nose. It cut off the visual of a flashing Motel 6 sign and Shanna dressed in nothing but elbow-length white gloves.

"A date. Now I don't have a date."

From her seat on the sofa, Isabel's hand dropped, her jaw following. She gazed up at him. It was like looking directly into the sun, and she returned the queer expression he offered moments before. *He couldn't possibly be asking . . .*

"I get that you think this whole gala thing is a stale tradition Catswallow can't let go of—like jaywalking or book banning. I hear you. It's an excuse for snooty wannabes to perpetuate a fantasy about not actually living in a barely four-corner town. Maybe that's all true, but I have to go, and I'd rather not go alone so . . ."

His ability to repeat her gala-loathing, *'rather stick a hot poker in my eye'* chant verbatim was striking, Isabel doubly amazed that he'd used *perpetuate* in a sentence. "Oh, Aidan, I don't—"

"You're right, never mind. I shouldn't ask. I know you turned down Jake Summerfield and Kyle Marsh. They couldn't figure out why until I explained your point of view."

"You do? You did?" she said, standing. She'd almost said yes to Kyle, but to what point? To spend $500 that could be used for tuition and books, not to mention the hours of her life wasted as an extra in Shanna O'Rourke's floor show. She took in his understated stance, hands shoved in the pockets of his jeans, a glum expression tethered to his usually charm-filled face. It was really such a simple request. And what excuse did she have to turn him down? It would be one friend helping out another. Nothing more. "If it's that important, I'll do it," Isabel said firmly, as if she'd just agreed to join the militia.

"You will?"

"Sure, what's the big deal?" While she did see the gala as something that should have gone the way of pearl necklaces and fat corsages, Isabel couldn't ignore the smile on Aidan's face. She supposed it was understandable. The significance of Catswallow's main event was lost on her. But to everyone born and bred in the tiny town, the late-summer gala was a beloved rite of passage. Isabel tucked a lock of hair behind her ear and smiled back. Inwardly, she wasn't as comfortable, uneasy about the idea of being Aidan's date. Distracted, she barely heard her name being called from the doorway.

"Bella! What in the hell are you doin', girl, all the way out here . . . with him?"

Rick Stanton, who'd opened the twisted door as if it were revolving, stood in the entrance of the farmhouse. Gala thoughts petered to a hard stop. She felt as if her sanctuary had been violated and looked at Rick, who was an imposing sight in every way: size, personality, money . . . male hormones. Initially, Isabel thought those were quality points. Her mother required somebody with an overwhelming allure. Eric Lang was like that; he had an innate ability to get along. Rick possessed this trait too, though differently, more like a smooth talker from the handshake forward.

"Carrie's been looking for you. I spent the last hour combing this side of town," he said, coming farther in.

"My mother?" Carrie, an x-ray tech, often worked a double shift, doing her best to excel at the county's new hospital. Promise of career advancement had been the clincher, drawing them to Catswallow in the first place. "Is something wrong?"

"Nah," he said, a concerned look traveling from Aidan to the cooler of beer. "We decided to take a ride into Birmingham for dinner. The three of us," he said, making it clear that Aidan was not on the guest list. "My boys, Trey and Strobe, are meeting us there. Carrie wants you to come home and get ready." More focused on Aidan than her, he stepped in his direction. "I've been meaning to ask. You're Stella Roycroft's boy, aren't you?"

"Yeah, you know my mother?" Aidan said, arms folding across

his chest. There was a thickness to him—physically . . . mentally. It seemed new, like it wasn't there yesterday, like those hairy legs.

"Everybody knows Stella Roycroft." Isabel's eyes flicked back, catching an upturn to his lips. "Me included." Her neck swiveled, seeing Aidan's mouth twitch. "Guess that makes you John Roycroft's effort. At least courtesy of a moment or two before he hightailed it out of Catswallow."

Isabel's head whipped back. "You knew Aidan's father?" She sensed that Aidan hated the question, if only from the way his stare was burning a hole through the back of her head.

"Some. I knew his mama better." The upturn widened. "In fact, his daddy and I had a scuffle over that very topic outside Cowboy Bill's," he said, referring to Catswallow's busiest bar. "Nasty right cross your daddy had," Rick said, a burly hand grazing his jaw. "'Course, not near as mean as mine. But yeah, I knew him. And you, boy, are the spittin' image. I'd bet you're just as smart-mouthed too." His taunt paused and he looked squarely at Isabel. "I can tell you this much, Bella, if he's got John Roycroft's blood in his veins, you'd be safer in the Crimson Tide locker room than alone with him. Now let's go." He closed the distance, touching Isabel's arm. Aidan moved the length of the room in a split second, jamming himself between them like a cement wedge.

"If Isabel needs to go home, I'll see that she gets there."

Odd ideas pulsed through her, not the least of which was requiring transportation assistance. She walked, Aidan walked; sometimes they drove in his truck. It didn't dictate a plan of action, certainly not an escort.

"That right, boy?" His linebacker frame stood inches taller and at least half a foot wider than Aidan. It was a fact that, suddenly, had Isabel concerned. "Seeing as the young lady's mama asked me to find her, I expect it's my responsibility to get her home. My vehicle is outside."

"Great, so's mine. Follow if you want." Aidan locked a vice grip around Isabel's arm, ushering her toward the door. "Who the hell does he think he is?"

"One sec, Roycroft." The bellowing vibration made them stop and do a double pivot. "Won't help your cause any when Carrie hears that aside from hiding out in your love shack—alone—you've been doin' it with a cooler full of beer. I'll see her home."

The observation seemed arrogant, especially since it was the same beer Rick offered her yesterday. "He hasn't been drinking . . ." *much*, she insisted. "For your infor—"

"Shut up, Isabel." And this was far different from the *shut up* she was issued earlier. It was commanding and in control. "I don't give a fuck what you tell Carrie. I'm taking her home." As if she might be unclear about the direction, Aidan hung on to her arm, moving them outside. Rick watched from the porch as the creaky doors to Aidan's truck opened, the two getting inside. There was a harsh look on his face during a silent ride. It didn't go with the Aidan she knew, or even an image bound to him like a fingerprint. As they pulled up to the Lang trailer, a two-bedroom model with a tidy front porch and central air, Isabel reached for the truck door handle. Aidan came across the seat, grabbing her wrist. The action was not pleasant nor cautionary nor territorial. It was protective. And with it came a feeling so powerful Isabel did not know it from anywhere: a book, the movies, or real life. He didn't speak, but he also didn't let go. Not until Carrie Lang was in full view, coming outside.

CHAPTER THREE

Catswallow, Alabama

I T WAS LATE WHEN CARRIE AND ISABEL ARRIVED BACK FROM BIR-
mingham. As promised, Rick's sons met them there. It wasn't
Isabel's first encounter with the Stanton offspring, and each time
they met she felt as if she'd landed in the audience of a cutthroat
game show. As everyone took a seat, the green flag dropped and
their amazing race began. Strobe was the older son. Different from
his father and brother, he was book smart and a physical opposite.
He had a slight build and a boy's body, but an intellectual's brain.
He also possessed a subtler, watch-your-back presence compared
with his father or Trey, both of whom led with their size. Isabel
assumed he took after his mother, who, according to her mother,
Rick Stanton divorced years ago. Trey, on the other hand, was
Rick's *son*—which wasn't to say that Strobe wasn't. It was just that
one was clearly cut from the same cloth while the other appeared
to be a genetic mutant. Rick had given each a dealership when they
turned twenty-one, then he let the bloodbath commence.

Out of the gate, conversation began with a comparison of sales
figures, a round that always went to Strobe. It was a fact that riled
both Trey and Rick, men who relied on fast talk and friendly

handshakes. Round two was dedicated to name-dropping. It was a point earner that had intensified with Rick's bid for state senator. As part of their due diligence the boys worked the voters, tapped as Rick's fundraising committee. Trey thought he had the constituent category in the bag when he announced that Catswallow's NRA and its very active Christian Coalition were both on board. In return, card-carrying members would be offered an enticing Stanton Motors discount. The hint of a bribe didn't matter as a thunderous slap of approval was applied to Trey's back, one that would have broken a vertebra in Strobe's. That didn't matter either as Strobe countered with a commitment from Southern Alabama's Junior League. It was a force guaranteed to draw a large and slightly more diverse group of voters. With rounds one and two going to Strobe, the competition segued to a swapping of he-man stories about whatever unsuspecting wildlife was in season. It was where Strobe, whose hunting skills were more cerebral, lost traction, Rick throwing the contest in his younger son's favor.

While all this happened, other parts of the evening took a different turn and Carrie Lang became the focus. Rick openly bragged about her as the younger Stantons responded with preprogrammed phrasing: "Ms. Lang, I do believe my daddy is smitten," and "Ma'am, we really enjoyed your company this evening." Downing a second Diet Coke, Isabel watched her mother revel in it, so animated that she would have won a matching washer and dryer had it been up for grabs. Though normally she only cooed at Rick, tonight she acted downright *motherly* toward his sons. Given a holiday gathering, she might have knitted them sweaters, Isabel thought. It wasn't reality TV or a game show, more like a cursory interview, and Isabel would later spend the ride home trying to put a reason to it. She thought about this and something else. Something she'd been trying to convince herself was a misunderstanding between Rick's hand and her brain.

After the Stanton boys left, Carrie excused herself to take a phone call from work. Rick paid the bill. Tucking his money clip away, Isabel felt his fingertips graze along her bare leg, right to the edge of her skirt, maybe underneath. When they arrived at the restaurant, the Stanton boys insisted that Carrie sit in between them. That put Isabel next to Rick. Had they all been sitting there when the check arrived, Isabel might not have thought twice. His touch was that slight, that *"pardon me"*-oriented, and at such a tight table. But with only the two of them and the check, well, there was elbow room to spare. As his fingers surfaced, wallet in hand, Isabel's head ticked in his direction. Rick looked blankly at her, as though he couldn't grasp her expression. She said nothing on the ride home, even less after Rick left.

It was a difficult call. Realistically, the man hadn't done anything but accidentally brush against her leg while paying for her dinner. He'd also spent much of the night making Carrie Lang feel like queen for a day—something Isabel thought about detailing on an envelope marked return to sender. *Hey, Dad, Mom's found a great guy too, thinks the world of her. Is finally indifferent to you . . .* But before she could decide what she saw or felt, the Diet Cokes hit bottom and she headed for the bathroom. As she mulled things over, all thoughts and actions were interrupted as Carrie knocked on the door.

"Isabel, we need to talk."

Okay, maybe I won't have to walk this very fine line after all. She stopped peeing midstream and listened.

"I want to talk about Aidan." That wasn't a promising start. "Maybe now is the right time to cut back on the time you spend with him." A terrific silence penetrated the bathroom door, like an ax. "Think about it, Isabel. You'll be heading to college."

"By way of the commuter lot."

"That's not set in stone."

"Why?" she said, holding back the rest of the Diet Cokes and reaching for the toilet paper. She yanked up her underwear and pushed down her skirt as she flung the door open. "Did the hospital make good on the raises they owe you?"

"Well, no, not a raise." There was an awkward glance, reminding both of the promised future that never materialized. "But there may be other options, plausible ones. We'll talk about that later. Right now, let's focus on Aidan. My point being that he's not going to college. Realistically, he's not going anywhere but Cowboy Bill's—perhaps as its entertainment, ultimately as its best customer. Certainly, he'll take a stab at the music thing; play every seedy bar between here and the Rocky Mountains. He might even hang in there until his perseverance, wallet, and hairline runs thin. But in the end he'll be back, looking to relive his glory days with whoever waited around. I don't want it to be you."

"That's ridiculous—all of it!"

"Is it? From what I heard about today's scene, he can check Shanna off his short list."

"Is that what this is about, Aidan and Shanna's argument? You weren't there. You don't know what happened."

"No, I wasn't. But it's all over town. And Rick, he felt obligated to tell me the rest. The circumstances when he found you, the farmhouse, the beer."

"Great, now we've crossed over to totally insane."

"Isabel, I have to butt in here, at least say my piece. Rick is only looking out for your best interest. He cares about you . . . like a daughter."

Moving toward her bedroom, she stopped and turned. "A daughter? Is that what you think?"

"What's that supposed to mean?"

"It means, on occasion, I've gotten a different vibe from your good ol' boy, Mom. I don't think Rick's interest is entirely fatherly."

There was a rapid blink from Carrie, as if trying to bring the innuendo into focus. "Isabel Lang, I'm not even going to dignify that with a response. I know Rick. Trust me when I say he's an honorable man."

Poised to go on, Carrie's quick defense made her hesitate. Random remarks and a gesture that, by her own admission, was subject to interpretation were weak accusations. "About Aidan," she said, choosing her battle, "the beer wasn't his. I brought it to the farmhouse. So if you want to be mad at someone, be mad at me."

"Beer is not what concerns me. It's more complicated than that. It's your unwillingness to let go of a relationship that, by now, you should have outgrown. That ugly scene at Higher Grounds, what does it say about Aidan? I heard it from three different people, his public lover's quarrel with Shanna O'Rourke."

"It wasn't a lover's quarrel," she snapped. "Aidan isn't in—" It was the wrong path. "Shanna O'Rourke is a shallow, overly pretty, self-absorbed—"

"And Aidan is . . . ?" Carrie countered, a hand sweeping past. "I understand that after Shanna caught him cheating he dumped her, right there, in the middle of Lovett Street. If you ask me, Aidan could benefit from a lesson in *honorable*."

A hand flew to Isabel's forehead. "This is so twisted I don't even know where to start! Shanna is not completely innocent. If you could just look at it from Aidan's point of view."

"I'd rather look at it from yours. Can you honestly tell me that you didn't go running to that farmhouse to comfort him, cocktails in tow?" And Isabel had no quick comeback for that. Carrie sighed, reaching out. Warm motherly fingers brushed through her daughter's hair, an empathetic smile edging onto her face. Isabel pushed her hand away, the gesture making her feel hopelessly awkward, hugely transparent. "Isabel, I'm concerned about the choices you're making to keep Aidan in your life. What you're willing to do for him. How far you'd go to . . ."

"It's not like that," she said quietly. "Not at all." She shook off Carrie's accusations, focused on the things she and Aidan did share. They were rock-solid things that didn't compare with something as intangible as romance. "Newsflash, Mom, not every relationship boils down to a sexual encounter. That's not what Aidan and I are about." But the delivery was lukewarm, and she tried again. "It's so much more than that."

"Isabel, it's all right. I understand how you feel. I can appreciate what it's like to love someone unconditionally. In return, they use you as a support system but are totally deceptive about what they're capable of giving."

"Are we talking about Aidan and me or you and Dad?"

It was a complicated connection, Isabel's astuteness surprising Carrie. She watched her mother tense, the fabric of her voice weaving into a patterned blend of hurt and humiliation. "Fine. But you could benefit from my experience. Look how many years it's taken for me to fall in love with someone else."

There was a hairpin turn. "In love? You're in love with Rick?" She wasn't sure why the shock value was so great. Somewhere in her head, Isabel believed Carrie Lang's fate was sealed. She would always love her father, a man she couldn't have. Isabel hesitated, trying to fit Rick, a man whose presence equated with a crowd-filled stadium, into their quiet corner-table life.

"This isn't the conversation I envisioned when we talked about it. But, yes, we're absolutely in love."

"That's um . . . That's kind of sudden, isn't it?"

"We've been together for eight months. See that? You didn't even notice—how long we've been together or how serious things are." Isabel nodded, racking her brain for the clues she missed. "So maybe," Carrie said, her tone gentler, "you can trust me a little when I tell you that I *get* someone like Aidan."

Isabel retreated into her room, her argument suddenly feeling weak. Her mother was right about one thing. Isabel didn't know anything about being in love. But as she recalled, Carrie didn't see Eric Lang's bombshell coming either. She supposed love could have that effect—leaving a huge margin for error. Isabel couldn't share any reservations about Rick. Not now. While they might be having this anchored conversation, Carrie's declaration said she was floating on a cloud, and Isabel would not be the one to paint a black horizon. She backtracked. "I'm happy for you, Mom. But really, Aidan and I, we're friends. Don't worry about me—"

"Don't worry about you?" Carrie had followed her into the bedroom, eyes widening at the remark. "You'd do better asking me to add your father and his *soul mate* to my Christmas card list." She arched a brow, the sarcasm penetrating through. "Isabel, do you remember how you used to swing so high, out in the backyard? I'd come out to the patio and tell you not to because I was afraid you'd fly off and break an arm or worse."

"I remember," she said, recalling the tidy brick house in New Jersey, its grassy fenced yard. The vision came with warmer feelings than she wished.

"Someday you'll understand it's only instinct to keep even your grown-up children out of harm's way."

"Mom, I hear what you're saying. But Aidan and I, we're just friends. That's all. I swear." And she could swear to this because it was the truth. Isabel bit her lip, hoping the poignant moment might be a softer spot to relay the rest. "Um, since we're on the subject, you should know. I agreed to go with Aidan, to the gala . . . as a favor."

With her girlish figure and hair like Isabel's but brown, Carrie usually looked younger than her thirty-nine years. Not at the moment. At the moment she looked troubled and worn through. "You haven't heard a word I've said." Carrie's eyes pinched tight, a hand wringing around her neck. "He's using you, Isabel. Can't you see that?"

A week's worth of clean wash sat on Isabel's bed and she deflected the accusation by turning away, stuffing socks in her shirt drawer and shirts in her junk drawer. "Look, I said I'd go, and I will. I'll pay for the dress myself if that's what you're worried about."

"A wardrobe budget isn't the issue. But this thought might be: You turned down not one but two lovely invitations to Catswallow's big shindig. An event you couldn't have cared less about. What suddenly put it on your to-do list?" She had no reply. "Exactly. You have a lot of self-worth, Isabel. You're intelligent, incredibly rational about most things. By agreeing to go, consider the message you're sending to Aidan."

Holding a fist full of clean underwear, she threw it back onto the bed. "We're just friends. Let it go! Maybe if I tattoo it across my forehead I'd convince you!"

"Only if you're willing to look in a mirror. Think about how it looks—"

"Oh, like I give a shit what anybody in this town thinks. Aidan and I know exactly what we are to each other."

"Fine. You're an adult—on paper. If this is what you want to tell yourself." Carrie walked the scant three paces to the edge of her daughter's bedroom. "But I see the kind of man Aidan is becoming. Whether it's some nightmarish betrayal or his ego, he'll use you until he decides to show his true colors. I love you, Isabel. You deserve someone special, someone who thinks the world of you. Hokey as it may sound, someone who'll put you on a pedestal for the rest of your life. Is that so awful of me? I don't want you to end up like this," she said, swinging her arms wide.

"I know, Mom." Out of words and warnings, Carrie retreated, Isabel going back to silently tucking everything away.

CHAPTER FOUR

Catswallow, Alabama

SECOND TO ERIC LANG, AND NOW IN ADDITION TO RICK STANton, Carrie had always been in love with the South. It was a distant, amorous affair. The kind where flaws were shadowed by wide leafy magnolias and the feel of romanticism was as inherent as the heat. In the days leading up to the gala this was a benefit. Carrie embraced one small town's custom, in turn, talking less about Aidan. At least Isabel hoped this was the circumstance. The only other possibility was that she was vicariously reliving her past. Isabel had considered this after finding an old photo album peeking out from beneath her mother's bed. She couldn't resist, flipping through its taboo pages. Pictures unfolded like a fairy tale, Carrie and Eric as high school sweethearts and at their college homecomings, the military balls they attended during her father's days in the Coast Guard. There were candid shots from their wedding, her parents slow-dancing into the future. The last picture was particularly bright and shiny, showing a very pregnant Carrie and a beaming Eric. His arms barely fit around her. Isabel closed the album, pushing it far under the bed.

On the night of the gala Carrie fussed with the snug bodice of

Isabel's dress, bedazzled by her daughter's appearance. If she was thinking about her former life, she hid it well. Her only fairy-tale thought seemed to be about the arrival of a pumpkin and a couple of field mice. "Doesn't she look beautiful, Rick? Just stunning," she said, admiring Isabel's reflection.

"Too good for the trash she's goin' with, if you ask me." He reached into the refrigerator, filling a glass from what appeared to be bottled iced tea. Isabel pursed her lips, corralling a smile. "What in the hell?" he said, all but spitting the concoction across the room.

She couldn't contain it, bursting into laughter. "Isabel," Carrie said, shaking her head. She looked in Rick's direction. "I'm afraid that's Aidan's signature preperformance elixir."

"Lighter fluid and honey?" he asked, retrieving a well-marked bottle of bourbon from the cabinet.

"Almost," Isabel said. The potion, a combination of iced tea, grapefruit juice, and honey, was fairly disgusting without its secret ingredient, which she would add just prior to showtime.

Rick and his fresh drink disappeared onto the porch, laughter fading as Isabel gazed into the mirror. Maybe *stunning* was the right word for the girl who looked back. Catswallow's best stylists worked a small miracle with every feature that fell short. Instead of swampy green, her eyes were bold and intense. A sprinkle of freckles were banished beneath a layer of powdery cover-up, and a nose, which she saw as a tad too long, was a pleasant complement to her face. And when, Isabel wondered, did she develop cheekbones? Though she was admittedly at a loss when it came to fashion, her hair lent itself to occasions such as this. Cascading ringlets were pinned delicately to her head, falling like beautiful curled ribbon. Between the hair, makeup, and the nail tips that looked strikingly real, there was a stab of panic. Would Aidan even recognize her? The dress, magazine worthy, was sheer luck, having just been returned to a boutique in Birmingham. Isabel thought the returning customer might have been Shanna O'Rourke, and was relieved to overhear the clerk say that its previous owner, a girl from Birmingham, was "too far along to squeeze into it." Isabel brushed a hand over the milky lavender skirt that flowed in sexy sheer layers. She'd never imagined wearing anything like it, not even in a dream. The saleswoman insisted otherwise, claiming the style flattered her natural curves. Needing no alterations, she said it looked custom-made for Isabel. She had to disagree when she saw the $800 price tag. To her surprise, Carrie had happily handed over a credit card, insisting the money wasn't a problem.

"Isabel," Carrie said, her tone less light. "Look, I understand the temptation. I'm not blind. If any girl your age were to custom-order the most magnetic, talented—God help me—good-looking male on the planet . . . Well, they'd get Aidan Roycroft parts in the box. Despite my feelings, I get it. But don't let the sheen fool you. You're smarter than that."

She nodded. Carrie Lang was immune. In an eleventh-hour attempt to keep her mother from a night of nail biting, Isabel pleaded her case once again. "Mom, I told you, I'm just helping him out. It's not like this is a real date. It's one night. Besides, Aidan doesn't look at me that way."

"Of course he doesn't." Busy smoothing the dress, she stopped. "That's not what I meant." A stark stare jerked to her daughter's reflection. "He should be so lucky. But I see what Aidan wants. Irresponsible hookups and girls who party twenty-four, seven. I'm only saying that's not you, Isabel. You're more practical, tradi-tional . . . sensible."

"Uh huh," she mumbled, deciding how many synonyms there were for *dull*.

Like a mole head from a carnival game, Rick popped back into the living room, where a lingering gaze passed over her. A shiver rushed down Isabel's back. It made her want to change into a T-shirt and baggy sweats. "You give her a time to be home, Carrie? My boys never went anywhere without a curfew. 'Course I never could get Trey to adhere to it," he said, downing more of his drink. "Tomcat and all that he was at her age."

Like father like son rolled reflexively through Isabel's brain.

"If she were my girl, I'd have that set in stone, be puttin' a glass slipper on her—somethin'." While Isabel ignored the comment, there was a vision of Rick hauling ass out to his man-size SUV, retrieving a rifle, maybe a chastity belt.

"Isabel and I talked about that, about Aidan, specifically," her mother said, shooting her a wary glance. "But there are a lot of post-gala activities and—"

"And exactly what activity she'll be participating in, that's what I'd be concerned to know. Guys like Roycroft have a way of sending even smart girls like Bella ass-over-teakettle. The next thing you know, she's on public assistance, her life chained to a place like this," he said, his glass sweeping through the trailer air, "hunting him down for child support."

"Seriously?" Isabel said, incredulous.

"How the hell do you think Roycroft got here? That kind of behavior is inbred. Trust me, Bella. There's more men looking to avoid that kind of responsibility than to take it on. I'm proud to say I'm one of the few who takes care of what's mine."

"I see," she said coyly. "So tell me, Rick, exactly how close did Strobe come to being your bastard son?"

"Isabel!" Carrie said. "Rick only wants to make sure you're safe. He's only trying to point out the obvious." She smiled at him, apologizing. "Sorry, honey." The endearment caused Isabel to blanch. The last time Carrie referred to someone as *honey*, she was married to him. "It's been too many years since she's had a solid male role model. It's hard for her to appreciate."

"No harm done. I could see where she'd be lacking after hearing about her daddy's . . . *choices*."

Before Isabel could tally the differences between Rick and her father, which, oddly, were stacking in Eric Lang's favor, there was a knock at the door. Rick's face was not the first one she wanted Aidan to see, but it couldn't be helped as he was closest. There was the exchange of manly grunts, Aidan brushing past. A swallow rolled through Isabel's throat. If she looked good, he looked a thousand times better. This, apparently, was what Aidan wore well. It was a standard black tuxedo, but he'd put his own spin on it with a pewter-colored vest, no tie, and an open wing-tip collar. Instead of shiny black rental shoes, he wore cowboy boots. Aidan bought them from a roadside vendor on their way to a show in Selma, a fine-looking pair of two-tone imitation-snakeskin boots. He always said when he made it big, really big, he'd own the best pair money could buy.

Isabel didn't know how many seconds had passed. But it was more than a few since Carrie was deep into a narrative of the drunk drivers she x-rayed on an ordinary Saturday night. Aidan didn't say a word, and Isabel thought she'd better. "You look nice." It hit the air with the sound of obvious information, as if saying that the sun rose. He still didn't speak, Isabel guessing he was saving his voice. On the other hand, maybe Aidan had taken one look at her and decided that this was the dumbest idea he'd ever had. Suddenly her hair felt too big, the dress too tight, thinking her lipstick looked as if she swiped it off a hooker. Naturally, Rick was right there with an *attaboy*.

"Uh, usually it's customary to compliment the female, especially when she spends an entire day gussying up for you. You really are cut from the same cloth as your skirt-chasing daddy, aren't you?"

Aidan's eyes veered from Isabel and onto Rick. His mouth

twitched and the silence turned ugly. "Isabel, you ready?" he said, shoving a plastic container at her. Inside was a beautiful spray of white roses surrounded by violets, a shade deeper than her dress. She'd been fully prepared to receive Shanna's already ordered bright orange corsage. It was to be expected, having guided Aidan past the soft pink roses in the flower shop, trying to convince him that someone so blond and fair would benefit from a kick of color.

"Wait," she said, grabbing the iced tea bottle and his boutonniere from the refrigerator. Handing Aidan a cellophane-wrapped rose, he didn't stop to put it on as he opened the door and they headed to his truck.

HALFWAY TO THE BANQUET ROOM AT THE VFW, WHICH CATSWALLOW residents had spent days transforming into a secret theme, Aidan's mood shifted. He hadn't said a word about the way she looked. Isabel ignored a swell of disappointment, reminding herself that this was no more than a friend helping out a friend. "Isabel, look in the glove compartment." She did, guessing it was a new CD, finding a fat envelope. "Open it."

She shrugged, peeling back the sealed flap. She looked at Aidan and back at the envelope. "Where . . . where did you get this? Is it real?" Onto the lap of her milky lavender gown, Isabel dumped more hundred-dollar bills than came in a Monopoly game. Only these were real, like from a bank heist, and suddenly she was wary of exploding dye. "How much money is here?"

"Ten thousand dollars," he said with a teasing grin.

"But I don't . . . Where did you . . . ?" It was more money than she'd ever seen, sure that the same was true for him. "Aidan, you tell me right now where this money came from!" Isabel didn't really believe he'd done anything wrong, but with Aidan you could never be completely sure. He pulled onto the side of the road. The grin disappeared.

"I inherited it. The check came registered mail from some lawyer in Boca Raton—a life insurance policy. I cashed it because I wanted to know what it looked like. Hell, I wanted to know if it was real."

"Inherited it from who?" As far as Isabel knew, Aidan's relatives were poorer than Aidan.

"My father."

"Your father? But that means he'd have to be . . ."

"Dead. Yes, that's what the letter said."

And Rick's comment seemed all the more vicious. Considering the news, she also fought a wave of guilt about Aidan not noticing her appearance. "Dead? Oh, Aidan, I'm so sorry—"

"What for?" he snapped. "He was just a man who called once or twice a year to see if I was still alive. That's not a father. I never knew the guy. He never cared to know me." His eyes jerked between Isabel and the money. "It's not like I got mail from him on a regular basis."

She ignored the comeback. "Yes, but in the back of your mind, surely you thought that someday—"

"No, Isabel. I didn't. And that, right there," he said, poking at the cash, "is about the nicest damn thing John Roycroft could have done for me. Do you understand what this means?" Isabel shook her head, though she was sure of the answer. "It means that I'm out of here. This money is my ticket to New York or L.A. or Nashville. Anywhere they make music. Anywhere that isn't here."

"Aidan, that's . . . that's incredible." Isabel put the money back in the glove compartment as Aidan pulled back onto the highway.

"You're the only person I told. My mother wasn't home when the letter came. From what it said, he left her his condo in Boca."

He nodded, satisfied. "She'll be a hell of a lot better off with that than she ever was with him. Anyway, I wanted to tell you first, before the night gets crazy on us. I played this gig last year and you won't believe the trouble one cracker-box town goes to."

Needing to move on from an answer about how long Aidan might hang around Catswallow, she said, "Hey, um, Katie Banks heard the gala is going to be a Spanish theme. You know, flamenco dancing and the running of the bulls. Kinda strange, but I suppose getting a bull is no big deal around here. Anyway, if it's true, if Katie's right, you could sing that Spanish song you're always working on at the farmhouse. Might be a nice touch, it's so emotion packed—like an opera."

"No," he said, shaking his head, "no way." Shifting in his seat, Aidan shrugged at her puzzled look. "That song isn't meant for a crowd. And the translation . . . well, I'm not sure if it works in English. Anyway," he said, retuning the radio, "whatever the theme is, you can bet it'll be over-the-top. I think they do it because, underneath, they know there's got to be something better than Catswallow. And this year, they couldn't be more right."

"In that case," Isabel said, focused on the passing scenery, "maybe the theme is bon voyage and have a nice life."

SHE WAS UNCANNILY CLOSE. EVERY YEAR THE CATSWALLOW GALA committee put forth a mind-blowing effort trying to outdo the one before—Disney, New York City on New Year's Eve, Hollywood, even a NASCAR-themed gala spectacularly done in white gloves and tails. This year was no exception, taking the recent Catswallow grads on a cruise around the world. Each table was dressed as a port of call, with Isabel docked in the Hawaiian Islands. Coconut cups and leis denoted her table, with mini lava cakes for dessert. But soon the world was moving as Cozumel mingled with the Greek Isles and a couple of girls traveled from St. Kitts to flirt with Lisbon. The partygoers in Hawaii drifted off too, leaving Isabel at a table filled with plates of chicken Kiev and poi, the native offering. Aidan went to work the moment they arrived, Isabel understanding his focus. She'd tagged along to enough country fairs and bar gigs to know the routine. He was in show mode, earning every dime he made. Sitting at the table, she closed her eyes and listened, something she rarely did. His voice was smooth, like twenty-year-old Tennessee whiskey over ice. At least that was the way she'd heard it described by one woman at a honky-tonk in Jasper. Tonight he entertained a peer-filled crowd with popular songs, slipping into one of his own every third or fourth number. All his music sounded like a bona fide hit. It hit her ears differently than when he practiced at the farmhouse, more finely tuned. Maybe it was the acoustics or the lights. Or maybe it was just Aidan in his element. At the farmhouse he could be less than sure, something that never showed in public. After playing a melody he'd written, Aidan would ask for a critique of the lyrics that were a work in progress. *"Hmm, I'm not sure . . . Dig deeper, Aidan. Connect it to something that really inspires you."*

Currently, he was the definition of confident. Aidan was in full rocker mode as he traded an acoustic guitar for the electric one, igniting a ring of fire that engulfed him and the crowd. Isabel admired him in the spotlight, the air heavy with hairspray, poi, and talent. It was fun for a while, listening to Aidan sing as he smoothly alternated with master of ceremonies duties. Always spot-on with the manners Stella instilled, he thanked the committee members, even noting Esther Womack, who'd served since the gala's inception in 1946. But eventually a sigh overshadowed the show, Isabel knowing it wasn't her favorite way to spend time with Aidan. She'd rather sit on the front porch of the farmhouse and watch the sun set, crickets dictating the melody. Or take a ride to

Tremont for soft-serve ice cream, Aidan harmonizing with the radio the entire way. The longer she watched, the more restless she felt. Along with admirable fascination came the reality of Aidan's imminent departure. Before tonight's windfall of cash, leaving tomorrow wasn't an option. But soon Catswallow would be his prior address, with sunsets downgraded to a scientific fact and ice cream just fattening. Watching the girls watch him, guys looking on with enviable awe, she knew it was the right thing for him to do. For anyone else success and fame might have the luster of a dream, but Isabel knew it would happen as well as she knew her own name. The same guilt she felt in the truck edged back. She wasn't being terribly fair or even a decent friend. Money was his only obstacle, and while it wasn't a king's fortune, a crafty guy who could survive on boxed macaroni-and-cheese could live off $10,000 for some time. Isabel sighed again, needing a break from Aidan's unfolding future—the one that wouldn't include her. She headed toward the ladies' room, which she'd put off since deciding that evening gowns should come with how-to-use-public-restrooms instructions. She took a last glance at the stage before running headlong into Kyle Marsh.

"Bella, you, um, you look incredible," he said, handsome enough in his tux. It was amazing how rented clothing could give the average boy the sheen of a man. "Would, um . . . Do you want to dance, being as your date's kind of busy?"

Aidan, who'd nodded in her direction, was well into the second chorus of Aerosmith's "I Don't Want to Miss a Thing." A crowd of girls puddled around the base of the stage, ogling him. She shrugged, shifting in her heels. "Sure, Kyle, but won't your date mind?"

"Katie? Nah, she went to the parking lot to smoke a joint. It's fine."

Isabel guessed that smoking pot wasn't on Kyle's to-do list, having won a full ride to the Citadel or West Point. She made a mental note to ask which one if they had to make small talk. But the beautiful ballad didn't invite conversation and the two of them just danced. A few moments in, as she was swaying comfortably in Kyle's arms, the music changed. It hadn't stopped, but Aidan wasn't singing anymore. The music had switched over to a CD, the real Aerosmith filling in. She moved with the melody, drifting to some dreamy place, positive that Aidan sang it better.

"Hey, Marsh, your date's looking for you." Startled, Isabel opened her eyes, finding Aidan standing next to them. "She looks really pissed, man. I'll take over, okay?"

Kyle glanced toward the door but didn't let go. "It's fine, dude. Katie's not into me, we're just friends—you know how it is," he said, his chin cocking at Isabel.

Aidan's eyes flicked between them and the stage, a hand running roughly over his mouth before moving onto Kyle's shoulder. Isabel recognized the grip; it was the same one that took hold of her wrist in his truck. "No, really, take off, man." They stopped dancing and Kyle, who boasted an athletic build but lacked Aidan's presence, let go.

"Whatever." He took a healthy step back. "But you can't have it both ways, Roycroft. Get a clue." Kyle shoved his hands in his pockets, disappearing into the crowd.

Aidan only stared, as though he had no intention of dancing. The *I feel pretty* moment faded, eclipsed by the whole hair, dress, whorish lipstick concept. Awkwardness intensified, the two of them standing still in the middle of a swaying dance floor. The tension broke as Aidan grabbed her around the waist. And again, there was nothing pleasant about it. "Why were you dancing with him?"

"Uh, because he asked and my legs were starting to cramp."

"You know I'm working this thing. I'm not letting you sit there by yourself on purpose."

"I know." But Isabel barely heard him, caught in the awesome sense of déjà vu that danced along with them. It was surreal; she knew it well, but she and Aidan had never danced before. It was like being pulled into a parallel universe. Her feet stopped moving, impeding the sensation, like a music box winding down. Aidan jerked her closer and everything wound tighter.

"Isabel, what are you doing?"

She willed her feet to move. As she did, déjà vu derailed. Breathing Aidan in, Isabel closed her eyes, her feet finding their footing while trying not to step on his. He smelled like Southern summer air, warm wrapping around her like the sun on her face. They'd been this close before, years of homework, playing tag Frisbee, sharing a bowl of mac-'n'-cheese. This was different, the simple solidness of his arms shifting boundaries. Anxiousness faded, Isabel feeling so very . . . *safe*. Her head drifted onto his shoulder, déjà vu marrying with current events. Like a roller shade, her eyes snapped open as her head jerked back. *I know this place! I know it from my dreams.*

"What?" he demanded, a huge bob swimming through his throat. He didn't look angry anymore, just in pain.

"Nothing." Her head drifted back onto his shoulder knowing quietly, softly, that she loved this dream.

"Isabel, I . . ." She felt his mouth press to her head, but it was hard to be sure between the bobby pins and hairspray. A voice interrupted. It put a fuzzy edge on a moment that was beginning to feel like reality. It was a man's voice, one she didn't know.

"Aidan. Aidan Roycroft." This time Aidan pulled away, blinking as if somebody flipped on a thousand-watt bulb. "Fitz Landrey," he said, shoving a fat hand in between them. Isabel thought if she had a knife—not even a terribly sharp knife—she'd chop it off. "How you doin', son?" The man was aggressively shaking Aidan's hand, the one that was wrapped around her seconds ago.

He led them to the edge of the dance floor. "My brother-in-law is Tim O'Rourke, Shanna's dad."

Super. He was there to call Aidan out for humiliating his niece, the one who showed up to Catswallow's grand gala with her cousin. But her uncle didn't seem angry, shoving a business card in Aidan's face.

"I'm here from L.A. My niece . . . Well, to tell you the truth, my niece couldn't hate you any more than a rabid hornet. But a few weeks back she insisted I come see you perform. Then she told me not to bother." He shrugged. "But I was passing through and I don't make business decisions based on pissed-off girls and something tells me that happens a lot. Right, cookie?" He gave her chin a squeeze, Isabel yanking her head back. "Besides, I'm stuck in this hole for the next three hours." Running a finger around the collar of his dress shirt, it was as if the confines of the Catswallow VFW were choking him. He was definitely a city dweller. He even smelled like something you'd never come in contact with in Catswallow. "My job is to find the next big thing. I'm always on a hunt for talent, looks, a singular presence. But mostly, I'm looking for an it factor." Aidan and Isabel exchanged a glance. "I can't tell you how many artists I've passed on, surely thousands. New faces with incredible talent, but nominal it factor. It's not something that comes with practice or a record label can manufacture. You either have it, or you don't. And, kid, I've got to tell you—your it factor is unlike anybody I've ever signed. I haven't seen this much natural talent since I signed Weak Need." Their mouths gaped as Fitz tossed out the name of a mega-hot band. "And, frankly, it takes five of them to produce as much raw charisma as you've got going."

The rest of the conversation was a blur, Isabel swearing that Aidan's eyes spun like a cartoon character's. Fitz Landrey explained that he was the head of C-Note Music: L.A., London, New York, and Tokyo. Doing most of the talking, he asked if Aidan had a demo. He obediently produced the CD he'd made in a second-rate Birmingham recording studio. It cost every penny he had. There were words about record deals, touring, and money, lots of money. He didn't stay long after that, telling Aidan that his handshake was as good as a signed contract. He'd be in touch. He gave Aidan another business card, telling him to call if he needed anything in the meantime, anything at all.

It was the moment Aidan dreamt of his entire life, Isabel forcing down *"Don't go!"* while summoning *"Ohmigosh, I'm so happy for you!"* She just stood, blankly staring. Trumping her Zen-like dance of clarity was money *and* opportunity, the night turning into a one-way ticket out of Catswallow and her life. The future flashed through Isabel's head: *Aidan gets his dream. I never make it out of here.* Years from tonight she'd chaperone a gala—the highlight of her year—accompanied by her flak-jacket-wearing husband, the manager of Goodyear Tires. The one Trey Stanton introduced her to. His occupation wouldn't be terribly obvious that night, having scrubbed the grease from under his nails and wearing his good short-sleeve dress shirt. The one without his name embroidered above the pocket. "Hey babe," he'd say, grabbing her ass, "didn't you used to know that guy?" Aidan would make a guest appearance, arriving as he lit cigars with hundred-dollar bills, the voluptuous flavor of the month hanging on his arm. He would look at Isabel, aghast, snapping his fingers as if he couldn't quite recall her name.

The music stopped, Isabel shaking her head, trying to dislodge the future. Standing at the edge of the dance floor, she looked at Aidan. She was sure he'd forgotten Catswallow's gala, certainly any moment they were on the verge of sharing before Fitz stepped up and realigned his universe. Aidan let out a howl like a crazed wolf, swinging her into the air. "Isabel, do you have any idea what this means?" A palpable electric current pulsed through him. No doubt you could see him glow from Birmingham. While happiness was hard to feign, it was impossible not to feel something. He was ecstatic. Isabel smiled, reaching for congratulatory words. They were there; she just needed a minute to get them out. As their wicked roller-coaster ride came to a jerky halt, Aidan's expression grew serious. He bent forward, snatching Isabel up into a ferocious kiss. It was incredibly soft and powerful, the absence of the sticky sweetness of a watermelon Jolly Rancher not an issue. For a moment she was caught up in the kiss. It was as if Catswallow were raffling off dreams and Aidan and Isabel held every winning number. But like an unexpected suitor, apprehension cut in. It silenced a force that was moving with the power of a tsunami. Isabel pushed him away. The last thing she wanted was for Aidan to kiss her because she was the closest pair of lips. Isabel didn't want to be the party kiss or, now, the *ain't-life-grand* kiss. If Aidan was going to kiss her, it had to be because kissing Isabel was the only thing on his mind. She refused to be his exclamation point. That job belonged to every other girl in the room. Isabel's desire not to be *one of them* exceeded her desire for him. If that was all he wanted, let Aidan Roycroft kiss the flavor of the month. She would not settle. Without a backward glance, or a congratulatory word, Isabel disappeared into a papier-mâché world, slipping out the side door of the Catswallow VFW.

CHAPTER FIVE

Catswallow, Alabama

ISABEL FINAGLED A RIDE HOME WITH KYLE MARSH AND HIS DATE. She held it together, even after Kyle informed her that an evening with him would not have ended like this. He had a point. Isabel said to drop her off at the entrance to Fountainhead. She'd walk the half mile to the trailer. In truth, she didn't want to take the dress off, the distance her only excuse to wear it a few minutes longer. The shoes she gladly forfeited, realizing her subconscious was a pushy ass. Isabel had chosen the stilt-like torturous things so if she and Aidan were to dance, or anything more, she'd be the perfect height. But bare feet and gravel were as painful as the night, and she ended up walking along the dirt edge. As she walked, she plucked bobby pins from her hair, dropping them onto the road. The cascading updo unfurled, leaving dangling curls caked in hairspray. She wiped mascara-filled tears, wondering if, after the ball, Cinderella felt this shitty.

The trailer was dark, but she did notice Rick's SUV parked nearby. *Super.* More than once he'd left in the wee hours of the morning. Aside from the obvious grossness of that, Isabel wanted her mother. Well, she wanted her to herself. She hesitated a few yards from the porch. Maybe she didn't. They were as snug as two bugs in a rug—after the split Carrie said it all the time. It was her mantra from the time they started driving on I-95 south, reassuring a younger Isabel about the beauty of the South, a terrific job, and the prospect of a happy life. But since the uproar over Aidan, since she wasn't that little girl anymore, maybe since Rick, things weren't so snug. She was home earlier than expected, that part being a small plus. She wouldn't have to play Juliet to his Mr. Capulet. Walking through the door, it occurred to Isabel that her mother's car wasn't out front. But that couldn't be right.

She tossed the high heels in a corner and grabbed some tissues from the breakfast bar. Blotting mascara, Isabel turned toward the dark living room and flipped on a lamp. She shuffled back, colliding hard with the breakfast bar. Rick was sprawled across the sofa, deep beer-gut laughter responding to her surprise. He scratched a hand across his chest where a thicket of hair protruded. Isabel was unable to keep from noticing his unbuckled belt, the open button of his trousers. "Where's my mother? What are you doing here?"

"Waitin' on you, missy. Busy night in the ER; Carrie got called in to work." It didn't happen often, but it did happen. "You're early," he said, glancing at the diamond-faced watch he showed off to anyone who would look. "Seems a bunch of you kids left the gala and got a little drunk. There was a wreck out on Old Station Road."

Isabel's mind leapt to Aidan. But there really wasn't enough time for him to go off and get drunk. On the other hand, with his newfound fame, who knew what he'd be tempted to do. "So why are you still here?"

"Your mother was worried, couldn't get you on your cell. I volunteered to wait until you got home. Just being helpful," he said, his shrug lazy and benign. It was at complete odds with Isabel's cautionary stance and the voice in the back of her head.

"Nice of you. I'm home. You can go." She turned toward her bedroom, but Rick was up off the sofa, following.

"Now, that's not too social, Bella." She froze as thick fingers moved up and down her arm. She'd rather it were fire ants. Isabel turned, wanting to tell him to get his hands off her. His penetrating stare stole the demand. "From the look of you," he said, a finger swiping through a tear, "seems your night with Roycroft didn't go so good. I didn't hear his truck—can't miss that hunk of junk." Caressing fingertips kept moving, closing around Isabel's arm. "See what I mean, him letting you find your own way home. That's not safe, sweetie, not safe at all." His gaze darted past her head. She was alone, and he knew it. "That's no way to treat a young woman, particularly one as special as you." She stepped back; her arm didn't follow. "You are special, Bella, you know? Pretty too. But not the kind of pretty that'll satisfy a tomcat like him. A little spitfire that's a touch more smarts than she is beauty. Roycroft, he can't help that. It's in his DNA. He likes 'em blond with big boobs, whether they can think or not isn't the point. Ever take a good look at Stella? I can tell you from experience she puts out after one drink. Not very classy. Not like your mama."

"You're disgusting, let go of me."

He did the opposite, inching closer. "You're nothing but a curiosity for Roycroft. Trust me. In the end he'll want the same thing as his daddy—the kind willin' to kiss his ass or anything else."

Isabel was about to say: *Just like you.* But she could see what an insult it was to her mother. "Aidan and I are none of your business!" She tried twisting away, but his hand was a sailor's knot. A body-skimming gaze moved decidedly south, his upturned mouth conveying every smarmy thought.

"You know, you're right. Forget him. Hell, by now Roycroft's busy dippin' his wick into something that's not quite so much work, like Ms. O'Rourke." Struggling was a moot point, Isabel recalling how much bigger and wider Rick seemed when confronting Aidan. "That's gotta sting, after the hours you put in. But I have an idea how to get back at him. I was entertaining a pretty good fantasy when you came in." His other arm wrapped around her waist, jerking Isabel into an iron-clad embrace. "And here you are . . . the star. I promise you, Bella, I'm at least one up on Roycroft when it comes to women."

They shuffled together, like some diabolical waltz, running out of room as the wood-tone paneling met with her back. He was drunk. It didn't register, not until Rick's mouth made razor-burn contact with her cheek. For once, he didn't smell like cologne; it was more of an 80-proof aroma. There was a furious pounding in her chest. Outwardly, Isabel forced herself to stay calm. "Get away from me!" she said, shoving her palms against his chest. It was like smacking cement. Rick grabbed her wrists and pinned them against the wall, the implication terrifying and real. His mouth moved hard over hers. It was raw and scratchy and beyond repulsive. Worse than that, it took the place of Aidan's kiss. Grinding himself against her, Isabel couldn't believe what she was feeling. There weren't enough layers of silky fabric on the planet. Calm was history as her body struggled against every part of his. *This is not happening. It can't be happening!* A bearlike hand pawed at the dress and the tear of fabric at the bodice informed her that, indeed, it was.

"Look, Bella," he said, his tone conversational, like he was trying to sell her a car. "I made an investment here, and I want the payoff—with interest. I watch you strut around this place in your short-shorts and tight T-shirts, like some kinda brainy trailer-trash tease."

"It's my home!" she shouted. "And what do you mean investment?"

He laughed but never lost an ounce of the power that was

riding against her. "Your dress, your day of beauty. You don't really think your mama shelled out for all that?"

"You? You paid for the dress, all of this?"

He shrugged. "All women come with a price tag. Hell, I don't mind. It made her happy. Besides, I admit it. I wanted to see spitfire polished up." He narrowed his eyes, his tongue sliding over his lips. "It's way better than I figured. 'Bout killed me to watch you waltz out of here with him." He pressed closer, whispering hotly in her ear. "But see how things work out? Roycroft's lived up to my expectations and here we are." He inched back. "So how's about we settle your tab? I'm a fair guy, Bella. We can have a good time if you give it a chance." Holding her wrists with one hand, with the other Rick wrestled for the zipper of her dress, which was on the side and he couldn't find it. His expression grew comical, as if a hide-and-seek zipper were part of Isabel's tease.

At a momentary standoff, Isabel hoped he'd back up an inch. That's all it would take for her to deliver a swift knee to his groin, which offered an ample target. Instead, Rick's mouth moved over hers again, Isabel clinging to a semblance of calm. It began to fade, Isabel struggling and gagging, wondering what, exactly, she'd done to deserve this. She'd never been so intimidated, not by any man. Physical force against her will; she was going to lose. "Please don't do this," she said, her head wrenching left and right, his mouth capturing hers.

"That's it, baby, you make me work for it. A little fight gets the blood movin'."

Turning her head hard, instinct urged Isabel to gather the self-worth her mother had talked about. Carrie was right. She had plenty. "Don't you do this!" Her head thumped hard against the wall, spitting into Rick's face. She watched a wad of saliva run across his broad nose, down his cheek. He looked stunned, the grin evaporating. In one angry motion Rick let go of the dress, wiped the spit, and backhanded her across the face. The sting was fantastic, delivering a brain-rattling reply. She wanted to scream, but just as fast her jaw was pinched between two vice-like fingers, her teeth cracking.

"It was my intention to ask nicely, but fuck that now. Take the dress off, Bella. Or we can just go around it." With angry intent, Rick pillaged through layers of dress, groping, until his hand made contact with her thigh, the dress bunched at her waist. Unlike at the restaurant, there was no margin for *"pardon me"* error, his hand thrusting between her legs. It was as if he had eight hands— or ten. One held hers to the wall. The others worked together, holding up the dress, grabbing at her underwear . . . unzipping his pants. "This will happen, sweetie. Promise, you'll like it more than you think." His liquored breath was hot in her face, his physical size consuming hers. "'Course," he said, exposing himself, "probably not as much as me."

But Isabel wasn't done fighting, impelled by the sharp image of her immediate future. "If you do this, I'll tell the entire town. I won't be quiet about it. I'll tell my mother and the sheriff, and anyone who will listen!"

His eyes creased, but his mouth bowed wider. "Try it, you little bitch. I've lived in Catswallow my whole life. Your word's nothing against mine. You'll be the Yankee slut who came on to me!" Additional spitfire worked against her, Rick surrounding her body, spinning her around. "But if you're that opposed, maybe it's better you don't watch!" Pressed between him and the wall, Isabel couldn't breathe. She couldn't get away. It was like being trapped under the cover of a swimming pool, the idea of everything going black suddenly having great appeal.

A truck door slammed. It was an earsplitting creak she'd know anywhere, more rust than painted metal. With her cheek pressed to the paneling, she screamed Aidan's name. Rick's hand came around, clamping over Isabel's mouth. She felt him jerk his pants up. Saliva and sweat oozed from beneath his palm. He whispered, "No worries, honey, I can take him—maybe make him watch." The front door burst open, Rick having no choice but to spin the two of them around. The knob went right through the wall, the force causing it to crash shut behind Aidan.

"What the fuck?"

He spoke and moved so fast Isabel couldn't comprehend how he absorbed what was happening. She broke from his hold, and Aidan rammed Rick like an opposing linebacker, putting his head right through the wood-tone paneling. Stunned and drunk, Rick staggered; Aidan rushed forward and hit him again. It was a small room with too much furniture. The two crashed over and into things, Aidan pummeling him with a ferociousness that was completely foreign to Isabel. Rick gained momentum, long enough to connect one terrific punch to Aidan's face. He stumbled, falling backward over the already toppled coffee table. Rick lunged, but not at Aidan. He dove for the bar stool where his jacket hung. Moving toward him, Isabel jerked to a halt as Aidan froze, prone on the floor. Rick stood over him, his gun aimed at Aidan's head.

"Those were some serious punches," he choked, spitting blood onto the carpet, "you swing harder than your daddy." Rick wiped the lingering drip from his mouth, holding the gun steady. "Didn't think that was possible. But I promise you, boy, this will pack an even bigger wallop." The trigger cocked. Isabel didn't think, she just moved. Layers of silky fabric were in motion, barreling at Rick, enough to knock him off balance and knock the gun from his grip. Aidan assisted with the tackle, taking him to the floor. A wrestling match ensued, punches flying again.

"Aidan, stop! It's over. You're going to kill him!" Isabel screamed so loud her words were a garbled shrill. But Rick wasn't fighting back. He was fighting off Aidan as he shimmied across the marble sculpted carpet. Lying a few feet away, the small revolver glinted in the light. Isabel scrambled for it, but the two of them and every broken piece of furniture they now owned was in the way. Aidan spied it. They snaked across the floor kicking and swinging. The grunting and grappling peaked as confusion mounted. Isabel couldn't see who had the gun—Aidan did. As she yelled again for it to stop, a short crack of thunder burst through the air, the smell of gunpowder filling the room. The sound was violent, louder than on TV, louder than she imagined something like that could be. But, maybe, the reason it was so loud was because of the horrific silence that followed.

CHAPTER SIX

Providence, Rhode Island
Present Day

THE STAFF MEETING DRAGGED ON, ISABEL OBLIVIOUS TO ANY agenda. She was too annoyed that she let herself be goaded into divulging a fact she shared with no one. She huffed loudly, which seemed to coincide with the vibe in the air. It was a brain freeze, the aftereffect of a late Sunday night, or, most likely, a desperate attempt to end the watercooler conversation about Aidan Royce. Thankfully, the confession hadn't mattered, neither of Isabel's co-workers taking a word to heart. She appreciated their skepticism. Had Tanya suddenly let it slip that she'd been present for any of Adam Levine's body art, how seriously would Isabel take that? The two women had chuckled all the way to the conference room, chalking it up to an eccentric sense of humor.

Station manager Rudy Shaw had called the meeting, and Isabel was content to let him have the reins. No one looked in her direction. Surely, the always conscientious Isabel was taking copious notes on market shares and ratings grabbers. For their conservative audience that meant nothing more shocking than giveaway tickets to *Antiques Roadshow* or sponsoring a Celtic Woman concert. White noise hummed guiltily in Isabel's ear. She shifted in her seat, staring at a *98.6—The Normal FM* notepad that had been reduced to scrap paper. Focused on random doodling, Isabel reminded herself just how far she'd come from the Aidan Royce she woke to that morning. Or more to the point, the one who'd dominated her adolescence. *The opposite of love was indifference . . .* And she'd been indifferent for years—an in-your-face media blitz notwithstanding. Isabel felt eyes shift in her direction, keeping hers on the notepad. She heard Rudy prattle on about the upcoming ratings sweeps and everyday profit margins. No wonder her thoughts were askew. Fighting for an audience in a pool as shallow as theirs was a never-ending battle—kind of like being the corner IGA surrounded by big-box stores. Whatever the crisis, she'd handle it. Problems at *98.6—The Normal FM* were manageable. Not like problems at Grassroots Kids. Isabel took a cleansing breath, redeploying her energy. Unwelcome angst drifted away, taking Aidan Royce with it. *Goodbye and good riddance . . .*

Grassroots Kids, now there was something worth thinking about, something that mattered. With her job at the radio station under control, Isabel had sought a greater challenge. For the past three years, *98.6—The Normal FM* paid the bills while she pursued a loftier goal, Grassroots Kids. Until it literally burned to the ground, the not-for-profit organization had surpassed fledgling-entity status, gaining momentum and even praise from the *Boston Globe*. In the project's most celebrated moment, last October, the Globe gave its stamp of approval, rewarding Isabel and the organization with an in-depth feature. The paper called Grassroots Kids *"a future voice in the world of social conscientiousness."* The article and photos, which Nate had framed as a gift, were a testament to what was—before everything turned to charred rubble. An Easter Sunday three-alarm fire had left its Providence site, the mainstay for everything, in ruins. For Isabel, the not-for-profit was more than a building, though it really couldn't function without one. Personally and professionally for her, it was a tangible thing, representing the capable, successful person Isabel's parents had intended. Before the fire, her days were rewarding, doing double duty at the radio station and acting as CEO of Grassroots Kids. The small nonprofit served as a haven, providing everything from medical expenses and after-school programs to counseling for children who were dealing with personal crises. The idea had spawned after years of reflection, Isabel's own past inspiring the concept for Grassroots Kids. If someone had been there to bridge the gap between her parents' divorce and the upheaval to their lives, and had Isabel not expended so much energy hating her father, she felt certain things would have been different. Secondly, what almost happened with Rick Stanton did happen in many cases, and a place like Grassroots Kids was poised to help. As it was, years removed, Isabel was still uncomfortable standing near any man of a certain stature, even if he was Santa Claus. *And if Aidan hadn't been there . . .* An involuntary hum rang from her throat, forced to acknowledge his single moment of honor. She flipped to a fresh sheet on her notepad, one that was crisp and even and blank.

Nate, she thought, smiling. *Now there's a man whose character is never in question.* Grassroots Kids was hardly a one-woman effort, and help had come from a surprising source. The two had met under much different circumstances, with Nate in his professional capacity as rheumatologist extraordinaire and Isabel not as patient but as concerned family member. Before long, feelings sparked beyond the scope of medicinal issues. Isabel, whose man-listening skills were honed to perfection, was just the right ear for Nate's troubles. He'd recently divorced from his wife, Jenny. She was a pediatrician who'd craved adventure, joining Boston's Doctors Without Borders. It sent her to remote regions of the planet, mostly to places where they'd never heard of Boston. Nate was blindsided. He'd assumed their married life was scripted and that altruistic medicine would be best served via the overflow of Mass General's emergency room. In the end he concluded that they'd married too young, too unsure about who they were as adults. Isabel appreciated the specifics of his circumstance. Eventually, Nate claimed indifference about Jenny, conversations moving on to Isabel's daydream of a place like Grassroots Kids. He encouraged the prospect, assisting via his well-to-do family's philanthropic ties by helping Isabel make initial contacts and connections. Raising awareness, she quickly learned, was paramount to raising money.

While she was thrilled by Nate's help, it was a subtle attraction that led to a goose bump effect. She supposed it could happen like that, a person enters your life with the concept of professional distance understood. But after exhausting his past and tending to her future, they realized that the wall had crumbled, taking practiced etiquette with it. Last night things kicked up another notch when a quiet waterfront dinner took a passionate turn. On other Sunday evenings Nate had returned to Boston and a busy patient load. But yesterday his plan changed, and instead of taking Isabel home, Nate took her to bed. As always, his touch was fiery. The echoed *I love you* were not new words. Nate had said them before, in the warmth of a bed with his arms wrapped around her, repeating the same, up to his elbows in grease as he changed a flat tire. *"Isabel, wait in the car . . ." "Why? I'm fascinated by an MD's ability not to depend on Triple A . . ."* His curly brown hair waved in the wind as he smiled at her from the raw rim of the jacked-up Audi. *"Because I love you, and inside the car is safer than the side of the highway."*

Last night presented no mechanical difficulties whatsoever, following a pleasant pattern. In bed, moments moved lithely until he reached the stitch where those words belonged. Instead, Nate asked a spontaneous question that startled Isabel, who replied with "What?" He'd laughed, kissing her. "Okay, no points for planning. I'm not a big-production kind of guy. But I have thought about this. I want this every night. I want two toothbrushes in one place. I want no hangers and six inches of room in the closet. I want you to tell me to take off because it's a Friday—and we do it. Would you . . ." And he hesitated. "Would you come live with me in Boston?" She was stunned by the invitation, knowing how wary he was of traditional commitment. "Your job at the radio station, I don't mean to downplay it, but Grassroots Kids should be your focus. That's your future. I . . . Well, I think I could be too." Before she could reply, his cell rang. While the interruption was frustrating, it only emphasized his point. On paper, it was fifty miles from Providence to Boston. But New England traffic moved like sludge on a good day, even at one in the morning. His feathery timbre shifted as he took the call, medical-jargon emotionless. Already out of bed, he hung up the phone, searching for his underwear. Isabel started to follow. "Don't get up," he said, almost tucking her back in. "Stay here. Sleep on it. Moving in with somebody is a big deal." He kissed her hard, honing his point. Nate glanced toward the dark living room. "I think I can discern my pants from your skirt." Smiling silly in the dark, she'd called after him, insisting he commit to memory the look on Mass General's staff's faces if he arrived in a flouncy summer frock.

Lost in thoughts of Nate Potter and the future, Isabel filled in the 98.6 logos on her notepad. She gave the thermometers raging fevers, attaching little red hearts to each one. The moment, the invitation, it still took her breath away. Isabel admired her adolescent tribute, pleased with a relationship that had matured to such a ripe, well-rounded point. It was steady and trusting and focused. Damn, it was practically an article in *Marie Claire*. Isabel sat up straighter, thinking she'd leave work early. She'd drive to Boston and surprise Nate with a candlelit dinner, bottle of champagne, and two new toothbrushes. It would be the perfect reply—less, of course, the voices seeping into her head. The ones coming from around the conference room table. Grumbling grew louder, disrupting her plans. Isabel jerked to attention, realizing something was amiss. She jammed the cap on the Sharpie, guiltily tearing away the heart-accosted sheets of paper. Like a middle schooler caught with a Nate Potter love note, she quickly hid it away.

"Isabel, this transition is unsettling for everyone, but I don't see how not sharing your insights," he said pointing, "is going to help. Maybe you've jotted a surefire cure down there. How about sharing your ideas with everyone?"

"Transition?" she said, taking in a table of shell-shocked faces. Everyone who worked at 98.6—*The Normal FM for Easy Listening* was in attendance. "Share my ideas," she parroted, feeling her face redden as though the principal had caught her. "Um, no. I'm pretty sure that I didn't write down any important ideas about the, ah . . . *transitional issue* we were discussing."

"She's just stunned," Tanya offered, patting Isabel's hand. "It's going to take a while for it to sink in. This is zero time to pull off a major promotion."

"The clock's ticking on you gals to come up with a brilliant plan. Isabel is always on point with these things. I was thinking a grandiose giveaway. Somewhere fantastic, like the *Wheel of Fortune* set." It was Rudy's long-standing fantasy.

"Forget game shows," said Mary Louise. "Start thinking bigger, like a trip to Europe."

"Or the moon," mumbled Tanya.

Isabel looked around the room, scanning for a hint.

"It could be worse," said Percy Harkins, who headed sales. "They could have gone classical. That's a death sentence. Ever try to sell airtime with a classical format?" Like a telltale note, hushed whispers passed around the room. "Funeral homes and dentist offices, that's where you peddle the goods. This could be okay, open all kinds of new markets. 'Course it's gonna mean connecting with a hipper crowd," he said, fingering the hairpiece everyone politely ignored. "I don't envy you ladies, though. Sounds like you're gonna need a miracle."

"Or an employment agency," whispered Mary Louise. "Nobody gives away anything that draws that big of an audience."

"Forget your audience," said Percy. "I don't think there are that many people in the state of Rhode Island."

"I think they did it so we'll quit and they can bring in their own people."

"Come on, Mary Louise," Tanya said, swinging into her positive postdivorce voice. "If they wanted to bring their own people, they would have done it. They've tossed us the ball. At least that means they want to see if we can play."

Ball? What ball?

"The three of us, we're a team," Tanya said, an arm firmly landing around Isabel's shoulder. "You, me, Isabel . . . If we put our heads together, we can get out of this jam." Isabel smiled vaguely. The last time she was this fuzzy on the facts, she'd just had three wisdom teeth removed.

The meeting broke up to a rumbling of exit noises. There was a mocking "Good luck," and a sarcastic "Nice knowing you." "Mary Louise," Isabel said, grasping her arm. "So, um, how do you really feel about all this?" She sat again. Mary Louise was adamant about articulating her feelings, particularly since Joe fell off the roof. She insisted it was a healthy way to keep things in perspective. Isabel was sure it alleviated unused energy.

"Well," she began, bearing down with an ultraserious expression. "At least the three of us get to keep our jobs—for now. That's a good thing. I can't imagine going home and telling Joe that I lost my job *and* our insurance. He feels bad enough being out of work. But you know how it is with new management. They'll make changes if we don't come through. And the kind of ratings they're after . . . Well—" She shoved a forecast sheet at Isabel. Seeing the number in print, Isabel was amazed her eyes managed to stay in her head. "It's exactly what Percy said: We're going to need a miracle. That or we'll be out on the streets, just like the DJs."

"The DJs?"

"Hello? Didn't you hear a word Rudy said? Where have you been for the last hour?"

Not here, apparently . . .

"Poor thing," Tanya said, rubbing her arm. "Your plate was already full with Grassroots Kids. Just what you need, another impossible problem." The empathetic look spurred a queasy feeling in Isabel's gut. "They let them all go. Tomorrow *98.6—The Normal FM for Easy Listening* goes on air as *104.7—The Raging Fever FM for Hot Sound.*" A massive gulp rolled through Isabel's throat—like she'd swallowed a watermelon. Her eyes peeled wide as Mary Louise delivered the entire bullet.

"It's the radio station nightmare and it's happening to us. We've been bought out, a complete format change: advertisers, music, demographics, and promotions. But I suppose the handwriting's been on the wall. Our format can't compete with any of the contemporary markets or talk radio, and let's not even discuss satellite. So starting tomorrow, we're all rock 'n' roll, all the time. The incoming regime wants a giant-size promotion to draw a new audience," she said. "You know the type, greedy capitalists. They'll want to rake in the bucks right away. And they won't care what kind of hype we use to do it."

"That's true," said Tanya. "Remember last year when *107.9 Providence Power* was bought out? To meet their new numbers, they ran that crazy promotion with Naked Rob, their morning DJ.

Listeners called in trying to outdo one another with the station's Hottest Place, Hottest Partner contest. First prize was $1,000."

"That's right. It went okay until some guy described, in detail, the woman he'd encountered and her prop-filled bedroom, top-of-the-line accessories. A page right out of . . . well, never mind," Mary Louise said, "you get the idea."

"Oh, yes," Isabel recalled. "The police found the guy the next day, naked, bound and gagged in his own garage . . . with his, um . . ."

"His, um, attached to fishing line that attached to the garage door opener," said Tanya. "Apparently, the man's neighbor was listening too. The woman and *accessories* belonged to him."

"But he won the contest, right?" In sync, Tanya and Isabel's heads turned toward Mary Louise.

Rudy Shaw, a man whose signature three-piece suit was his calling card, popped back through the door. More train conductor than overseer of a rock 'n' roll station, he opened his pocket watch again. "Ladies, I suggest you get busy—pronto. What I mean is you'll come up with something, right?" Rudy Shaw was a nervous, post-middle-age man with chronic indigestion and little tolerance for change. It occurred to Isabel that his job was in real jeopardy. He was the perfect fit for *98.6—The Normal FM*, having surrendered back during the British invasion. Chances were he had one shot to prove his worth. "This buyout came as a shock to me. I didn't even know the station was for sale." He looked expectantly at the wall clock. "The minutes are ticking. I'm sorry. I know this is practically impossible." He unraveled a Rolaid and disappeared out the door.

"Eight weeks," Mary Louise sighed. "He's right. It's zero time to pull off a major ratings grabber."

"Especially with zero connections," Tanya said, fingers dragging through a thick bob of hair. "It takes years to develop those kinds of contacts. Our usual go-to options, a telethon from Ned's

Bowlarama or a trip to Mystic Seaport, they're not going to cut it." Three heads nodded in agreement, Tanya's face suddenly brightening. "Hey," she said, grasping Isabel's shoulder. "Maybe we do have a connection, a real ratings grabber." Isabel's head ticked around, wondering if she was looking right into it. "Isabel, don't you know people in Alabama who own a bunch of car dealerships? If they could hook us up . . ."

She stopped midsentence, Isabel's appalled expression ending the query. She'd put herself, Mary Louise, and Tanya on a street corner to solicit listeners before she'd ever ask—Well, like that would get them there. "Gimmicks aren't going to cut it, Tanya. Did you see those numbers?" she asked, pushing the forecast sheet toward her. "We'd have to give away a luxury car every day for a month to draw that kind of audience." Isabel leaned back, chewing on a thumbnail.

"Mmm, I suppose it would be hard to get anyone to give us a car every day for a month." Isabel stared, her eyes meeting with the layer of denseness that translated into Tanya's three children. "So you think it needs to be something bigger. Something with a massive guaranteed draw."

"Yes, something with a huge draw."

"Something people want," Mary Louise added.

"Like a lightning-in-a-bottle kind of thing," said Tanya.

"Lightning in a bottle," Mary Louise echoed.

"Wouldn't a huge concert be that kind of draw, generate those kinds of ratings?" Tanya said, her chin resting on her fist.

Sometimes, at the worst possible moment, denseness managed to hit the nail on the head. Isabel's teeth bore down into the flesh of her thumb as a careful gaze rose. She suspected that direct eye contact might give her away.

"Yes, hosting an event like that would be a slam dunk," said Mary Louise. "But so what? Even if we scraped together the talent from every past *Normal FM* event, it's all wrong. Kidnapping Neil Sedaka, Paul Anka, and most of the headliners at Foxwoods wouldn't be close to the firepower we need."

"I guess not." Tanya sighed, her stubby nails thrumming the table. "Maybe you were right, Mary Louise. Maybe we should spend the time looking for new jobs."

Isabel kept her focus on the tabletop, Mary Louise's stare penetrating. She was supposed to be in charge, the leader, the idea person. She didn't make a sound. She didn't move. "Still, we need to make some kind of effort. Don't we?" Isabel ignored the verbal nudge, pressing deeper into her chair. "Okay then." Mary Louise's gaze edged off Isabel. "Listen, here's what we'll do. I'll start putting together some potential ideas. Tanya, you call over to *Providence Power*. See if you can find out the exact limits of liability, if anyone tried to sue after the, um, fishing line incident." Tanya nodded, ready to take direction. "Who knows what we'll have to do to make this happen."

Tanya and Mary Louise gathered up their belongings and burdens and headed out. At the door, Tanya lingered, maybe looking to cure whatever ailed their usually competent supervisor. "Hey, Isabel," she said, smiling. "It's too bad you don't really know Aidan Royce." Isabel gulped hard, swallowing down whatever thing that was one size larger than a watermelon. "Imagine what we could do if you had a connection like that."

Keeping a firm hold on her poker face, she shrugged. "Yeah, just imagine."

CHAPTER SEVEN

Catswallow, Alabama

AIDAN PULLED INTO THE DARK DRIVEWAY OF THE FARMHOUSE, jerking the truck into park. He couldn't get Isabel inside fast enough. He needed to take control of the situation, and the only way he knew how to do that was to get her somewhere safe. That meant the farmhouse. Seconds after the gunshot, a moment after he took Stanton out, Isabel was telling him to get in the truck, start the engine. Dazed by the fast and furious events he followed the instructions. It was a habit, forever listening to whatever Isabel said. Aidan thought she was right behind him, but she'd scurried out the door moments later. No one said a word as they drove, not until he'd reached to his cheek, dabbing a bloody bruise. "Here, turn here," she'd said, pointing to a convenience store. Isabel hopped out of the truck, the dress rustling as she hurried inside. He could see her moving from aisle to aisle, orderly, the way she did everything. Even after Stanton . . . *What?* Coming through the trailer door, the scene inside was evident and forever bound to his brain. But Aidan didn't know if he arrived just in time or seconds too late. It could have been either. Composed and in control, that was Isabel and it made it impossible to tell. She could always take care of herself. But in that circumstance . . . Aidan scrubbed a hand over his face, the thought too heinous. Through the stark light of the convenience store he stared at Isabel, who was conversing with the clerk. To his point, outside she was a mess, yet her poise was unflappable. He was overwrought by the possibility of a ripped ball gown being the least of the damage. *What do I say? How do I handle that?* With his fingers in a death grip on the steering wheel, Aidan closed his eyes, convincing himself that he'd come up with the words—whatever Stanton had done. Moments later she climbed back into the truck, not saying anything, handing him a bag of frozen peas. And for a split second Aidan thought she'd lost it.

"For your face," she said, guiding the bag toward him. It molded perfectly to the swell of his cheek. "The ice machine was broken. This will work."

A few minutes later they arrived at the farmhouse. They sat in silence, the truck idling. "Aidan, turn the engine off."

He obeyed, still blindsided, dropping the bag of peas onto the seat. He couldn't get it out of his mouth, what he needed to ask. Monstrous visions stole his voice: Rick Stanton . . . Isabel tight in his grasp—his pants wide open. With the spark of an electric shock, he scrambled out of the truck, pacing in a small circle. It was so horrifically . . . *real.* Aidan squeezed his eyes shut. His swollen fists, his cheek, his head, it all pounded like an anvil, but it was Isabel's fate that caused the most livid pain. He forced down the bile that rose to the edge of his throat. Looking across the hood of the truck, his gaze followed Isabel as she reached the rickety porch, peas in hand. "Isabel!" he shouted. It was the loudest sound since the gun had fired. She stopped, turning. "I need to know what happened. If I . . . if he . . ." The idea of Isabel suffering something so awful, and the word, it was too grotesque. He couldn't make himself say it.

"I'm okay, Aidan. He didn't . . ." She hesitated, arms wrapping tight, a hand sliding to the torn bodice, holding the fabric in place. "You got there in time."

Bending forward, he murmured, "Thank you, God." With his hands clamped to his thighs, Aidan exhaled so deeply he thought he'd knock himself over. He let the affirmation sink in, dragging himself along to the door. Isabel said nothing more as she moved about the worn kitchen. Aidan began to calm, soothed by the familiar sight—less the ball gown. She belonged there, a bright moon enhancing a glow that was ever-present and bound to her. But his brow knotted as Isabel opened her purse, shoving a watch and a fat money clip into a drawer.

"Here they are," she said, pulling candles from a cabinet, setting one on a plate.

As she lit it, Aidan's gaze adjusted to the ambient flicker. It linked with a stream of moonlight that poured through the dirty cracked windows. Everything poured into the farmhouse, everything that mattered. They'd accumulated a lot of stuff over the years. It made no sense—it had nothing to do with his plans—but Aidan often found himself lost in the idea that one day they'd show up to the farmhouse and never leave. The Kessler family had lived there for generations; there was even a family plot. There were more than a dozen headstones adjacent to the front orchard. It was land that Aidan had walked a thousand times. Even in its defunct state, the old farm had a real family vibe, the two of them bonding over the thing they desperately lacked. It was a concept that everyone he knew viewed as archaic and irrelevant. Aidan felt differently, fascinated by the idea of a home with two functioning parents. John Roycroft didn't have the decency to own up to his common-law marriage to Stella, never mind considering the kind that came with a license and ceremony. Not even after he had a son. In turn, this made Aidan wonder what, exactly, you'd need to feel for another person to make that kind of commitment. Being there, at the farmhouse, stirred a lot of thoughts. But right now, it only made him realize where he was. He was where anyone would want to be after such a wicked night—he was home.

Tossing the match into the sink, Isabel turned. Beyond the chaos of the trailer, closer than she'd been in the truck, he saw it, candlelight illuminating the harsh red of one cheek. "He hit you?" It was dull and stupid, but it was the only thing that would come out of his mouth.

"He hit you harder." She handed Aidan back the peas, putting the candle down. But her eyes were wet, the confident line of Isabel's chin quivering. Aidan dropped the frozen bag onto two crates that served as a makeshift table. Before, he wanted to kill Stanton; now he wanted him alive. Aidan wanted to drag him through the center of town, butt naked, and string him up from the flagpole at city hall. Isabel's voice broke the intent, angry vision. "Before I came out to the truck I called an ambulance."

"What the hell did you do that for?"

"Aidan, he needed medical attention."

"He needed a bullet through his head!" he shouted, turning away. With his hands on his waist he shook his head. "But I wasn't man enough to do it. Was I, Isabel?" he said, speaking to the wall. "After what that son of a bitch did, the best I could manage was to put a bullet through the wall and my fist into his face."

"He was unconscious. You did enough, you kept him from . . ." She clasped his arm and as he turned her voice steadied. "Aidan, are you crazy? You think it would have been better to have shot Rick Stanton? We're probably in enough troub—"

"You think I give a damn about that?" Aidan edged closer, looking past her red cheek, her ruined dress. Even so, he saw how beautiful she was, standing there, shivering in moonlight and candles. Damn, why hadn't he said it earlier when a compliment would have mattered? *"Isabel, you're the most beautiful thing I've ever seen . . ."* It was his everyday opinion, that being why he could manage even less tonight. She was the most beautiful piece of music come to life. And he'd come so close to saying as much. Aidan almost blurted it out on the dance floor, everything that he'd kept quiet about since the disparity had dawned on him. It was the day Aidan understood the difference between wanting other girls and loving Isabel. But things were best this way, and he was mindful of that. Aidan Roycroft was his father's son. There was no gray area. For a man he never knew, he saw the stark resemblance. He'd heard it from everyone—Shanna O'Rourke to scum like Rick Stanton. He knew what Isabel's own mother thought of him. He'd seen what his father's philandering had done. It broke Stella Roycroft. And Aidan guessed he'd rather die before hurting Isabel that way. Besides, Isabel was wise to him, her romantic disinterest clear. They were great friends, best friends, closer than kin. It was so important to her. Aidan was sure that if he even hinted at the truth, she'd slap him upside the head and never speak to him again. Tonight, though, he was determined to tell her. He was just about to when Fitz Landrey showed up, spinning his world out of order. *So don't think, you idiot. Just do.*

Aidan shrugged off his jacket and draped it over her shoulders. Isabel gathered it willingly, but it didn't help. The shaking didn't stop. "Here, sit." The two of them sunk onto the sofa, the creaky springs groaning. Aidan closed his eyes, the despondent noise repeating in his head. It was a house rule, never to sit on the sofa with Isabel. Visions of where it could lead were taboo. But now, tonight after what happened with Stanton, Aidan needed her to know. "Isabel, I need to ask you something. Before what happened with Stanton, earlier, why'd you run away from me? You know . . . when I, um, kissed you."

There was an odd look on her face, as if it was so removed and long ago she didn't remember. Her fingertips inched toward his face, but she snapped them back. "When you kissed me, I didn't know what to do. I didn't expect it."

"Was it so awful?" One long arm reached toward the red of her cheek, seeing that both sides had turned crimson. She laughed and looked away. It wasn't the reaction he usually got.

"No, of course not. It wasn't awful. Like I said, it was just . . . unexpected. You kiss lots of girls, all the time. I don't want to be *one of them*—ever."

One of them. She couldn't make that any clearer. "I see. I'm sorry." He could barely get the words past the boulder in his throat. "It won't happen again."

"Oh . . . okay." They were both silent. He watched Isabel take a deep breath, her eyes meeting his. "Thanks, Aidan, for doing what you did. I told Stanton to leave, but he was all over me," she said, plucking at the tattered fabric. "He said he'd paid for this dress, the beauty salon—everything." There were tears, big puddling ones. He'd never seen Isabel cry. Despite her less than ideal family history, she was the strongest person Aidan knew. The sobs intensified as the story spilled out. Stanton had hinted at this before, offering Isabel beer, making vague remarks about the way she was dressed, wondering if she had a boyfriend. When she got to the part about Stanton's roving hand in the restaurant, Aidan was ready to kick the crap out of him again. "I told myself it was nothing," she gulped, wiping a hand across her nose. "That it was just my imagination. You've seen him with my mother. He's another person around her." There was mocking laughter, half a smile crossing Isabel's lips. "You have to admire her consistency, between Rick and my dad she's two for two."

"Two for two?"

"Choosing men who possess two different personalities."

"Isabel, your father's personality has nothing to do with . . . Never mind, go on. Tell me the rest."

"Tonight when Rick started in, it wasn't completely obvious. Then," she said, a shaky sigh expelling, "it was. Even so, I thought I could handle him."

"He's more than twice your size and he was drunk. Why didn't you tell me this before? Why didn't you tell your mother?"

She was almost hyperventilating, the words barely coherent. "I tried. I was here, at the farmhouse, one night last week. I wanted to tell you then, but you'd gone to Jasper or Cullman . . . I don't remember."

"Good Hope," he whispered, guilt rushing him. Ironically, he'd gone to He's Not Here, an always packed bar. The owner called with a last-minute opening, and Aidan jumped at the chance to feed his indulgent aspirations with a hundred bucks and a crowded room. Had Aidan turned him down, he would have been at the farmhouse. Isabel would have told him everything. And *this* would have never happened.

"She, um . . . my mother, she says she's in love with him. I started to, but I couldn't tell her. Not after everything with my father. But tonight, Rick made me so . . . so damn mad." And despite her tears a flame lit; a fire that said Stanton would have had a hell of a fight on his hands. "Aidan, I swear, he would have had to kill me first, before I let him . . . But the worst part, when he kissed me . . ."

"He kissed you?"

Isabel's fingers trailed over her pouty lips, clasping gingerly around her throat. "I couldn't breathe. Not because I was afraid of what he was going to do. But because it was gone."

"What was gone?" Aidan asked, wondering if reliving it was even worth it. He just wanted to find the thing that would make it all go away.

"You . . . your kiss. The way it felt, the taste, he took it away."

Aidan Roycroft thought he could handle anything any girl

threw at him. Then it occurred to him that this was what made her so hard to handle, so impossibly different. Isabel wasn't like other girls. Not really meaning to, but so confused, Aidan could only close his eyes and laugh. "Isabel, you just told me you don't want to be *one of them*—ever."

"I don't." But her body said otherwise, coming closer, her forehead tipping against his. "I can't be one of them, Aidan."

His mouth pressed to the tears, kissing them away. He'd fought it for so long, everything he felt, and this much he could not resist. What the fuck was wrong with him? She said she didn't want this. Was he going to be the second man to attack her in one night? A low hum pulsed from her throat. Aidan inched back. Her lips were pursed, eyes closed. He couldn't read it. Isabel was all about words and precise direction, making it foreign and strange when she simply reached for him.

"Isabel," he cautioned, "wait."

"Why?"

"Because I don't know if this is right. If after what happened with Stanton we should—"

Her fingertips pressed to his lips. "Aidan, it's the only thing I want . . . I swear."

He kissed her fingers, Isabel's hand cupping his face as his mouth curved gently over hers. The trembling stopped and he felt a terrific surrender. Isabel's body eased calmly into his, telling Aidan that this was where she wanted to be. She tasted of salty tears and a trace of lipstick, which so wasn't Isabel. Aidan dared himself to open his eyes, making sure it was really her. Tears stained her face, but she was smiling. With fists full of her hair, that beautiful hair, his body leaned into hers, laying them down on the sofa. Silky lavender fabric rustled beneath his chest, Aidan's mouth tracing the line of her throat, needing more as it met with the edge of the gown. But he hesitated.

"It's on the side," she said, "the zipper."

His mind wasn't on a zipper. "Isabel, are you sure? Maybe we should talk about it . . . I don't want either of us to make a mistake here."

"You . . . *this*, it's the only thing I can imagine erasing Rick Stanton's touch. Please, Aidan," she said, her voice steady and sure. "I just want you to make it go away. Would you do that for me?"

The gown was quick to comply, the ruined thing slipping to her waist. Isabel kissed him again, less gently than he had kissed her moments before.

Between dim candles and moonlight he saw how beautiful she was, his gaze flowing over every curve. "Jesus . . ." he mumbled, unable to get enough air in to get the rest of his reaction out. *You are so incredibly beautiful . . .* Wicked emotions collided, words derailed by the reality of seeing every part of her. The moon, while mood setting, was reduced to nothing more than a teasing glow. He cupped one breast in his hand, taking the other in his mouth. There was a hint of submission, Isabel's body arching against his. Giving in to things was not her usual behavior. He backed away and she stood, the gown falling to the floor. As it hit the dirty hardwood Aidan fought a flash of anger, Isabel tugging at his hand. But he was fixated, thinking he'd really like to set the damn thing on fire, knowing whose money had paid for it. Maybe she'd lend him the lighter.

"Aidan," she said, hearing his thoughts. "Just don't go there." Nimbly, anxiously, her fingers worked the buttons of his shirt. He undid the last one, sending the white dress shirt sailing across the room. Aidan watched her hands, flush to his skin. Those beautiful delicate hands. For a while, he'd convinced himself he was only in love with her hands, the way they moved, calculating math equations, cradling worn paperbacks, penning smart essays. It was safe and respectful and an epic fail. While he'd never admit it to a breathing soul, Aidan often woke from this exact moment satisfied by some damn wet dream. Her mouth mimicked her touch, gliding over his chest with an ease that felt natural and right. Aidan responded in sequential reply, his hand slipping inside her panties. He corralled a grin as his mouth met with hers again and again. The panties were lace. Even his dreams had never been so bold as to conjure up lace. And Aidan wondered what else he didn't know about Isabel. She kissed him harder, the hum from her throat intensifying. Aidan had never worried about a girl wanting him, and he sunk into a wave of relief finding her more than ready. Her legs moved apart as he stroked her, Isabel's delicate fingers transformed, digging decisively into his back.

Having fed a rush of hunger, kissing could only do so much and suddenly she stopped. Isabel's mouth turned away from his, her head resting on his shoulder. It was another unimagined act when her teeth nipped at him—so spontaneous it caused Aidan to gasp out loud. He kept the rhythm steady as even the air around them changed. The simple space that buffered their adolescence filled with sensual aromas, two adults repurposing this room. At the last second, her hand pushed between them, crushing hard into his. "Oh . . . Oh, Aidan . . . I . . ." It was an idyllic breath that gushed forward, consuming her. He didn't want it to end, but after a few moments the wave crashed, Isabel's body washing into his. Through locks of tousled hair, his gaze caught on the shadowed wall, which mirrored the moment. He thought he'd like to paint a mural of the whole damn scene. Looking back, he saw the expression on Isabel's face. It was intense, truly awed. And Aidan got the distinct impression that, perhaps, this had never happened before. Apparently, the same thought was on her mind.

"Aidan, is, um . . . Is the rest going to be like that? Because if it is, I'm not sure I'm going to survive it."

"Yeah, Isabel," he said, his voice wavering. "It's going to be just like that."

There was a small nod, a glance briefly connecting with his. "Okay," she said. "As long as I know."

There was no further discussion, nothing about intent or tomorrow, Isabel reaching for the zipper on his pants. He didn't want to know if this was once or forever. Either way, caution edged into Aidan's conscious and he reached for his wallet, retrieving a foil wrapper. The wallet dropped with a thud to the floor as her hand wrapped around the aching length of him. Aidan closed his eyes, nearly giving in to her touch. And this, he knew, did not happen with other girls. He grappled for composure, guessing it was the risk of a fantasy coming to life. Aidan kissed her once more, the lacy underwear shuffling from her body. Slow had never been party to these actions, but now it was all he wanted, resting at her feet. He needed it to last, absorbing every barely lit line. The images in his head, they dulled in comparison and he tried to tell her as much. But he couldn't find the sentences, words wedging between this moment and the one that nearly happened at the trailer. While it was enough to throw his romantic senses off balance there was also a swell of remorse, Aidan regretting every other girl he'd touched. Two incongruent things clicked into a perfect union, like the solid sky-blue pieces of a complicated puzzle: the respect Aidan had and wanting Isabel like this. In return, a smoky gaze wrapped around him, making him feel as if he was the only man she'd ever want to do this with. The thought was powerful and sublime—and something he thought impossible. Intuitively, his hands caressed her body, from her ankles, between her legs, across her stomach. He wanted to touch every part of her. He wanted to erase the night, just like she'd asked. Each time he touched her, even if it wasn't a place synonymous with arousal,

Isabel responded with sounds—emotions he'd never before heard. She pulled forward, the two of them knee to knee on the old sofa. He understood this. Intentional and direct, it was the way Isabel did things—even, apparently, things that were uncharted.

Her mouth grazed hotly over his, kissing his neck, avoiding the bruise on his face. Aidan reached to the crate where the condom had landed and Isabel tugged at his trousers. He stood, kicking off the cowboy boots, dropping his pants to the floor. He needed it to happen before Isabel considered other things, saying that doing this broke the rules by which they lived in this house. But as he tossed the pants aside, underwear fast to follow, a siren wailed. Streaks of red invaded the room, popping passion as if it were a delicate bubble. A whirl of angry lights flashed across the candlelit walls of the farmhouse, across Isabel's beautiful face and his naked body. And instead of Isabel calling his name, instead of this poignant moment coming to fruition, it was a bullhorn announcing the arrival of the Catswallow Sheriff's Department demanding that Aidan come outside.

CHAPTER EIGHT

Catswallow, Alabama

HOURS HAD PASSED SINCE THE HOLDING ROOM DOOR SHUT, and Isabel was no closer to getting Aidan out of there. Two sheriff's deputies had slammed him face-first into the hood of a cruiser, handcuffed him, and shoved him into the backseat. After the car sped away, they told Isabel to get in a different one. She did get a glimpse of him when they arrived at the Catswallow sheriff's station. He was on the opposite side of a glass wall with his back to her. That was all she saw, eight solid seconds of Aidan's backside, hands cuffed, bloody and swollen from the beating he gave Stanton. A female officer hustled her away, locking Isabel in the holding room before she could call out to him.

Officer Denton said she'd be back, only sharing that Stanton identified Aidan as the person who beat him. She refused to answer Isabel's questions. Watching the last fifteen minutes tick by, Isabel wished she'd paid better attention in high school history. Wasn't there a law about detaining a person without charging them? On the other hand, Isabel suspected that if you were being held in the Catswallow, Alabama, sheriff's station, civil rights weren't a given. In between worrying about Aidan, Isabel relived what was about to happen before the sheriff showed up. Her eyes closed, arms wrapping tight, amazed by how apprehensions had melted away. Even in the quiet chaos of that barren room, she could feel his touch, the way he tasted. Only in a small corner of her mind did she wonder if she'd dreamed it. Silky fabric scratched against the chair, Isabel thinking that Cinderella didn't have a damn thing on her. Since putting the dress on, the night had segued from one mind-boggling moment to another. Isabel's gaze drifted onto the locked steel door. Fairy-tale endings, though, those she wasn't so sure about.

The lock tumbled. Officer Denton, a beefy woman who appeared primed for a jailhouse reality series, came inside. Isabel wrenched her neck looking past the officer, surprised that her mother wasn't there. Her gaze jerked back as the officer pulled out the metal chair opposite hers. As the feet scraped along the cement floor, Isabel assuring herself that it was only the noise sending a shiver up her spine.

"Isabel," she said, placing a small tape recorder on the table. "It's time to talk about what happened. Start from the beginning, the moment you arrived back at your trailer."

She nodded, anxious to set things straight and to get Aidan out of there. Rick Stanton was the one who belonged in a jail cell. Methodically, she took the officer through the events of the evening, her voice deliberate and rational, as if it had happened to someone else. Calm had always driven Isabel's comfort zone, serving her well as she relayed the details. She told the officer that Stanton was on his way to raping her, and that Aidan arrived just in time. Isabel spoke about the gun and how Rick Stanton was going to shoot Aidan. Purposefully, she used her steadiest tone, explaining how they wrestled for it and how it fired into the wall. She insisted it was an accident, but that was a small lie and the only part she stumbled through. For a split second, Aidan did have the gun in his hand. She saw it. Anger, frustration, an accident, one of them made him squeeze the trigger. "After it fired, Aidan threw the gun across the room. He, um, he hit Stanton . . . again," she admitted, acknowledging Aidan's bloodied hands, which she could not hide.

As she came to the last sentence, Officer Denton kept up, jotting notes on a clipboard that Isabel couldn't see. She took a long breath, staring across the table. Her doughy face and a mouth that was bordered by several chins were expressionless; tiny blue eyes scanned hers. "You tell that story very calmly. Most young women allegedly attacked by their mother's boyfriend aren't as poised." A fervent nod stopped, Isabel realizing that composure was working against her. Eyes on the running recorder, she wanted to ask if they could start again. Perhaps a hysterical state of mind wouldn't have led to the word *allegedly*. "I'll be honest with you, Isabel. With the exception of Aidan's physical attack, your story doesn't square with Mr. Stanton's version."

"His version?"

"Yes, the moment Rick Stanton regained consciousness he told us what happened. In fact, he's already made a statement to the district attorney. Isabel, it's imperative that you tell the truth."

"But I just told you . . . Wait. What, exactly, did Rick Stanton say?"

She flipped up a page from her clipboard, paraphrasing, "Rick Stanton states that he'd gone out to run an errand at one of his dealerships. He returned a short while later and found Aidan Roycroft attacking you." Isabel's body stiffened against the chair as *allegedly* came clear. "Mr. Stanton said that when he came to your aid, Aidan turned on him."

Her head shook rapidly, faster than she could get the words out of her mouth. "That's not what happened! Not at all. He's lying! I told you what happened. Aidan will tell you the same thing!"

"Isabel, please, we are professionals. We're trained to see through situations like this. The fact is that the two of you were found together at the old Kessler farm, a place where Aidan had ample time to coerce you into cooperating." Her robust shoulders shrugged. "It's a classic scenario, a girl who'll do anything because she's obsessed with a guy—even after he attacks her. I've seen it a hundred times. Consider this an early intervention. Usually, I conduct this interview from the ICU ward when the victim has finally, mercifully, wised up to the abuse. Don't be one of them, Isabel."

And she couldn't calculate the number of stings associated with that. "I am *not* one of them."

"If you say so," Denton said, her patronizing tone based on what she perceived as impaired judgment. "But it doesn't take a PhD in psychology to grasp that you'd lie for Aidan."

"Okay, how about you grasp some common sense."

"A smart mouth won't get you anywhere," she snapped. "If this were a simple assault charge, our conversation might not be so serious. But we're talking about attempted murder here, a felony offense in the first degree. It's a very serious charge. Get your mind around it, girlfriend. We're talking about one of Catswallow's most prominent citizens, a man running for public office, possibly paralyzed for the rest of his life."

Isabel rolled her eyes. "Are you kidding? You want me to believe that a wicked right cross left Rick Stanton paralyzed?"

She plunked the clipboard onto the table, her stubby fingers folding. "No, of course not. The beating only left him bloodied and bruised . . . toothless. It's the bullet Aidan Roycroft put in his spine that will be responsible for that—as if you didn't know."

Isabel's body jerked into the metal edge of the table. "A bullet? How did a bullet . . . What are you talking about?"

"Ah, so now you're going to play dumb. Isabel, we know that Aidan shot Rick Stanton point-blank."

"Aidan did what?" Isabel's mouth dropped open as the accusation rang in her head. "They wrestled for the gun and it fired—into the wall! I told you that!" she said, pointing to the tape recorder. "Okay, maybe Aidan had the gun for a second, but he—"

"Ah, the story shifts again." She picked up the clipboard, making a fresh note. "At least we're making progress. Interestingly, not even Roycroft has denied shooting Mr. Stanton." Her voice was calm while Isabel's skipped toward hysteria.

"Aidan confessed to shooting Rick?" And suddenly Isabel wondered if any of them were in the same room.

"No, currently he's exercising his Miranda warning," she said, sounding sure a confession was forthcoming. "But he hasn't denied it. Aidan Roycroft is not putting up the vigilant protest you are."

Her eyes closed, thinking back. *Yes, Aidan had the gun. It was in his hand. I admit that. He fired it . . . Into the wall!* They opened, focusing on the tabletop. *Maybe I only thought the bullet hit the wall . . . maybe . . .* Isabel's gaze shifted onto the officer. *I know what I saw . . .* Aidan shot faux-wood paneling, not Rick Stanton. So why wasn't Aidan screaming as much from his jail cell? "Aidan hasn't denied it?" she repeated, utter confusion settling over her.

"No, he hasn't. Think it through, Isabel. You might want to get your story straight before your mother arrives. She was at the hospital when they brought Mr. Stanton in, but I understand she's on her way here."

"My mother . . ." It explained her absence, also telling Isabel what version she'd already heard. Isabel was unsure if she'd convince Rick's girlfriend of hers.

"Be reasonable. Let's do this the easy way. You haven't been charged with a crime. Not yet." She shut off the tape recorder. "Wasn't it more like this: Rick returned from his errand to find Aidan assaulting you. Fill in the backstory, Isabel. Perhaps it began friendly enough between you and Aidan. Then you changed your mind. You told him no. But Aidan didn't take kindly to your rejection. Mr. Stanton attempted to intervene, and in that effort drew his weapon. Then," she stated with a certainty that said she *was* in the room, "Aidan went berserk and attacked him. In his frenzy, he managed to get the gun away from Mr. Stanton and . . ." Her burly arms rose upward. "The rest seems clear to me. In addition to beating him senseless, Aidan Roycroft shot a defenseless man."

"Listen to me," Isabel said, palms pressing down on the table. "I know what happened in that trailer. The bullet in the wall will prove it."

"We found the bullet in the wall. *After* finding the one in Mr. Stanton. The first shot hit the wall, the second hit Stanton. Isn't that what happened, Isabel?"

"That's not what happened. This doesn't make any sense."

"Aidan is being charged with attempted murder. As soon as you decide to wise up and cooperate, we'll be adding attempted rape to those charges, maybe kidnapping."

"Attempted rape? Kidnapping? That's insane! Aidan didn't—"

"Isabel, don't make false statements to protect him. You can go to jail for that. You will go to jail for it. Girls like you . . ." There was hesitation, Officer Denton looking Isabel over as if she was decidedly *one of them*. "You're all so easily swayed. Get a clue. Don't let him use you like this."

"Use me—" She leapt from the chair, fingers digging through tresses of sticky hair. Isabel's brow crinkled so tight she thought her head might turn inside out. She looked between the door and Officer Denton, unable to explain any of it. "I have no idea how Rick Stanton ended up with a bullet in him, but Aidan didn't do it!"

From her seat at the table, the officer's gaze settled on the torn bodice. "Okay, Isabel. We'll go with that for the moment. Sit down here and tell me how your dress ended up in that condition." She turned the tape recorder back on.

"Fine with me." She sat hard in the chair, ready to drive home her point.

"Explain how Aidan isn't responsible. Explain it to me especially after what you told the clerk in the convenience store."

"Clerk in the conven—"

"Tell me about your conversation with him," Officer Denton said coaxingly, her tone saying she knew the whole story.

"The clerk."

"Yes, Isabel, the clerk." She blinked wide, staring. "And don't bother denying that you were there, we have it on video. Aidan concurred. The clerk described your appearance in detail. The torn dress, the red mark on your face." Isabel's hand rose, wondering if it had faded. "And the bruises on your wrist."

She peered down, splotches of red that were already turning purplish black. They were definitely there, but they didn't name her attacker. Things had spiraled so far out of control, Isabel wasn't sure if Aidan had a prayer.

Officer Denton pushed the tape recorder closer. "What did the clerk ask you, Isabel? What did you say in return?"

Isabel closed her eyes, picturing Aidan and reaching for the safe haven that was not anywhere in the room. "First . . . first I asked if they had any ice. I couldn't find it. Then the clerk asked if I was all right." Deadpan, the rest of the statement was devoid of emotion and surely matched the clerk's. "He saw my cheek; he whistled. He asked if I'd been to the gala or a boxing match. Then the clerk said that the ice machine was broken. He, um, he suggested frozen peas."

"And?"

"He was nosy," she said, wanting to make it clear the man's

query was about the sordid details, not her welfare. "He wanted to know if I'd been in a wreck or if somebody did this to me."

"And your reply was what?"

"I don't remember." She pulled in a long breath. "I said I got into a little scuffle."

"And what did he ask next?"

Isabel's head tipped back as tears slid down her face. "He pointed out the window of the store wanting to know if the guy in the truck, *my boyfriend,* did it."

"And what was your answer? What did you tell the man?"

"I wanted to get out of there! I didn't want to have a discussion with some meaningless store clerk about how or why . . ."

"What did you tell him, Isabel?"

Her mouth closed; her head bowing dejectedly. "I told him, 'Yeah, sure, you guessed it. It was something like that.'"

"Once more, please, a little louder."

Her head jerked up. "It doesn't matter what I said to the clerk! It wasn't true! I just wanted to get back to Aidan—" It was too late. The officer's doughy face had risen to a smug look of triumph. Short of picking Aidan out of a lineup, Isabel had slam-dunked their case. She shook her head, attempting speech-like words: "Officer Denton, you've got to listen to me. I came home and Stanton was there, sprawled out on the sofa. He's the one who came on to me! It . . . it wasn't the first time!"

"Do you have proof of that? Have you ever confided a specific incident to anyone?"

"Specific?" she said, thinking about what she implied to Carrie. "No, not exactly specific."

"I didn't think so. Isabel, Rick Stanton is a respected member of this community. That's a fact. People will not take kindly to slanderous remarks. Something else you might want to consider is Aidan Roycroft's reputation with girls . . . women, a fact for which we can get plenty of testimony."

For the first time since she'd known Aidan, Isabel didn't know what to do. "I want . . . I want to see him," she said, hoping he might. "I *need* to see Aidan."

Officer Denton rose and crossed to Isabel's side of the table. A hand gripped her shoulder. While the gesture was empathetic, she jerked away. "You can't. Aidan's waiting to be arraigned. We'd really like to get the rest of these charges straightened out. You don't have to lie for him, Isabel. What he tried to do wasn't your fault. When you're ready, we have someone you can talk to, a counselor trained to deal with the emotions of assault victims." Isabel cringed. It wasn't worth explaining again. Apparently, Rick Stanton's word was law. Didn't he tell her as much just hours ago? "Think about it," she said. "But we won't need your cooperation for the aggravated assault or the robbery."

"What robbery?" Isabel looked at the officer, guessing she was about to accuse Aidan of knocking over the convenience store.

"At the farmhouse, after Sheriff Sanders arrested Aidan, they found Rick Stanton's Rolex, his money clip." Isabel's hand flew to her mouth. "That's right, Isabel. It wasn't enough that the young man shot Mr. Stanton, beat him senseless, but he had to steal from him as well."

"I took the money and the watch!"

"What for? What possible reason could you have to take his money and watch?"

She'd never felt such a panic, not even at Rick Stanton's mercy. And for this reason, Isabel's confession continued on a blind ramble, "I sent Aidan to the truck, ahead of me. Then I checked Rick's breathing to see if it was steady. It was. I dialed 911. Then, I don't know, I freaked . . . thought about how it all looked."

"That's the first rational thing I've heard you say."

Her neck wrenched back, realizing she was only digging a deeper hole. "I never imagined anything as horrible as this. How could I? Taking the money and the watch," she insisted, "it was a lame attempt to make the whole thing look like a robbery."

"I see. Maybe we'll have to revisit the robbery charge." Then she offered a pitiable look. "It only bolsters our position, you staging a robbery to try to cover up the despicable things Aidan did, dialing 911 in an attempt to save him from a murder charge."

"Wait . . . what? That's not what I'm saying at all." Then Isabel shut up, invoking her right to remain silent. So far, all she'd managed to do was admit to confessing to a convenience store clerk that Aidan tore her dress and hit her. That, in fact, Aidan did fire the gun. Now there was the robbery she'd staged to deflect suspicion from the guy she was hopelessly in love with. The one for whom she'd, apparently, go to any length. If she kept this up, Aidan would get the death penalty. She needed a different plan. Isabel shifted her tone. "I'm sorry, Officer Denton. Can I . . . Is there any chance I can go home? Maybe things will be clearer there. I need time to think."

After a last warning to reconsider, the door was unlocked. The Catswallow Sheriff's Department was willing to release Isabel. Before she could leave they photographed the bruises on her wrists, the tear in her dress. Passing back through the booking area, she did pick up a helpful piece of information. A judge was being dragged out of bed to preside over Aidan's arraignment. In the exchange she heard something about him being an old hunting buddy of Stanton's. *Super.* Isabel looked around for Aidan, who was nowhere in sight. But a familiar face did rush toward her as Carrie Lang came through the jailhouse door.

CHAPTER NINE

Catswallow, Alabama

ON THE RIDE HOME, CAREFULLY, BUT WITH MORE EMOTION than she'd used in the holding room, Isabel recounted what happened. Carrie said nothing, concentrating on the road. As they turned into Fountainhead, Isabel asked if this was different from the story she'd heard. "Very," she replied. Isabel waited for realization to dawn. There was only the fumbling of keys and a shaking of hands as they made their way inside. Carrie surveyed the room full of broken furniture, one long stuttering breath pulsing from her. Isabel looked on, thinking how many years it took for her mother to acquire the garage sale possessions. She'd worked so hard for everything to amount to this. Picking up a toppled bar stool, she asked, "Who do you believe?" Carrie didn't answer, staring at pieces of their coffee table, which was now kindling. Isabel was quiet, letting her process the facts: Prince Charming, as it turned out, was nothing more than a sleazy car salesman.

Isabel excused herself to the bathroom. Her gaze panned the dingy space that they'd tried to brighten with sun-colored paint and frilly throw rugs from Target. The crinkle of fabric amplified in the tiny bathroom, morphing from a shimmering rustle to a

crackle of doom. She couldn't get the damn thing off fast enough,
flinging it into the tub, grabbing a pair of dirty jeans. Angrily, she
yanked on a bra and a T-shirt that hung from the back of the door.
Slumping onto the floor, Isabel racked her brain for words that
would convince her mother. Given her already poor opinion of
Aidan, a positive outcome seemed grim. Isabel's head pounded.
Big surprise. She opened the door to the vanity with her big toe.
Inside there was a plastic crate. She picked through, still with her
toes, rooting around for something stronger than Tylenol, a smidge
less lethal than cyanide. Tylenol PM, generic Tylenol. She bent
forward on her knees, weeding through with her hands . . . expired
Tylenol. *Geez, do we not own anything outside the acetaminophen
family?* Then, past the crate, far toward the back, she saw a box.
Retrieving it, Isabel sat hard on her behind. Where was a vat of
cyanide when you needed one? It was a home pregnancy test—a
used home pregnancy test. Inside the box were the contents. It
didn't require any detective skills, much less a high school education to interpret the results: bright blue and positive.

While different scenarios raced through her mind, Isabel
decided to go straight to the source. Only two people lived there.
She hurried out of the bathroom, box in hand. "Would you mind
explaining this to me?"

Carrie Lang sat on the edge of her bed, shoulders slumped, her
exhausted appearance gripped with new meaning. She looked up,
eyes as round—well, as round as a baby's bottom. "Isabel, where
did you get . . . You weren't supposed to find that!"

"Clearly! You . . . you're pregnant, now, today?" she demanded
as if this were an event she'd merely overlooked. Her mother nodded. "You're pregnant and Rick Stanton is the father?" She nodded
again and Isabel's stare bore down, incredulous and distraught.
*Tell me this isn't the complete reversal of every mother-daughter
confrontation on the topic.*

"I was going to tell you tomorrow, after all the gala business calmed down. I wasn't sure how you'd feel about it." She laughed, swiping at a tear. "Of course, the gist of that conversation, my announcement, has changed a bit."

"Announcement, like you were thrilled to tell me?"

"I was hoping . . ." She rose from the bed and moved toward her daughter. "Like I said, I was going to tell you after this weekend. Rick and I—"

"Rick and you what?" She took a giant step back. "Does he know?"

"Of course he knows. Rick has asked me to marry him. Like I said, Isabel, he's an honorable man. That dinner with Strobe and Trey, he wanted to tell everyone then. I convinced him to wait. I wanted to tell you privately, being as the news . . . well, being as the news included something more than an engagement announcement."

"And you're happy about this? I mean, before tonight, this is what you wanted?"

"I can't say I'd given much thought to having another child. But it is Rick's and I . . . I do love him, Isabel.

So she's said

"And . . ."

"And what? Accidents happen?"

"Even at thirty-nine," she said, chagrined. "Rick was so excited when I told him. You should have seen him. Happy, talking about our future . . . together." Isabel turned away. "Anyway . . . I won't say it didn't speed up a proposal, but we've already set a date. Next month, September. Everything was going to work out just fine until a few hours ago."

"You mean until Rick attempted to . . . until you found out what he tried to do." Isabel's eyes moved from her mother to the mirror where Carrie reflected on herself. Fingertips slid from her cheek to her jaw, following the line of a face that was drawn, burdened. "Mom, you do believe me? You know that Aidan and I are telling the truth, right?"

Carrie never deviated from her reflection. It was trancelike and frightening. "Isabel, there are so many things to consider. This baby in particular." But her voice was lost, her stare fixed on her midsection. "These last years have been difficult, harder than I might have imagined when we came here. My, um, job for one. It never panned out like I expected. I don't have to tell you that." Her gaze stuttered onto Isabel. "I don't want to have this baby without Rick. By myself."

"You'd have me."

A weak smile crept across her face. "And you'll what? Give up college, take a job at the Jiffy Mart to help support me and the baby? I've made some precarious choices, but absolutely not, Isabel. Absolutely not," she said, shaking her head. "That much I'm sure about. But I can't go it alone either. I don't want to. I'm better at being married. When I left your father, or he left me, I thought I'd prove myself to the world. That's what I set out to do. That was my intention, to make a better life for us. But I'm not like you, independent and full of fire. If it makes me a horrible person to say I want a life that doesn't rest on cinder blocks and rely on twelve-hour shifts, well, I suppose I am. I've done alone. It was challenging enough with a teenager. I've zero desire to try it with an infant."

The fear on her face was even plainer than her words. She clung to the bedpost as if it possessed human comfort. Isabel understood that much, piecing together the aftermath of Eric Lang and her mother's fears. None of it was without merit. The two of them, they'd barely scraped by, the hospital making cutbacks instead of expanding. It had tempted Carrie with the world, and she'd uprooted them for the promise of a future. In the end, she was lucky to hang on to her job. A baby with no Rick would be tantamount to disaster. Maybe it would be worse than what happened to Isabel that night. It was one thing for Carrie to cope with a teenager in a *modular home community*. She couldn't imagine a place like Fountainhead being all she knew. Damn them both: her father for leaving them and Rick Stanton for showing up. Her mother's body trembled, though Isabel couldn't bring herself to be human comfort. She was as distraught as the night they'd arrived home to their house in New Jersey. The same night Carrie Lang found her husband with a man.

She and Isabel had returned, unexpectedly, from a Girl Scout camping trip. Isabel threw up first, after the hot dogs, before the s'mores. Then Carrie threw up after finding Eric with Patrick Bourne. Isabel had crawled onto the sofa. Her mother went upstairs. There was a scream, awful and eye-opening, she supposed. Absorbing Carrie's lost expression, a well-worn flash of anger pulsed through Isabel. Her father was still with Patrick, and they were in this mess. "You're choosing not to believe me," Isabel said, pushing her father away, feeling anger shift.

"Oh, Isabel, if only it were that simple. If what I thought made any difference. You know what the sheriff thinks. You see how it looks. All of Catswallow will side with Rick. It's clear enough that Aidan beat him to a pulp, and whether it's intentional or accidental, Aidan will take the blame for the shooting. If he's smart, that's what he'll say, that it was an accident."

"And you're okay with that, knowing he'll go to prison, that his life will be ruined."

"Better his life than yours." Isabel's head inched forward, eyes widening. "You know my feelings about Aidan. It's only a matter of time until he devastates you. If it takes something this drastic to get him out of your life . . . so be it."

"Do you hate him that much?"

"It has nothing to do with hate. It's not black-and-white. Whether you admit it or not, I see how lost you are to Aidan, willing to do anything. I don't want this," she said, arms swinging wide, "to happen to you. I don't want you to wake up a dozen years from now and find yourself living in Stella Roycroft's trailer while Aidan is out with whoever . . . well, whoever does it for him. Hear me, Isabel. Aidan Roycroft will do that to you."

Isabel paused, calculating just how alone she and Aidan were. Lips pursed, she tried to follow her mother's skewed logic. "And what about Rick? Is it your plan to stand by your man—no matter what?"

"There's another interesting complication." With renewed energy, Carrie rose from the bed and tugged on a sweater. "Who knows what Rick's future will be. Or did you forget that he has a bullet in him?" She moved toward the living room as Isabel followed.

"Where are you going?"

"Back to the hospital. I was there when they brought him in. I saw the films. I've seen my share of bullet wounds. When Rick comes out of surgery, I don't think it's going to be good news. I want to be there when they tell him." Her eyes filled with tears as she moved toward her daughter, hands reaching. Isabel couldn't back away fast enough. "Think about what I've said. Tonight has altered four lives. Yours, mine, Rick's," she said, placing a hand over her abdomen, "and this baby's. It's my job to protect both of you. I know it doesn't seem like it, not right now. But I really am doing what's best for all of us."

As she left, Isabel whispered, "Five lives, Mom. What about Aidan's?"

Gravel spun, then the roar of a bad muffler faded. One worry disappeared with her. In a strategic move to bolster, or buy, her confidence Isabel guessed that Rick would have her in a new vehicle by week's end. Something safe and reliable for her and the baby. Falling onto the sofa, she considered her mother's situation and Aidan's. Both were unnervingly real, though an adamant allegiance no longer felt as firm. Carrie's choice had seen to it. While Isabel's decision was not painless, it was also not difficult. Rising to her feet, she followed her mother's cue. She slid on a pair of flip-flops, slinging a macramé purse over her shoulder. With a short backward glance and sides chosen, Isabel took Rick's keys from the bar and headed toward the Caddy Escalade.

CHAPTER TEN

Catswallow, Alabama

IN MOST SOUTHERN-SET MOVIES AND ALMOST ALL NOVELS, THE courthouse sat opposite the jailhouse. She guessed it was a cliché derived from fact. Isabel parked, on the jailhouse side, hurrying through the light of a tired moon and into the building. A couple of sheriff's deputies milled about; the same ones who'd corralled Aidan. Not surprisingly, his arraignment was the only activity. She slipped inside the courtroom and stood at the rear in a dark corner. The emergency hearing was already underway. Aidan sat with his back to the courtroom, Isabel deducing that the cranky-looking man tapping a pen against the desk was the DA. Once he started talking you'd never know it was the middle of the night, his accusations against Aidan sharp and succinct. Much of it was legal jargon, but Isabel caught the formal charge: attempted murder in the first degree. A man dressed in rumpled khakis and a polo shirt, as if it were casual Friday, stood next to Aidan. Isabel surmised that he was the court-appointed lawyer. He didn't exude much confidence as the judge peered at him over bifocal lenses. He asked the lawyer if Aidan had any prior arrests or convictions. In response, the attorney assured the judge of Aidan's spotless record. Out of all the things going against Aidan, she guessed it was one small thing in his favor. Aidan leaned over, saying something to his lawyer, and the man vehemently shook his head. From there the DA talked about the violence of Aidan's purported crime, his blatant disregard for human life, his unprovoked attack on Rick Stanton. Isabel literally bit her tongue to keep from launching into a vigorous defense. But it wouldn't do Aidan any good. They'd lock them both up and throw away the key.

Aidan's mother sat behind him, shoulders jerking as she sobbed into a wad of tissues. This had to be killing Aidan. It was generally all Stella Roycroft could do to handle the day-to-day stuff. Last winter, Aidan's truck skidded on a patch of ice and hit a guardrail. He ended up with a mild concussion, but it was Stella who left the hospital with a sedative. It was one reason Aidan didn't depend on her for much of anything. Isabel was unsure how much help she was going to be.

A few moments later, when the judge actually granted bail, setting the price of freedom at $80,000, she knew exactly how much help—none. Stella Roycroft didn't have that kind of money, not even the ten percent she would need to post. Aidan turned and said something comforting, her arms thrusting around him as if he was headed to the gallows. Her cries escalated, carrying on about how they should have moved to Boca Raton years ago, that she should have given John Roycroft one more chance. Isabel heard him say, "It's all right, Mom. Just go home. Everything's going to be okay."

The exchange was upsetting from so many angles, not the least of which was that, right now, someone should be comforting him. A guard pried them apart, putting handcuffs back on Aidan. Facing the courtroom he looked around, and Isabel knew he was looking for her. In one fast motion she stepped into the light. She'd been looking at Aidan for a long time. She knew every expression his ridiculously handsome face made. This was new, and she realized that this was fear.

Needing to make a decision fast, Isabel climbed back into the Caddy Escalade, curious as to how much trouble she'd be in if she drove it over the state line and sold it to a wholesaler for cash. It would serve Rick Stanton right. But then she figured if there were a charge for brainwashing, they'd slap that on Aidan too. She thought about Stanton's money clip, but surely it was locked in the evidence room. There was the twenty-four-hour pawnshop on Beaumont Street, though all hers and Aidan's possessions combined wouldn't make a dent in the sum. Isabel knocked her head against the steering wheel. It jarred something loose. *I'm an idiot.* "Thank you, John Roycroft," she whispered, grateful for a man Aidan never knew. She turned the key, screeching toward the farmhouse and Aidan's truck.

PAYING AIDAN'S BOND IN CASH MADE THINGS A RELATIVELY EASY process. Isabel signed a few papers and handed over $8,000. The desk clerk told her to wait on the other side of the glass partition. She felt as if she hadn't seen Aidan in weeks. Isabel glanced at the clock; six a.m., surely Carrie would be home soon. She had until then to get Rick's vehicle and herself back. It didn't leave much time for the two of them to figure out what came next. The idea of Isabel and Aidan conferring over a bowl of Cinnamon Toast Crunch when Carrie walked in wasn't terribly plausible.

A buzzer sounded and Aidan walked through the door. He didn't look bad, just worried, even a wrinkled tux unable to completely dishevel him. Isabel wanted to fall into his arms. But she was unsure if he expected the same, the horrible portion of the night having greater sticking power than any notion of them as a couple. She offered a sympathetic smile, keeping the grand gesture to herself. It proved to be a wise choice when he didn't even smile back. He walked out of the sheriff's station, Isabel following. Aidan blinked into the bright light of day. "This way," she said, motioning toward the Caddy. He stopped, the blink morphing into a wide-eyed look of confusion. "If we get it back in the next twenty minutes, I don't think they'll add grand theft auto to your rap sheet." He got in and they drove toward Fountainhead.

"How long did it take you to remember the money?"

"A few minutes longer than I would have liked. I'm not at my sharpest at four in the morning." He leaned his head back and closed his eyes. "The rest is in my purse."

After a moment, Aidan's body wrenched forward, his head turning sharply toward Isabel. "I understand why you did it. Like I said at the farmhouse, I'm an awful coward. You stayed behind in the trailer to do what I couldn't. Just so we're clear, I *will* take responsibility for shooting Rick Stanton. I'd never let you . . . It should have been me," he insisted with warrior determination. "I wanted to confess back there, at the arraignment, but my lawyer said it was suicide. He told me I needed to stay calm until he could arrange a plea bargain. But I am curious; I never heard a gun fire before you came out. Did . . . did you muffle it somehow?" Isabel glanced between Aidan and the road. Then the obvious fell from the sky and through the Caddy Escalade sunroof, smacking her on the head. She screeched onto the side, gravel pinging against the SUV, dust clouding around them. "Here's how I think we should say it went down," Aidan said, plotting her alibi. "The simpler, the bet—"

"Aidan," she said sternly, making sure she had his full attention. "You'll confess to no such thing because I didn't shoot Rick Stanton either." He stopped talking, though his mouth hung wide. "I robbed him, I checked his breathing. I called 911. But I swear to you, I did not shoot him."

Thoroughly confused drifted to clearly relieved. "Then how . . . ?"

"I have no idea. I haven't really had time to think about it. Rick's shooting was as much a surprise to me as it was to you."

He started to say something else but sighed, nodding absently. "Good. That's good, Isabel. I didn't want you to have to live with that. It's bad enough, everything that did happen." She pulled back onto the road. "How long do you think it took for that ambulance to arrive?"

"I'm not sure. There was a wreck on Old Station Road. The county only has one ambulance," she said, knowing this from her mother's hospital talk. "If it was at the scene of the accident, it probably slowed their response. Why? What are you thinking?"

Aidan's hands, less swollen but still bruised, scrubbed over his face. "I'm thinking that somebody had enough time and motive to shoot Stanton before that ambulance arrived. The question is, other than me, who wanted that chance?"

And right there, glancing at his ink-stained fingertips, was the mother of all quagmires. Who, other than Aidan, would the police even think to look for? They drove the rest of the way in silence, turning into Fountainhead, bypassing the cutoff to Aidan's trailer. She knew he didn't want to go home. Returning the Caddy to the exact place she'd found it, Isabel was relieved to see that her mother's car wasn't in its spot either. "Aidan—"

"Yeah, I know. What am I going to do? You wouldn't think something so great and something so awful could happen in one night."

Aware of the negatives, she was unable to pinpoint if the something so great was Fitz Landrey, the record executive who promised him a future, or them. For now she thought it best to avoid the subject entirely. "Actually, I was going to say, what are we going to do?" He stared out the open window as a fly buzzed through, summer heat and irritation already mounting. "I . . . couldn't believe the other things they wanted to charge you with. You know I did everything I could to convince them otherwise, that I'd never . . ."

"Isabel, you don't have to say it." He didn't turn from the window, but his hand reached over, blindly covering hers. "I trust you with my life."

"I wish . . . I wish it had happened. I wish Stanton had done it, that you hadn't gotten there before he—" Aidan's head whipped back, his face incredulous. Staring at him through filmy tears, Isabel was at peace with the notion. "If he had, we'd have all the proof we need."

Aidan's body moved toward hers, his hands cupping hard around Isabel's face. "Do not . . ." He paused. There wasn't even a twitch to his mouth, his lips pursing so hard. "Do not ever say that or think that again." She'd never heard his voice make such a sound. "Do you hear me?"

She nodded and he let go, turning his gaze to the tin can horizon. He was so very quiet, though Isabel could feel the scorching anger radiating from him. The rest of the story, the part he didn't yet know, would send an icy chill up his spine. "Aidan, I have to tell you something else . . . something important." His head moved slowly, looking at Isabel as if she were about to tell him the whole Fitz Landrey thing was a practical joke. "My mother is pregnant." She said it fast, like ripping off a Band-Aid. "She's going to marry Rick Stanton." A practical joke might have gone over better. There was a fierce wide blink, as though he couldn't bring it into focus. "I know; it's, um, weird . . . unbelievable. She said she was going to tell me after the gala. I found out—well, it doesn't matter how I found out. But she is . . . *pregnant*," Isabel said, still trying to absorb the fact. "I've tried to tell her, Aidan, everything. But because of her . . . her situation, despite anything I've said, she believes . . . To tell you the truth, I'm not sure what she believes. Circumstance is demanding that she take Rick's side."

"You've got to be . . ." But he saw that she wasn't, slinging his head hard against the seat. "That's just great. Perfect. Your mother and Stanton can stand arm in arm at my sentencing. How many public officials do you think Stanton will have in his pocket by then? How freakin' old do you think I'll be by the time they let me out?"

Isabel wanted desperately to reassure him that none of this would happen, but Aidan had had enough hours to process the facts. He understood Stanton's influence and his endless connections. It was hopeless. Maybe that was why Isabel said the next thing that popped into her head. "Walk away from it, Aidan. All of it. You didn't do anything wrong and you still have $2,000. It's enough to get you out of Catswallow and clear to the other side of the country. It's not like you don't have somewhere to go." It was an outrageous solution, but so was the entire situation. To her amazement, he replied with something even more extreme.

"Only if you come with me."

"If I what?" She heard him but stalled. A part of Isabel wanted to give her mother another chance. Maybe she'd come home and come to her senses. Glancing down the gravel road, early waves of heat skewed the horizon. It was a predictable effect that she guessed was unavoidable. With only minutes to decide, Isabel debated a choice that would turn a rift into a ravine. "Aidan, I—"

"Come with me, Isabel. There's no way I'm leaving you here. What's here for you? Why would you stay? There's the farmhouse, but this," he said, motioning toward a sea of manufactured homes, "has never been where you belong. I'm sure as hell not leaving you here to move in with your mother and her new husband."

She hadn't thought about that. Isabel couldn't get her mind

around the concept. She couldn't believe that Carrie would demand as much. He was right about the farmhouse. Despite Carrie's snug-as-a-bug efforts it was the closest thing to home she'd known since they left her father and New Jersey. *Dad* . . . As fast as Eric sparked in her head, she snuffed him out. She belonged with Aidan. And whether he was asking out of friendship or fear, it didn't matter. She wouldn't let him go alone. "All right," she said, nodding, as if he'd only asked her to take a ride to Tremont for ice cream. "Let's go." Isabel dropped the keys onto the seat of Rick's vehicle, the two of them running for Aidan's truck, which was still at the farmhouse. They'd take it to the airport. They wouldn't be adding grand theft auto to the only crime he was about to commit: jumping bail.

CHAPTER ELEVEN

Providence, Rhode Island
Present Day

ISABEL SLAMMED THE DOOR TO HER APARTMENT AND FLIPPED THE deadbolt over. She leaned her weight against it, trying to keep the day from following. And because she could, she kicked the cat-shaped draft stopper across the room. From his sofa perch, Rico eyed her. He offered a token Halloween greeting, his raccoon tail ticking as though she'd wounded a close cousin. "Sorry," she grumbled, straightening the stuffed cat. "But you wouldn't believe the day I've had." If cats could gesture, Rico would have offered a middle-finger salute, hopping down and slinking toward the kitchen.

Not even the cat wanted to lend a sympathetic ear. It didn't matter, she didn't have time to chat; Mary Louise and Tanya would be there any minute. They'd accomplished nothing that day, Mary Louise running off to a doctor's appointment with Joe, and Tanya leaving to pick up a sick kid at school. Seeing messages on her machine, Isabel considered a fanciful solution. Maybe kismet had called with a message from Taylor Swift saying she didn't have a thing planned for the third week of August. She snorted a laugh, flipping through the mail. "Ha! And I thought this day couldn't get any worse." Isabel fired junk mail, a newsletter from a Vegas tattoo parlor, into the wastebasket. The damn undeterred thing had followed her everywhere. Hitting Play, she hit Skip upon hearing Carrie's voice. Surely she'd seen the loop of a handcuffed Aidan and was calling to validate old opinions. "Thanks, Mom, but I'm all set." While they'd become expert at avoiding any mention of the Catswallow debacle—like a relative with a prison record—this, she suspected, Carrie could not resist. She moved onto the next one. It was from Nate. It wasn't the *"Call you later"* she was expecting, not on her landline. There was a flash of panic, thinking he was calling in his professional capacity. But he'd never break patient-doctor confidentiality—not even for her. His next sentence confirmed as much, saying he was calling about Grassroots Kids. His mother, who was friendly with the Providence city attorney, had called with a heads-up. Unless Grassroots Kids began construction within sixty days, the city would invoke its right to sell the land. "Are you kidding?" He didn't interrupt to say that he was, reminding Isabel they hadn't settled on an architectural rendering, let alone secured the money to start building. Isabel sat down on a bar stool, listening harder. The probable land sale was tied to the grandfather clause that won them the prime location in the first place. Since the building no longer existed, the city council had the right to rescind the clause, and they planned to do just that. Nate called it a bitch of a catch-22. As the news sunk in a hand pressed to her cheek. "And here I thought déjà vu junk mail was the kicker." Nate said he was sorry to leave the message, but he thought she'd want to know. He was crashing after fifteen hours at the hospital but she should call if she wanted to talk—it didn't matter what time. Isabel grabbed the phone. Of course she wanted to talk. Nate would have great input about which thing she should tackle first—the radio station buyout, an idea for a mega promotion, or Grassroots Kids.

Poised to dial, second thoughts interrupted. Maybe he'd say none of the above, telling her that the answer was staring her right in the face, and pointing out that she was just too much of a coward to pursue it. On the other hand, Nate would never say such a thing, because Nate didn't have a clue about Aidan and Isabel. Coming full circle, she put the phone down. Quietly, as if not to emphasize the one guilty omission that marred an otherwise mature, steady, focused relationship. Isabel closed her eyes, shaking her head at the absurdity. If the phone hadn't rung last night, if Nate wasn't called away—had this day never happened—she'd be busy giving the land- lord notice. Isabel would be poised at the edge of the rest of her life. Glancing at the trash can, she tucked it tighter under the bar and out of sight. She'd call Nate later, after Tanya and Mary Louise left. By then there'd be a savvy list of ideas that she could talk over with him, none of which would include Aidan Royce. Seeing one last message, Isabel listened to a meaningless advertisement from Stan- ley Steemer. It was running a summer special: three rooms for $99.

She headed to the bedroom changing into sweatpants and an REO Speedwagon reunion T-shirt, mulling over a day's worth of bad karma. There was plenty to go around. Her thoughts wandered past pop-up images of Aidan Royce. For instance, she ventured, flinging her work clothes into the hamper, she could have called her mother back, enduring an, *"I told you so,"* conversation. Along with the past, they also avoided present-day conversation about Aidan. Despite those two taboo topics, they'd made positive mother-daughter strides, Isabel even visiting Carrie Stanton and her wheelchair-bound, seasoned state senator husband on occasion. That only came after Jack was born, Carrie all but begging Isabel to consider a relationship with her half brother. After soul-searching that rubbed so raw it left a blister, Isabel acquiesced, returning to Alabama for two Thanksgivings and a few of Jack's birthdays, the most recent early last spring. That trip had started out promising;

Rick, accompanied by Trey, was in Montgomery, tending to state business. For two days the future was different, Isabel, her mother, and Jack acting like the family they might have been less Rick. They ate dinner together, Jack's mother and his big sister tag-teaming him about eating his vegetables. Admittedly, however, dinner would not have been served in a well-appointed kitchen or a home where the housekeeper had just left for the day. At night, Isabel read to Jack the same books her mother had read to her. Mercifully, he didn't resemble Rick, making it easier to ignore his paternal DNA. Jack even insisted that Isabel drop him at Cannon River Academy. He held tight to her hand through the private pristine campus, all the way to his classroom, where Jack offered a proud toothless smile and "'*Sabel*" to Mrs. Babcock, his teacher.

That day, Isabel and Carrie had gone to the Summit, Birmingham's most upscale shopping area, her mother insisting on a lavish spa treatment after lunch. On the way home, there was lively chatter about their purchases, the two of them agreeing that their mutual curves were ill-suited for the pencil skirts they were showing. They shared dark chocolate truffles left over from dessert, joking how the indulgence was a detriment to their seaweed-scrubbed faces, never mind ending any hope of wearing trendy skirts. Pulling into the driveway, Jack came running. He and his sometimes sitter Leighanne were kicking a soccer ball. Rick, who'd also arrived home, watched from his wheelchair. His chin cocked in Isabel's direction before heading up the ramp, seeing his wife and son inside. Not eager to follow, she turned to the bubbly blond college student who was tucking money in her backpack. "Rick paid you?"

"Yep, I'm all taken care of," she said, smiling. "Your step-daddy sure is generous. He asked if I wanted to intern for him this summer."

"Did he?" Isabel said, taking in the girl's tight T-shirt, low-slung jeans.

She cracked her gum and smiled. "He did. He even asked if I'd be interested in serving as his personal assistant," she said, sliding into her cute-as-her convertible. "I wouldn't mind bragging about that. Leighanne Dunbar, personal assistant to Rick Stanton, state senator."

Isabel didn't reply. Caution and warning would fall on deaf ears. Besides, it was residual fear, the senator's permanent sitting position eliminating any physical threat. "Well, good luck with that." She turned and headed toward the house. Halfway there, Isabel stopped. She didn't want to go inside, not with that tidbit on her mind, positive what was on Rick's. Looking at the beautiful house, thinking about the prestigious private school Jack attended, Isabel found herself at the juncture where she couldn't make peace with the price. She tried to force herself, even negotiate. In a few hours she could escape to Strobe's for the night. Over the years he'd been amiable, if not inviting, insisting Isabel stay with him when she visited. It worked out well, each glad for an ally. Strobe remained the underdog of the Stanton clan and the two of them made for a lovely pair of black sheep. But Strobe wouldn't be home for hours, giving Isabel no choice but to go inside. She took another step, hearing Rick's deep belly laugh, charming his son and taunting her. Glancing through the open car window she saw Carrie's keys in the ignition. She pulled out her cell phone. "Mom, I'm going for a ride . . . I don't know, a while."

It seemed unlikely that a person could drive for an hour and never consciously decide where she was going. Yet, Isabel did just that, ending up in a place walled in comfort. She stood for a time in misty rain, shoes sinking into the muddy red-dirt driveway of the farmhouse. Tentatively, she approached its rotted front porch. Along with the floorboards, indifference weakened, meeting with a momentary lapse. Isabel was overwhelmed by the notion that if she went inside Aidan would be there. She'd find him sitting on one of those old crates, strumming a guitar—like he'd never left. Smelling air that she attributed to the unique combination of apple orchard and graveyard, Isabel nearly swore she could hear the chords. Maybe it was that Spanish thing he only played there. Almost too easily it led to Aidan's wide lazy grin, the one that said, *"Isabel, quit with the debate team talking points and tell me what you think of this . . ."* She reached for the rusty knob and the music stopped. She didn't go in. On her abrupt retreat, Isabel saw a Sold sign, passing construction vehicles that were on their way up the drive. It rattled her, imagining other people, strangers, calling the farmhouse home. In the rearview mirror her eyes met with a road that ran like a gray snake, glancing one last time toward the past.

Afterward, Isabel cut the trip short, saying a fast goodbye to Jack and her mother. Carrie was disappointed but didn't question it, Isabel forgoing the obligatory grunt at Rick. Instead of driving her to his house, Strobe drove her to the airport. While they'd never discussed *that night*, he did make a telling remark. Grabbing her suitcase, he held on until there was solid eye contact, airport noises roaring in the background. "If it helps, Bella, my daddy got what he deserved that night. Never let it bother you—I don't." During the flight to Providence, Isabel debated if she'd heard right, amazed by what Strobe had all but confessed.

Not unlike her trip to the farmhouse early last spring, this day had only aggravated the past and Isabel was angry about that. In the small hall of her apartment, she took a cleansing breath, stopping in the bathroom to pop two Excedrin. After an exchange of food for ardent meows, Isabel passed on anything that could be construed as dinner. But she did spy a stash of beer in the back of the fridge. Still not her beverage of choice, it was something new since Nate. She grabbed one, popping the top and guzzling a long mouthful. It hit the back of her throat, cold and bittersweet. The doorbell rang, Tanya and Mary Louise arriving together.

Wonderful . . . Tanya also brought all her children, including the one who vomited a couple of hours ago.

"You don't mind, do you, Isabel?" Tanya hustled past with Lucy straddling one hip, two pizza boxes in her free arm. Her boys, Josh and Eddie, followed. Mary Louise brought up the rear, carrying a plate of sushi and tofu disguised as something mirroring meat. "I couldn't afford a sitter and none of their dads were home." Four-year-old Lucy was a keen shade of green, clinging to her mother, whimpering. "I'll just lay her in your bed. It's closest to the potty, right?"

"Close as anything else," Isabel said. Tanya deposited the feverish-looking child onto the bed. In a 700-square-foot apartment, they'd probably all be diving for the commode before the night was over. But she couldn't object, Tanya would only think she was slacking off if she'd stayed home. It all went to her well-meaning but questionable judgment. "Have the boys eaten?"

"Oh, don't you worry about that. The boys are all fed. They're going to play on your jungle gym. We won't even know they're here."

She didn't mind. Eddie and Josh were great kids, though not without their issues. Josh suffered from acute asthma and Eddie was diabetic. Many days, it was all Tanya could do to juggle her kids' medical appointments and work. Besides, Tanya's boys liked to visit. There was a great recreation area, all of it visible from Isabel's living room window. Tanya lived in subsidized housing where the amenities weren't as nice—or existent. Isabel had only been there a few times. There were no trailers, but the air of desperation was the same. Places like that led to a coarse reminder of the moments before Aidan arrived and him beating Stanton to a pulp, followed by Rick's shooting. Once there, it was a slippery slope, moving on to Aidan's arrest before the two of them ran away from everything. Currently complementing that was the present-day image of Aidan in handcuffs, nearly identical to the scene from the Catswallow sheriff's station. Opening another beer, Isabel suspected you couldn't make up a scenario like that.

She dropped the pizza boxes onto the kitchen table, finding the first one empty. She supposed the boys had eaten. Clearly, medical issues did not affect their appetites. She didn't know how Tanya managed. Their fathers were sporadic, at best, when making child support payments. The spunky airtime scheduler barely made enough to support herself, never mind four people. Isabel gave each boy a juice box, which she specifically kept on hand for them. As their mother prodded, they offered a quick hello and thank-you, heading out the door. "So how's Joe?" Isabel asked, hoping for good news.

"He's okay. A little depressed." Mary Louise settled onto a bar stool, opening her signature sports bottle of tap water.

"Why's that? I thought they were taking one of his casts off today."

"They were, but the orthopedist wasn't happy with the way the bone is healing. It's going to be a few more weeks. When Joe called work, they said they weren't sure if they could hold his job at the shipyard. He was pretty upset; he's worked a lot of years there. I'd hate to see him lose it. I didn't have the heart to tell him what happened today."

"Won't he get suspicious when your clock radio goes off tomorrow and 98.6 is nothing but static?" Tanya said.

"I mentioned the format change. I didn't tell him the rest—us having to come up with an entirely new audience in ten seconds or the fact that we're going to get canned if we don't. If he knew we might lose our health insurance, it would put him over the edge." Isabel offered a sympathetic hum, realizing she'd downed her beer as if entered in a chugging contest.

"I'll take that," Mary Louise said, snatching up the empty

nickel-deposit bottle. "Add 'em up and it's a large soy latte, Isabel. Thriftiness is something you might want to embrace, considering what's in front of us." Mary Louise made her way to the sink, rinsed the bottle, and dropped it in her tote bag. "You know, the more I think about it, if Joe had angled his fall a little to the left, not hit the fence on the way down, it would have been a cleaner break."

"For heaven's sake, Mary Louise," Tanya said, reaching for a slice of pizza, "take some responsibility. If you paid for dirty movies like everybody else he wouldn't have fallen off the roof at all."

Isabel's appalled stare volleyed between the two women. Like Tanya's questionable judgment, they did not berate Mary Louise's frugality. It was one reason they got along, their ability to accept each other's quirks, or at least not skywrite the flaws. "Mary Louise, I'm sure she didn't mean anything—"

"Humph! I know what I heard. Tanya called me cheap! Do you agree with that, Isabel? Do you think it's my fault that Joe got hurt, that he might lose his job because of me?"

She was saved by the sound of a gagging four-year-old, a disoriented Lucy unable to find the bathroom. It was almost worth the river of vomit on the bedroom carpet to end what was heading toward a nasty confrontation. In three years, Isabel had never seen Tanya take such a cheap shot at Mary Louise. The stress of delivering an out-of-thin-air feat and looming unemployment was taking a toll. The quiet was palpable as Isabel helped Tanya clean up the mess, curious what Lucy ingested that would turn beige carpet bright green. Scrubbing away, Isabel could see that Tanya felt awful. The inconsequential Stanley Steemer message occurred to her, Isabel insisting that all her carpets could use a good cleaning. From the edge of the living room, where she vigorously applied hand sanitizer, Mary Louise said she'd see if the number was still there. She replayed the messages, including the one from Nate.

"Isabel, why didn't you say anything?"

"You guys have enough to worry about," she said, blotting the stain. "Grassroots Kids is my problem, not yours."

"That's not true," Tanya said, leaning back on her heels. "Both my boys' medical expenses have been offset by Grassroots Kids, and Lucy loves the after-school program. More important, Mary Louise and I both know what it means to you."

"One problem at a time, okay? We've got enough to deal with." Finished with the mess, she headed toward the kitchen.

"It didn't sound that way to me," Mary Louise said, following. "It sounds like the problem with Grassroots Kids is as urgent as the radio station—maybe more."

"I'll handle it. Nate will help. You two don't need to worry about it." Putting away the bucket and disinfectant, the silence resumed. She popped up from the sink, smiling. "Look, I've had my share of challenges with Grassroots Kids. Both problems are the perfect opportunity to test my skills, think on my feet." She smiled wider. "Besides, you guys know my parents. They didn't raise a quitter!"

They smiled to appease, Tanya adding, "You're right about that. Where do you think my best parenting tips come from?"

A couple of hours later, Tanya made use of that advice, taking her ninth or tenth pass by the window, watching her boys play under a giant spotlight. Lucy had fallen asleep and Isabel returned to the breakfast bar where she made three mental notes: The pizza was gone, they'd made little progress, and she'd drained the last beer. That one was most surprising. There was plenty an hour or so ago. Especially surprising since Mary Louise rarely drank and Tanya, who had to drive, stuck to diet soda all night. She was spot-on with short-term judgments. Isabel didn't feel drunk, but a good buzz had segued to numbness, which, considering the circumstances, wasn't such a bad thing.

"I put a call in to my friend JJ Reese, he works promotions at *JMX-Classic Rock* in Dallas," Tanya offered. "They're huge. They sponsored two major shows last year. He'll know somebody. We just have to wait for him to call back."

Isabel didn't have the heart to tell Tanya that a weekend at a radio station conference, spent mostly in bed with a stranger, didn't translate into the kind of LinkedIn relationship they'd need. In fact, they were all relieved to find out that it didn't link him to being daddy number four.

"He might know people, but unless he's super chummy with Beyoncé or moonlights as Bon Jovi's booking agent, I don't know how that's going to help," Mary Louise said. "Those shows are booked months, even a year in advance. This is going to take the kind of personal connection we don't have."

You mean, like, once upon a time having run away with a rock star? But instead of speaking up, Isabel clamped her hand over her mouth, silencing a burp. She slumped against the wall, sliding, until her bottom found the floor. Mary Louise's conjecture was fact, having gone through every connection, every possible marker owed them. Except for a few unreturned phone calls, which wouldn't amount to a thing, they were screwed.

"Maybe we should be using this time to find new jobs. I can appreciate how upset Joe is, just the thought of being unemployed and having no insurance. I can't afford to be out of work for a day."

"For heaven's sake, Tanya," Mary Louise said, folding her arms, "if you'd just used some birth control, like everyone else, you wouldn't have such a problem."

The residual sarcasm wasn't lost on Tanya, her face turning as red as her hair. It was a callous remark and Tanya, who had odds in a catfight, looked as if she might come right across the bar top.

"What a horrid thing to say, Mary Louise! I was only talking about your cable bill. Those are my children!"

"I'm just saying, nothing against your kids. But if you'd been a bit more frugal with your sex life, maybe the idea of potential unemployment wouldn't be scaring you to death."

"Is that right?" Tanya seethed, stomping around the bar. "Well, at least I'm a real enough person to have had children. Unlike some people who can't get their mind around anything messing up their health-crazed, sterile existence!" There was a stunned gasp from Mary Louise, Isabel's eyes volleying from her spectator spot. "And at least when I was married my husbands were very much alive and kicking. Unlike a man who personifies his name—Mary Louise *Bland*!"

Things were getting out of hand, Isabel picturing one of them showing up to work and going postal on the place. She struggled to her feet, trying to get between them, the half-dozen beers impeding her accuracy. "Hey, come on, guys, don't do this. It's not going to help." They edged her right out of the argument. Isabel had never seen them behave like this. Tanya and Mary Louise had worked at the radio station longer than her, been friends for years.

"You take that back, Tanya! Just because some of us have a moral code, instead of an area code followed by *do-me-Tanya*, doesn't make me a cold fish. At least if I ever have children, the school won't have to cross-index them by last name."

"Really?" Tanya said, stretching her curvy five-two frame against Mary Louise's fishing rod stance. "Well, when you find that new job, good luck acclimating your co-workers to your habits."

"Habits? What habits?" demanded Mary Louise, who prided herself on perfectionism, which, in truth, was her most irritating habit.

"The ones that require years of conditioning—like not looking twice when you use a tea bag for the third time or order water when we go out for lunch. Then," she said, thrusting a hand in Isabel's direction, "ask Isabel to *'be a sweetheart and make a secret trip to the salad bar'*—so you can pick!"

But as she pointed, Isabel was darting away. She exited to her bedroom, where the argument reverberated through the walls. She moved with her usual calm cadence, albeit visibly tipsy. This morning the changes at *98.6—The Normal FM for Easy Listening* threatened their livelihood, now it threatened a friendship. Isabel dragged a chair across the wet carpet, teetering, as she climbed up, widely acting under the influence. Grasping the closet doorframe, she paused, swallowing down a rush of alcohol and angst. The decibel level rose and Isabel pushed forward as Tanya ranted to Mary Louise about the harsh realities of single parenthood. Mary Louise countered, wanting to know if Tanya had a clue what an orthopedic surgeon charged per visit.

Isabel could see how things would play out, bad for her, worse for them. Providence was a limited place, their jobs tough to duplicate in the New England market. It wasn't as if you could get another one at the radio station across the street. If they lost them Tanya would end up on welfare or working at Walmart. Her kids would grow up somewhere worse than subsidized housing. She could picture Joe Bland, who wasn't the most resilient guy, spiraling into a deep depression. The loss of another income and their medical insurance would be devastating. Isabel rummaged past a couple of baseball caps, a blanket she'd attempted to knit, and old copies of *Wuthering Heights* and *Pride and Prejudice*. Tanya's and Mary Louise's circumstances were real. Hers was unpleasant history. If anything like that happened, Isabel couldn't live with herself, especially when the answer might be buried—like all good skeletons—in the back of her closet.

The two women didn't realize she'd left the room. They didn't see her come back, going at it like two feral cats. Even Rico had retreated beneath the sofa, his posh tail flicking at the edge. They'd moved on, from personal to professional grievances.

"You know what, Tanya, if you spent half as much time beefing up promotions as you did your roots, we might have a name. Somebody we could go to in this situation."

"Don't you put this on me, Mary Louise! Promotion is only part of my job. At least I didn't have to google Lady Gaga to figure out who or what she is. At least I own an iPod! You don't have a clue what's hot or happening."

Mary Louise stood stiffly, her librarian looks accentuating Tanya's claim. "Until today hot or happening wasn't in my job description either!"

"They don't have to be." Isabel slammed an envelope onto the bar top. "I can fix this. Just stop it, please, both of you. Don't do this." Their mouths stopped moving, but steam continued to hiss from every orifice as they looked at Isabel. Tears streaked through Tanya's painted-on blush, the fine line of Mary Louise's powder-pink lipstick quivering as she pulled her glasses from her nose, blinking fiercely. "Go ahead, open it." They hesitated, then grabbed for it, Mary Louise's long reach winning. She turned the envelope over, and onto the breakfast bar spilled Isabel's past, three official-looking pieces of paper along with a random strip of images, the kind you'd get in a photo booth. Indifference rattled and wavered, Isabel's hand clamping on to the bar top. Alcohol-induced fuzzy faculties. That's all it was. The pictures registered first, Tanya's eyes bugging as she picked the strip up.

"Oh my gosh, Isabel, where did you . . . These are pictures of you and Aidan Royce!"

Mary Louise snatched it from her hand, examining the telltale images. "You and Aidan Royce . . . less his tattoo!"

"Yes, the last photos of Aidan pre–body art." She laughed.

"What do you think I could get for them on eBay?" Neither woman replied, Isabel's stab at humor missing. "They were taken right before we visited one of Vegas's hippest ink-art establishments." She reached down, plucking junk mail from her trash can, adding it to the evidence. "Like I said, I was there. It was about an hour after we—"

"Got married!" Tanya said, shoving a marriage license at Isabel, as if this were news to her.

Isabel picked up an even more official-looking piece of paper, the blue-backed document that nullified any marriage license. From there she aimed at the quickest explanation, mostly because it wasn't her point. "Married and divorced faster than his first gold record." Mary Louise put down the pictures, picking up the remaining piece of evidence. Indifference flat out faltered as Isabel took in the singular flow of Aidan's bold signature, the one on a letter insisting that a quick divorce was for the best. Goodbye and good luck. She blinked blankly, unable to deny the residual sting of his curt dismissal.

Tanya had a different reaction. "This is amazing! To think you and Aidan Royce . . ." Her voice floated away, the dreamy whisper they heard every time she fell in love.

"You were married to him?" said Mary Louise, her tone far more pragmatic. "Seriously?" she pressed. "But how . . . when?"

"Before I married Aidan, he was my best friend—when we were kids, after my mother took a leap of faith and took a job offer in Alabama." She pulled in a breath, thinking how the job never panned out, though the move had decidedly affected their futures. Blindsided, Tanya slumped onto a bar stool, Mary Louise's forehead crunching as she internally organized the information. And for a moment, Isabel thought that might be it. Asked and answered. But the absurdity of that sunk in as they continued to stare. "I, um . . . I guess you'd like to hear the whole story." A gulp rolled through Isabel's throat, wondering if time had changed her delivery. She'd only told this story once before, to two men she would have never fathomed on the receiving end. She started to speak, resigned to explaining the inexplicable.

"Wait." Mary Louise came around the breakfast bar, reaching into the cabinet above the stove. From it, she retrieved a lone bottle of gin.

"For me?" Isabel asked.

"For me," she said, unscrewing the cap. "Something tells me this isn't a tap-water kind of story."

CHAPTER TWELVE

Birmingham, Alabama–Las Vegas

STANDING IN THE BIRMINGHAM AIRPORT, AIDAN'S FIRST INSTINCT was to head for Los Angeles. Inside his pocket he'd been rubbing Fitz Landrey's business card like a lucky charm. He hoped the man wasn't full of shit. It was the only card he had left to play. Two thousand dollars wasn't going to last forever. While Isabel visited the vending machines, he tried to buy two tickets to L.A. There was one seat available on a flight that left in thirty minutes. He didn't consider it. But the two of them did need to get on a plane to somewhere fast. It wouldn't be long until everyone in Catswallow realized they'd gone missing.

He looked over the posted outgoing flights: Seattle, St. Louis, Montreal, Dallas, Orlando—it didn't matter. He'd go anywhere as long as Isabel was with him. Doing this without her was unimaginable. There was a flight to Akron. He thought about that. Surely somewhere in Akron there was an abandoned farmhouse. Maybe they could move right in and go on as if none of this ever happened. Aidan's fingers brushed again along Fitz's business card; the desire for that chance was nearly as strong. Damn, why did it have to be a choice? Then something caught his eye, something that would make the last twelve hours seem like a trip to over the Catswallow County line. A few minutes later Isabel returned. Her arms were filled with a cellophane-wrapped buffet. In his hand were two boarding passes. "Ready?" he asked, feeling at ease with his decision.

"Yeah, I'm good to go. Maybe when we get to L.A., we can get something that doesn't come with yesterday's expiration date."

"Definitely." Aidan took the prepackaged consumables, which did appear questionable. "You can get whatever you want. But we're not going to L.A."

"We're not? But isn't that where Fitz Landrey is?"

"Yes, but we're taking a detour first, to Vegas."

"Vegas?" she asked worriedly. "What's in Las Vegas?"

Aidan started prodding her toward the gate. "Not sure, never been. My guess is casinos, desert, Elvis impersonators, and wedding chapels."

She laughed, pushing a lock of hair behind her ear. The laughter was nervous, so was the habit. "Let me guess, you're going to bet what's left of your inheritance on the roulette wheel because your luck's been so great in the last twenty-four hours."

"Some of it has. And no, nothing so crazy." Aidan paused as they got to their gate. He tucked her hair back on the other side, making solid eye contact, never having felt so sure about anything. "I'm interested in the chapel. Marry me, Isabel."

LESS THAN TWENTY-FOUR HOURS AGO, AIDAN ROYCROFT WAS STANDing in front of his bedroom mirror, cursing at a bow tie. In the end he'd shoved the thing in his pocket, thinking it might inspire a look. Just for fun he'd traded in the shiny black rental shoes for imitation-snakeskin boots. It felt like the last real thing he'd done. Now he stood in front of a justice of the peace, the bow tie, and the rest of his inheritance, and an unlikely note from John Roycroft in his pocket, marrying Isabel Lang. And out of all the incredible and hellish things that had happened in the last day, this was by far the most calming. He only wondered when it might feel something other than surreal.

Aidan slipped a thin gold band on her trembling finger. Isabel had chosen it herself from the display case out front. They repeated vows that were too simple for everything he felt. While the marriage was spontaneous, his feelings couldn't be more grounded. Surely she understood that. Isabel was the one person who understood everything about him. The ceremony was over in minutes, Isabel shying away from a kiss that he'd intended to be a whole lot more. Yet, he had no regrets. But Aidan wasn't convinced Isabel felt the same way. Everything considered, he guessed that she might be feeling a bit overwhelmed.

Isabel hadn't said much during the flight, not answering until the plane landed. As passengers jammed the aisle, she'd stayed in her seat. She sat for so long Aidan thought she was going to say she'd take the next flight back to Birmingham. She'd barely spoken, certainly not a word about his proposal. *"What? Oh . . . yes, thank you . . . a Diet Coke would be nice."* And that was to the flight attendant. Aidan started to wonder if what happened between them at the farmhouse was just fear, a panicked means to erasing Stanton's attack. In the moment, he'd worried about exactly that. He didn't know much about those kinds of things, but he supposed it was possible. It was one scene out of sync with their entire relationship. Isabel always talked about their friendship as if it was the most important thing in the world. What if she was right? Isabel was always right. Who goes to bed with their best friend— or better yet, proposes?

Determined to go with his gut, Aidan inched forward as much as an airplane seat would allow. He was prepared to ask again.

He was prepared for the answer to be no. From a trancelike stare at her tray-table, Isabel reached over and wrapped her hand around his, answering, "Yes, Aidan. I'll marry you." They'd taken a taxi to a chapel on the old Strip.

After the ceremony their motel room wasn't ready and Aidan suspected that this was a good thing. Picking up where they left off at the farmhouse was definitely on his mind. But letting her get used to the idea was more important. He chuckled. Since when did Aidan Roycroft think more about the girl than himself? It reaffirmed his vow. Marrying Isabel was the most perfect thing he'd ever done. "Let's go for a walk."

"Now?" She stood opposite him, twisting the ring as if it were a foreign object, suddenly adhered to her body.

"Well, if we take the $1,150 that's left into the casino, we might be broke before dinner. So, how about a walk?" Aidan pulled her into his arms and for a moment he felt her relax.

"A honeymoon walk?" she asked, her head resting on his shoulder.

"Sure, it's part of the whole Vegas honeymoon package. Didn't you read the brochure?" She laughed. That felt good. He hadn't heard her laugh in hours. They headed out of the hotel, side by side, just like always. Not touching, not holding hands. Give it some time, he thought. On their way they passed a photo booth. "Hey, a wedding picture. That's what we need, something to commemorate the event."

"Oh, Aidan, I don't . . . I'm a mess. My hair is full of sticky hairspray and I haven't slept all night. I probably look like the bride of Frankenstein!"

But he insisted, pulling her into the narrow booth, where she was forced to sit on his lap. The multi-shot strip captured the essence of the union: goofy faces, Aidan's eyes closed, Isabel's eyes closed, cheesy smiles, Isabel laughing as he tickled her, and the last shot:

Aidan stealing a kiss, smaller than the one she offered at the altar. Even so, there it was, on film.

Continuing down the street, weaving in and out of shops to avoid the summer heat, silence nudged him. He couldn't get used to it. There'd been more silence in the past few hours than the last five years. Finally, she asked, "Did you check your cell phone? Did you call Fitz Landrey?"

"Of course I checked." Since he was ignoring a dozen hysterical messages from his mother, and several more ominous ones from Catswallow law enforcement, Aidan figured he'd spare Isabel as well. "Nothing important, no message from Fitz yet. But he'll call, I'm sure."

"Do you really think so? Aidan, what . . . what are we going to do if he doesn't call?"

"He'll call," he snapped. She stepped away, putting a body width between them. "I'm sorry. I'm tired—cranky, that's all." And she laughed again. "What's so funny?"

"This may be the first honeymoon in history that starts with a nap." He smiled. It was on her mind too. Isabel stopped in front of a tattoo parlor—*Rico's Tattoos*—distracted by the goings-on inside.

Aidan peered through the window, where a man sat in a chair. The tattoo artist was putting the finishing touches on a colorful design on his forearm. The entire scene made him think of root canal, only this was voluntary pain.

"Do you think that hurts?"

"Nah." He used his best macho grunt, shrugging as he looked harder into the window. "Yeah . . . I guess . . . a little."

"Probably not as much as childbirth." Their eyes met in mutual alarm, Isabel quickly turning back to the window. "I didn't mean anything by that. I mean, I wasn't talking about you and . . . I was just making an observation, that's all. About other people . . . not us."

Aidan shoved his hands in his pockets, tipping back on the heels of his imitation-snakeskin boots. "Not ever?" She didn't answer, forcing a hand through her hair. The nervous gesture didn't smooth anything, sticky hairspray and the moment making things more difficult. Aidan took a harder look at the tattoo in progress. "Why don't we find out if that's true? In ten or fifteen years we can compare notes." She didn't look at him, but he caught a small smile curve around her mouth. "Come on—at least it's air conditioned. Let's go inside."

It was a grand distraction from everything. They spent the next hour flipping through clip art, the thousands of possibilities. Isabel flat-out rejected the first few hundred: tigers, all birds, cartoon characters, an array of symbols, and anything resembling a heart bearing her—or anyone's—initials. Aidan was about to give up when she saw it. "That one," she announced to Orlando, who was the proprietor of Rico's, and with whom they were now on a first-name basis.

"*Buena elección,*" he said, raising a unibrow at them.

"You think?" Aidan wasn't as convinced.

"Yes, that one." Isabel pointed to a snake that coiled with sinister appeal. It was as unpredictable as her. She looked at him. "Unless you think it's too out there."

He laughed. "Nope, no way. I'm in. *Orlando, a mi esposa le gustaría marcarme con una serpiente enrollada.*" Her forehead crinkled. "I told him *my wife* would like to brand me with a coiled snake." And the bend in her brow turned to a smile on her face. Aidan was pleased by how natural the word sounded—in either language. Somewhere in his head, between the music and lyrics, he'd been thinking of Isabel that way for some time.

"*No hay problema,*" Orlando agreed. "But you haven't said where?" His eyes grazed over the rumpled tux, Aidan not having thought about where the tattoo might go. Isabel had an answer.

"His neck."

"My neck?"

"*Tiene cojones,*" Orlando said, slyly grinning.

"Yes, your neck. It'll be your thing, you know, when you're famous—like an insignia. It's sexy and dangerous. Aidan's going to be a famous rock star, Orlando."

Aidan admired her confidence. "From her lips . . ."

"I surely hope, *mis amigos*, because putting that thing on your neck does not say nine-to-five employment." Orlando leaned back in his chair and in an accent thick with folklore, explained its meaning. "I will tell you more about the *señora*'s choice. Rico," he said, pointing to a flashing sign, "the once owner, said the coiled serpent was the great protector of true love. The story goes that the venomous snake guards the *princesa* while keeping all other suitors away—his and hers." His singular brow furrowed at their curious expressions. "*¿Que?*" He shrugged. "Rico insists it is very powerful. The snake, he will stand guard until the *príncipe* returns from war and suffering. As long as it is there, others may try, but no one will come between them." He leaned in close, his finger tapping against the clip art. "I know this is so, because once that snake is on your neck, you will never be without it . . . or her."

"Mmm, interesting," Isabel said, nodding. "Though I don't believe Aidan plans on going off to war. I think we have enough going on right now."

Orlando offered a grunt of agreement, moving some paperwork toward them. "You need to sign here," he said, pointing. "And once more, here." Aidan picked up a pen, ready to write. Isabel's hand clasped hard over his.

"Wait, aren't you going to read it first? You can't just sign it."

Aidan shrugged. If you were going to trust a guy enough to take a needle to your neck, what harm was there in a signature?

"Standard release," Orlando explained, pointing to the first two signature lines. "Says we followed the health department rules, instructed you on how to take care. What you do after that . . . *es tu problema.*"

"My business," Aidan translated.

Isabel nodded. "And this one?" she asked, absorbing the fine print.

"That one is for Rico's newsletter."

"A newsletter?"

"*Sí* . . . Body art is a come-again, word-of-mouth business. I am strict about keeping up with my clients. People return to Las Vegas . . . *y hacen locuras.*" Orlando turned away, beginning the prep work for the tattoo.

Isabel translated this time, spinning a finger at the side of her head as Aidan nodded. "Makes sense," she said, letting go of his hand. "Aidan, you really need to take the time to read things before you sign them."

He signed distinctively, *Mr. and Mrs. Aidan Roycroft.* But he hesitated at the address line. "Isabel," he whispered, feeling like the fugitive he was. "What should I put here? I don't think it's a smart idea to . . ."

"No, I suppose a Catswallow address would be like leaving a trail of bread crumbs. Just leave it blank."

"I don't know; he's pretty into his newsletter. What if he asks?"

She sighed, thinking. "Give it to me." Aidan watched as she wrote, 7 Charles Street; Boston, Massachusetts, even including the zip code. Finishing, she glanced at Aidan's curious expression, shoving the papers back to him. "I burned a couple of hundred letters. Can I help it if I accidently memorized the return address? At least it proved useful."

"At least," he said, shuffling the stack into a neat pile. Over the years they'd talked about everything, though they didn't talk much about that. Aidan's initial reaction to Isabel's story, her father's startling *coming out,* was that of any uneducated heterosexual boy—not polite or pleasant. It certainly wasn't a comfortable topic in rural Alabama. But over time his perspective had matured. From the amount of letters the man wrote he certainly appeared anything but indifferent to his daughter. And Aidan envied that, the one and only communication from his father coming after his death. But every time he brought it up, trying to convince her to read the letters and give her father a chance, she wanted no part of it. Isabel could never see it as any more than a slap in her mother's face. With all due respect to Carrie Lang, Aidan had a different point of view: If that's who Eric Lang was, so be it. Of course, it was easy for him to say. It was Carrie and Isabel, not Aidan, who had to forgive and get past the lie he'd first lived. Aidan's outlook trended more toward gratitude. If not for Eric Lang's lie, his confusion, his misstep . . . whatever the man's reasons, there wouldn't be Isabel.

With the paperwork in order, Isabel sized up both sides of Aidan's neck. "Every happening artist should have a tattoo with some mystery. But we need it out front, up close, where all your fans will see it. What do you think?" Isabel hesitated, looking hard into Aidan's eyes. "It's not too late. We can get you a sequined smoking jacket instead."

"Are you kidding?" Aidan said, unbuttoning his shirt. "Like Orlando said, it's *una idea muy cojonuda*."

STANDING IN FRONT OF THEIR MOTEL ROOM MIRROR, AIDAN HAD to agree with Orlando's observation. It was very ballsy. Leave it to Isabel to make the perfect choice. He often thought his golden-boy looks were a detriment to the image he wanted to convey. Once or twice, he'd thought about shaving his head, just to toughen that pretty-boy shell. Although Aidan knew he lacked the nerve, at least he had a grip on his vanity. This was better and lower maintenance. He ran a hand along the venomous creature that now coiled from his collarbone, up the left side of his neck, the split tongue licking the square bone of his jaw. The snake was edgy and dangerous and only slightly hurt like hell. He'd definitely have no trouble comparing notes with Isabel in ten or fifteen years. And that thought brought him back around to the other thing, the thing that had wandered into the hotel room with them. Aside from an edgy snake, sex seemed to be taking on the unlikely form of a giant pink elephant.

They only had the clothes on their backs when they arrived in Las Vegas. At some point, Aidan suggested they stop and buy a few things. Since then, since the tattoo, Isabel had hardly spoken. Standing on the opposite side of the room, she folded and refolded the clothes. She looked exhausted. She looked like she was sorry she ever left Catswallow. She looked like she was going to cry.

"Hey, you hungry?" She shook her head. Not a good sign. Isabel could eat anywhere, anytime. "Tired?" She shrugged; then she nodded. He crossed the room, pulling a sweatshirt from her arms. It was stamped Property of Las Vegas County Jail. At the time, he thought it was funny. Now it was tough to find humor in a moment that was growing weightier by the second. "Sorry you came with me?" Her forehead crinkled, but her head shook harder. He sighed, relieved. She glanced up. Aidan's arms slipped around Isabel, pulling her close. She shuffled begrudgingly into his hold. "Sorry you married me?" It still felt strange, to touch her like that, like she was his.

Isabel's head, resting on his shoulder, shot up like a rocket. "Are you?"

He smiled wide. And in an attempt to be cunning and suave, Aidan Roycroft tripped right over his own ego. "Are you kidding? Not only do I get to marry my best friend, but I get to take the virgin bride. Good thing I've had practice."

The idea was to sweep her into his arms and onto the bed, proving she was a great deal more. But clearly it wasn't going to go that way. Pushing away, Isabel narrowed her eyes. It was the look he earned whenever he said or did something that met with her disapproval. She stomped around the bed, fishing through the clothes. Screwing up with Isabel, he knew he'd find a way. "I'm sorry. I didn't mean that the way it came out. Isabel, listen to—" His cell rang and he glanced at the caller ID. "It's Fitz." All day long and *now* he called. Isabel's face was angry. She looked like she didn't give a crap who was on the phone. Aidan had no choice; he had to talk to him. Snatching up the toiletries she'd bought, Isabel headed for the bathroom.

"I'll give you some privacy. I'm going to take a shower." The door slammed as she went inside.

CHAPTER THIRTEEN

Las Vegas

S HE STOOD IN THE SHOWER WAITING FOR THE HOT WATER TO clear her head. *Am I really married to Aidan?* "Isabel Roycroft," she whispered. *Damn, if I had a pen, I'd practice it on toilet paper.* Isabel held up five seriously pruned fingers. Sure enough, there was a thin gold band on one of them. "And to think what every girl in Catswallow would have done for his class ring." It didn't seem real. Any moment she'd wake to discover that this was one of those dreams. "That or Aidan," she said, mercilessly wringing a washcloth, "will jolt from a sound sleep and thank God his nightmare is over."

The blunt observation and lack of hot water snapped her into a state of semi-reality. Shutting off the spigot, Isabel reached for a skimpy motel towel, positive she'd felt smoother sandpaper. She didn't hear anything on the other side of the door, guessing Aidan was off the phone—or he'd simply left. It was a blunt prospect, hitting harder than the insult he'd lobbed at her before she ran away to the bathroom. Isabel pressed her ear to the door. She heard nothing and braced for the worst: jilted on her wedding night in a chintzy Vegas motel room. Isabel was about to fling open the door when she heard the TV turn on.

She needed to stop that. Aidan would not have proposed, much less gone through with it, if marrying her wasn't what he wanted. Okay, maybe he was scared, freakishly so, like never before in his life. And maybe Isabel was his go-to girl when he was feeling lost or down. What did it matter if, on occasion, Aidan expected her to hold things together for him? This was different. *So's what happened to him in the last twenty-four hours.* Maybe being married to her was just a tad safer than the alternative: Catswallow County lockup and a cellmate named Gus.

"Isabel," he called. "Are you okay? About before, I didn't mean anything by that. I was a jerk." She shrugged and nodded. "Can we . . . can we just talk about it?"

Yeah, that's what I want to do, talk about it. Isabel stalled, saying she'd be right out. Why rush into the immediate future? The one where Aidan would elaborate on the details of every beautiful girl he'd slept with in Catswallow. And in return she could inform him that before last night no guy had ever kissed her like that . . . touched her like that . . . wanted her like . . . Isabel clutched the rough towel tighter. "Oh my God, what am I doing here?"

"Isabel, did you say something? I didn't hear—"

"No . . . nothing, just hang on a sec." Leaning against the bathroom door, she thought she might pass out. Just remembering what nearly happened at the farmhouse brought on a wave of heated sensations. Oddly, they still felt as good as they did new and curious. But what happened there, it was more natural than this. There was no discussion; it just grew organically out of the moment. And whatever made Aidan act that way, whatever spell he was under, well, he truly seemed to have wanted her as much as she did him. Now when Isabel went out there it would be like performing a duty—like when Stella made him sweep the mice turds from the kitchen cabinets.

On the other hand, spending the rest of her married life in the bathroom of the Crazy Eights Motel wasn't a realistic option. Isabel looked in the mirror where the fog had begun to lift, searching for some courage. She'd found enough to marry him. That or she was selfish enough to pounce on a moment of intense vulnerability. In all seriousness, if the last twenty hours hadn't happened, where would marrying her have fallen on Aidan's to-do list? Isabel shuddered at the amount of zeros attached to that figure and moved on to the one in the reflection. She grabbed a hand towel and with broad, brave strokes revealed the girl in the mirror. She concentrated on her face. What would Aidan see? There had been prettier girls, she had no illusions. Beautiful girls sprouted like wildflowers in Catswallow, Alabama. She was from New Jersey and it showed. Before last night, Isabel never pictured Aidan having sex with them. It was foolish and naïve, Isabel realizing how clueless she'd been. The moments on the sofa, in the farmhouse, exceeded any book she'd ever read, any dream she'd conjured up.

She sucked in a breath and in one fast motion let the damp towel drop, examining what Aidan would. Tangled wet hair hung like a cape, falling past her shoulders. It was long enough to shroud parts of her, and Isabel thought of Eve—equally tempted. She pushed it back, exposing everything. Like an expired fairy tale, Isabel was restored to her former self—a smattering of freckles and muddy green eyes. They were not striking or even interesting, only accentuating a nose that was definitely a tad too long for her face. Aside from thick waves of auburn hair that she could attribute to no one, she looked like him, like her father. And for so long that had not been a good thing.

Through those eyes, which registered twenty-twenty vision, Isabel took a fluorescent-lit inventory of what Aidan had seen by

candlelight. She sighed. *Maybe the Crazy Eights will lose power . . .*
Unlike the girls in Catswallow, she didn't boast a belly that could
pass for an ironing board. The kind with a navel primed for a ring.
Expanding her line of vision, she reflected on the ring she did possess. It set off a wary thump in her chest and Isabel's eyes panned
top to bottom, the mirror capturing just about everything—
including hips that had a definite shape. It was all okay; more
hourglass than willowy pine, but it wasn't a *Cosmo* cover waiting
to happen. She stared harder, knowing it wasn't a one-to-ten scale
of physical beauty, not really. It was more about her desirability
quotient. Isabel didn't come across like other girls; sexual allure
was not her dominating factor. Even her own mother saw it, unable
to believe someone like Aidan would want her. And if Rick Stanton did, what did that prove? She could arouse a middle-aged car
salesman with seedy political aspirations. *Gee, wouldn't girls like
Shanna O'Rourke be jealous of me.* With a hand to her throat,
Isabel's fingertips traced downward, past her breasts, across her
stomach, inching lower and pausing where Aidan did. It sent her
hurling toward a moment Aidan certainly knew how to induce.
Her other hand braced against the cold tile of the sink as his voice
penetrated—from the other side of the door.

"Isabel, open the door—now."

Everything stopped. Isabel gasped for a breath, staring red-faced
into the mirror. She was pathetic, more comfortable with the fantasy than the reality of any pending wedding night. But she was
also distracted, realizing a different problem. She had no clothes.
She left them in the other room. To put the clothes back on that
she wore into the bathroom seemed asinine. Of course, wearing
the skimpy towel out was ridiculously obvious—like she was looking for *it*. Wait. Couldn't she look for *it*? After all, she was Aidan's
wife. *Aidan's wife.* Could anything sound more absurd? He knocked
again.

"Isabel, here." She pinched the door open and through the crack came Aidan's arm, Isabel's undergarments, sweatpants, and T-shirt dangling from his fist.

Okay, that answers a few things.

"We have to go."

"Go? Where are we going?"

"To Caesars Palace. Fitz Landrey is meeting us there."

"Fitz Landrey . . ." Did he already get Aidan a gig? "Why, what are you talking about?" She shuffled into the underwear and pants, flinging the door open and hooking the bra. A giant gulp slid through his throat. *Desire or despair?* Ignoring both, she yanked the T-shirt over her sopping-wet head.

"It's good, Isabel, really good." He smiled wider than she'd ever seen. And *that* she could decipher; Aidan was definitely beaming. He'd also changed into the jeans and shirt they bought. Isabel's gaze traveled from his face to the snake. For some reason, she thought the tattoo would vanish with the tuxedo. But it appeared to be hard at work, adding a layer of recklessness to his *Brad Pitt is my ugly brother* looks.

"When I more or less explained things, Fitz told me not to worry and to meet him at Caesars. He's booking a room for us. He said that he gave my demo CD to a bunch of execs at C-Note and they're all on board, big-time. He was in Reno, so he'll be there soon." Aidan rushed around the room, stuffing their few belongings into bags. "Come on, I don't want to keep him waiting." He buzzed past her, heading right out the door. He stopped, glancing back. "Isabel, let's go. What's the problem?"

And to answer that would clearly stop Aidan's world from spinning, so, dutifully, she followed.

CHAPTER FOURTEEN

Las Vegas

THE INSIDE OF CAESARS PALACE WAS A SMALL CITY, ISABEL TRYing to ignore the fact that they were dressed like its resident vagabonds, their worldly possessions tied up in two plastic bags from Joe's Strip Souvenirs. They didn't have to meet Fitz for a half hour, though Aidan was anxious, and Isabel told him to go ahead without her. She'd catch up after taking the *bags* up to the room. As Fitz promised, there was a reservation waiting in Aidan's name. Aidan left her by the elevators, telling Isabel to meet them in the Seahorse Lounge.

The hotel room was a jaw-dropping improvement over their prior accommodations. A fast glance into a Caesars Palace mirror suggested she make an effort to improve her appearance as well. A head of damp hair, cheap sweatpants, and a tacky T-shirt surely fell short of the famous casino's dress code. Isabel went into the bathroom and used the hair dryer. The result wasn't much of an upgrade, her hair resembling a mop that'd stood in a corner for a week. She had no makeup with her, just a tube of lip gloss. Isabel was tempted to go to the shops downstairs. Surely one of the boutiques sold a head-to-toe, five-minute makeover kit. But the only money she had was Aidan's, and she wasn't comfortable spending it without telling him. Tucking the handful of twenties away, it occurred to Isabel how dependent on Aidan she was going to be. Yesterday, paying for college was her biggest concern. Now, who knew? Scavenging through her purse, Isabel thought she might have some forgotten cash. She only came up with a lint-covered Life Saver and her cell phone, which she'd purposely ignored.

Isabel tossed the phone back into her purse but seconds later guiltily retrieved it. As expected, there were messages from her mother. The first ones were panicked pleas to tell her where she was. By the third, she'd figured it out—or at least her version. Aidan jumped bail and he'd coerced Isabel into going with him. From what she said, everyone assumed they were driving. Good. They hadn't found Aidan's truck at the airport. She'd never guess they were in Las Vegas. Damn, Isabel would have never guessed it twelve hours ago. The fourth message was a recap of how Aidan was going to ruin her life. Couldn't she see how he was using her? *Gosh, Mom, must be a gene I inherited from you* . . . Her tone shifted considerably in the fifth message, a tongue-lashing like Isabel had never heard. She was furious, almost rambling. She'd worked so hard, sacrificed so much to make a decent life for the two of them. And, oh, by the way, the Catswallow sheriff was now looking for her, although Isabel guessed not in Las Vegas. Carrie eased up in the next message, saying that this wasn't how things were supposed to work out, and would Isabel please come home—at least call? "Come home to what?" she muttered, hitting Delete. "Rick's house? And you can politely ignore it when he suggests I take the bedroom across the hall. Better yet, maybe he can pick up the tab for college. Imagine what I'd owe him for that? No thanks." There was one more message, a number Isabel didn't recognize. But the man's voice sent a wicked jolt through her—heart rattling.

"Is, it's me . . . It's your father."

She hadn't heard his voice in nearly six years. Not since their last conversation when he told her he'd halted visitation proceedings. He said he wanted to give Isabel time to adjust. That hopefully she'd come to him. The trouble she was in crystallized. Eric Lang could have called only if he'd spoken to her mother. And for that to happen, Isabel thought she'd have to be dead.

"Listen, Is . . ." He was the only person who called her that. "I heard what's going on. Well, I heard your mother's side of it. I'd like to hear your side of things, if you'll let me. This . . . this sounds serious, Isabel. I know you're a smart girl, but you need to talk to someone. I can help. You know I can, but you have to let me. Call me back, Is—please."

Tears pooled in reply. For a moment, Isabel wanted to call him. His voice was so genuine, so concerned, so like the dad she knew the day before that night in New Jersey. The phone rang again. It was Aidan.

"Isabel, are you coming? How long does it take to drop two bags in a hotel room?"

"Sorry, I was listening to my messages." He didn't say anything right away.

"And?"

"And it's about what you'd expect. Do you want me to elaborate?"

"No, not right now. Let's just talk to Fitz, see what happens."

"Okay. Aidan?"

"Yeah?"

"My father called. He left a message."

More silence. "Your father? That's, um, that's incredible. Geez, he must have talked to your mother. For that to happen I thought you'd have to be . . ."

"Dead?"

"Pretty much. Are you going to call him back?"

"No, of course not." She hesitated, twisting a lock of hair around a finger. "Well, it would just be a conversation, right? Maybe. I'd . . . I need to think about it."

"Oh. That's, um, that's surprising." There was another pause. "I, uh . . . listen, Isabel. I think you should . . . Damn, here comes Fitz. I have to go. Just get down here as quick as you can."

Her father wanted to help. It was more than Carrie had offered. Isabel stared at the phone, imagining the conversation. Where would it even start? *"Hi, Dad. It's me, Isabel . . . yeah, it's been a while. How are you? How's Patrick?"* And that's where it stopped. She'd met Patrick Bourne once. Twice, if she counted the night in New Jersey, but that was more of a frantic blur. To this day she had no idea what her mother walked in on. Although she supposed it left zero room for interpretation. Isabel's second encounter with Patrick Bourne occurred not long after her father moved out. She was twelve and understandably confused by the turmoil. Other than Carrie doing a lot of crying and the overnight upheaval to their lives, no one had filled in the blanks. Not to Isabel's satisfaction. On a hunt for answers, she took a public transit bus from the neighborhood where they lived to Princeton University, where Eric worked in admissions. Patrick Bourne was a visiting lecturer at the law school, but she didn't know that. Isabel managed to find her way to her father's office. She poked her head inside, seeing Patrick there. The two men were drinking coffee, talking. They didn't see Isabel as she listened at the door. There was an odd cadence to their conversation. It wasn't the way Eric Lang spoke to the men in their neighborhood or his golf buddies. It wasn't even the way he spoke to her mother. It made Isabel think of her older cousin, Jennifer, the warm way she talked about her fiancé. David was in the army, stationed in Afghanistan. They hadn't seen each other for a year. That's how Patrick and her father spoke, longingly and unsure about the future. The two men were startled to find her there,

Patrick leaving quickly, but not before saying he hoped to see her again. He said he was sorry about her parents, very sorry. She remembered thinking that he was tall. His voice was soothing and at the same time in charge—like a teacher whose manner made you take notice. Still, she was unable to come up with a reason why he was so interested in Isabel or her parents' divorce.

After he left she came around to her father's side of the desk, spinning in his big leather chair. He took the seat on the other side. A half-dozen spins in he asked Isabel to be still. She did—mostly, just swaying a few degrees left then right. Eric started and stopped. Finally, bluntly, he asked if Isabel knew what the word *homosexual* meant. The chair stopped as if the wheels seized, knowing it as a nasty synonym some of the boys in her school used, sometimes kidding around, sometimes to be mean. Logan Kraft and Chad Hollis, they said it about Ben Strickland, calling him *gay* because he took dance lessons and didn't care much for sports. And the year before, when she was in the sixth grade, there was incredible fuss over the fact that Miss Lewis, the science teacher, was living with Miss Saperstein, the assistant principal. Isabel didn't understand that either. Not until Naomi Britton, whose father was a Baptist minister, clarified. The two women didn't just share an apartment; they shared a bed—like Isabel's parents. Naomi went on to assure her that the depraved lifestyle meant that their eternal address would be Hell. God and the devil would see to it. So when her father asked what she knew about homosexuality that was her answer. It left Eric Lang with a lot of explaining to do—particularly since God and the devil seemed to be in joint agreement. She listened, her discomfort growing upon asking if he kissed Patrick the same way he kissed her mother. The way couples, men and women, sometimes did in movies she really wasn't supposed to see. In the end, the facts were more than Isabel was prepared to take in or on. Not long after came the job offer in Catswallow, Carrie assuring Isabel that her father had a new life and they would have theirs.

Considering everything now, a Las Vegas hotel room was the last place she expected to encounter Eric Lang. His voice unearthed feelings that Isabel believed to be long since buried, or at least charred into windblown ashes. She picked up the phone, tempted to hit redial. She could just tell him that she was alive, that he needn't worry. That whatever her mother believed, well, she had it all wrong—again. He, of all people, should be able to comprehend the thing about Carrie Lang that kept her from seeing the truth. He could tell her mother that Isabel was alive . . . that she was fine . . . that she was—*ohmigosh*—married to Aidan. It froze forward motion, imagining how she'd take to the news. It would be salt in the wound to have married the boy Carrie believed would ruin Isabel's life, hearing the news via her ex-husband, the one who left her for a man. Isabel cringed, eyes squeezing shut. While Isabel was angry about her mother's blind loyalty to Rick, she couldn't humiliate her like that. Now wasn't the right time for any of it. Yet, Isabel sat on the edge of the bed holding the phone. Her thumb hovered between erase and redial until the joint ached. She hit Save and headed for the lounge.

CHAPTER FIFTEEN

Las Vegas

THE INTERIOR OF THE SEAHORSE LOUNGE WAS DARKER BUT NO less glitzy. From what she'd seen of Vegas, Isabel wasn't sure they were meant for one another. They were definitely out of sync when it came to wardrobe. She was the polar opposite of glitz in gray sweatpants and an orange T-shirt stamped with a silk screen of Sin City's original Strip. Awkwardness mounted as scores of women passed by. They were stunning: gamblers, tourists, and showgirls—even the locals looked as if they'd been bred for this ultra-sheen lifestyle. They sparkled from head to toe, like Christmas trees parading along in glamorous dresses, breasts spilling over into the next casino. Every woman towered over her and if you turned them sideways, Isabel swore they'd be invisible, except for the breasts and sequins. Bottom line: They made Shanna O'Rourke look like a starter kit.

No one noticed her, but as she finally spied Aidan it was obvious that they'd seen him. Two girls—women—sat on the edge of their bar stools, batting a collective false eyelash in his direction. Another threesome sat at an adjacent table. Isabel guessed a Vegas wager was being made as to which one could hook up. Aidan saw them; she could tell by the casual smile that flirted through the air. It had to be reflex, learned behavior, Isabel finding that she wanted in on the bet, positive which woman had the best chance. She'd almost forgotten she was his wife. He reminded her by leaping from his chair as though she'd caught him fondling the native wares.

"Isabel, I was worried," he said, meeting her halfway. "What took you so long?"

"Um . . . I was in the bathroom." She rolled her eyes at her inability to come up with a more attractive excuse. Certainly the only reason these doe-eyed beauties used the bathroom was to reapply lipstick. On the way to the table she heard one girl remark, *"She must be a personal assistant . . ."* "How's it going?"

"It's going. So far we've talked about music and," he said with a deep breath, "the trouble I'm in. Fitz says he can take care of it, Isabel . . . all of it."

"Really? That's great." She wondered if he'd told Fitz about them, but from the sincere look of confusion on the man's face the question was answered. He composed himself, standing, as Aidan pulled out a chair and she sat.

"Ah, Aidan, I don't under—Isn't this the young lady . . . your date from the other night?"

"That's what I was getting to, Fitz. This is Isabel. Isabel Roycroft. We got married this afternoon."

"Married," he said, like the word was a cement anchor. He sipped his drink and inhaled deeply. "Seriously?"

"Seriously," Aidan said, an arm slinging around Isabel's chair. But the back was too low, making it an awkward fit.

"You'll have to excuse my confusion. I didn't realize the two of you . . . This seems kind of sudden." As he spoke, he turned his full attention on Isabel. "Your idea? To come to Vegas, get married?"

"No, actually, it was mine," Aidan said.

"Is that right? Correct me if I'm wrong, guys, but back in Catswallow wasn't my niece Aidan's date until five minutes before the big dance?"

Okay, I can totally understand why that's a valid question.

"Yes, that's true. Aidan and I . . . You see, it's like . . ." Isabel sucked in her own deep breath, attempting to explain the upgrade from substitute date to Aidan's wife. "You see, Aidan and I have been friends for a very long time." Brilliant reasoning, she thought, wanting to smack herself in the head.

"Friends, I see. That's nice. Well, I'm sure there have been Vegas marriages based on less." The silence around the table was palpable.

Aidan leaned forward, folding his hands in front of him. "Like I said, there was a lot to tell you. It's been a surreal twenty-four hours. I was just saving the good part for last."

Shouldn't that be the best part?

Taking better aim, Aidan wrapped an arm around her shoulder, hugging Isabel—kind of the way you would any good buddy. To shore up the effort his lips moved toward her, but she leaned too far and the kiss connected with the side of her forehead.

Fitz shifted in his seat, his gaze jerking from Aidan to Isabel. "I'll be, how fantastic!" he exclaimed, extending a hand to Aidan. "This calls for a celebration. Congratulations, both of you!" He gave Isabel's arm a fast squeeze and ordered a bottle of champagne from the passing waitress, who didn't ask for ID.

Fitz seemed to accept the marriage news, not mentioning it again as he prattled on about the kind of songs Aidan would record, the lightning speed with which they planned to release his first single, and how every executive at C-Note Music was sold on his demo CD. He even agreed that Aidan's newly acquired tattoo was a savvy marketing tactic. Finally, Isabel interrupted, "Mr. Landrey—"

"Please, it's Fitz," he said, filling her champagne glass again.

"Fitz. I know Aidan explained what happened before we left Catswallow—and I swear to you that Aidan did not shoot the man— but I'm wondering how you can be so sure about things. I mean, they did charge him with attempted murder and Rick Stanton—"

"Stanton, your mother's boyfriend, right?"

"Yes, the man who attacked me, that Aidan was defending me against."

"Yes, yes, he told me the whole story. Awful circumstance, lucky for you he was there. Don't give it another thought. I've already got my people on it. You can't run one of the world's largest record labels without a few piranha-like attorneys. They'll have Aidan's situation resolved in a couple of days. I guarantee it."

"But I don't understand. How is that possible?"

"Isabel," he said, in a firmer tone than she'd heard so far. "I'm a powerful man with many connections. It's my job to make things happen or to make them go away. I assure you, it will go away— all of it. You needn't worry." He excused himself from the table, saying he'd be right back.

"Isabel, can you believe this, everything he's said?"

Really, she couldn't. But Isabel kept the reservation to herself. The fear that was hanging over him like a guillotine had lifted. Every dream Aidan ever had was about to come true. "It's wonderful, Aidan. I can't wait to see California," she said like it was a trip to the science museum.

He nodded, folding his hand over hers. She stared, thinking how solid it felt. "Everything's going to be fine, I'm sure of it." He smiled, but she couldn't muster the return gesture. "Isabel, are you okay?"

She felt wet eyelashes, blinking fast. "Yeah," she said, an impassable lump in her throat. "I'm fine. Everything's going to be fine. It's just . . . just been a wild couple of days."

"Tell me about it." The grin vanished as he rolled his finger over the wedding band, which was a little big, not so secure. "Isabel, I need to tell you something before this goes any further, especially before we go to California." Aidan's face was so serious, leaving Isabel anxious about his next thought. "When we got married this afternoon—"

Unlike his first interruption on the VFW dance floor, she was now glad to see Fitz. She wasn't sure that she wanted to hear her new husband's declaration about their spur-of-the-moment marriage.

"Aidan, I spoke with the manager; he's an old acquaintance of mine."

Of course he is.

"The stage is free this evening," Fitz said, pointing to a small platform area that was dark until a moment ago. Bright lights cut through the blue hue of the room. They beckoned to him, like a piece of Aidan that was missing. "I'm wondering if you would treat the crowd to an impromptu performance."

"There's no band," Isabel remarked.

"There are a couple of spare guitars backstage. I'm sure Aidan can find something he's comfortable with. A small audience in a place like Caesars isn't a bad place to start. What do you say? I'd really like to hear something you wrote."

Isabel wanted to say it was a dare, Fitz wanting to see if Aidan was willing and able to perform on cue. She wanted to insist that Aidan not open his mouth until there was a signed contract—in triplicate. She wanted to protect him. But what Isabel had to say didn't matter. Aidan was up and out of his seat at the mere notion of performing at Caesars Palace. She suspected it was an irresistible lure, not to mention a major step up from the Catswallow VFW. As if to prove he could hit the mark, Aidan firmly planted a kiss on her cheek before heading backstage. "Any requests?"

She felt foolish. Isabel knew all Aidan's music, the slow love songs that she could listen to while finishing a chem lab and the edgier rock stuff that made the walls in the farmhouse vibrate. There was that Spanish thing he did on occasion. But she'd never bothered to learn the titles—she didn't have to, he played them for her every day. "Um, do the one you wrote the day it rained so hard we thought the farmhouse would slide off its foundation. You know, when there was all that mud." He laughed at her awkward interpretation of a beautiful ballad he'd penned on a dreary Saturday last spring.

"Slip Away with Me."

"Yeah, that one." He nodded and disappeared backstage. Fitz tapped her on the arm.

"Why don't you and I move to the back? The manager has a table waiting. I'd like to see how the crowd reacts."

Isabel knew how the crowd would react. But if he needed proof, it was fine with her. She followed Fitz away from the swell of the main room. A tall cocktail table was set on a riser offering a bird's-eye view of the small but packed venue. There was general disinterest and a smattering of applause when the manager came out and introduced Aidan—Aidan *Royce*. She leaned over, whispering, "He got his name wrong."

"No he didn't," Fitz said. "Aidan Roycroft is a kid in a whole lot of trouble from some backwater hole in Alabama. Aidan Royce is the next superstar."

Isabel wondered about this bit of spin. Perhaps he had a point.

For a solid fifteen seconds there was nothing. People continued to drink, laugh, and carry on their conversations as if Aidan was nobody. Then, as predicted, heads began to turn. The chatter

petered out to a soft hush. And the hush hung on to the mesmerizing texture of Aidan's voice. The only sounds left were curious
whispers asking, "Who's he?" Naturally, it was the women who
fell first. The ones who'd openly ogled him reveled in their discovery. Not only was the dreamy guy next to them drop-dead gor-
geous, but holy crap, he could sing too. A gaggle of older women,
definitely not in Aidan's demographic, became equally aware.
Isabel smiled as the men caught on, tuning in to Aidan Royce. It
was a proud moment, his voice caressing the room, captivating the
audience like a hypnotist and his subjects. But there was also regret.
Isabel felt something physical give way, relinquishing to the masses
what had belonged completely, selfishly, to her.

No performer was more comfortable onstage than Aidan,
deftly switching rhythms to something with a stronger beat.
Instead of politely listening, the men swayed in their seats, thrumming fingertips on tabletops at the harder rock sound. It was doubly impressive considering Aidan's only accompaniment was a lone
guitar that didn't even belong to him. With the entire room
engaged, Isabel glanced toward Fitz. He appeared to be taking
serious mental notes, confirming the *Eureka!* of his discovery. She
settled into her seat, feeling more at ease. Maybe Aidan was right.
Maybe everything would be fine.

Well into his third or fourth song, Fitz tapped her on the arm,
gesturing that she should follow. They moved to a cylinder-shaped
room. There was an aquarium on one side, the other offering a
two-way mirror view of the lounge and stage. She could still see
Aidan, but the crowd noise dulled, his voice muffled. "What is
this?"

"When not using it to feed the fish, they utilize it for security.
You can't have too much security in a casino." He shoved his hands
into his pockets, giving her a long once-over. Isabel had almost
forgotten her inappropriate attire and makeup-less face. Curling

her toes into the soft rubber soles of her flip-flops, she twisted the gold band around her finger. There was a flutter in her stomach that wasn't there before. "Isabel, we need to talk."

"About what?" But her throat went tight, not really wanting to know.

"Do you see that crowd, the way they're reacting?" She nodded, inching closer to the glass. "That's nothing, Isabel. That's without a record on the shelf, zero promotion—not even an afternoon with a good stylist. Imagine what's going to happen to him when we put the polish on his package."

"He's very talented."

"Yes, he is. And his life is about to change in ways that he can't possibly fathom."

She glanced at Fitz, ready to stand her ground. "It's good then, that I'll be there for him when it gets crazy. He'll be surrounded by strangers; he'll need someone who understands him."

Fitz smiled. "We hire someone for that."

"I mean someone who knows him—knows the old Aidan."

"Perhaps, for however long the old Aidan exists. This business, it changes people. Success changes people, and not always in a good way."

This time she turned her whole body. "Maybe I should tell Aidan that, suggest he think this through if it's going to have a bad effect, if he's going to wake up one morning and not recognize himself."

Fitz pursed his lips, his head nodding in agreement. "I don't doubt your influence, Isabel, not for a moment. While I'm not convinced you could talk him out of it, I am positive he'd give ample credence to anything you say." He paused, even muffled applause proving thunderous. Isabel turned back, seeing the golden carrot dangled before Aidan. He tried to leave the stage but was easily coaxed into an encore.

"Isabel." Fitz waited, watching her turn from the window. The look on his face was doubtless. "I want you to leave him." Isabel's mouth dropped open as her heart plummeted past her feet, plowing right through the floor. Fitz, on the other hand, possessed Isabel's usual sense of calm. "And I want you to do it in a way that doesn't leave him with any uncertainty, so he can move forward with C-Note and his career."

"But . . . I . . ." Shaking her head furiously, Isabel wanted to pack Aidan up and take him home to Catswallow. She took a half step toward the door but stopped. *Wait—I can't. They'll put him in jail.* She turned back, cornered in a round room. "Why . . . why would you ask me to do that?"

He ignored her question. "You're not pregnant, are you?"

She sighed, squeezing her eyes shut. While the answer to that was not-a-prayer-in-the-world no, admitting that she and Aidan hadn't consummated the marriage was better news than Fitz could have hoped for. "No," she hissed. "I'm not pregnant."

"Excellent," he said, smiling. "That will save us some trouble."

Fitz's words rattled through her head: "*It's my job to make things happen and to make them go away . . .*" Isabel suspected she was in the latter category. "I don't understand. I love Aidan." She found this easier to admit to Fitz than her own mother, herself, or even Aidan. Maybe because, before now, the stakes weren't as high, and girls like Shanna O'Rourke were no threat to her. "Nobody wants to see Aidan succeed more than I do. I'm not going to jeopardize his success."

"On the contrary, you're the one thing that will keep him from succeeding. Come, sit down over here." He led her to a chair away from the two-way glass. "I want you to listen to me carefully. Look, I've got nothing against you personally. I'm sure you're a lovely young woman with the best of intentions." It came out of his mouth as heartfelt as a hooker making a date. "Let me make clear a few precarious things about this business. Things that drive the beast, so to speak. The world that Aidan is about to step into has rules, a certain criteria for success. Societal rules, on the other hand, are almost taboo, irrelevant in some instances."

"You mean like going to go to jail or standing trial for attempted murder or whatever else they want to pin on you?"

"That's right, Isabel. There are privileges and pitfalls to what he's about to embark on. It's my job to guide him, to make sure he follows the rules, avoids the pitfalls, and meets the criteria. Now, there are artists, even rock stars, who've made it based on talent alone—I'm not saying that can't happen. But it's not the way it's going to happen for him and let me tell you why. As musically gifted as Aidan is, a large chunk of his appeal is going to be based on an inexplicable it factor. In his case, that it factor wholly revolves around his raw magnetism. The way he looks, if I need to be blunt, an aura that drips off him like liquid gold. His female audience is what's going to ignite his rocket to stardom. That's not some fantastic notion I've dreamt up, it's simply the way it works." Isabel's chin tipped higher, her thoughts transparent as the aquarium on the other side. "I'd also bet it's not something that comes as a great surprise to you."

The girls of Catswallow heaved through her head. Isabel didn't know it had a name, but Aidan's *it factor* is what drove the juggernaut, the thing that made him so popular, elevating him to his godlike status. She saw it as an anomaly, something that wouldn't matter beyond the superficial boundaries of their adolescence. She'd misjudged. Apparently, it counted for everything in this superficial world. "So what are you saying? If Aidan were coyote ugly, or had a *sorta* factor, he'd have a much tougher time making it?"

Fitz's answer was cold and decisive. "If that were the case, you and I wouldn't be having this discussion at all. I don't represent possibility. I represent a sure thing. It's artificial . . . it's unfair . . . it's shallow. It's how it is."

"I still don't see what that has to do with me—with us."

"Everything, Isabel. Aidan needs to be available to his fans and not just on tour or for a photo op. Aidan needs to be available for the fantasy. It will be especially important in the beginning, the make-or-break stage. It's crucial that Aidan be unattached, particularly unattached to a conventionally attractive girl from Catswallow, Alabama."

"I'm from New Jersey," she countered with a narrow-eyed hiss.

"Whatever. The point is that Aidan can't be married to some insignificant girl who, if she hadn't attached herself to Aidan's star, would be enrolled in vocational training, maybe community college. Being married to you is career suicide."

Fitz's blade twisted through, a shaky breath pumping in and out of Isabel. She didn't want to give his theory credit, but she knew there was truth in it. Even so, she wasn't about to be bullied. Fitz Landrey might be in the process of purchasing Aidan, but he didn't own her. "Maybe we ought to see what Aidan has to say."

"I'm afraid Aidan doesn't get a vote," he countered. "To be honest, how he feels about you is of no concern to me. But maybe it should be to you. I'm clear enough on Aidan's love life to know that a couple of weeks ago you two weren't exactly a hot-and-heavy couple. Whatever spurred this sudden marriage isn't real. You have to know that." Fitz was onto her like a Svengali lounge act in a thousand-dollar suit. "Aidan's grasping at straws, panicking over his situation, clinging to something familiar when nothing around him makes sense. But I'm here to fix all that for him. I'm going to set his world right and then some. I'm here to make a sizable investment in his future and things *will* run according to my plan— nobody else's."

It was every fear she'd had in the last eight hours verbalized, the rational reasons why Aidan asked her to marry him. Isabel rose from the chair, returning to the window. No wonder Rick Stanton was of no consequence to Fitz Landrey. Situations, unpleasant or otherwise, were his business. Aidan had stopped singing. She smiled in the midst of Fitz's brutal life lesson. He was signing autographs. Isabel's eyes drew wide, transfixed on the scene. She was watching Aidan's dream—and it was beautiful. Just days ago Isabel forged his signature on a town job application. Catswallow was hiring that fall, road crews and the like, just part-time. She hadn't gotten around to mentioning it, suggesting to Aidan that supplemental employment, no matter how off target, might prove useful. It was just as well, she thought, smiling. Her attempt to duplicate Aidan's handwriting was completely off, unable to reproduce the singular sway of his signature. The one destined to be an autograph.

Stunning women surrounded him. One slipped a piece of paper into his pocket, a phone number, maybe a late-night invitation to her room. In the past, which was admittedly just that morning, Aidan's ability to resist was finite. She wondered how much a person could change over the course of a few hours and a couple of *I do*s. Her stomach rolled on a wave of reality, Isabel clinging to the solidarity of what she and Aidan shared. She whipped around in a vain attempt to—*unbelievably*—save her marriage? "What if we keep it a secret? Why does anybody have to know?"

"Is that what you want? To have less status in his life than his personal masseuse or the roadie who'll stand backstage handing him a towel as he darts into a limo?" He hesitated, inching back a bit. "Interesting, you struck me as hardier than that." He joined her at the window. "Those women pawing him, they're bottom feeders. He's going to have his pick of movie stars, models, celebrities. He'll go to parties and clubs, travel all over the world. That's not to mention the groupies that will be waiting outside every stage door, willing to perform any act of indecency. Will you really want him to come home to you after that?"

"Aidan wouldn't do that, he'd never hurt me like that—now . . . now that we're married."

"Mmm, maybe not at first, maybe not intentionally, but maybe not at all? I sincerely doubt it. My guess, observing that scene, is he doesn't have the willpower." She watched, focused on the layers of women circling him. The girl who slipped the paper into his pocket repeatedly touched his arm. She was the one Isabel would have bet on earlier. "Look, my niece and I aren't close, but I can see that she's an exceptionally beautiful girl." His eyes glossed over Isabel. Forget the sweatpants, she felt absolutely naked. "If Aidan cheated on a girl like Shanna, what makes you think you can hold his attention? Straying from *your* marriage will come easier than his first hit single." He looked her up and down. "Said you're from New Jersey, right?" She nodded. "Hoboken?" He was wrong, but she didn't correct him. "It would be Frank and Nancy all over again."

While she didn't get the reference, she did see a grim picture of their future. Aidan rolling through the door at three a.m. covered in stinky perfume, lipstick on his face or more intimate body parts. The vision was clear because she'd already seen it to some degree. Honestly? It sucked when they were only friends. Isabel could imagine the humiliation on their second or third wedding anniversary. But part of her wanted to keep fighting. Why did Fitz Landrey, a man they didn't know forty-eight hours ago, get to decide? "I could go to Aidan, tell him everything you've warned me about, explain it all the way you've explained it to me—just like you've explained it to me. Do you think he'll appreciate it, undermining him like this? Sticking your nose in what is so clearly none of your business!"

His worldly calm was daunting, particularly when he agreed.

"You have an excellent point. Like I said, *hardy.* You could head right down there and repeat our conversation verbatim. Perhaps Aidan will be so furious he'll tell me to go to hell. It's an interesting risk. I won't stop you. I'll be on my way to the airport catching the next flight back to L.A.—without Aidan. Refresh my memory. Exactly where would that leave him?"

Aidan stood at the edge of the stage accepting the fervor of adulation, a man from the audience buying him a beer. Staring through the window, Isabel understood why Fitz Landrey got to decide. "It would leave Aidan as a wanted fugitive, as the person who shot Rick Stanton. He wouldn't be on his way to stardom. He'd be on his way to jail."

"And whose fault would that be?"

"Mine," she said, gulping hard. "Everything that happened back in Catswallow *and* taking away his dream. It would all be my fault."

"Uh huh, and how would Aidan feel about you then? For how long, under those circumstances, do you think you'd be married to Aidan Roycroft?"

Isabel nodded, a single tear breaking through a hardy barrier. "You know, if I wasn't a vocationally bound, insignificant girl from Catswallow, I'd say that almost sounds like blackmail."

"Well, I guess you'd almost be right. Except it's hardly my fault that Aidan beat the crap out of Rick Stanton in the first place. It wasn't me who set this in motion, Isabel. And while I'm happy to believe yours and Aidan's story about the shooting . . . Well, I suspect law enforcement may not be as compliant. And so we're clear, as some added incentive, if Aidan were to go to trial, I can imagine the Catswallow DA will go full throttle. Can't say for sure, but I suspect jumping bail won't bode in his favor. He'll be looking at the maximum sentence and then some. He won't get a recording contract. He'll get twenty years in a maximum-security

Alabama correctional center. I'd hate to picture who he'd be married to in that case." He shrugged at her horrified stare. "It's what will happen if Aidan Roycroft leaves this hotel with a wife on his arm. It's a far cry from MTV's *TRL*. But, hey, you know him better than I do."

Incredulous, she absorbed Fitz from this angle, curious where they kept the shark tank. Her gaze dropped to the gold band encircling her finger. It was a noose around Aidan's neck. Not unlike her jailhouse confession, she'd done nothing but make things worse. By marrying Aidan, Isabel sabotaged the most important relationship she ever had. More to the point, she wouldn't be responsible for Aidan spending the next decade or two in prison. And she certainly wasn't going to be the reason his career nosedived before it ever took flight. Brushing away the tears, laughter rumbled from her throat. "You're very good at your job."

"I'll take good care of him, Isabel. I promise. By stepping aside, look at what you'll be doing for him. He's going to have everything he's ever wanted. And don't worry, it won't take long."

"What's that, Aidan's rise to stardom?"

Fitz shook his head, frowning. "No, until he forgets about you."

With a breath of surrender she turned toward Aidan. Without casting a die, playing a card, or pulling on a slot machine, Isabel had managed to suffer the biggest loss in Vegas history. Even when common sense said she'd get over him, that they were too young for this anyway, Isabel knew she'd never love anyone the way she loved Aidan. "What, um . . . what should I tell him?"

His tone never deviated from the sound business maneuver he was negotiating. "Tell him what he needs to hear. You realize what a mistake this was. That while you wish him well, you can't possibly stay married to a man you don't love. You have other plans. The glitz and fast track of what's about to happen is his dream, not yours. Most important, Isabel, be very clear."

She nodded, guessing she was about to discover how deep that hardy well of calm went. "Can I have some time alone with him?"

He studied her for a moment. "Fine—I don't suppose I have much choice there. Our flight isn't until morning. Mind you, I don't want him getting off the plane looking like he hasn't slept in days. He'll need to make a good impression at C-Note tomorrow. That *it factor* needs to be in top form, understand?" She nodded again and turned to leave, but as she opened the door Fitz offered something else, a consolation gift. "It wouldn't be right to leave you here, stranded in Las Vegas. A one-way airline ticket will be at the front desk for you. Just tell the concierge where you want to go. He'll make the arrangements. Anywhere but California," he said, putting a fine point on things. "Isabel, I don't want to give you false hope, but there's a remote chance this won't work out. It happens. The wind doesn't blow right; the song doesn't break the hot one hundred. If he doesn't catch on like wildfire, doesn't make it, say, within a year, it's likely we'll be returning him to you."

Isabel looked over her shoulder, knowing she had a better chance of being pregnant. "That just goes to show you, Fitz. You don't know the first thing about Aidan Royce."

CHAPTER SIXTEEN

Las Vegas

BECAUSE IT WAS APPROPRIATE, ISABEL SMILED AS SHE AND AIDAN rode in the elevator, chatting with a couple who'd been in the audience. Aidan was on such a high he couldn't see the cement wall that had dropped between them. And maybe it was better this way, that he didn't see it coming. As the couple gushed on, Isabel's smile dissipated. Who was she kidding? Among the scenarios Fitz had laid out, her worst fear wasn't any future unfaithfulness on Aidan's part. Her worst fear was the present, telling Aidan that she was leaving him. No matter his outward reaction he'd only be relieved. Before exiting the starstruck twosome insisted on an autograph, thrilled to shake Aidan's hand. The elevator doors closed and Isabel cued up calm. Aidan buzzed in her ear, ecstatic about performing in front of a real crowd, people who'd pay money to listen. He was a sweaty, stunned golden statue of awe, claiming it was more exciting than the Selma County Fair, a place where he'd filled every seat. "Did you hear them, Isabel? It's one thing for people to get into a cover song, something they already love. But they went for my stuff." Forcing the smile back around, she listened as his voice softened, the everyday Aidan falling slightly short of the consummate performer. "At . . . at least I thought they did. They did . . . right, Isabel? They liked my music?"

The smile turned genuine. "Yes, Aidan, they loved it. The world is going to love everything about you." The elevator doors opened. Isabel self-comforted by guessing her only wifely act would be not to stand between Aidan and his one true love.

After arriving in the room, Aidan took a shower. He was running on pure adrenaline. Isabel moved out of pure fear. She didn't dare lose sight of the plague-like prophecies that would befall him if she didn't follow through. She needed to put things in motion, thinking hard but not for very long. Her assets amounted to a one-way plane ticket and a lint-covered Life Saver. She reached for the human lifesaver that had been offered. While Aidan was in the bathroom, Isabel made two calls. The first went to voicemail. She almost left a message, but what for? It wasn't like she had somewhere else to go. The second call was to the concierge, informing him of her travel plan, which did not include California. Methodically, she packed her things into one of the bags from Joe's Strip Souvenirs, putting most of Aidan's cash back into his wallet. She kept thirty dollars, just in case. Isabel executed each move deliberately and with composure. It was a warm-up for what came next.

She turned. With the abruptness of a scream in church, their marriage license interrupted. It and the strip of pictures from the photo booth sat atop the dresser. She told herself it was just a piece of paper. It didn't mean anything. She considered throwing it in the trash, but her hand veered left at the last second, slipping it inside the bag. Isabel tore away one photo—the one of them kissing, tucking it inside the pocket of Aidan's tux. It was symbolic. Besides, he'd never find it. But she did think about it for a moment, the kiss. Aidan did kiss her. Not the other way around. And what happened at the farmhouse . . . This time Carrie interrupted, Isabel hearing her warning about such foolishness. The thought was punctuated by Fitz's logic. The scene at the farmhouse was fear seeking comfort, not unlike the past few hours. Aidan was upset, they both were. Comfort is what he expected from Isabel. How could it be anything else? He wasn't in love with her, not like that. Even if the world had tipped off its axis and Aidan did love her, like a wife . . . Well, it was a moot point. Fitz Landrey had seen to that. Really, it was a huge blessing. Isabel couldn't imagine the devastation if Aidan's feelings amounted to any more than friendship. Of course, the alternative, Aidan in jail, was even more disturbing. She'd follow through with whatever it took to keep that from happening. She couldn't do anything less. Not after Aidan was prepared to do the same for her.

Shoving the strip of pictures into her purse, Isabel's first instinct was to take the coward's way out. She could leave a heartfelt note and vanish. No, it was too open-ended. It would fall short of Fitz's instructions. *"Tell him what he needs to hear. Most important, Isabel, be very clear."* There was zero margin for error. Aidan needed to believe everything she was about to tell him. Counting on hardy calm, Isabel waited, constructing the framework of her manifesto. Like Aidan said, he trusted her with his life. That was a good thing. It would make it easier for him to swallow the whopper of a lie she was about to tell him.

AIDAN CAME OUT FROM THE BATHROOM, A TOWEL AROUND HIS waist, another draped over his shoulders. "Where were you and Fitz while I was singing? I couldn't find you in the crowd." As he spoke Aidan peered in the mirror, thinking about how it would feel to wake up to the snake for the rest of his life. A wedding ring and marriage license; it was nothing. Orlando had it right. Every glance at the tattoo would make him think of Isabel, forever bound to her. Patting it dry, he tossed the towel onto the floor. "Isabel?"

he said, watching her in the reflection. A wide-eyed gaze was trained on him. She leapt to her feet. It was as if Aidan in a towel, or perhaps less, was the furthest image from her mind. Damn, maybe he should have put his pants back on. "Isabel, are you okay?"

"Yes, yes . . . fine," she said, pulling a hand through a tangle of hair. She brushed by, picking up the discarded towel. "I, um, I just didn't think you'd get out of the shower and be, you know, naked—half-naked."

He shrugged. "Is there a way to get out of the shower and not be naked?"

"I suppose not." Isabel kept moving, returning the discarded towel to the bathroom, picking his clothes up off the floor. Coming back around the corner, she stopped. She leaned tight against the wall, clutching his pants. Short of standing in the tub it was as far as she could get and still be in the same room.

"Anyway, where were you? I was going to sing the Spanish song I usually do at the farmhouse. I thought tonight was the right occasion. I was going to sing it in English. But I couldn't find you." It was the perfect opportunity to tell her how he felt. But when he couldn't find her, Aidan didn't follow through. He'd purposely written the song in Spanish, never translating it, explaining its evolution, or how it applied to them.

"Really? I thought you said that song didn't fit with your usual set. That it didn't belong."

"It doesn't. It's not meant for a crowd, but I did want to sing it for you."

Isabel cocked her head, an annoyed look on her face. "That's ridiculous, Aidan. All the gigs you played back home and you never sang it, not once. Why waste Caesars Palace on some meaningless song—in Spanish no less. I don't think C-Note plans on promoting your Latin side. You're going to have to be savvier than that. Every song counts from here on out."

The romantic notion was lost on her and, just once, Aidan wished she'd weaken, maybe even succumb to his charms. He turned from the mirror, facing her. "What are you getting so upset for? It's one song."

She popped away from the wall and stalked to the opposite side of the room. "Sorry, I didn't mean to snap. I was in the back. Fitz and I were watching from the back of the room." She folded the pants, placing them neatly on a chair. Her gaze drew to his. "He believes in you, Aidan. I can't even begin to tell you how much. He's going to do everything in his power to make this happen. He told me that, exactly that."

"Yeah, I hope," he said, a thick wave of Isabel's hair catching his eye. He was done performing, working the room. He didn't want to think about anything but the two of them. There was zero pressure to perform with Isabel. He loved the stage, but he enjoyed shedding the persona almost as much. And there was no better place for that than Isabel's company. To her, the everyday Aidan mattered so much more. In turn, he loved everything about her. Isabel's quirky nervousness, it was a rare phenomenon that overrode her serene exterior. On occasion, in the right circumstance, there was a sweet and sexy appeal that affected him like nothing else—certainly no other girl. Tonight he'd get the chance to show Isabel exactly what she meant to him. But slow. He had to approach this slowly. Aidan didn't want a repeat of this afternoon, and thought that maybe he should get dressed. He hesitated. No, let her mull it over. "Hey, do you want to order more champagne?" he asked, knowing she really didn't care for beer. "They don't seem too concerned with checking ID in this place."

"Not right now. Listen, Aidan, we need to talk."

"Yeah, I know. I've been trying to talk to you all day. But it's just been, you know, crazy."

"*Crazy*'s a good word. Insane might be another." Isabel sunk onto the edge of the bed and Aidan didn't hesitate, sitting next to her. He watched her eyes brush over his chest, inching toward a tented towel that was showing sure signs of man waiting to stake his claim. An alarm-filled gaze shot to his. "Aidan?"

"Yeah?" he said softly, stroking her arm with his fingertips, anticipating the moment.

"Could you put your pants on?"

"On? You want me to put them on?" He sighed, fighting a nudge of frustration. "No, Isabel, I can't. I don't wear pants when I go to bed. In fact, I don't wear anything at all." He crossed his arms, staring. If they sat and stared at one another for the next eight hours, fine. But he wasn't putting his damn pants on.

"I see, I guess," she said. "But let me talk first, okay? What I have to say is important and it will save you the trouble."

"What trouble?" His hand rose, fingertips touching her hair.

"What are you doing?" She grasped his wrist, pushing it away.

"I was going to kiss my wife." Aidan didn't wait for her reaction, guessing it might call for some assertiveness on his part. He was stunned by the intensity with which she resisted, pushing hard against his shoulders.

"Oh God, Aidan, don't do that!" she gasped, stumbling across the room, wiping her mouth with the back of her hand.

He followed, dumbfounded. Nervous, yes, but this was just weird. "Don't do what? Kiss you?" She nodded, her hand clamped over her mouth like a shield. And he fought the absurd image of Isabel spending their entire marriage that way, her legs crossed too. "Isabel," he said, forcing her hand away. "What's going on? Maybe we do need to talk. I don't know about you, but it was my intention to finish what we started at the farmhouse."

"It . . . it was?" She blinked widely, frantically tucking her hair, like two ears weren't enough.

"Well, yeah," he said, hands firm to his hips. "I thought that getting married made it a no-brainer. Jesus, I don't know, really insane people might call it a honeymoon!"

"A honey—I . . . But Aidan—" Her mouth dropped open, then shut. It was as if the concept was utterly mystifying. "Aidan, we need to stop this. I think it's time we quit playing house and admit what a mistake this was." Isabel took a huge step back, standing out of his reach. "It's only a honeymoon if two people are in love."

Two people. Air wouldn't move in or out. Had she stabbed him through the snake with an ice pick it couldn't have hurt any worse. There, she said it. Isabel wasn't in love with him. Aidan felt the man drain out of him, a boyish tear stinging at his eye. He forced air in, running a hand through damp hair. Staring past her, he squinted into the distance. No, he wasn't going to give up that easily. He didn't believe it. There was no way he could feel so much for her and she feel nothing . . . nothing but friendship. His gaze jerked to Isabel, reaching for the right words. Elaborate lyrics flowed effortlessly, melodies following freely. But it was plain prose that Aidan needed and it wouldn't come. "What . . . what about the farmhouse, what we were just about to do, what we did before . . ."

"What about it?" she snapped, as though it were nothing more than a vague irritation.

"Don't tell me that didn't mean anything."

"I'm sure it was as sincere as all the other girls you've entertained there." She hesitated, shrugging. "We both know I'm not the only action the farmhouse sofa has seen. Seriously, I bet you can't even count the number of girls there before me." She folded her arms. "Go ahead, give it a guess."

"Zero," he replied, and her mouth gaped wider, the idea that she assumed as much causing a searing burn. "I'd never take a girl to the farmhouse. Maybe that's not what you and I were about then. But that place, it belongs to you and me—no one else." There was a fast blink, her mouth closing.

Apparently, he ranked even lower than he suspected. There had been other girls, most suggesting they go to the farmhouse. But he'd never disrespect Isabel that way. He wanted to tell her again, prove it, but she was onto other things. "What are you doing?" Aidan watched her flit about, arranging his belongings, as if organizing his life.

"I'm leaving."

"You're . . . but you can't. We just got married." Everything was moving so fast, Isabel rushing by like a passing comet. Leave him? She couldn't. She held everything together. "Wait!" he shouted, grabbing her arms. "Just wait a damn minute. You're not going anywhere."

She wouldn't look at him, her head turned hard. "Let go, Aidan. This is ridiculous. Our marriage is ridiculous. Look," she said, offering him the courtesy of eye contact. Those smoky green eyes, he'd never seen them filled with so much fire. "Everything is going to be fine. Tomorrow you'll get a brand-new life, everything you've ever wanted. You won't need me to fix your screwups, confirm your gigs, or program your cell phone. I understand they have someone for that. But, Aidan, please . . . I can't stay married to you!"

"Why the hell not? I need you, Isabel! Don't you know how much? I can't do this without you. I don't want to!"

Her face scrunched to a serious look of indignation, the one she used whenever she was busy holding his life steady. "Grow up, Aidan. Don't be an idiot. Of course you can."

If he hadn't been scared to death, he might have laughed. It was classic Isabel—blunt-force trauma resulting in corrective action. But fear won out, sparking an odd anger. "Goddamn it! Why are you making this so difficult? For the last year it's been impossible! And somehow, now that we're married, it's even harder to say."

"What . . . what's harder to—never mind. I don't want to know."

Isabel blew past, signaling that she was through with the conversation. Like hell. Aidan grabbed an arm and yanked her back, maybe harder than he meant, his towel slipping to the floor in the process. She gasped, struggling to get away from him and his very naked body.

"Prove it, Isabel. Prove that you don't want us." He kissed her hard, his arms clutching tight around her. There was a groan from her throat that he couldn't place. Under any other circumstance he would have thought it was a hungry growl of desire; now he wasn't so sure. Then, slowly, the closed fists that pushed against his shoulders eased and opened, her fingertips reaching for him. Her body followed the surrender, curving into tense muscles. Her lips replied, without words, melding into his. Instinct said to just keep going, no pausing for idle chatter. But Aidan knew this would require a more cerebral appeal. "Give me a chance, Isabel. Let me show you how wonderful this can be." He held on with everything he had. "You did marry me. And I swear, when I married you I meant it . . . all the words." She didn't respond, but she wasn't pushing him away. It was like she couldn't figure out what to do. No doubt his reputation was to blame. "If I had thought for a second that you wanted . . . well, that you ever would have come to Vegas and married me." Aidan's grip eased to caution, the way you might hold an exotic bird. He touched her face, ending any distance, his mouth nuzzling against her hair. "None of those girls meant anything, Isabel. Not one. I'm so . . . so very sorry."

Her head bowed, breaking from his touch, stroking his cheek with her thumb. "I know that, Aidan," she said as if it was long ago understood. Looking down, he watched tears splash onto her painted toenails. From its somber position, Isabel's head rose and their gaze met. A soft bob pulsed through her throat. "All right, Aidan. If that's what you want, take me to bed."

His brow knotted tighter. Shouldn't she at least have been smiling when she said it? Then a bit of the old Aidan emerged. A confidence that he was glad he possessed. Clumsiness and virginal hesitation were the last thing he needed. The way Aidan saw it he had one shot to get this right.

He kissed her, his mouth fluttering over her wet cheek, the soft line of her throat. Deftly, he slipped the T-shirt over her head. A small shiver was the solitary response as he unhooked her bra and it fell to the floor. Though she was more beautiful than in the light of dim candles, Aidan reined in the desire he'd lived off, searching for a pace that would suit her timidity. Maneuvering them toward the bed, he tugged at the drawstring on her pants. There was a spark of reassurance as he caught Isabel's expectant stare, a long drifting gaze taking in his bare body. Stopping to thread some ambiance through the moment, Aidan dimmed all but one light. It cast a golden glow around them. "I promise, Isabel, this will be incredible. You'll see."

She was tentative, the same way she'd shied away from his kiss at the altar. And, actually, he loved it. Even if she hadn't been waiting for him, the idea that she'd waited was enough. Every girl he met threw it away to him or the next guy. And the guys, they were no better. It was what made sex so meaningless. But she was choosing to give him something that she hadn't shared with anyone else. That alone set her apart from any girl he ever knew. And on her wedding night, how rare was a moment like this—in Las Vegas, no less. Admittedly, he'd never thought about marrying Isabel before they had sex, but the old-fashioned notion seemed appropriate. Maybe fate had seen to it that this was the way it would happen for them. Maybe it was something they'd tell their grandchildren someday. Well, maybe not. But it was incredibly special all the same.

Having eased onto the bed, Aidan tried guiding her hand toward his throbbing erection. She snapped it back, unwilling to be coaxed into participation. It was okay; she'd be more comfortable next time. But at the farmhouse, hadn't she touched him then—willingly? It was as natural as kissing, which she also seemed to be avoiding, meeting his mouth with a lackluster effort. He kept at it, trying to entice her body, if not her mind, toward the place he desperately wanted to take her.

Flashes of passion would emerge, like a switch with a short in it. She'd almost lose herself to him. He could sense it, an unbridled jerk toward the heat between them and then retreat. If he hadn't wanted the moment so badly, it might have been frustrating, even disappointing. He hesitated, trying to get his mind around what was in her head, wanting to do the right thing. "Isabel, if . . . if you want to wait until tomorrow, it's okay. I understand." He didn't, not really. But Aidan guessed it was the mature thing to say.

Her eyes met his with fresh determination—intense. He knew that look. Something had set her off. "No," she insisted. "I can't wait until tomorrow."

It was all he needed to hear. Aidan wasn't about to let something as negligible as doubt squeeze in between them. Dragging the sweatpants and underwear from her body, it startled him when in return she plunged recklessly into the moment. Her arms entwined around his neck, holding tight. Isabel kissed him with a passion that was unknown to Aidan. He could barely take it in, how this differed from the physical act he associated with locker room banter and girls that he didn't care to think about again. A shapely leg hooked hard around Aidan's, almost a staking of territory. He loved her legs, remembering the first time he'd seen Isabel in a dress. It was seared onto his mind. It was at a funeral.

A few years before, a teacher from Catswallow High had passed away. Aidan recalled his perplexed embarrassment, the overt physical response as Isabel arrived at the funeral home. He wanted to stand, it was the polite response. But he couldn't get up. Coming through the doors, unbeknownst to her, a waning sun saw through her dress—as did Aidan. She approached the casket, his thoughts so far from the dead, Aidan was sure he was bound for Hell. He sat, dumbfounded, absorbing Isabel in a much different light. It was the onset of an avalanche of emotions, random things he began to notice without cause. Things about Isabel that accumulated until Aidan could no longer deny the feeling, his dense brain finally putting a label on them.

And now they were married, on their honeymoon, her mouth meeting passionately with his. But it wasn't a seamless fantasy come to life, Isabel's slingshot behavior altering the well-worn images. "Wait," he said breathlessly. "What's the rush?"

"Nothing," she whispered, fingers weaving through his hair, anxiously tracing the angles of his face, the line of the snake. "I just need you to do it, right now. Okay?"

He could only assume it was a panicked virgin plea. "Okay." He kissed her again. Aidan shimmied over the side of the bed, coming up with his wallet. Retrieving a foil wrapper, he tossed the wallet back on the floor. His eyes widened as he opened it. "We're still on the ten- or fifteen-year plan, right?"

"I—" She stared at the condom as if debating the wisdom. Aidan stared back. Surprise drifted to satisfaction, knowing if that was what Isabel wanted, he would not deny her. It didn't even need to be a conversation. A late but vehement reply said he was mistaken. "Yes, absolutely," she said, taking the condom from his hand, tearing open the packet. "That would be the last thing you need right now."

He was so counting on this moment, ignoring every feeling that was telling him something wasn't right. Quickly sheathing himself, he positioned himself over her but hesitated. "Isabel, you know the first time . . . it can be, well, kind of uncomfortable." She only nodded.

It was tense for a moment, Isabel burying her head in his shoulder as he did his damnedest to ease into her with a finesse that he guessed might escape most guys his age. The idea of Isabel having to endure that had invaded more than one thought, Rick Stanton turning into his worst nightmare. After only a few careful thrusts, he realized how ready she was. Even if Isabel wasn't responding like the fantasy in his head, her body wouldn't lie. But she was so silent, not hinting at anything as they stumbled into a sweet rhythm that he couldn't have written.

With an odd urgency she clung tighter to him, grabbing fistfuls of his hair as her face burrowed into the snake on his neck. He wanted to kiss her, but Isabel wouldn't relinquish the space. It was as if she couldn't get close enough, fiery friction sparking between them. It wasn't what he envisioned, always imagining something lusty and romantic, definitely slower. But he wasn't going to let the moment slip away. Struggling against the firm lock she had on his body, Aidan inched away, their faces but a breath apart. He'd never used this moment to convey anything so honest. In truth, he'd never used this moment to convey much of anything at all. And an unexpected rush of tender emotions nearly stole his ability to say the words. "I . . . I love you, Isabel. That's what I've been trying to tell you. Since Mr. Renner's funeral, since the dance floor and the farmhouse . . . since we got married. Since we got on this damn roller-coaster ride. I've always loved you."

He'd never seen her eyes go so wide. There was a whimper from her throat, an aching gasp as if her heart had stopped beating. Isabel's fingers dug into the muscle of his shoulders. He could feel the shudder, reeling, like his words were a massive punch to the gut. It rippled through her body. He knew this because the steady Isabel, the one who was the center of his gravity, trembled violently, as if the earth had quaked under her. Her heart pounded against his. He could feel it. He didn't know what to make of it. She couldn't be that surprised. Aidan pulled farther back. "Isabel . . ." She didn't make eye contact, staring past his shoulder. "Isabel," he said more forcefully. "Would you look at me?" Her gaze moved onto his. "Did you hear what I said? I love you. I want to be with you as much as I want the whole damn music thing, the career, the money, the fame." He shook his head. "No. I want you more."

"Me," she gulped, a blank expression anchored to her beautiful face. "You want me? You want me more than . . ."

"Without a doubt. The song, *"Mi Todo,"* that's who you are. That's what it . . ." He felt as bewildered as she looked. "How can you not know this? You know everything about me."

She didn't answer, not replying or matching his heartfelt sentiment with her own. Instead, she asked, "Aidan, would you kiss me?"

He did, hoping the kiss would erase any blur between the lines that separated friends from lovers. It seemed to be working. She kissed him back. Moments later, Aidan could feel the intensity climb to a level he'd never experienced—Isabel clawing at his back with sharp little strokes, their mouths meeting with a heated luster that surpassed his best fantasy. It was as unpredictable as all of her. With her legs gripped tightly around him, the rhythm mounted to a thunderous threshold Aidan couldn't control. "Jesus, Isabel . . . if we don't slow down, I'm not . . . you're gonna make me . . ." She still didn't speak, grating against him with throaty gasps that he took as a sign of excitement. Passion reached a pinnacle he did not know existed, and he gave in to it. As her body shuddered against his Aidan smiled, believing the moment was the same for her as it was for him. It was a sure sign of a perfect union.

But when the writhing didn't stop Aidan suspected that even he couldn't induce an orgasm of that magnitude. It was almost like a seizure.

And then Aidan realized this wasn't anything good. Though Isabel still held firm, he pushed up over her, horrified by the tears she'd been masking. The silent hysterical sobs that she finally let escape. "What the hell? Did I hurt you? God, Isabel, why didn't you tell me to stop?" He didn't think such a high could plummet so fast, a free fall from somewhere above Heaven. Aidan couldn't focus, trying to comprehend how anything so perfect could be replaced with such gut-wrenching fear. Terrified by what he'd done, Aidan bolted from the bed. Isabel darted in the opposite direction, taking the sheet with her. Clawing his hands through his hair, Aidan heaved heavy breaths that he wanted to attribute to their fiery union. But common sense told him otherwise. This had nothing to do with passion or love. *This was the aftermath of what Rick Stanton had intended.* "Isabel, tell me what's wrong! What's happening?"

Crying harder, she gathered the sheet around herself, retreating—repelling from him in every way. Isabel turned toward the wall. Shoulders slumped, she pulled the sheet tighter. Her head drew back as if pleading upward for an answer. "I'm sorry, Aidan. I tried to tell you, but you wouldn't listen." Slowly, Isabel turned. "I'm not in love with you. Can't you see that? Do you honestly believe I would have hung around, watched you hook up with all those girls if I was? How pathetic would that make me? It . . . it was disgusting . . . awful, what we just did—like having sex with your brother. I didn't want this," she said, her arm flailing toward the used bed. "Marrying you," she said, firm and sure, "having sex with you! It's what I always do. Isn't it, Aidan? Take care of your every need." He wanted to say something, but he couldn't get a word between the explosions of her rant. "Running to your rescue, giving into every imaginable need, everything from my advice to my virginity! This time it went too far. You'll have to find another way to soothe your mistakes and celebrate your highs, because you're done using me."

She wiped tears with the edge of the sheet, the anger in her voice clear as furious breaths puffed in and out. It was vivid and real, but he could not, *did not*, want to believe this was the effect of what they'd shared. That he'd done something so heinous it resulted in this. "Isabel . . ." he gulped. "You don't mean that. You're just . . . just upset." He couldn't move, a wave of self-loathing ripping through him. "We're going to California tomorrow. We're going to have everything we've ever wanted!"

"No, Aidan, everything *you* ever wanted! You think that's what I want? Have you even asked me? Of course not! We're far too busy focusing on you. What makes you think I want to spend my life waiting for you to climb down off your ego or polishing it back up when someone bruises it. And like that won't be the bane of my existence, being Aidan Roycroft's pacifier. No thanks." Yanking the gold band from her finger, she threw it at his naked body. "I want a life that doesn't revolve around you and your indulgent needs."

"It wouldn't be like that, I swear. I won't let that happen. And what about . . . what I just told, what I said. I love you, Isabel." He tried to come toward her. She backed away, grabbing her clothes as she went. "Without you the rest doesn't mean anything. If that's what it takes, fine. The hell with all of it! I won't go to California with Fitz. You and I, we can go wherever you want. We can go to Akron." Her mouth opened, but she had no response, moving another step away. "We can go back to being friends. Just tell me what I have to do to make you stay." His breaths were anxious, the promise certain. "I don't need Fitz or C-Note Music or that life—but I do need you." The tirade stopped and for a moment the Isabel he knew stood before him. It faded fast, the sheet billowing around her as if she were an apparition that was sure to vanish. He couldn't let that happen. But she was even less interested in alternate scenarios.

"Aidan," she said, speaking in a blunt tone he recognized. "First of all, put your pants on." Scooping up the neatly folded jeans, she rifled them at him. "And secondly, that's the stupidest thing I've ever heard. Nobody gives up their dream for somebody else. Especially when it's a dream like yours and it's about to come true. Even if you did love me, how long would that last on $1,150, nothing more than a high school diploma between us, and several outstanding warrants for your arrest?"

"I'm willing to find out," he said, shuffling into the jeans, zipping the zipper, buttoning the button. And for a moment, Aidan thought he had her. Isabel inched toward him, looking tempted and broken, as if she might fall into his arms. Then she shook her head, fists squeezed tight. "You're good at a lot of things, Aidan. Taking care of me isn't one of them. Go with Fitz. Go be somebody famous. You'll be good at that; I know you will. I care about you, but it's not enough. Don't throw this chance away to chase after something you'll never have. I'll . . . I'll never love you like that." Without a tear in her eye, Isabel's gaze was fixed on him. "Let it go . . . let *me* go. We're not worth it because *we* don't exist." Wrapped in a white sheet, Aidan's heart firmly tacked to the train that followed, Isabel walked past and disappeared into the bathroom.

CHAPTER SEVENTEEN

Boston

S HE NEVER MADE A SECOND PHONE CALL. ISABEL DIDN'T KNOW
what she'd do or where she might go if he told her not to come.
The hour spent in the Las Vegas airport was the longest of her life.
She didn't think about Aidan. She didn't dare. Curled in a duct-taped
ink-stained chair, Isabel was obliterated by her own actions. She
just sat, peeling off nail tips, biting one fingernail until it bled. Isabel
watched a parade of CNN crawls, amazed that she wasn't among
them: *Girl Suffers Catastrophic Loss. Loses Boy to Fate . . .* She
spent the last few minutes staring at an exhausted, bawling, hysterical child. She was envious and devoid of sympathy.

Boston was cool. It already felt like fall. It was the first thing
to hit her as she stepped from the maze-like Logan Airport. She
thought about city streets and how warm sidewalk grates would
soon be well-staked territory. During the flight, Isabel tried to
calculate the magnitude of the last two days. There was no scale
large enough. Cause and effect, she felt like a science experiment
run amok. In the end, there were only two proven facts: one, Aidan
loved her . . . *like a wife*. And two, she was homeless. The span in
between those specifics was cavernous. Isabel forced her attention

onto a man with a thick Middle Eastern accent. He asked where she wanted to go. Nuggets of black eyes reflected in the rearview mirror. She blinked blankly into them, uncertain how she'd arrived inside the cab. Isabel repeated a return address label in a deadpan tone that sounded like familiarity. In truth, she had no idea where she was going. Fortunately, he did, speeding toward Charles Street and Beacon Hill.

Standing at the door of an immaculate brownstone, Isabel wondered which was worse: her appearance or her story. Except for dozing on an airplane, she hadn't slept in two days. Back to wearing filthy jeans and the T-shirt of the Vegas Strip, surely she looked like she'd rode in cargo. Then there was her story, which by comparison, made her appearance look pretty damn good. The brownstone's fancy carved door and neatly potted urns were inviting and homey. They reminded Isabel just how homeless she was. It didn't matter. Home was a person, not a place. And he was decidedly gone. So with that nonnegotiable fact, Isabel scraped together her courage. It was starting to feel thin, like a cotton sweater in the arctic. Aware of the alternatives, which included seeking shelter at some church-run facility, she tapped at the door. Maybe she could just ask for directions. On the second attempt she knocked harder, realizing it wasn't quite six in the morning. She'd lost track. While debating between the cold streets and ringing the doorbell, which seemed too bold a move, lights began to turn on. She heard footsteps, thundering footsteps. The door flew open and before Isabel could speak a man pulled her inside.

"Isabel! Thank God. I was so worried!" He was holding her . . . crushing her. She could feel a heart pound. It wasn't hers. That was impossible. It was in too many pieces. He finally let go. Isabel backed up and gazed into a manly mirror image. She watched him get hold of himself. It was where her calm came from, and even years later it was strange to see it ruffled.

"Dad," she said, but it sounded foreign and lost, like she might have addressed the cab driver the same way.

"I saw that you called. I called back right away but you didn't answer. I'm so glad . . . relieved that you came." A hand reached out and grazed along her chilly arm. It was as if something lost had been returned, though his uncertainty showed. And why shouldn't it? Along with the last two days there were the past six years.

"I didn't know what else to do. I—"

"You did the right thing, Is. You absolutely did the right thing."

She nodded, feeling slightly surer about not having to master the fine art of panhandling. For the first time Isabel saw that they were not alone. Patrick stood near the bottom of the staircase, wearing pajamas and a bathrobe. Isabel's face burned. Her early morning arrival had drawn them out of bed. *What did you expect? It's five-thirty in the morning . . . And it's who he is.*

"Hello, Isabel." The greeting was emotionless, which she guessed was intentional and something Patrick was good at, being he was an attorney of some sort.

"Hello," she answered back, matching his unreadable tone. She concentrated on her father, who was dressed, though he looked as if he'd slept in his clothes. Isabel decided this image worked best, bypassing a flood of discomfort. She turned toward him, ignoring Patrick. "Like I said, I didn't know what else to do. I can't go back to Catswallow. I know what Mom told you, but she's wrong. Rick Stanton, her boyfriend, he said that Aidan attacked him, that he shot him. But that's not what happened. No one believes anything I've said. We were going to California, but the flights were full, so Aidan asked me to go to Las Vegas, and Fitz Landrey . . . And, oh God," she gasped, a hand raking through her hair, unsure how she'd ever get the entire story out. "Aidan and I, we got—"

"It's all right, Is. Just take your time, gather your thoughts."

Her wild-eyed glare met a look that was all fatherly intent. And for one hideous second she thought he was going to side with Catswallow, accusing Aidan of everything they were trying to pin on him.

Patrick stepped closer, forcing himself into her line of vision. "Isabel, may I ask you a question?"

"Patrick!"

"Eric, we talked about this. We agreed if Isabel came to you that you'd let me—"

"Yes, but does it have to be this second?"

Her gaze volleyed between them. "What?"

"Isabel," Patrick said, his voice lawyerly and direct. "Did Rick Stanton try to rape you?"

She was stunned and embarrassed. The mere idea of this man asking such a question caused her to repel back. She couldn't share that horrible experience with him. Why would she? Then Isabel looked at her father, grasping the reason. He couldn't manage the question. She knew this about him. At the age of twelve it would crush him to know she fell off her bike and skinned a knee. Seeing her hurt, it was the only time that calm demeanor turned flappable. "Did the Catswallow police or my mother tell you I made it up? That I lied to protect Aidan?"

"We heard something to that effect. But your father felt there had to be more. We had the police report faxed here yesterday. We read your statement, Isabel. We'd just like to hear it, again, from you."

This surprised her on many levels. Not only that they'd go to such lengths to learn her side of things, but because there was such unity in his *"we."* It was comforting, people who were willing to listen, or at least not turn a blind eye to the facts. "Yes, he did." Her reply was unwavering, making firm eye contact with Patrick. There was a golden brown flex to his irises, his face, which was strikingly handsome, was filled with question. Patrick's expression shifted, the two men exchanging a look as if this one phrase made things crystal clear. But it also opened a floodgate for which Isabel was unprepared. Thoughts of Stanton's attack barreled back— what would have happened if Aidan hadn't been there, the images in her head rolling randomly from her mouth. "Everything I told Mom and the police, it's exactly what happened. When I got home, Stanton was there, lying on the sofa, his belt and pants undone," she said, recounting the details. "He said he'd been *entertaining a fantasy, starring* . . . me. It wasn't the first time he'd said stuff like that, but it was definitely the most direct. He was drunk, which only added to his nerviness. Rick said he paid for my dress and the beauty salon and that I owed him. He . . . he made it clear what he wanted . . . expected. You have to know him . . . see him," she said, speaking to both men. "He's a big man. I couldn't get away. He had me pinned to the wall, kissing me. His hands were every-where," she told them, offering her bruised wrists as proof. Eric's face paled, a closed fist pressing to his mouth; Patrick moved closer. "If Aidan wasn't there, Rick Stanton, he would have absolutely . . ." The pitch of Isabel's voice hit a shrill, unable to finish the story, sobbing, coming undone as she fell into her father's waiting arms.

SHE DIDN'T KNOW IF HOURS OR DAYS HAD PASSED. TIME WAS THAT elusive. Isabel woke to a strange bed wearing a T-shirt she didn't recognize, the air heavy with the scent of lavender. It soothed her for a second before sitting up. She smelled different too, like sham-poo, fragrant shampoo. Any sharing of skin, any remnant of Aidan was gone. Isabel hugged her knees to her chest, eyes closed, soothed by a clear vision of him. The last thing she did recall was a hot shower, reality reforming in her head. After her breakdown in the foyer, they moved into the living room, where Isabel conveyed the rest. As the facts came clear, she thought her father was going to bolt from the brownstone, hijack a plane to Catswallow, and finish Stanton off. At one point, Patrick had to physically restrain him. He was the voice of reason, even using humor to assuage the anger. "Eric, I appreciate your feelings, but consider what you're suggesting. You, an openly gay man, want to storm ultraconservative Catswallow, Alabama. Go there and accuse a favorite son of attempted rape and false swearing to a DA. A former star of the Crimson Tide no less. A man who, from what Carrie has said, will be paralyzed." Her father returned to the sofa as Patrick sat in a chair where his stature pulled tight, his bearded face doubtful. "Did you not hear the part where the town's most popular heterosexual boy, its very own Conrad Birdie, is being railroaded for the crime? Yes, Eric, that would end just splendidly. Let me know what tree to find you swinging from." And with that, humor evaporated.

Isabel reiterated the gun portion of the story, that she had no idea how Rick Stanton ended up with a bullet in him. A fervent pace slowed as she told them about Aidan. She came clean with everything—everything less the particulars of her Academy Award–worthy farewell scene. Isabel explained how she and Aidan went from best friends to a chapel on the Vegas Strip, describing their impromptu marriage, "On the surface, you'd say it was completely unexpected. Underneath, it felt exactly as it should be." Isabel paused, waiting for the rolling of eyes and shaking of heads. She assumed their disbelief, remarking that she didn't guess they'd understand how something like that could even make sense. From the leather wing chair that Isabel presumed to be Patrick's spot, he listened. On a side table were reading glasses that she could not see her father wearing and a novel by Proust that she could not envision him reading. For the second time since she'd arrived Patrick Bourne caught her off guard. He insisted that theirs was a no-judgments home—at least as far as consenting relationships were concerned. Taking in the comfort of the room, plush furnishings, woven throws, and even-tempered voices, Isabel saw that this, their brownstone, was just that—home.

Looking as though it hadn't registered the first time, Eric said, "You're married?" The last time they were in a room together she was thirteen and not really thinking about marriage. In fact, she was about as ugly and unyielding as a daughter could be. And for the first time, Isabel felt shame shadow that mindset. When Eric asked about the marriage, Isabel reached for the sack from Joe's Strip Souvenirs. From it she produced the piece of paper that proved as much. She was almost as surprised as him to see it. Equally engrossed, both men listened as Isabel explained Fitz's involvement. It was Patrick who summed things up, "So you left Aidan to protect him, to assure everything this Fitz Landrey promised, and to keep him out of jail." She only nodded.

Not long after, Eric showed her to a bathroom, handing Isabel a stack of thick towels—more than one person could need, asking if she wanted something to eat. Sleep, she told him. She just wanted to sleep. Isabel had shuffled around the unfamiliar bathroom, cringing at her haggard reflection. She searched for pain reliever, the cursory kind that came in a bottle. Her head felt as if it weighed more than her entire body. She looked through the medicine cabinet, accidently knocking a half-dozen prescription bottles into the sink. Shoving them back inside, she hung on to a bottle of Excedrin PM. Even their choice of pain reliever was better than her mother's.

Now shuffling from the bed, Isabel saw that it was dark. But whether it was that night or the next, she wasn't sure. There was a light on in the hall, muffled voices coming from downstairs. Finding a lamp, she turned it on. She glanced around a room that seemed decorated in anticipation of her, maybe a younger her, with sweet rosebud wallpaper and bright white furniture. The décor was magazine perfect, the attempt to make her feel at home obvious. The result, however, was a bit off. It really wasn't Isabel at all. She looked around again. It was an arrogant assumption. Maybe Patrick had a daughter too, one who was off at college with Isabel invading her space. She knew nothing about Patrick, and Isabel was proof that it was feasible. If he did have a daughter, what would that make them? Stepsisters, she guessed, in the most modern terms. Isabel sat on the end of a chaise, a twinge of jealousy sitting down with her. What if Patrick's daughter accepted the two of them years ago, her own father closer to her than Isabel? She shook her head. Enough difficult facts were in play; she needn't borrow any. Draped over the back of the chaise were her sweatpants, neatly folded and smelling freshly laundered. Isabel tugged them on and padded toward the stairs. Eric's and Patrick's voices came from the first-floor study, a room she'd passed on her way through the foyer. Isabel didn't make her presence known, eavesdropping from the bottom step.

"For the last time, Patrick, I don't want you to go. She'll be fine. And this is your home."

"So is the Cape," he said, his voice too casual. "I'll only be at the beach house. It's temporary, and this is too important."

"Isabel is a strong girl. She can handle us."

"Can she, Eric? She hasn't been able to handle it for nearly six years. You just got her back. I won't interfere with that. I'm the reason you lost her in the first place."

He cut him off, "No, Patrick. I'm the reason I lost her in the first place."

"Regardless, consider the incredible circumstance it took for Isabel to come to you. She didn't decide to suddenly give us a chance and show up for Thanksgiving dinner. She's been traumatized, nearly raped. And not to change the subject, but please tell me you understand why I was so abrupt with her earlier."

"Yes, I suppose. Though it about killed me to hear her say it, what almost . . ."

"Well, it wouldn't have killed you any less when she wasn't exhausted or as fragile. I had no choice. You don't spend years in my profession and not know the most opportune route to the truth, cruel as it may have seemed. As her father, it's your job to trust what she tells you." Then in his lawyer voice, which was now obvious, he added, "I'm not her father, and we had to be sure. I won't let anyone use you, Eric. Not even your own daughter." Isabel's eyes widened at the protectiveness with which he spoke. She'd heard it before, experienced it herself. The day Stanton came to the farmhouse, Aidan grabbing her wrist in the truck. Patrick's maturity expressed in words what she felt in his grip. "But after listening to Isabel, hearing it firsthand . . ." Her breath didn't move awaiting judgment. "I don't have any doubts either."

"And you don't think being here would be helpful to both of us?" There were a few seconds of silence and she heard Patrick sigh. All this time and Isabel could still distinguish her father's sigh from another person's.

"Maybe. I don't know. This is difficult for a lot of reasons. You know I want to be here, and not just for Isabel."

"Let's not go there." Uneasy laughter rumbled from her father. "One crisis at a time, okay?" And Isabel wondered about that.

There was another bout of silence, a throat cleared. "Just take some time, see how things go. A few weeks or whatever it takes, I won't be far. You know that." Intimate quiet followed and Isabel backed away. It was still disconcerting, though less confusing. She shook her head, embarrassed—at herself. Isabel was the one out of line, eavesdropping on a private conversation. There was shuffling, maybe a suitcase being moved. "Listen, aside from what happened with Stanton, which we've had time to absorb, Isabel did arrive with unexpected news. Perhaps you'd better start there, find out more about her impromptu nuptials and this Aidan."

"What's your gut telling you?"

"Rationale, experience . . . society, that all tells me it's a doomed preposterous relationship, an absurd marriage." Isabel took a massive step toward the study, ready to defend everything she felt for Aidan. But then Patrick said something else, repeating her words, " '*Unexpected on the surface, but exactly as it should be.*' Where have I heard that before? I've lived awhile now, Eric, witnessed more than most people, decided a few fates. I saw the look in your daughter's eyes, heard the sincerity in her voice. I can't speak for this Aidan, but she feels no differently about him than I do about you. In which case, rationale, experience, and society can all go to hell."

CHAPTER EIGHTEEN

Boston

TIME WAS A FUNNY THING. IT LEFT YOU WITH MEMORIES; IT allowed you to forget. Isabel had forgotten that her father was allergic to peanuts but remembered that he was a huge Red Sox fan. So for many reasons, she supposed Boston suited him. He was passionate about modern art, David Hockney especially, something Isabel was reminded of roaming around the brownstone. All three floors were an eclectic blend of Patrick's finer sensibilities, complemented by her father's love of Hockney's work, conceptual and personal. Eric Lang was the dad on the block who could teach you how to swing a bat while coaching you on the importance of diversity. Peeking into the study, Isabel was reminded how good he was at his job. In her first days at the brownstone Eric only left to keep interview appointments at Boston University, where he was now dean of admissions. She'd also forgotten his lack of fashion sense, maybe a little color-blind, unable to coordinate suits, shirts, and ties. On her fourth morning there she found him fussing in front of his bedroom mirror, debating between a green striped tie and a brown speckled one. Neither matched the blue suit he was wearing. Initially, he appeared grateful for her assistance. But as she dove into the closet, his voice took a nervous turn, "Isabel, don't. Never mind, I can . . ."

The walk-in closet was neatly divided, its impact immediate. Everything in this closet belonged to a man. *Duh* . . . Patrick's clothes were meticulously arranged, pants that would be inches too long and a waist size too small on Eric hung next to an array of expensive suits and laundered shirts, all of which were coordinated by color and season. Her father's side didn't look much different than it did in New Jersey. Suits, fewer in number than Patrick's, hung haphazardly, bunched sweatpants and sweatshirts stuffed on a top shelf. Patrick knew what he was doing by going to the Cape. It allowed Isabel to, at least temporarily, erase him from the equation. The reality of the space validated the facts. A fact she was incapable of dealing with before then. Isabel backed out of the closet, snatching a tie as she went. She backed right into her father. She turned and faced him. Identical swallows swam through their throats. What more could he say? Isabel held up the tie, which by chance was a perfect match. She smiled. "Patrick usually helps with this, doesn't he?"

And that was where threads began to weave into fabric. From there they talked in short bursts, her father slowly letting her in on things that were beyond Isabel's comprehension at twelve or thirteen. They were things she might have realized had she read the letters. Most, he told her, were just, *"Hi, how are you,"* notes. Others, he said, went into finer detail, admitting to her what he could not admit to himself. At least not until it was too late. "You have to remember, Is, it was a different time. People weren't as open or accepting as they are nowadays. As it is, your Aunt Denise, my own sister, considers my life nothing more than a sinful choice. She hasn't spoken to me since . . . well, since I moved here." He'd married Carrie at twenty-one, hiding his true sexuality from her and himself. It was something about which he still harbored great guilt, but insisted he did not regret. "It gave me you, Is. And I wouldn't change that for anything." Eric Lang explained that back in New Jersey he was wholly committed to his life. Or so he thought, until a visiting lecturer arrived from Boston. Yes, the affair had been ongoing, and something for which Eric took complete responsibility. But the night Carrie found them together it was Patrick who'd come to break things off. As much as he wanted to be with Eric, he couldn't accept what he was doing—having an affair with a married person. From there, she supposed, goodbye escalated into something more. And what Carrie walked in on, well, he insisted that her mother had every right to every feeling. Eric said it took that event to realize the gross unfairness of the circumstance, not to Patrick or himself but to his wife. "What I did to your mother, I'll never forgive myself for that. But in many ways, I suspect I've paid for it." In return for his candor, Isabel talked about her perceptions. Had she always known this about him, had there always been a *Patrick*, her response would have been far more everyday and not so acute. But learning it with models of traditional families set in her head, they agreed, had made things significantly more difficult.

Eric took that conversation as a cue, coming home early from work. He was quiet at first. There was too much on his mind and he didn't know where to start. Isabel knew this because she felt the same way. Since Patrick left they'd been living in a safe, if not bogus, hollow of normal. In addition to Patrick's absence there wasn't a word, not one conversation about the circumstance that brought her there. But the look on his face said time was up. Perhaps she'd sensed the pending conversation, having made lasagna for dinner. It was old comfort food for both of them. She set the table in the dining room, the two of them managing a few bites and more benign conversation. Eric talked about college, asking if her plans were flexible. Maybe instead of a small satellite campus, she'd consider one of New England's many colleges. It was late, but he had solid connections in admissions. If she was interested, he'd be glad to make some inquiries. "Of course," he said, moving on to his point, "much of that depends on what you plan to do about Aidan."

His name resonated, Isabel shoving the plate away. Lasagna was a damn waste of time. "Nothing."

He waited, sipping a glass of wine. It wasn't Proust but an interesting switch from the black and tan beer he always drank. "You can't do *nothing*, Is. You're married to the boy . . . man," he corrected, allowing Aidan the benefit of the doubt. This, she assumed, was out of respect for Aidan doing to Rick Stanton what her father would have done, and keeping his daughter from certain harm.

"I don't know, *nothing* sounds pretty doable."

"I can tell you from experience that mindset only works for so long."

She also knew it wasn't going to work with Fitz Landrey. A look at the Catswallow online police blotter proved as much. The charges against Aidan were still pending along with the warrant for his arrest. She had a good idea what it would take for them to go away. "Dad, does Patrick handle divorces? He handled yours, right?"

He put down the wineglass and leaned back in his chair, arms folding. "I guess that's an obvious assumption. But no, Isabel, Patrick didn't handle my divorce. For one, he's not that kind of lawyer. Patrick's an investigative attorney for the government, the Department of Immigration." Her eyes widened at the information. "More to the point, he would have considered it highly unethical." He smiled, sipping more wine. "You have to know Patrick. He's undoubtedly one of the most honest people I've ever known." She supposed he said this in defense of that night in New Jersey when the wheels came off their lives. "But that's not what you asked, is it?" He didn't wait for a reply. "Is that what you want, to divorce Aidan?"

"I don't think I have a choice."

"That's not true. There's always a choice," he said, voicing experience again. "You don't have to let Fitz Landrey blackmail you, and that's exactly what he's doing. Worse than that is the lie Rick Stanton is perpetuating. To think what that son of a bitch is going to get away with, what he . . ." He paused, regrouping. "I feel for your mother in this situation. I really do, but not at the expense of the truth."

"Dad, I appreciate what you're saying, but between Fitz Landrey's power play and Rick Stanton's word, I don't see where we'd have a prayer."

"I didn't say it would be easy, Is. Or even turn out the way you want. It's definitely a risk. But you can stand up to Landrey and Stanton. I'd back you all the way, so would Patrick."

"I thought you said he's not that kind of attorney."

"He's not. But lawyers know lawyers. I'm sure he'd find Aidan one of the best defense attorneys in the country."

It was tempting. Isabel thought a few days without Aidan would give her some perspective. It did, just not the one that would have helped. Isabel hoped that she wouldn't miss him so much. Or realize that being married to Aidan wasn't as nifty as it sounded in Vegas. But all she could hear was Aidan's voice, telling her that he loved her. That he'd always loved her. All she'd considered while awake or asleep were those moments when she allowed herself the fleeting pleasure of being Aidan's wife. He was right; it was incredible. *Miss him.* How obtuse. You miss fresh air, a favorite sweater, a friend. Since leaving Las Vegas she'd done little more than watch the gap in her soul grow wider and deepen.

In the dim dining room, Isabel looked across at her father. He looked tired. Actually, he'd looked weary since she arrived, paler than she recalled. Frankly, he didn't look well. While his features still matched hers, though the hair was darker, gray at the temples, there was something decidedly different in his face. Whatever it was, Isabel took it as her cue to be a big girl, maybe even a married woman. She retrieved her cell phone, which she'd purposely let die. Today she ventured out to a Verizon store and bought a charger. Isabel plugged it in and put the phone on speaker. There, inside the brownstone, they'd had time on hold. They were about to be brought up to speed. The first messages were from her mother. Eric said to skip them; he'd do her talking with Carrie for now. That sounded like a plan and she accepted the reprieve. In between there were numerous messages from Aidan. First, he begged her to listen, to give things another chance. "Please, Isabel, just call me back. Tell me where you are. I won't let you leave like this. I don't believe what you said."

Eric tipped his head, looking perplexed. "Is, what exactly did you say when you left him?"

She didn't answer. Some things were just too personal. There was a span of time between the fourth and fifth message—almost a day. Isabel assumed the latter message came from California. It began differently, Aidan demanding to know where she was, informing Isabel that if she'd gone back to Catswallow he'd be on the next plane to get her. There was a flash of panic as the call abruptly ended, Isabel picturing the Catswallow sheriffs, guns drawn, manacles readied. Then she saw the next message, left only minutes later. Aidan said he just got off the phone with her mother who told him that she was not in Catswallow. His guess was that she'd gone to Boston. There was a shift in his voice at the end of the message. Aidan told her what was happening in California. A limousine took him from the airport to C-Note studios, and that despite the sun on his face and the very real sway of palm trees, he believed he was dreaming. As upset as he sounded there was a gust of happy fascination. In the last message there was a lot of noise in the background. Aidan talked about a photo shoot and the zillion people buzzing around him. He'd done a magazine interview. Along with his first single, it was to be the launch for a massive C-Note campaign introducing Aidan Royce to the world. Isabel smiled, picturing his suave exterior, sure that he was bursting inside from head to toe. After that the sentences slowed, the wave of exhilaration gone. He reverted to talk about them. "Isabel, please . . . this is crazy and nuts and wild . . . and it's nothing—"

Fitz Landrey boomed from the background, "Aidan, let's get a move on. They've just finished mixing the last song we're considering for your first single. We need your input—pronto."

She hit End, not wanting to hear anymore.

"Listening to that, Is, I'd say Aidan really wants to talk to you."

There was a soft hum from her throat. Yes, there was genuine upset, but there were also gusts of happiness, bordering on delirium. And why not, how many people saw their wildest dream come true? Even if she had an army of lawyers would she seriously take that risk? Force a showdown between the life on the other end of that phone and the fast track to an Alabama correctional facility? And for crimes he didn't commit. No, she wouldn't be that person—not twice. It would only make Isabel slightly more selfish than when she took her best shot at destroying the man sitting across from her. "Dad?"

"Yeah, Is," he said, poking at his lasagna.

"You, um, said that Patrick knows other attorneys."

"Dozens, I'm sure. Maybe not personally, but he can find what you're looking for. Should I call and ask him for the name of a top-notch defense lawyer?"

She shook her head. "No, ask him for a decent divorce lawyer." He put down his fork, not looking terribly pleased. "And ask him one more thing."

"What's that?" he said softly.

"Ask him to come home."

⊗

ACCLIMATING TO ERIC AND PATRICK, WHO WERE LEGALLY MARRIED in the state of Massachusetts, proved more fluid than Isabel imagined. Perhaps it was their acceptance of her that made it so seamless. After all, she was the third person in a household built for two. Patrick had no children, Isabel's first assumption being correct. The bedroom had been decorated in hopeful anticipation of her. About a week after returning from the Cape, Patrick leaned against the doorframe as Isabel put away the clothes they'd shopped for that afternoon. "We dressed this space for a thirteen-year-old girl. It could use some updating, wouldn't you say?"

"It's fine . . . pretty. I don't want to be any more trouble than I already am."

He didn't move into the room, his tone didn't warm beyond two people just getting to know one another. That was his way. He was thoughtfully reserved, compassion seeping out from under a refined edge. Above all, Patrick Bourne possessed a debonair confidence that simply pulled you in. "Don't think that way, Isabel. You're Eric's daughter; from the beginning I've been prepared for that. I don't have any firsthand experience with parenthood, but I don't have any illusions either. I'm here to help, just as much as he is." It didn't take many more conversations before Isabel found herself confiding in Patrick. She asked if he would help retain a lawyer to handle the divorce. If that was truly what she wanted, he would not assist but see to the matter himself. "Why bring a third party into this?" he said to Eric as Isabel listened. "I can file the papers, quick and efficient." Her father disagreed, urging Isabel to be honest with Aidan before taking such a drastic step. She could not, in good conscience, take the risk or advice.

It took a few weeks to move the matter forward, but on the same day Aidan's first single was released the papers were ready. Isabel and Patrick were home alone, reviewing the blue-backed petition in the study. After explaining the details, he showed her where to sign. Like a dive from a cliff, Isabel did so without pause—otherwise, she'd surely think second thoughts. Patrick would file it later that day. The doorbell rang and he excused himself. Holding on to the paperwork, Isabel followed to the edge of the study. A man entered the foyer, introducing himself, a large envelope in hand. Vince Ederly said he was looking for Isabel. He peered down the hall, making eye contact from a dozen feet away. She didn't respond. Patrick took charge, ushering him toward the door. From there she heard her name and Aidan's, Patrick having forced Vince onto the front stoop, where she couldn't hear anything else. After he left, Patrick stood with his back to Isabel, examining the envelope's contents. He turned, Isabel fraught with the sinking feeling of a doctor delivering devastating news. In his hand was a blue-backed document that mirrored the one in hers. Gently, he offered a layman's interpretation of what Aidan had done. He'd trumped her petition with a divorce of his own, a detailed note agreeing with her most private wedding-night conclusions. Isabel was right. She was always right; he did want that life more than them— a few weeks of his new reality woke him up to as much. A quick divorce was for the best. He wished her well. Isabel was visibly shaken, internally annihilated, and Patrick reached out, offering the comfort any parent would.

CHAPTER NINETEEN

Providence, Rhode Island
Present Day

BLISSFULLY INDIFFERENT, RICO HAD EXERCISED HIS INHERENT right to catnap, curled in Isabel's lap. Everything that occurred during those confounded August days had no effect on him. Well, other than the misguided flub of his namesake. In stark contrast, Mary Louise and Tanya remained keenly aware. Hunkered down on Isabel's kitchen floor, Mary Louise had wrung a dishtowel tighter with each twist of her tale. Tanya sought refuge against the stove, knees balled to her chest. Her white-knuckle grip didn't ease, and her wet face dipped to her jeans as she was moved to tears by the familiar end to another marriage. At least that one wasn't hers.

"To this day, it's the one thing my father and I disagree about, how I handled things." Determined to remain indifferent, she moved on to the details of a positive post-Aidan life. After settling in Boston, she attended Northeastern University, which was commuter distance from the brownstone. Isabel made friends and found her footing, getting a degree in social science and political thought. There were ideas about graduate school, but when a radio station internship at NPR led to the job at *98.6—The Normal FM*, the urge to be on her own won out. The framework for Grassroots

Kids, which was her thesis project at Northeastern, temporarily took a back burner. She moved to Providence and got an apartment, remaining a frequent visitor to Boston and the brownstone. Then, about a year ago, at a black-tie fundraiser for Mass General that Patrick chaired, Isabel met Nate Potter. He was her father's new doctor, Eric having been diagnosed with lupus only weeks before Isabel's arrival in Boston. Since then, Patrick had been on a continuous hunt for the best and brightest. At the fundraiser he was introduced as Dr. Potter. But it was Nate, newly single nice guy, who'd asked Isabel to dance. At first there was *just coffee*, the two negotiating the extenuating doctor-patient circumstance. So taken with each other, they agreed early on that Eric's condition would be the one off-limits subject. It worked out fine, Isabel and Nate easily sharing everything else. Everything less the one other off-limits subject. And it wasn't because Aidan was a taboo topic; he was simply a piece of the past to which she was, by then, indifferent. "Until today's turn of events at the radio station it had no place in my life. It wasn't worth telling—to you guys or to Nate." They nodded in what seemed like thoughtful agreement until Mary Louise brought the point back around.

"And you've never wanted to pick up a phone and call Aidan?"

"Actually, I did," she said, never having admitted that part out loud. "I needed to know how he could . . ." She stopped, clearing her throat, forcing a smile. "Well, maybe I just wanted the last word. Either way, it didn't matter. The number had been changed. And consider this, Aidan's never picked up a phone to call me. It kind of speaks volumes."

"And the attempted-murder charge against Aidan, and Fitz's demand?" Mary Louise asked.

"Interestingly, they were dropped regardless," she said, feeling the welt of a scar that traveled deep into pride. "In the end," she said, owning it, "my great sacrifice wasn't even necessary."

"Ouch! Talk about adding insult to injury."

"Even so, I don't know how you could keep something like that to yourself," Tanya wondered. "I mean, he's not your average ex—believe me, I know average. Aidan Royce is so . . . so . . ."

"In your face?" Isabel shrugged, the idea being old news. "You grow up; you accept it for what it was. Remember, Aidan Royce wasn't quite Aidan Royce back then. He was a headstrong, closet-insecure nineteen-year-old boy who, in a fleeting moment of passion, said that he loved me. It's how any guy would process things at that age—in moments. First ours in Las Vegas, then, just as fast, the life that he left me for." She sighed, offering anecdotal clarification. "The first time I saw Aidan with another woman, Patrick and I were in the checkout line at Stop & Shop. A package of biscotti, a carton of milk, two prescriptions, and tampons," she said. "That's what was in the basket. It was only a couple of months after I'd arrived in Boston. I was joking with Patrick when I saw them together—on a magazine rack. At the time, laughter and my heart plummeted right through the high-traffic linoleum floor. Aidan was on the cover of *Rising Star* magazine, a candid shot of him lip-locked with Fiona Free." She smiled at Mary Louise. "The starlet who was *not* the muse behind his tattoo." In return, there was a sheepish glance. "Anyway, they looked like rocker Barbie and Ken. Aidan had one hand around her, a drink and the good life in his other," Isabel said with a mocking smile. "It only proved to be the first of many such photos, sincere and steady behavior that said Aidan's feelings were something less than till death do us part."

"But still . . ." Tanya said, drawing a dreamy breath. "I don't know if I could keep something like that to myself."

"Tanya's right. I think I'd shout it to the world, maybe write a tell-all book."

"And forever label myself *one of them*? No thank you. I put the right perspective on it years ago. As Patrick pointed out in the middle of that grocery store, either, A) I would have been holed up in a hotel room, waiting for Aidan to return from said party and God knows what temptation. Or B) the photo op would have been a nonexistent, nonevent had Aidan's arm been wrapped around me. He told me to take solace in C. At least he wasn't awaiting trial from the confines of an Alabama correctional facility." Isabel's gaze, having lost focus, jerked back to Tanya and Mary Louise. "I never wanted that, no matter how it ended. So I left him there, on the magazine rack in the Stop & Shop, right where all Aidan's fans could find him. It was a turning point and a giant step toward indifference."

Isabel didn't bother telling them the rest, how days later indifference was facilitated by a new and disturbing event. Isabel, Eric, and Patrick had gone to the Cape, just a weekend away from everyday life and magazine racks. Upon returning to the brownstone, they found an ugly reality had slipped inside. There'd been a break-in, the brownstone ransacked, walls spray-painted with homophobic slurs. It was beyond disheartening, the study in ruins, much of Eric's art destroyed. The police concluded that the break-in was aimed at Patrick. They suspected it was retribution, undesirables or their stateside counterparts retaliating for a case he'd prosecuted. In the aftermath, Isabel's respect for Patrick grew and deepened. It was a dangerous job with words like *terrorism* and *national security* cropping up regularly. It enhanced her perspective, keeping her focus on things that mattered and dismissing people who didn't.

"So," she said, standing, dumping a disgruntled Rico onto the floor. "Now you know that despite Aidan Royce, life did go on. He doesn't mean anything to me. He hasn't for a very long time." Glances passed from woman to woman. "The only reason I told you is because . . . well, because I'm willing to see if Aidan will help us out. I'm sorry I didn't bring it up earlier."

"Bring what up earlier?" asked Tanya, swiping a stray tear.

"Oh, Isabel, you can't," Mary Louise said, also standing. "After everything you've told us. After how he . . ."

"Dumped me? It's okay. I've had plenty of time to develop a thick skin," she said, fingers grazing over the evidence.

Tanya scrambled to her feet. "You'd seriously be willing to ask Aidan if he'd be our ticket out of this mess? That would be, um . . . We can't ask you to do that. Can we, Mary Louise?"

"You can," Isabel said, putting up a hand to halt any incoming protest. "And I will ask . . . *him* . . . Aidan . . . his people."

"But could he . . . would he help us out?"

"I have no idea. I really don't." She looked at the matched set: marriage license, divorce decree, and curt letter from Aidan, each bearing his unmistakable signature. Sequestering a twinge of spite, she picked up the drink Mary Louise had poured and downed it. "I won't let this happen to the two of you. Not if I can help it." She plopped the empty glass onto the bar top. "As your boss, I've made an executive decision." Isabel's management style was more laid-back than governing, and their faces were perplexed. "We're going to contact Aidan Royce and that's final." *Final, unless I can get a psychic to contact Elvis . . .* She shrugged off the cowardly option and focused on the plausible as her co-workers mumbled words of appreciation. Tanya picked up the strip of photos. "Hey, we're looking for ratings, right? Just ratings."

"Unbelievable ratings, the kind of numbers they'd draw in markets like New York, Chicago, Los Angeles."

"If *104.7—The Raging Fever FM* was to host an Aidan Royce concert, that part would be a sure thing," Mary Louise said, looking at Tanya, their expressions plotting. "So what happens to all the money?"

"Aidan cashes in, buys a new private jet or whatever," Isabel said, cringing at the idea of enhancing her ex-husband's profit margin.

"You're right, Mary Louise, the proceeds would be incredible."

"People will pay top dollar to see a show like that. And forget Providence venues," she said, referring to the 1,200-seat setting where they held most events. "Aidan Royce sells out stadiums." Mary Louise's expression grew ultraserious, the same way it did when she was figuring her to-the-penny share of the lunch check. "I can hardly do the math—millions, it must be millions."

"I'm sure an army of accountants keeps a tally," Isabel said. "Aidan was a whiz with numbers, but he never could be bothered."

"Isabel!" Tanya said, grabbing her arm. "Don't you see?"

"See what?"

"The phone message from Nate: Grassroots Kids . . ."

"The money you need," said Mary Louise. "We're only looking for ratings, but Grassroots Kids needs the cash!"

Isabel didn't think her eyes could open so wide and remain in her head. "Oh no. No way. You can't possibly be suggesting that I ask Aidan . . ."

"Why not?" they replied in unison.

"No one could argue the worthiness of the cause," Mary Louise said, pointing to the answering machine. "I should think Aidan Royce would be thrilled to help out."

"Aren't you always saying that philanthropy is key? If anything, Grassroots Kids should be even more incentive. Celebrities love to pin their name on a cause. Think George Clooney," said Tanya. "Name one tragedy where people like that didn't line up to answer telephones or perform on cue."

"Yes, but Grassroots Kids isn't a tragedy on a national scale."

"Maybe not," Mary Louise said, fingers tapping on the papers that detailed Isabel's past. "But how could he possibly say no once you explained the circumstances?"

"Explain the circumstances . . . *to him*," she repeated, looking at the papers. "But that would mean actually speaking with . . .

Seriously, I was thinking more third-party contact, like his booking agent or manager." Under normal circumstances those would be her go-to sources. But this wasn't a normal request, a single conversation pitting indifference against contact. A sigh labored out. She didn't want to think about him. Aidan was uninvited, doing it again, taking up every inch of breathable space—and he wasn't even in the room. She didn't say yes or no, just saying that she needed to think about it, more than ready to end the evening.

Not long after, the two women, with three children in tow, were ready to head home. Mary Louise put aside their earlier argument and insisted on following Tanya, helping her get the children into bed. Isabel was relieved to see that much had already repaired itself. She'd done the right thing. As they shuffled out the door, Isabel bid goodnight to an achy story that had no better end than it did back in Vegas. But before the door closed, Tanya poked her head back through.

"Isabel, can I ask you one more question?"

"Sure," she said, rubbing a hand around her neck, leaning against the frame. Everything about Aidan exhausted her. It always had.

"It's kind of personal."

"What hasn't been in the last few hours?" She laughed. "It's fine, Tanya, whatever you want to know."

"Okay, well, just remember you said that." Isabel inched back, wondering where Tanya was heading. "Before, you said, '*Aidan said he loved me . . . in the moment.*' Exactly what moment are we talking about?" Isabel shook her head, not quite following. A bob of red hair and the lingering scent of pepperoni and Pine-Sol drew closer. "Specifically," Tanya insisted with the bluntness that defined her. "What were you and Aidan doing when he said that to you?"

Isabel felt something inside push against her. "I don't remember."

"Yes you do."

"How would you . . ." Lips pursed, her hand tightened around the doorframe, tempted to slam it shut. Instead, a dull delivery made "We were in bed" sound like *We were in church.* "Look, let's just concentrate on getting Aidan to perform for *104.7.* If we make that happen, it would be the one positive to come out of a very dusty, very doomed relationship. It doesn't matter when he said it."

"Oh, but I think you're wrong. If you could just tell me, was it right in the middle of . . . well, you know, before he, um . . ." she said, her finger twirling dramatically through the air.

Wanting to grasp at a fast lie, Isabel was too weary to come up with anything but the truth. "Uh, yes, before anybody . . ." she said, a finger twirling the opposite way. "In the middle," she said, fingers locking in a demonstrative gesture.

"Hmm, so interesting." Biting on a nubby nail, her cheery expression grew serious as she stepped from the front stoop, moving toward her car.

"Wait," said Isabel with the restraint of a hiccup. "Why did you want to know that?"

She spun around, her hair iridescent in the moonlight. "It's nothing, just a theory." Tanya's gaze moved up and down, as if measuring the accuracy of her supposition. "Look, I might not know much. My life isn't exactly an example of Sunday school morals. I don't need Mary Louise to tell me that," she said, glancing over her shoulder. "But I have learned a thing or two about men along the way. Most will tell you they love you to get you into bed. A handful might say it afterward. You know, like a cigarette or any other cliché. But the guy who tells you he loves you *in the moment* . . . when it's a sure thing. He's the one who means it." They exchanged a wide-eyed blink. "For heaven's sake," she concluded, "why else would he say it?"

"Tanya that's . . ." While *absurd* was on the tip of her tongue, "Really?" is what fell from her mouth.

"Really," she insisted back. "You said he doesn't mean any-thing. I heard you. I also know you have a great thing going with Nate. Anybody can see you're two peas in pod."

"Meaning?"

"You're made for each other. You and Nate are the textbook definition of a perfect relationship."

Nodding along, Isabel's head jerked to a stop. "I was thinking more an article in *Marie Claire*."

"However you see it. But there's something in your voice when you talk about Aidan. I'm sure it's exactly what you said, that he's a bygone memory. On the other hand . . ." As she spoke, Isabel inched farther behind the door. "I can also see where it would scare the bejesus out of you. That sound in your voice; it's not your style, Isabel. You're all about calm and confident, and that's not what I heard." As Isabel began to defend perfection, the three-time divorcée held a hand up. "I'm just saying, according to my theory, Aidan Royce meant what he said." Heading toward her car, she turned. "Of course, I've never had a chance to prove it. It's never happened to me."

CHAPTER TWENTY

Los Angeles

AIDAN ROYCE ROLLED OVER, BURYING HIS BLOND HEAD beneath a thick goose-feather pillow. The sun drilled through a crack in the curtains of his hotel suite. He rolled to the other side of the king-size bed, yet the narrow beam of light followed. For seven solid years, that's the way it went, the spotlight always finding him. "Damn it!" There was that—the spotlight— and the impossibility of sleeping in the middle of the fucking day. Exasperated and wide awake, Aidan swore again, firing the pillow across the room. It made deathly contact with a crystal lamp, sending it crashing to the floor. He sat up and flipped on the light. "Shit," he muttered, stretching to look at the lamp, which now appeared to be a pile of jagged ice chips. From the bedside table, a full glass of scotch flirted with him. Hurling it instead of drinking it stood a better chance of easing the swell of shit he'd taken to bed.

Though, really, what would be the point? Housekeeping would only blab to the kitchen staff. In turn they'd zip-line the info to the concierge. From there a smashed lamp would lead to the smashed rock star in the penthouse suite, the story morphing into salacious fact. In the end it would result in the room Aidan Royce trashed, shredding the mattress with a machete for kicks—the one that he carried along with his collection of exotic sex toys. That part would be purported by the turndown maid, who'd become a witness after being offered cash to participate. Inevitably, and for the right price, the tainted tale about the perverse behavior and subsequent tantrum thrown by the Royal Beverly Crowne's most special guest would be leaked to the media.

Welcome to fame.

Aidan thrust himself flat onto the mattress, grimacing over an image for which he and he alone was responsible. Aside from the one on his neck, Aidan Royce was a six-headed serpent with an endless amount of lives. He sat up, eyes locked on the glass. He couldn't believe he filled one. What was he thinking? He was damn angry about last night, that's what he was thinking. Scenes like the one at Pure Oxygen, he didn't fucking need it. He'd asked Kai Stoughton, road manager turned personal assistant, to look into it. There had to be more. After Kai bailed him out of an L.A. County lockup, in an effort to avoid the deluge of media that had converged on his Malibu home, they decided to check him into a hotel. Maybe, by now, he'd unearthed some answers. A fist pounded to his forehead. Aidan unfurled it, examining the puffy knuckles on one side, the clean fingertips on the reverse. He pumped it open and closed. The bruise was eerily reminiscent, fingerprint scanning an improvement over ink. A substance that had left its mark in more ways than one.

Running a hand through a trendy haircut, the contents of his head felt worn and outdated. There was a time when drugs and alcohol would have been the cause and the cure to last night. A tremulous breath pushed out. Aidan dragged his naked body around, sitting in silence. For the first time in a long time he felt like nothing. He raked a hand over his unshaven face, staring at the glass. On the other hand, *nonentity* sounded pretty damn good. Who would know? Hardly a soul knew he didn't drink. Rule one, if you wanted something to stay private, trust no one—no matter how much you were paying them. Aidan dipped a finger into the tea-colored liquid, swirling the rim until it mimicked a bad sound check. Goaded by the whole fucking mess, he drew the drink to his lips. As the cool glass made contact, numbness a swallow away, he caught a glimpse of himself in the mirror. He put it down. Once again, the kid from Catswallow was coming dangerously close to the much ballyhooed life of Aidan Royce.

That was where he'd landed when the earth tilted the other way, catapulting him from his former life into this one. Looking back, he appreciated the cliché of the lure. Women and drugs, they were the means to making the costume fit and a surefire way of banishing the past. A couple of years ago, last night wouldn't have mattered. Fitz and a team of C-Note lawyers would have bailed him out adding another *"You owe me"* chip to his stack before dropping Aidan at the Beverly Crowne to lie low. Of course, back then, he wouldn't have lain low alone. Aidan would have conveniently forgotten Miss October, a woman who in that case he would have certainly picked up. He would have whiled away the time with her, and maybe her interchangeable counterpart. The next day, the personal assistant du jour would have quietly whisked her or them away. From there he would have gone about the business of being Aidan Royce. It was time-consuming, body numbing, and deceiving from every angle. It seemed to be what the unbridled icon was supposed to be doing. There sure as hell wasn't anyone objecting—definitely not his ex-wife. Isabel didn't give a damn about him; Aidan had seen to that. There were no boundaries, not as long as the music sold and stadiums filled. But when the last hints of perfume, ambient aromas of a meaningless existence, faded, Aidan discovered the pit that was the bottom of alone. He came to hate it more than he hated Aidan Royce. And by then, he hated Aidan Royce quite a bit.

It was a crossroads, the place where anyone who had too much too soon swan-dived off the cliff, landing headfirst on the jagged rocks below. It could have easily happened to him. But as Aidan plummeted he scrambled for the brakes, help coming from an unlikely source. Along with his inheritance, enclosed with the check, was Aidan's own letter from his father, who'd succumbed to AIDS. He'd carried it in the pocket of his tuxedo pants to the gala that night and directly into this life. *"Look what it took for me to earn ten grand. Don't be your old man, son. Don't blow it on women, or drugs, or worse. Be something, do something, with it."* For years he'd remained indifferent, mocked John Roycroft's use of the word *son*—like he had a right or a clue. But he never could bring himself to throw away handwriting that mirrored his, words that eventually reflected his life. Finally, one good party shy of those razor-sharp rocks, he heeded the advice. Otherwise, Aidan Royce surely would have foundered in his own waste. And that's what it was, a waste of a life and the complete waste of an opportunity. He started there, fixing what he could, which wasn't everything since he also accepted the fact that C-Note Music owned about half of who he was. An ironclad seven-year contract saw to that, C-Note being a serpent unto itself. But he could retool his lifestyle, put an end to the extraneous drugs and women. While there was accomplishment in banishing both, the bad-boy persona had adhered like . . . well, like another tattoo. Much to C-Note's pleasure, there was no shedding an image that loomed larger than the snake on his neck.

His personal reinvention began by taking the $1,120 he left Vegas with and replacing the rest of the original inheritance. By then it was a pittance compared with his fortune. But it was important money, family money, earmarking it as seed money for Aidan Roycroft's future. From there he didn't rush but carefully considered what he wanted from life. It was another reason the girl . . .

the cop . . . the arrest had so thoroughly pissed him off. Reinvention wasn't an overnight evolution. It took years to craft the rock star into somebody Aidan was willing to live with, though it was the musician he'd learned to love. Last night was a giant step back, like falling off the wagon. He'd worked hard to stay away from that kind of press. He didn't need to remind the world—not now. "Wait," he said, shuffling through the sheets for a remote. Maybe he was too out of touch. Maybe the world had more important things to do than gawk at Aidan Royce. He aimed the remote with magic-wand expectation, and a wave of disappointment lapped over him. He flipped through the channels, finding his supposed drunk and disorderly ass everywhere. He paused on the booking desk scene, where he caught eight solid seconds of his backside, hands cuffed. His stomach lurched and he escaped to the Weather Channel. It was a safe haven as apparently weather forecasters didn't give an atmospheric shit about Aidan Royce.

Calmer, he tossed the remote aside, wondering where Kai was. He wanted out of that hotel, and he sure as hell couldn't do it without security. With the heavy drapes drawn, Aidan realized he didn't have a clue about the hour, the internal clock of a rock star never in sync with real time. He found the clock, which he'd kicked under the bed. Late afternoon. Aidan reached for his cell. No call from Kai, just messages from his people and from Fitz. No doubt he was calling to revel over a media-induced surge in sales. Good or bad, Fitz would squeeze every bit of energy out of the situation. Hell, no doubt the other messages were requests for an exclusive with *Maxim* magazine, maybe a sit-down chat with Piers Morgan. *"Tell us about the new woman, Aidan—the one from your wild ride. A former Playmate. More your type, wouldn't you say? Last we heard you were engaged to Anne Fielding, that stunning attorney of yours . . . What's she say about all this?"* Aidan squeezed his eyes shut and his imagination closed. Deleting the messages, his finger hovered over one from Anne. What *would* she say about all this? He could tell her he'd been punk'd or that he'd simply reverted to the Aidan Royce of old. Why not? Clearly the world had tuned in to watch him fuck up. Either way, he had to call her. Before he could dial, Kai's ring tone intervened. "Where are you?"

"Outside your fucking door. I've been banging on it for ten minutes. Wanna let me in?"

"On my way." Aidan rose from the bed, avoiding the trail of glass as he grabbed his pants, forgoing a shirt. The living room of the suite was equally dark, drapes drawn. He turned on a lamp, making his way. On the other side of the penthouse door was Kai, who looked as if he'd been present for last call—an image that was permanently adhered to him. The former bass player for an '80s mega band, Kai was a pro, who, in many ways, lived the rock 'n' roll existence Aidan strategically sidestepped. He'd ridden his wave of indulgence and when he finally washed ashore he'd turned to the business end of music, managing tours for some of its biggest acts. Hired to do the same for Aidan, he'd recently segued into a more personal role. Having been there, done that, Kai got it, and Aidan appreciated it. "You look like hell," Aidan said.

Kai's hand grazed over gray stubble and tour-weathered skin. He was the vintage version of *rock star.* "You think?" Kai strode across the room, opening enough drape to confirm a sharp but aging sun. "Take a look at yourself by the light of day."

It was the other thing Aidan liked about Kai, his blunt, sometimes necessary, candor. Squinting into stinging light, he recalled his unhappy glance in the mirror. He pressed forward. "What did you find out?"

"Not much more than the media's version of things. That you and Miss October were about to make an evening out of it when you decided to reenact a scene from *The Fast and the Furious.*" At the well-stocked bar Kai surveyed the wall of liquor. "Aidan,

I've got to ask. Are you sure it wasn't more than you thought? The Breathalyzer did register .12, and I know what that Porsche tops out at. I saw the cop's face, which is hard to miss since it's on every damn channel." He turned on the TV, easily finding a visual. "Mind telling me where you learned to land a punch like that?"

"Inherent, apparently," Aidan said, recalling the Catswallow event where he'd discovered as much. He pumped his fist again. The television focused on the officer's swollen mouth and missing tooth, but it was a different rerun that looped through Aidan's mind. His hand scrubbed around the snake on his neck, resting there. In the span of two paces he was at the bar, reaching for the gin.

"Hey, take it easy." Aidan grabbed the bottle, staring wild-eyed at Kai. The déjà vu in his head made one of them seem hugely out of place. "Whatever went down last night, it's not worth it—you know that." Kai knew a lot, but he didn't know everything. While he was angry about last night, Aidan's unease had nothing to do with the current event. "Even if it's true, your lawyer will handle it, which brings me to the main reason I'm here. I thought you'd want a heads-up that—"

"I wasn't drunk," Aidan defended, pushing the bottle away. "You know that." Kai nodded at the undisturbed bar. "It was a long studio session, the guys convinced me to go blow off some steam. And not for nothing, but where were you?"

He looked sheepishly at his employer. "I got a last-minute call. The Fray was trying out some new material at a small club. Their bassist was out of town; they asked me to sit in. I'm sorry, Aidan. Had I been there, none of this would have happened."

He didn't begrudge him the lure. Hang around and watch or be part of the rush. "I was just asking. It's not your fault. When you took this job I made it clear you weren't my fucking keeper. I take care of me. Anyway, I can't explain the Breathalyzer or the girl's story. We were talking . . . just talking when her boyfriend, the club owner, assumed it was more. He threatened her, grabbed her by the arm . . . hard. He was twice her size. She asked me for a ride. I couldn't walk away, leave her there. And if you call doing sixty in a forty a high-speed chase . . . Well, yeah, then I guess that's what it was. But the cop instigated the fight, threw the first punch. Not that it will matter. Not that anybody's going to believe me."

"Aidan, this will blow over. I don't know about Anne, but the fans will forgive you. And if you do end up doing time, C-Note will put the right spin on it. They'll sell tickets, a chance to win an Aidan Royce conjugal visit. It could be the new meet-and-greet. Imagine the line."

"You're a pig," he said, eyes narrowing. "Move on."

"Okay. Here's my theory, the former centerfold and her boyfriend pounced on an opportunity. Thanks to last night, a trendy club becomes an instant L.A. shrine. It's the place where Aidan Royce, who you have to admit hasn't suffered press like this in some time, slips back into those dangerous habits. They saw you coming, buddy, and they went for it. Unfortunately, it also sounds like you ran into a cop who was looking to spank the rich and famous."

Aidan shook his head. "Maybe . . . I don't know. The whole thing reeks of—"

"Just stay loose until your lawyer gets here. What's the worst that can happen? You reclaim your crown as rock's king of the badly behaved. It won't come to anything more than a few hours in an overcrowded cell. Maybe some time under house arrest with a nifty ankle bracelet."

Aidan's mouth dropped open, hands thrusting into the air. "But I didn't fucking do anything! I gave a girl a ride because it's what any decent person would do!"

"Maybe so. But Aidan, you're not any decent person." Kai laughed. "You know what I mean."

"Unbelievable, I order fucking club soda and I end up with the mother of all hangovers!" Pacing in a small, somewhat trapped, circle he talked more to himself than Kai. "This can't happen, not now."

"Assuming we have to deal, you can always turn the tables, go on the defense and say they slipped you something. Your lawyer can manufacture a blood test that says as much." He looked at Aidan, gesturing with a look that said *money and celebrity can fix anything.* "Speaking of which, counsel is on its way."

"I won't plant one lie on top of another. Not that C-Note's PR people wouldn't love that angle." Hands thrust to his waist, he continued to pace. "And that's the first thing I want to make clear to C-Note attorneys. How many did they send? Maybe we should move this thing to a conference room."

"Uh, Aidan, I didn't say C-Note attorneys were on the way." He stopped, listening harder. "I haven't even talked to Fitz; he's been on a plane on his way back from Japan. But there is a lawyer on the way, a really good one."

Aidan's head cocked at the innuendo, his gaze bearing down. "She's not?"

"She is. That's what I came to tell you. Anne is on her way. She called off the C-Note attorneys herself, said she'd handle things."

"Here? She's coming here?"

"Is it that surprising? I know she's been in New York and traveling since the Asian tour ended, but I thought that was just logistics."

"It was . . . it is. You know I've been stuck here in the studio."

"Okay, but your Facebook status hasn't changed, has it?"

Aidan walked to the window, absorbing the scalding view. "No," he said, then glancing over his shoulder, "of course not."

"So it doesn't take Dr. Phil to figure that Anne wasn't keen on waking up to footage of the new lady in your life."

"There isn't . . . That woman was def—This is total bullshit." Aidan turned, looking hard at Kai before his gaze darted away. "Believe me, if there was someone else, it wouldn't be *Miss October.*"

"Whatever works for you, man, but I'd review my story before Anne gets here. You know how these things take on a life of their own."

"Anne won't jump to conclusions. But DUIs and assault charges aren't her forte. She's a business attorney, Kai. She handles my personal business matters, my new contract with C-Note. Besides, Anne's a busy woman. I just wish she'd talked to me before she got on a plane."

"Apparently she saw this as her most urgent priority." His phone rang. "Damn, there's Fitz now. Let me run some interference." He answered, but put his hand over the phone, adding, "Just so you know, she'll be here any minute."

"Terrific," he muttered, wondering if Xanax was a staple in the Royal Beverly Crowne's minibar, not for himself but for her. Anne's concern would be resolute. He returned to the bedroom, avoiding the glass, rummaging through the linens until he came up with his shirt. Buttoning it, he adjusted to the news: Anne was on her way. Capable, sharp-minded, accommodating Anne. Beautiful, though she didn't lead with it. He dropped onto the edge of the bed. Aside from those facts, what he couldn't gauge was his reaction. Aidan wasn't sure how he felt about Anne descending on the situation.

CHAPTER TWENTY-ONE

HIS RELATIONSHIP WITH ANNE FIELDING BEGAN HONESTLY enough. Aidan had hired the savvy East Coast attorney to handle his affairs, not with the intention of having one. A few years older, she was versed in finance and law, and in solid possession of a focused life. It made her the perfect choice to handle a variety of business matters. The then-firm of Reinhart and Phelps was known for its celebrity clientele. Today it was Reinhart, Phelps and Fielding. Entertainers, professional athletes, new money of all sorts eagerly sought her out. They'd dabble in vineyards or look to add to a collection of vintage vehicles, maybe buy real estate in up-and-coming markets. While negotiations and contracts required lawyerly expertise, Anne referred to them as show-and-tell acquisitions—investments that her clients could brag about at parties but involved no real risk. Aidan surprised her by wanting to do the opposite. With his inheritance, he'd set out to build his own portfolio, one that didn't include anything in Napa Valley or bear an Aston Martin insignia, not even part ownership of a condo in Dubai. It was the cornerstone of his reinvention, a way of making Aidan Royce accountable. At first his wildly small investments perplexed Anne, but as his portfolio grew so did her interest. A guy who could have bought and sold pro sports teams or start his own record label, he went for the minuscule long shot. Aidan was drawn to start-up companies and quirky inventors, small ventures that had everything but big capital. Capital that, in time, he could provide. In the beginning he stuck to what he knew, ideas and tangible commodities related to the music industry. He grew bolder, trusting his instincts and a head for numbers that, until then, he'd generally ignored. His efforts did make Aidan Royce accountable, adding a layer of self-worth to Aidan Roycroft, businessman. But only in the last year could he confidently claim that the two had merged into one.

So it was the thrill of the chase, the rush of the win, the comfort of an occasional loss that became an aphrodisiac. As needed, Anne offered Aidan legal guidance, financial advice, and, eventually, her bed. It seemed like an appropriate segue. Although with Anne, a dark-haired beauty with snow-white skin, tethered to New York, and Aidan in almost constant motion, the relationship had an odd structure from the get-go. This did not concern him as his life had a decidedly odd structure of its own. They saw each other when they could, Aidan trying harder when Anne complained that time together resulted from rare open calendar dates or him mixing business with pleasure. He was determined to prove her wrong, the desire for a substantial relationship something he wanted to renew as much as his image.

Then, last fall, she'd flown to Boston to meet him before a sold-out show at the Garden. It was a singular performance, a mistake really. There were certain venues a rock star simply preferred not to play. And while he didn't deal the card often, it was the only explanation someone so famous need offer. But when the show sold out in less than fifteen minutes he felt obligated to see it through. A rain-soaked October day had Aidan holed up in his hotel room waiting for time to pass. Anne was late, weather delaying her flight. He'd turned on the gas fireplace and flipped through local newspapers. In whatever city, reading them had provided Aidan with leads for some of his best acquisitions. When she finally arrived, he was sitting on the sofa. The business section of the *Boston Globe* lay open in his lap, his gaze fixated on the flames. In his hand was a near-empty glass of scotch, on the table sat a bottle with a terrific dent in it. Aidan recalled having to tell himself to breathe, pumping air in and out with the synchronicity of a machine.

"You look toasty," she'd said smiling, tossing her coat on a chair, curling up next to him. She inched back. "Or make that just toasted. Aidan, what's going on? You . . . you don't drink."

That was all she knew, Aidan having explained *alcohol-enhanced nothingness* to a good therapist, but never to Anne. "I made an exception. I forgot how much I fucking hate Boston—and everything connected to it." He finished what was left, his hand gripping until the glass squealed for mercy. "How was your flight?" he asked, a peripheral glance darting from the fire onto her.

"Fine, if you like flying in a monsoon. Aidan, give me the glass." She eased it away, her head tipping curiously. "Was it your intention to just do the show drunk or did you want the stitches too? I know you weren't looking forward to Boston, but you'll be gone—"

His head whipped from the fire to her. There was one giant breath, the kind a body might take before expiring. "What would you say if we took this, us, to the next level?"

She shook her head, not in a negative gesture, just trying to keep up with his mood swing. "Us? The next level, as in we move in together?" She reached for his other hand, which was clutched around the paper. "Aidan, this is unexpected, I—"

"Not move in. Get married," he said, staring. "Marry me, Anne." She was uncharacteristically silent. "I don't want to just live with somebody. It's too fucking easy to walk away. I want forever, permanent . . . a real family."

"Forever, permanent . . . a real family?" She blinked widely. "Like the kind with children?"

"And a dog. Even a mortgage . . . if I needed one."

"Because rock star lends itself so beautifully to stable marriages."

"It's not a fucking joke, Anne. I'm ready for this. Marry me." Her facetious smile faded.

"Aidan, I . . . Are you serious?" She quieted, perhaps weighing blood alcohol versus legitimacy.

He only hesitated long enough to toss the newspaper aside. "Incredibly serious."

"Listen, let's get you some coffee—or tea, you prefer tea before a show. Kai will be here soon." She left him on the sofa, finding tea bags and filtering water through a coffeemaker. Silence pulsed, the faux fire not offering the crackle of much needed background noise. A timer beeped through, signaling hot water and Anne's opening. "Aidan, you caught me off guard," she said, arms swinging wide. "My gosh, I'm not even spending the night!" But her tone shifted as she filled a cup, dunking a tea bag like she was trying to drown the thing. "Of course, we could adjust that plan. We could talk," she said, a spoon swirling. "Not that anybody needs to send out invitations or alert the media. Well, not yet. But after Boston, there's only Philadelphia and Cleveland, and then you're done touring. To be honest, I didn't realize you were such a fan of marriage. But it might be the perfect time to explore the idea."

Aidan, whose gaze had returned to the unchanged flame, looked over. "Absolutely, perfect timing . . . "

"Your tea's ready. I don't know the concoction though." She glanced over, so anxious to get it right. "Honey and some kind of juice . . . Pineapple?"

"Grapefruit, but that's only if it's cold." His gaze shot to hers. "Besides, it's missing an ingredient, and I don't know what it is." Focusing on small motor skills, Aidan neatly arranged the newspaper pages—all except one, which remained in his hand. On his way to the bar, where the future steeped and stirred, he stopped at the fireplace. He looked at a photograph that was surrounded by paragraphs of text. It swam in his drunken gaze. A couple stood in front of a downtown building in Providence. It was a place called Grassroots Kids, the *Globe*'s business section featuring the unsung heroes of nonprofits. This story was dedicated to a Boston doctor, Nate Potter, and his girlfriend, who'd spearheaded the Rhode Island–based project. In the interview, Dr. Potter spoke not so much about the cause but about its architect. He talked about her commitment to the fledgling nonprofit while maintaining her day job at a radio station. How it was an honor to be a part of her life. His words read passionately, the way you'd speak about someone you loved. *No, that isn't right. Say it, Aidan, admit it. Put an end to it, because you'll never take that risk.* The good doctor's words, they were the way you'd speak about someone you were in love with. Crouching in front of the fire, Aidan felt the alcohol rush back up his throat. How rock star and poetic, he thought, to lose it right there, all over the Four Seasons' imported Persian carpet. He forced the booze back down. Straightening the crumpled page, Aidan mirrored an old ritual by turning unwelcome emotion into blistering ash. He couldn't get the hell out of Boston fast enough.

Time was on Aidan's side, waking up to the City of Brotherly Love the next afternoon. He closed out the tour two days later before a record crowd in Cleveland. There he'd played a special set, paying homage to the Rock and Roll Hall of Fame. HBO was taping it for a spring special. It had taken Aidan's complete focus to memorize the lyrics to a half-dozen vintage songs, knowing he had one take to get it right. He put all his energy into nailing cover versions, hits that belonged to Sam Cooke, the Doors, Springsteen, Van Halen, and a few others. Not long after he was back in California, far away from Boston's depressing weather. From there he thrust himself into forward motion by asking Anne to work from the West Coast. While she readily agreed, she didn't suggest setting a wedding date or moving in. Instead, she sublet an upscale condo a short drive from his Malibu home. He was touched by her respect for his feelings about living together. Aidan didn't want his parents' life. He wanted forever after, and a careful approach stood a better chance. While it was a piece of paper that held no guarantee, it was a tangible thing that symbolized the commitment he wanted. After unpacking her personal items, before buying a houseplant that, according to Anne, would only be a death-row prisoner, they went about the business of exploring the next level. They did couple things, like walks on a private stretch of beach, Anne on Aidan's arm for any public outing. They adjusted to each other's quirks, which included his extreme hours, as well as Anne's love of Fabcrgć glass and golf. It was something she excelled at and he loathed, though Aidan viewed this as a plus. Anne had her own interests, separate from his. That was important. The glass collection he didn't really get. Yet, on her birthday, Aidan presented her with a rare and lavish addition. He helped her choose a car, which he insisted on buying since California living required as much. She balked at the gesture, but eventually selected a limited-edition Mercedes coupe. Delving into familial tasks, she tried her hand at cooking. "Seriously, Aidan, I'd love to cook for you. How hard could it be?" The law, golf, and vintage Fabergé glass were her fortes. Cooking, they discovered, was not. It was an odd spot for the overachieving Anne, who appeared dumbfounded when a delicate seafood dish became permanently encrusted to a pan. Aidan joked that she should have started with foolproof fish, like sticks that came in a box. He felt bad afterward, Anne sulking,

Aidan making it up to her by hiring a personal chef. But those ripples appeared to be the biggest bumps, Aidan set on the idea of a singular relationship. Eventually, he decided a ring would make things more concrete, fulfilling a desire that seemed to be insatiable. So it came as a shock, mostly to himself, when in the midst of nurturing a relationship that was striding toward permanent, he agreed to an impromptu Asian tour.

Fitz suggested it at a roundtable of C-Note executives. The group gathered quarterly to marvel over the pot of gold that was Aidan Royce. There they would scheme future plans as to how they might further exploit their product. Fitz and company had grumbled about Aidan's Far East following, insisting that greater exposure would translate into increased earnings. "They'll spend money if you're accessible—CD's, merchandising, and shows . . . spectacular live shows."

Fitz was prepared for an all-out argument, including the fact that Aidan had recently completed a thirty-city U.S. tour, and he was taken aback by his response. "It's fine. I'll do it. I'll go," Aidan said, swallowing hard. But he couldn't keep the sentences from flowing. "It's easy to lull yourself into the security of a homegrown fan base. You have to be smart, you have to play to the world like it's one fucking stage."

From across the table, Fitz removed his glasses, looking queerly at Aidan. "That's what I was going to say."

Kai went to work directing the nonstop multicity tour: Manila, Beijing, Seoul, Singapore, Shanghai, Bangkok, Hong Kong, the Philippines, and Malaysia, a place where they were ecstatic to welcome rock royalty. Anne did not feel the same, his decision causing a volatile argument. In the heat of it, Aidan almost put the tour on hold. But the fiery moment faded when Anne acquiesced, agreeing how important it was to promote the public side of Aidan Royce.

There were phone calls and video chats, along with plans for Anne to join him as soon as she could get away. But it was difficult to put a career on hold for the express purpose of popping in on a rock 'n' roll life. Tour demands mounted, further interfering. And although he gave every performance one hundred percent, Aidan's focus was askew, his mind not on the business of being a rock star. Midway through the tour, surrounded by throngs of fans, hordes of media, and endless entourages, Aidan found himself, once again, in the pit that was the bottom of alone. He turned to the thing that had saved his ass the first time around, concentrating on business ventures removed from the world of rock 'n' roll. It kept him busy, kept him functioning. But when he got to the penthouse balcony of a five-star hotel in Kuala Lumpur, Aidan knew it wasn't enough. That's when he decided to jump. It was a wild leap, making a risk-filled purchase that he couldn't explain, completely unsure what he would do with it. But he did know the moment he put the deal in motion an insatiable need no longer felt as urgent. Days later, he finished out the tour, returning to L.A., not quite as ravenous and temporarily at peace. He should have known the feeling wouldn't last.

Now, sitting on the edge of the Royal Beverly Crowne's California king, Aidan knew that any shred of serenity was decidedly gone. It was time to deal. He heard Anne's voice. She was there, sounding lawyerly, like she had a plan. He considered his circumstance. Maybe her presence was necessary. Of course, Kai also had a point, the media frenzy surely playing into her decision to rush to his side. He could hardly blame her. As Aidan finished buttoning his shirt, he stopped listening, stopped thinking about last night. It wasn't the point. It didn't matter. He headed into the bathroom.

Standing in front of the sink, Aidan brushed his teeth and splashed icy water on his face. He rarely made eye contact with the mirror. He could shave with the skill of a blind man. For the past seven years it was the way he'd completed those tasks— avoiding what was irrevocably bound to him. Admittedly, it was the same way he'd gone about his life. Today he took a deep breath and forced himself to look. There was the expected flutter in his gut. He allowed himself to feel it, the predatory reptile meeting his gaze. He stared, head-on, facing all the things that were never going away. From there he patted the last drops of water dry. He was ready, prepared to make peace with a coiled snake and everything connected to it.

CHAPTER TWENTY-TWO

Providence, Rhode Island

GETTING IN TOUCH PROVED TO BE A TAD MORE DIFFICULT THAN it was in Catswallow. Back then, Isabel might have left a message scraped through mud on Aidan's windshield: *Farmhouse, later.* He was there every time. But they weren't kids anymore, and this was grown-up business. Determined to go forward with that approach, she filed Tanya's absurd theory where it belonged, under *Hopeless Romantic.* The only mission here was to contact Aidan Royce, rock icon, and see if he'd consider helping out an old friend. Given that context, it seemed plausible. They might have been married for five minutes, but they were friends for years, and she thought Aidan would honor that.

In that effort, Isabel considered serious ideas and fanciful ones, everything from hard-core publicists and management companies to Aidan Royce's official Facebook fan page. All of it led to a dead end. Reluctantly, she narrowed her scope and moved on to plan B: Stella Roycroft. A perusal through Catswallow information turned up nothing. It wasn't surprising. No matter the depth of Aidan's flaws, she was certain he'd secured his mother's future.

Eventually, the Boca connection occurred to her. Isabel guessed that Stella might have viewed the Florida locale as her last chance to be with John Roycroft, even if it was his final resting place. Dialing information, she was amazed to find Stella listed. From there a computer prompt took charge, a crackle of nerves overtaking Isabel who yelled, "*Wait,*" into the phone. Technology didn't respond to hesitation, though an answering machine did. Curiously, anxiety abated the moment she heard Stella's voice. It was the same infectious drawl she remembered, more genuine than most. The message was identical to the one she used to get at their trailer: "*This is Stella, I'm not home, leave a message.*" Aidan would always tell her not to say, "*I'm not home,*" that it was dangerous. She'd laugh, telling him it was okay if people thought she was out living it up. She couldn't remember how to record a new one anyway. Isabel left a simple message explaining that it was her, and she was trying to get in touch. It was important. Could Aidan call back? She'd hung up, uncertain if it was the most natural thing she'd ever done or the most insane.

The latter thought seemed like fair reasoning, especially after the day led to an out-of-sync evening with Nate. With so much in motion, he made the drive to Providence. Over dinner, they talked about Grassroots Kids and the radio station crisis, though Isabel didn't mention how or why Aidan Royce might be a viable solution to either. She decided it would be wiser to explain after speaking with Stella, after there was something meaningful to say. Instead, she padded conversation with questions about his day and asking if he'd given any more thought to a fall trip to Maine. Afterward, Nate said goodnight at her apartment door. That was when culpability kicked in, Isabel darting after him. "Nate, wait!" He turned back, a step closer to his car than her. "I'm so sorry! We never talked about . . . I haven't answered your question."

"What question?"

"Your question," she said, grasping his arm, "about coming to live with you in Boston."

"Oh, that question," he said, playing dumb to her clumsy behavior.

"That's if you still want to share living space with somebody so self-centered and dense."

He hesitated, looking her over. "Well, you have a point." And her mouth dropped open. "I'm not sure I want to live with someone who so easily forgets a two a.m. merlot-laced offer to shack up."

"Is that all it was?" She smiled, meeting the offended tone.

"Hardly," he said, pulling her into his arms. "No reply to my chivalrous invitation, and for what? To save your co-workers' jobs, not to mention a well-meaning nonprofit. And here I thought tonight would be all about which side of the medicine cabinet you get and how many drawers this is going to cost me."

"Clever and understanding," she said, kissing him. "But I am sorry."

"I'm not. I wouldn't have expected anything less of Isabel Lang. As long as . . ."

"As long as what?"

His arms, encircling her, let go, Nate's fingers brushing along her face. "I can understand as long as that's what kept you from answering."

A knitted brow met his. "Of course. How could it be anything else?" Claiming he had no idea, Nate kissed her goodbye before heading back to Boston, Isabel telling him to drive carefully.

Days later, despite Nate's easy demeanor, Isabel still felt guilty. The entire mess was distracting her from their future. Sitting at her desk, she invoked desperate measures by willing her phone to ring. She wanted to get on with a solution, in turn getting on with her life. There was an internal vow to come clean—five-minute marriage and all—the moment she heard from Stella. That way she could give one cohesive explanation about the Aidan from her past and why he'd suddenly turned up in her present. Staring at the phone, she even went as far as to project positive outcomes. Isabel pictured herself and Nate attending a benefit concert where she and Aidan would exchange pleasantries, briefly reminiscing about bygone days. Maybe she'd mention that the old farmhouse had sold, and how nice it was that the abandoned place would have a future after all. With Nate's arm securely around her, Aidan would shake his hand, everyone satisfied that things worked out just as they should. Heck, perhaps things would end so amicably she'd even add Aidan to her Christmas card list.

After a week passed, with her phone call to Stella unreturned, Isabel felt markedly different. Amicable, pleasant, and satisfied shifted to perturbed, embarrassed, and plainly pissed off at Aidan's continued dismissal. She should have taken her ex-husband at his word. His abrupt end to the marriage had come with clear messages, including the one about severing any lingering ties. Giving him the benefit of the doubt was a mistake. It was a fresh opportunity for Aidan to say: "Was me divorcing you in any way unclear?" The media's portrayal of a spoiled rock star with no boundaries was spot-on. Indulgent, lazy, and slightly self-centered were manageable teenage flaws. Obviously, as a human being, he'd peaked back in Catswallow.

As other ideas surfaced and sunk, Isabel found herself preparing a *"We gave it our best shot . . ."* speech. And she might have delivered it if Tanya hadn't shown up to work distraught over two out of three child-support checks bouncing. Mary Louise trailed behind with more bad news. Joe had, indeed, lost his job at the shipyard. Failing at this task trumped any bruised ego. She had no choice but to keep at it. Forcing down a bitter dose of humility, Isabel threw the Hail Mary pass she'd been dreading. She called

Fitz Landrey. She never got past a personal assistant, who listened as Isabel painstakingly explained who she was and what she wanted. Hiding a belly laugh, and not very well, the assistant remarked about the number of women who called claiming to be an ex-girlfriend of Aidan Royce—though ex-wife, she admitted, was a far more grandiose pretense. Isabel hung up with a thud, her self-esteem pummeled. Seven years removed from Aidan and she'd achieved the one thing she was determined to avoid. She was officially *one of them*.

CHAPTER TWENTY-THREE

Long Island

Fitz Landrey attributed the majority of his success to knowing talent when he saw it. The rest he viewed as an innate ability to cut the right deal at the right time. This was that time. Having waited patiently for Anne Fielding to return from California he suspected his bargaining position would be at its most malleable point. With that in mind, he watched Anne choose the club with which she would handily beat him. Firming up his stance, he prepared to make the sacrifice.

"I'm surprised at you, Fitz," she said, eyeing him before swinging. "I can't believe you think rolling greens and a Bloody Mary will get me to acquiesce on Aidan's contract." Her golf ball traveled like it had built-in radar, landing midway, perfectly aligned with the green. "Sorry," she said, smiling, "but I can't be anything less than myself."

"I'm counting on it, Anne." Glancing at his caddy, Fitz's hand hovered between two clubs, taking the nod as to which one he should select. "You love the game. There's no reason we can't enjoy the weather and a round of golf while we chat." He took minimal aim, his shot looping lamely across the fairway.

"Seriously?" she said, watching the disastrous drive. "Eighteen rounds in a conference room might have been less painful. Besides, you have the list of amended items. For the amount of future income Aidan is worth, it's a fair deal. This is, um, pleasant but unnecessary." She winked, Fitz remaining behind as Anne advanced toward her shot, saying over her shoulder, "If you think bargaining on *my turf* will get me to budge, then I'd say it's a weak-willed move. Maybe you're losing your edge."

He waited until the distance was enough that shouting would be appropriate. "You think so? My apologies, Anne. Let me be more direct. I invited you here to ask if you'd like a hand in putting Aidan Royce in your bed—permanently."

The nine-iron she marched along with became a third leg and she nearly tripped over it. As Anne pivoted, Fitz watched the spikes of her golf shoes tear into tufts of grass, his words snagging, as he'd anticipated, on her heart. The caddies backed away as business turned personal. "Don't be ridiculous," she said, flashing a ring. "Things are fine with Aidan. Our lives are insanely busy." But even from the distance he could see her coax excuses into valid reasoning. "It's a complicated relationship."

"Complicated to what end? Personally, I think you're on the cusp. Things could go either way." He approached, his golf club resting lazily over his shoulder. "I've watched the ebb and flow between you and Aidan. He wants it. I'll give you that much. But something is keeping him from closing the deal." She began to launch into a defense, Fitz raising a hand to stop her. "Don't get me wrong, I'm impressed with what I've observed. You handle Aidan well. When you realized he'd basically run away to Asia, you made a brilliant countermove." She narrowed her eyes, arms folding. "Most women would have stuck to him like glue— canceled their lives to protect their interests. Instead, you made the tough choice and retreated. But after his very public Pure

Oxygen encounter with Miss October, things changed. It was enough space and you decided to make your presence known."

"Really, Fitz, do you have a telepathic link to what I'm thinking, how Aidan's feeling?"

"No," he said bluntly. "I have a commodity worth hundreds of millions of dollars. It's my business to know exactly how it's functioning. Identify any potential glitches and take whatever action is necessary to protect its earning potential. But I'll admit, even I don't know everything. So, enlighten me, Anne. Did your trip to the coast result in what you'd hoped? Will you be booking the grand reception hall at the Four Seasons, entertaining offers for exclusive rights to the wedding footage?"

"You bastard," she said, firming up her stance on the high road. "How incredibly offensive!" Fitz didn't flinch, the epithet being old news. "I was sure the Fourteenth Amendment and Oprah Winfrey had moved us past that mentality. Is it so incomprehensible that an accomplished woman could take action without an ulterior motive?"

"With a man she didn't want to marry? Sure," he said, shrugging. "And I'll take that as a no." Silence and a mutual glare alluded to an agreed-upon point. "Listen, I have complete respect for your fierce talents as an attorney and businesswoman. We wouldn't be standing here if I didn't. But I'm not a bad businessman myself, capable of recognizing a personal agenda. Along with bastard, you have to give me credit for that." She snatched up her club, marching past him. "Before you stomp off this course, Anne, consider your position . . . and mine. I won't reach out a second time. Don't allow pride to prevent you from getting what you want. I assure you, that trait cost the last woman in your position dearly."

She stopped, the club digging hard into the earth. "Assuming you're not completely off the mark. What, exactly, are you after, and how does it involve me?"

An hour later they sat on the country club terrace drinking Bloody Marys, Anne absorbing every morsel Fitz offered. As he suspected, she had no knowledge of Aidan's brief marriage to Isabel. It was a taboo topic for C-Note's number one property. After confessing their honeymoon catastrophe, the details of why Isabel left him, since taking it upon himself to end the marriage, Aidan hadn't spoken of it. But Fitz was surprised to learn that Aidan had never even mentioned an Isabel Lang. Not as an old friend, not even in passing. It was a telling tidbit. "Recently, Isabel Lang tried to contact me. My assistant took the call. It was uninvited and very out of the blue."

"What did she want? Money?"

He paused, sipping his drink. "In part, but if that was her only motivation I'd hardly need to involve you."

"True." Lawyerly speculation faded as women's intuition kicked in. "Aidan," she surmised, "she wants Aidan."

"It's in the realm of possibility," he said, waiting for an emotional follow-through. It came via body language. There was a physical shift in alertness, like an animal sensing a predator. The fingertips of her folded arms tightened, nails paling as they pressed into her flesh. "Isabel could very well have a hidden agenda and it would be unwise to ignore her. This girl is determined . . . *hardy*. I know what she's capable of when faced with a task; I've seen the result. She'll get to him eventually. I can't have that. Isabel Lang represents serious risk."

"Risk for you? Why?" she said. "This might concern me, but what do you care about Aidan's love life?"

"I told you, brief as the marriage was, he was humiliated by it. For Christ's sake, he's Aidan Royce. He doesn't need to deal with the sudden reemergence of Isabel Lang."

"Mmm, maybe not, but I should talk to Aidan first. You have to know my loyalty is to him, not you."

Fitz leaned back, his body relaxing. "Right, absolutely. Good answer," he said, pulling forward, hands folding. "I certainly give you plenty of credit there, Anne."

"For what?"

"That level of kamikaze loyalty. I can only imagine how Aidan will react when you remind him how poorly he fared on his first trip on the marriage-go-round. Of course," he said, wagging a finger at her, "there is a chance any negative impact will be offset by shock."

"Shock?"

"Yes, when he learns about your sudden in-depth knowledge of information he, clearly, didn't want to share." Allowing doubt to hover, Fitz continued, "You're here, Anne. You've already laid down in the bed. We're talking about a man who covets loyalty, craves privacy. You've compromised yours by having this conversation. That's how he'll see it. You know it is."

She breathed deeply, studying him. "Tell me more. What does this woman want, specifically, and where do I come into play?"

"Isabel claims the attempt to get in touch is because she needs Aidan's help. From what my assistant said, she's the CEO of a nonprofit that will go belly-up without a major financial shot in the arm. She wants Aidan to put on a benefit concert, the proceeds going to some charity called Grassroots Kids."

"Never heard of it, sounds desperately altruistic. Why the concert? Why not just hit him up for a mega donation?"

"Apparently, the nonprofit is the backend of her proposal. Her day job prompted the call. She works at some lame radio station that recently switched to a rock 'n' roll format—must have been a real dinosaur." He paused, watching Anne's face fade to a decidedly paler shade. "Anne? Something wrong?" She shook her head, pulling more erect, fingers tightening. "Anyway," Fitz continued, "she wants Aidan to headline a promotional concert."

"I, um, I didn't realize there were any dinosaur markets left . . . radio station, you say?"

"Yes, *104.7—The Raging Fever FM for Hot Sound,* if you can believe that, in Providence, Rhode Island, of all places. A speck on the map."

"Interesting," she said, taking a long sip of her drink. "The New England area, not somewhere Aidan cares to be."

Fitz leaned back, considering the observation. "You're right, he detests the region."

"Maybe she's the reason. Maybe if you tell him this Isabel Lang called, Aidan will do nothing more than ask for a restraining order and have you tell her to go to hell."

"Are you confident that would be the outcome?"

There was a rhetorical sigh, Anne plucking sunglasses from her face. "What do you want me to do?"

"I want you to go there, confront Isabel, and put out this fire. As Aidan's attorney, a visit from you would be appropriate. Your presence will send the right message."

"And as Aidan's fiancée that adds a nice postscript."

"Why it hadn't occurred to me," he said, smiling. "What an appealing plus!" He leaned forward, his fingers tapping the table. "On the other hand, we wouldn't want your visit to appear rogue or random. Take some C-Note representation with you, that way we cover all our bases."

"Kai Stoughton brings a nice presence to things, business smarts and industry glamour. Too bad he's on Aidan's payroll."

"To a point. While I don't think it would be wise to send Kai, we never like to completely relinquish a viable connection at C-Note." Fitz finished his drink, hesitating before smiling slyly. "Do you really think it was fate that Aidan ended up at Pure Oxygen without his trusty sidekick?" Her eyes widened at the vague confession. "It's not every day a yesteryear '80s bass player gets a call to perform with one of the hottest bands around."

"You? You orchestrated the whole incident? The girl, the boyfriend . . . the cop?"

"Me? I was in Japan. But know this, that timely windfall of publicity resulted in an across-the-board spike in Aidan Royce numbers. Listen," he said, a celery stalk swirling through ice. "Aidan operates like a thoroughbred racehorse, always has. Sometimes a blindfold is necessary to get him where he needs to be. His talent takes it from there. His image sells the merchandise. A media blitz was exactly what he needed." Fitz avoided Anne's cool stare, concentrating on the open green. "It's not like anyone could have predicted he'd haul off and punch a cop."

"Fitz that's—"

"That's show business, Anne, and you're not innocent to the culture." He downed the rest of his drink, the glass hitting the table with a definitive thud. "Look, C-Note will back you with an appropriate entourage. Are you interested in assisting with this Isabel Lang issue or not? Because my other choice involves getting some group like Weak Need to help her out. They're past their prime, plenty of open dates. But that's a fluid solution. We'd both fare better with a permanent one."

From the edge of the high road, a slim finger tapped her chin. "I suppose I could justify intervening. As you pointed out this girl is . . . What did you call her, *hardy*? Who knows what her scheme is."

"I agree. You have to anticipate with these situations. Strangers would take advantage of Aidan's celebrity. Imagine the damage someone could do with a real connection. Isabel Lang might decide to write a tell-all book about their marriage, however brief. Look at the public reaction to a single incident involving Aidan; imagine the uproar if there was an entire book. He'd be at the center of scrutiny and scandal while Ms. Lang would survive comfortably in the profit margin."

Anne nodded along, Fitz watching the seeds of speculation take root. "As Aidan's attorney it would be negligent if I didn't protect his interests—all of them. At the very least, it's reasonable that I investigate the situation." She reached for her cell phone.

"What are you doing?"

"Making some travel arrangements," she said, dialing. "You're not the only one who got where he did by seizing the moment."

Fitz leaned back in his seat, relaxing, ordering another drink from the waiter.

CHAPTER TWENTY-FOUR

Providence, Rhode Island

Tom Danvers, the architect who'd volunteered to design a new Grassroots Kids facility, had just left. Aside from his professional expertise, Tom was a kind man. He'd never make a point of noting that a meeting was a complete waste of his time. Isabel sat with her eyes closed, embarrassed, feeling like a fraud. Nate's hand was clasped over hers, the two of them sharing a private moment in the rather public, glass-walled conference room of *104.7—The Raging Fever FM*. "Isabel, it was all right to take the meeting. You didn't do anything wrong. Tom's designs will still be there, not if but when Grassroots Kids has the money to move forward. You'll figure this thing out. You did it the first time."

She shook her head, mouth bent to a frown. "Yes, I'm sure I sounded so promising, 'Thanks for all the hours you spent on this, Tom. We'll let you know when we have two nickels to rub together, never mind the money to actually start building.'" Nate laughed softly, Isabel's head dipping onto his shoulder as he kissed the top of it. "Between the radio station and Grassroots Kids, I'm starting to feel like a one-woman disaster."

"Hey, not to change the subject, but I saw Eric the other day—"

"Why? A flare or something worse?" she asked, sitting upright. At the moment it seemed possible, her bad luck spilling over to him. "I'm sorry, that was unfair. I know the rules. If my father has anything medical to share, he'll tell me himself." She sensed a sliver of hesitation, but it waned like a crescent moon as Nate smiled assuredly.

"Actually, he wanted to know if you had plans for this weekend. I told him you did—with me."

"Don't tell me I forgot something else," she said, fingers flying to her forehead. "I still feel awful for not answering right away about moving to Boston."

"No, you didn't forget. But, Isabel, I was thinking . . . What if we took a break?" She inched back, guessing he'd tired of what seemed like endless issues. He smiled wider. "I meant together." She sighed, shaking her head at her runaway imagination. "We spend a lot of time on the serious side of life. Let's get out of here, hop on a plane. We could take an evening sail in tropical waters, dine by candlelight, make love until we pass out. Let's just go, even if it's for the weekend."

She smiled. "Kind of like running away." It was tempting, an escape from everything. Isabel leaned in and kissed him. "Have I mentioned, Nate Potter, that you are one incredible man? How about if we . . ." But Isabel's idea petered out, her peripheral glance catching on her co-workers at the conference room door. Tanya looked as if she'd won the lottery, Mary Louise not quite as remarkable, as if maybe it was just a two-for-one special at Stop & Shop. Behind them was a beautiful woman dressed in a sleek cream-colored suit, her dark hair pulled into a stylish upsweep. Two people followed. A young woman who had the essence of a capable gal Friday, and a man who appeared all seasoned Hollywood glitz, like someone you might recognize but didn't.

"Isabel, this is Anne Fielding," Mary Louise said, ushering

them all in as she and Nate stood. "She's an attorney, just in town for the day. She's here to see you." Isabel reached out, shaking a hand that felt like fine bone china—cool and expensive. Her smile was pearly, though there wasn't anything particularly friendly about it. "And this is, um . . ."

"Business associates of Miss Fielding," the man answered. Isabel detected a West Coast vibe, the rail-thin girl wearing a sheath-like dress that would be barely appropriate in California—perhaps never in the state of Rhode Island. There was a quiver in her belly. It linked things in her mind a step ahead of the confirmation that came from Tanya's mouth.

"They're with C-Note Music," she said excitedly. "They're here because of Aidan Royce!" The quiver morphed into a punch, Isabel stumbling directly into Nate's arms. While she was in no danger of falling, she felt him hang on tight.

"Oh, I'm sorry," Mary Louise said. "This is Nate Potter."

"Isabel's . . . Oh, what's the trendy phrase, *significant other*," Tanya chimed.

Anne Fielding's smile warmed, extending a hand. "My pleasure, I'm sure."

"Nice to meet you," he said, looking curious. Isabel appreciated his confusion, wanting to turn and ask, *"How about if we hop on that plane right now?"* Instead, she stood wedged knee-deep in guilt, Nate's schedule rescuing her from an on-demand explanation. "Isabel, I have to go. I have a ton of patients this afternoon." His glance volleyed from his watch to the glamorous entourage and onto Isabel.

"Patients? You're a physician?" The question from Anne sounded more like a wish.

"Uh, yes, I'm a doctor at Mass General."

"Really? How wonderful."

"My mother seems to think so," he said, moving toward the

door. "Again, nice meeting you. Isabel, I'll call you tonight." Her gaze, which was adhered to the group, peeled away.

"Absolutely . . . of course." She followed, making certain he didn't leave without an answer. "You're right. A tropical getaway sounds perfect."

"We can talk about running away later," he said, squeezing her hand before heading down the hall.

Language seemed elusive, Isabel nodding hard, not turning back until Nate and every safe harbor he brought disappeared. Reaching for the door, Isabel quieted a trembling hand, dipping deep into that hardy well of calm.

A courtesy call, that's how they referred to it. Anne clarified that she wasn't with C-Note, not like her two associates, but as a group they were, indeed, there representing Aidan Royce. Having received word of 104.7—*The Raging Fever FM for Hot Sound* and Grassroots Kids' request, they'd come to address the matter. In a businesslike tone, Anne proceeded with the impromptu meeting. She explained how Aidan Royce received endless appeals for him to appear at charity functions, most of them worthwhile and moving causes. She continued to dominate the dialogue, her companions nodding sporadically, more adamantly when she came to her point. Since the request involved a bygone *friendship* they felt obligated to offer a personal regret. Bottom line, the calendar simply wouldn't cooperate. Anne hoped they understood. There was a groan of disappointment from Tanya and Mary Louise saying they did. Isabel wasn't feeling as compliant, her ex-husband sending henchmen—henchwomen—to do his dirty work.

"So if you don't mind . . . Isabel?"

"Mind what?" She'd already dismissed Anne and her last thought, focused on the one gnashing through her head.

"A private word before we're on our way."

"Sure, whatever," she said. The gal Friday was first out the door, Mary Louise and Tanya following the man. Isabel heard Tanya offer him a cup of coffee, a doughnut, quite possibly her phone number.

A buffed fingertip tapped against Anne's painted mouth. "This, um, this is a difficult point to make. I don't want to cause you further embarrassment."

"What makes you think you caused me any in the first place? It was only a question; you answered it."

"Of course . . . my apologies, my assumption." Her head tipped humbly. "If I may, I'd like to be perfectly candid." Isabel's hand swept through open air, not intimidated by the beautiful and clearly accomplished Ms. Fielding. "You should know, not unlike your past, I share a current personal relationship with Aidan." Except for the reflexive gulp, Isabel stood stone-faced. She hadn't put it together; she was *that* attorney. "Naturally," Anne said, her mammoth diamond ring and fingers brushing between them, "ours is more significant—certainly more complex than some ancient five-minute marriage between two teenagers."

"You know about that?"

"Of course I know. I also don't mind telling you that you can't imagine the difficulties of nurturing a relationship in a world that's, essentially, rigged to destroy it."

"I have an idea."

"I'd be grateful, Isabel, not to further complicate things."

"I'm not sure I follow. Whatever the excuse, schedules or commitments, you said Aidan wouldn't help. I get it. I don't see—"

Anne's fingers fluttered through the air, halting Isabel's words. "If I can make a snapshot observation. You're fortunate to be in a relationship where you don't have to deal with that kind of stress." Isabel's head cocked. "Your *significant other* . . . Nate, was it? I caught a glimpse of the two of you. He struck me as stable—committed. I admit; I'm envious."

"Are you?"

"Don't get me wrong. I love Aidan very much."

"Do you?" Isabel said, a breath sucking in until she found there was no more air to take.

Anne smiled. "I wouldn't be here, have hung in there if it wasn't meant to be. It's a lot of give and take—on my part. The recent incident in L.A. is a perfect example, Aidan's encounter with that girl, his arrest. One of many, I'm afraid. Lord knows this time I should have kicked Aidan to the curb. But I can't. I think I'm good for him. And we're both dedicated to working things out. Aside from the bad-boy behavior, he has many wonderful qualities. He's, um . . . Well, he's . . ." She laughed. "My goodness, he's Aidan Royce. What more do you need to know?"

And out of Isabel's mouth tumbled the thought in her head. "He's extremely protective." Her eyes squeezed shut, stunned by the staying power of a deep-rooted fact.

Anne's eyes narrowed, the smile looking a tad forced. "Naturally. I just meant there were too many to list. Anyway, his career, the pressure, it's hard on him. The demands are endless. Personally, I feel it's important to be forgiving with Aidan. You know, give him big boundaries, ample leeway in life."

Isabel looked blankly at her. "Funny, I never thought so."

She cleared her throat, tucking a stray lock that had slipped from the chignon. "Regardless, as I've explained, Aidan simply cannot meet your request. In addition, I wanted to offer insight to Aidan's life—for you to know that he has one beyond the stage and fans and chaos."

"If you're implying that my motive was personal, I assure you it wasn't. I moved on from Aidan in the instant I signed those divorce papers. The request was nothing more than what it appeared, the radio station format change and Grassroots Kids."

"I'm so very glad to hear it," she said, her face softening. Anne turned for the door but pivoted back around. "Oh, of course, your charity case. I'm sure Aidan would be glad to make a donation. Generosity, it's one of those great qualities, right?" Isabel didn't respond, an inward storm clouding outward calm. "I can give you a prime example of that! After Aidan insisted I move to L.A. to be closer, he bought me the car of my dreams."

Isabel's arms widened, hands slap-landing together. "Well, there you go."

"I know; it's overwhelming. Generosity like Aidan's is hard to imagine."

"To be candid with you, Ms. Fielding, I don't imagine anything about Aidan." Isabel moved toward the door, not knowing her own voice, gravel bitten, perforated by the conversation. Bodily reactions continued to disobey, Isabel blinking fast, mortified to find her lashes damp.

"When I get back to New York, I'll see to it that a check is written on Aidan's behalf. Would, say, $100,000 be helpful and bring this query to a close?"

"You tell Aidan," she said, spinning back, jaw clenched. Isabel paused, grasping for indifference while letting go of a person who, clearly, did not exist. "You tell Aidan that would be lovely. Grassroots Kids would be appreciative of any monetary support."

"Wonderful," she said, smiling broadly. "I'll take care of it. Best of luck, Isabel, with everything, your job . . . your cause . . . your life."

CHAPTER TWENTY-FIVE

Los Angeles

DAYS LATER FITZ WAS MORE THAN READY TO BRING THINGS full circle. "Where the fuck is he?" he groused, sitting behind a mahogany desk that took up a fair chunk of his L.A. C-Note office. "I spoke with Kai. He assured me Aidan would be here. I want those contracts signed—today!" He slammed his fist atop a healthy stack of legal documents flagged with bright Post-its. They marked the numerous places Aidan needed to sign. He tossed an aggravated look at Anne and resumed knocking his knuckles on the desktop. "Just what I need today, the rock star version of Aidan Royce! It's not like I don't have a fucking major record label to run!"

"Calm down, Fitz. He'll be here," said Anne, who'd arrived that morning. She'd been on a coast-to-coast jaunt, beginning with her business in Providence. Sitting on the opposite side of Fitz's desk, her attention shuffled between him and a duplicate set of contracts.

"You'd better be right. He'd better be sitting in fucking L.A. traffic or being mobbed in the lobby! His tardiness better have nothing to do with—"

"Don't be so paranoid," she said, though Anne did check her

watch. "I told you, my trip to Providence panned out better than expected. My presence was hardly necessary. Isabel has moved on—her exact words. She has a lovely boyfriend with whom she can play doctor while she lives out a contented, albeit, pedestrian life. Add to that my personal insight on Aidan and I doubt we'll hear from her again."

"Doubt?"

"Certain . . . I'm certain we won't hear from her. You were her best shot at making contact. She has no recourse. And to be honest, she didn't strike me as the type who longs to be labeled a stalker."

"Perhaps, but maybe we should have—"

"It's already in place, a backup measure," she said, not looking up. "If Isabel Lang so much as contacts your office or mine, an army of lawyers will descend, slapping her with a most embarrassing cease-and-desist order."

"Good, that's good, Anne."

"Besides, once he signs this contract, Aidan won't have time to bother with relationships that date back to his yearbook." Anne waved a portion of pages at him, denoting C-Note's segue into the motion picture industry. It gave Aidan a starring partnership, as well as a share of the profits.

"Speaking of said contract, I can't believe you didn't ask for one amendment. For the next seven years, when Aidan's not meeting C-Note commitments his professional life will be consumed by our new production company."

"He'll look great on the big screen." This time she made solid eye contact. "Like you said, Aidan operates like a thoroughbred, every once in a while you have to blindfold him. He'll appreciate it in the long run. Fortunately, he isn't much for fine print. He relies on me to convey contractual details."

The thrumming stopped. "Don't get too cocky, Anne.

Publicity stunts and circumventing an ex with an ax to grind is one thing. Aidan's not the same naïve kid I plucked out of Catswallow, Alabama. He's older . . . wiser." He raised a brow. "Certainly capable of reading fine print if it's in front of him. That's not a tactic I'd pursue nowadays."

"Thanks for the advice, but I have a good read on how to handle Aidan."

"If you say so." Silence filtered through, Fitz clearing his throat. "Um, Anne, it's not my business, but here's a thought. Should you find your personal progress stagnant, there is an old-as-time method of securing a place in Aidan's life."

She looked up from the documents, frowning. "Really, Fitz, I don't think my father offering a dowry of two goats and a mule will sway Aidan."

"Not quite that archaic."

"Seriously? You think he'll read fine print, but you don't think he'd see through something that . . . *accidental*?"

"What difference would it make after the fact? The point is Aidan's persistent sense of right and wrong, that loyalty we spoke about. In my experience, it's never been in step with today's easy standards." He shrugged. "It came in handy enough when he thought Miss October was in peril. Think about using it to your advantage, that's all I'm suggesting."

Incredulous or curious, either way, her expression was awed. "Don't be ridiculous. I'd never . . ." She paused. "On the other hand, he certainly had an aversion to living together less a marriage license. Who even thinks like that nowadays? Maybe you have a—"

A ringing phone interrupted. "There he is," he said, mashing a finger into the speaker button. "Aidan, where the hell are you? You were supposed to be in my office a half hour ago!"

"Sorry about that, Fitz. Something came up, we'll have to reschedule."

Anne inched forward in her seat. "Aidan, I don't understand. The plan was for us to meet this morning, have dinner this evening. I have all the contracts here, ready to review."

"I've already done that. There are details we need to discuss, but we can do that later." Fitz shot Anne an *I-told-you-so* look, the two of them leaning closer. "While I was on the phone with you last night my mother left a message."

"Your mother?"

"Yes, she'd been on an extended trip to Hawaii with some friends. You know, Fitz, that crowd of ladies that makes it to every show we do on a swing through Florida."

"Not really, but if you say so. What's the problem, Aidan? Is she ill?" A few seconds of crackling silence passed.

"No, nothing like that, but thanks for the concern. Instead of heading home, she decided to take a detour, Big Sur, Monterey. Seems she's always wanted to do the tourist thing. I decided to drive up and spend a few days."

"Are you fucking kidding me?"

"No, I'm not," he replied in a lazy, *"Why is this a problem?"* tone. Over the years, more so in recent ones, he'd used it for what seemed like the express purpose of annoying the living hell out of Fitz. "It's the perfect opportunity with the break in my schedule." As Fitz shook his head, Anne's posture slumped dejectedly. "Hang on, there's some traffic."

"You're driving yourself?" she asked, jerking upright. "Do you think that's wise?"

"Anne, you worry too much. I can take care of myself."

"Of course, I didn't mean—"

"Never mind that," Fitz said, a hard glare passing across the desk. "Aidan, you want to postpone signing your C-Note contracts so you can take a personal day?"

"No, I *am* postponing signing for a personal day." Fitz's arms lifted into the air, acknowledging how little hands-on control he had over Aidan Royce. "Besides, those contracts aren't due for a couple of weeks. What's the rush? My relationship with C-Note and you is solid, right?"

"Absolutely, very solid, but that's not the point. We're busy people, the three of us. It's not easy to coordinate a meeting like this."

"I suppose. But out of the three of us, you'd have to concede that I'm the busiest—certainly the most in demand."

Anne held up a hand, calming Fitz's protruding veins. "Yes, of course we understand. You're Aidan Royce. How, um . . . how long do you expect to be away?"

"Just a few days. You'll hardly have time to miss me. Promise."

Calming hand or not, Fitz couldn't be stopped. "That's just great, Aidan, fucking great. I leave for Europe tomorrow. I won't be back until the end of the month—"

"Hey, Fitz, I can barely hear you. Kai has my calendar, Anne's right there, put your heads together and come up with a new date. I'll be there to sign. No problem. But, really, you're fading. And I shouldn't be talking on my cell while I'm driving."

He hung up. Fitz and Anne were left with unsigned contracts and the real-life spin of an irreverent, iconic rock star.

⁂

"EXCUSE, MR. ROYCE, BUT DID YOU JUST SAY YOU WERE DRIVING while on your cell phone?"

Aidan grinned, dropping his phone onto the seat next to him. "Yeah, I guess I did. Sleight of hand I learned courtesy of Fitz Landrey. At the moment, I need a high-profile life to fly very under the radar."

"I know privacy is paramount to you," he said, filling Aidan's coffee cup. "Speaking of flying, the pilots estimate a late-afternoon landing." Henry was his in-flight Kai, more formal but friendly, handling anything that his employer might need while en route on his private jet. He lingered for a moment, finally remarking to a still-grinning Aidan, "If I may say, you do seem rather upbeat today."

"I am, Henry. I definitely am." He took the steaming cup, sipping it, pausing. "I don't mind telling you, I've logged a lot of hours on this plane, in this life. Parts of it have been an incredible wild ride. I'd never claim otherwise. But always," he said, his gaze drifting toward the window, "something huge has been missing."

"I'd have to agree." Aidan looked back, surprised by a feeling he assumed was well guarded. "It's my job to observe, Mr. Royce, to anticipate needs. I've worked for you for a while now, watched you spend a great deal of time staring out that very window," he said, pointing. "Whatever's missing, I've always suspected it was far removed from fame, well beyond anything a staff member could deliver."

Aidan nodded, breathing deep. He cleared his throat, needing to change the subject. "Tell me, how's your sister doing?"

"Kara's doing beautifully, thanks to you. She has her son back; she has a job. Every time I see her, she asks me to thank you. My family asks me to thank you. We never could have afforded a treatment program like that."

"I've seen the toll drugs take, especially heroin. It's bad news. I'm glad I was in a position to help." Aidan's eyes traveled the opulent interior of the aircraft. "And what I did, it's not as selfless as it sounds."

"Sir?" he said, gathering the lunch Aidan didn't eat.

"The good life, Henry. It's not a simple thing to justify. It carries a lot of burden for a guy whose job it is to carry a tune. Doing things like helping your sister . . . Well, it doesn't balance out, but it lets me sleep a little better at night."

"For the record, Mr. Royce, I can't carry a tune in a bucket."

Sipping his coffee, Aidan offered a curious glance. "But I am a jack-of-all-trades. My previous employers, all well-known, well-to-do *people,* demanded as much. Allow me to assure you, you should sleep well."

Henry retreated to the forward cabin, a place normally jammed with the Royce entourage. Aidan remained where he usually did, in the rear section of the aircraft, a private space that was off-limits to just about every other human being. He squinted into a pre-painted canvas, mountains of cumulous clouds drilled with telltale signs of light. On any ordinary day, the heavens unearthed might be inspiration. Enough to pick up a guitar and sell his soul for three minutes and thirty seconds while keeping it radio friendly. Not today. Today he picked up his phone and dialed his voicemail. As he told Fitz and Anne, his mother had called, like he told Henry, the need for privacy was paramount.

"Hey, sweet boy, I'm home. The girls and I had a wonderful trip—private tours, the best hotels . . . You're spoiling me, son! But listen, sweetie, that's not why I called. I had a message here, on the house phone. It was from Isabel. Surprised the devil out of me! Anyway, it was just a short message, saying it was her, and that she needed to get in touch—that it was important. I . . . I know you don't like to talk about her, Aidan, but you know how I feel. It sounded like she really needed you. Of course, truth be told, I've always thought of that as the other way around."

And this, Aidan knew, was the truest statement of his life. In the midst of an Asian tour, on a balcony in Kuala Lumpur, from the pit that was the bottom of alone, Aidan finally let it in. He finally accepted that his divorce from Isabel was a complete and utter mistake. The feeling had chased him across continents, since the moment a story in the *Boston Globe* triggered an avalanche of emotion. In the end, it was her noted place of employment that provided a serendipitous fact. And from that Far East balcony, he put in motion an acquisition that was meant to be a symbolic gesture. Silently, anonymously, without Isabel ever knowing, he'd be a part of her life—even from as far away as Kuala Lumpur. It was a way to let her go, bringing closure to a tumultuous past. He had no hope of winning her back. What he'd done to her on their wedding night made it a certainty. It was his intention to move on. The fact that he was engaged to another woman gave the concept credibility. But the gesture had turned on him, his feelings fucking up the best-laid plans. When Aidan returned stateside, the tour over, he found himself fixated on his new acquisition, curious as to how it might translate into common ground. And for every second Aidan spent telling himself that it was an absurd fantasy, he spent one more pursuing the prospect. His purchase put him in the ballpark, but he needed a reason to get in the game.

That's when Aidan began to wonder what might happen if Isabel needed him. Maybe nothing. Maybe she'd reach out. And before he knew it, Aidan was turning gesture into possibility. He made the executive decision that *98.6—The Normal FM for Easy Listening* change its format, giving the outrageous order that the radio station prove itself with an on-demand audience. In turn, it made him the only viable solution to the problem. It was an incredible risk. Aidan couldn't fathom the devastation if Isabel rejected any notion of him coming to her aid. The waiting had left him on edge, his ridiculous arrest the last thing he wanted on Isabel's mind. He shifted restlessly, thinking he should have been more direct. Maybe he should have showed up on her doorstep with his heart and a mega check in hand. Why not? It seemed like a slam-dunk move. Slam-dunk if it was anyone but Isabel. She'd see it as a flashy attempt to buy her, and arguably she would be right. Dropping in on her life would have led to a lopsided ten-second opportunity to reconnect. He needed to be invited. And much to his amazement, according to his mother, he had been. He understood that it was just an opportunity. That he could end up doing nothing more than performing a benefit concert and Isabel writing him a lovely thank-you note. There was a man named Nate Potter, someone who, in a heartbeat, could render him meaningless. He sucked in a breath, the image harsh in his head. Aidan rubbed a hand around the snake, expecting to find an ink-stained hand. It wasn't the obvious that haunted him: body art, marketing tool, branding, sexy fodder, a universal danger sign in the world of rock 'n' roll, but the symbolism about which he'd been warned. Neither the snake nor Isabel was ever going away. Aidan was aware of the uncharted future. For a guy who'd never suffered a bout of stage fright, the approaching moment was wildly unnerving. He couldn't recall the last time anything had sparked such a buzz in his soul. It was never money or fame or even thousands of people screaming his name—it was always Isabel. Exactly as he'd told her. As the plane pushed east, on a physical course bound for Providence, Aidan leaned back and closed his eyes, praying for the same destination.

CHAPTER TWENTY-SIX

Providence, Rhode Island

NORMALLY, TANYA AND MARY LOUISE WOULD BE GONE BY
five o'clock, but they'd hung around, recapping the last of
the *104.7* brainstorming ideas. A few minutes after five, they unan-
imously agreed that every reasonable option had been exhausted.
At the very least, they would go down together.

"I guess that's it," Mary Louise said, straightening an unusually
disheveled desk. "I'm going to tell Joe everything tonight." She
smiled at Isabel. "Did I tell you that his brother's fishing business
in Florida has really taken off? Maybe tonight we can talk about
how nice it would be to spend next winter there."

"Florida. That means you'd have to move."

"It's just an idea, Isabel."

"But Joe gets seasick, which is why he stuck to building boats,
and you fry like a lobster," she said, a hand flailing at Mary Louise's ghostly skin.

"There's always Dramamine and 80-plus sunblock. We're only
exploring our options, even if it means relocating. Maybe this is
for the best. I happen to know a gem of a guy who'd love it if you
changed your address."

Finishing a cup of coffee, a hum rang from Isabel's throat. Before she could add words, Tanya cleared hers, drawing their attention. "I, um, meant to say something before, Isabel. I'm sorry my theory about Aidan was so off the mark. I just thought . . . Well, we all know I'm the last person who should be tossing around her two-bit theories on romance."

"It's okay, Tanya. Obviously, I couldn't have been more wrong about him—across the board. No harm done." Isabel turned in her chair, round-filing scraps of paper where hope had been scribbled.

"I've got to get going too. Big Eddie has all three kids. He's been a huge help with the midnight oil we've been burning. He really was the best of the lot."

"He was," agreed Mary Louise. "If only he could have quit taking the rent money to Foxwoods."

"If only," Tanya wondered, her romantic ideals decidedly intact.

"Oh, I nearly forgot," Mary Louise said, moving a stack of papers. "Patrick called while you were in with Rudy." Another hum radiated out of Isabel, having delivered their epic fail to a dismayed station manager. "He asked if you'd call him back on his cell."

It barely registered. Her mind was still reeling from the letdown of not coming through. "Okay, I'll call him." Retrieving her cell phone from her purse, Isabel saw three missed calls from Patrick. "Damn," she murmured, "how did this end up on silent?" Isabel sat up straighter, trading an anxious glance with Mary Louise. "With everything going on here, I haven't talked to my dad since early last week. Patrick probably just wants to know what's up."

"Yeah, that's probably it," Tanya said, smoothing a crumpled Dunkin' Donuts napkin. "I'm sorry; I forgot too. He called this morning. I was here early thinking my contact from *JMX-Classic Rock* in Dallas might have left a message. I wasn't awake." She handed her the chocolate-smeared napkin, Isabel reaching for a more reliable landline. A call to Patrick went straight to voicemail. A call to her father brought the same result. She dialed Nate. When that went to voicemail, she tried his apartment. He was supposed to be off after spending the weekend on call. She almost hung up when a woman answered. There was a brief exchange, Nate having mentioned that Jenny would be in town. She'd spent the last year living out of a duffel bag, and she was coming by to collect the rest of her things. After identifying one another, she said that Nate had returned to the hospital early that morning. It was all Isabel needed to hear.

"I can stay," Mary Louise said. But her tote bag was in one hand, a pile of Sunday circulars that Tanya brought in bulk stacked in the other. With three children to gather, Tanya was already at the door.

"No, it's okay." Dialing Patrick, she missed a number and started over.

Mary Louise turned as she exited the office. "Call if you need me. You know . . ." she said, backing out the door. But before Isabel could reply or dial she heard Tanya gasp. It was like she'd seen a ghost or a unicorn or maybe a snake. Waxy circulars flew through the air, wafting around the doorway. There was an audible "Oh my God!" from Mary Louise as Isabel rushed to the door. Crouched outside were three bodies, one wearing a ball cap. It was a tight huddle, everyone grabbing for the loose pages of Sunday circulars.

"Here, sorry, let me help. I didn't see you ladies coming." Isabel propelled backward—about seven years—one, two, three giant steps, until her backside was pinned against the desk. She summoned every form of apathy. But the voice in the air was having none of that, challenging indifference. "I'm looking for Isabel . . . Isabel Lang."

"There . . . in there," Mary Louise squeaked.

Isabel's fingers gripped the desk's edge. Her heart pounded out an old coded rhythm, her brain insisting it was residual and passé. A thought flashed through her head, something about running away to Las Vegas or Boston. But before she could breathe another breath, or locate a safe exit, it happened. She and Aidan were face-to-face.

His eyes were brighter than she remembered or maybe it was the Dodger blue of the ball cap he wore. It struck her as odd. Isabel didn't recall Aidan being the ball-cap-wearing type. He grinned, revealing something she did recognize, a feature stitched to that runaway rhythm. "Hello, Isabel."

"Aidan," she said, though it came out raspy and unsure.

"Sounds like you haven't said that in years, or maybe even thought it."

"Oh, I don't know about that," she said, glancing at documentation that confessed as much. She wanted to burn the evidence. Clearly, old habits died hard.

"My, um . . . Stella . . ." She watched him draw a deep breath. She couldn't read him, like a forgotten parlor trick, and she hung tighter to the cold metal edge of the desk. "My mother gave me your message." Before she could reply with, *"That's okay, I already got the one from Anne,"* he changed the subject. "You look . . . You're as pretty as the night of the gala." There was a slight bob to her head. "I'm sorry," he said, sounding as if he'd come all that way to say as much. "I never told you that night, and I should have."

"Didn't you?" she said, lying. "Well, nothing really went as expected that night. Did it?" He smiled at humor that seemed to have lost its rhythm. "Your mother, how is she . . . Stella?"

"She's great. She lives in Boca Raton."

"I know. I mean, I thought of it after I tried Catswallow information. I remembered that she talked about Boca, that your dad left her the condo. It was a shot in the dark. There weren't too many ways of getting a hold of you. You, um, changed your cell number."

"A few hundred times."

"I'm sure. Anyway . . ." She stopped, not wanting to review any more desperate measures. "I hope I didn't bother her."

"You didn't. She'd been away in Hawaii with some friends."

There was a nod from Isabel, anxious to conclude six-degrees of separation from Aidan Royce. "I figured the one thing you'd take care of would be Stella." There was a pause, the remark hitting the air more accusatory than complimentary. "I mean, I bet she's seen the world thanks to you."

"The better resorts anyway. You know Stella. Give her an umbrella drink and a conga line. But you're right. It's been one of the perks, doing that for her. She called with your message."

"My message," Isabel repeated, as if one of them was speaking another language.

"Yes, your message. That you, um, needed me."

Isabel blinked wide, her bottom slumping onto the desk. For a second she was utterly confused. Anne and her entourage had made things perfectly clear. Then she recalled the exceptions to the Aidan Roycroft rules, honor thy mother being the only item on the list. Scattered sweet Stella always had a soft spot for Isabel, and her son was standing there out of respect for his mother, maybe a good browbeating—something she might dole out if Aidan showed too much swagger. Suddenly, her message to Stella seemed more pathetic than her Hail Mary pass to Fitz. "Okay, even so, I thought you'd call . . . like, on the phone," she said, pointing to the one on the desk. Her fingers flitted fast, tucking her hair behind her ear. "And what do you mean, *I needed you*?" She untucked her hair, deciding she didn't care for the sound of that.

"That's what she said. That you needed me to come right away."

"I didn't say any such thing." Isabel popped up from the desk and scooted around to the inside. "I only asked if you could call back."

"Okay, either way," he said. "Here I am. You know it's not my nature to do things halfway. I took it as urgent, your need to see me."

"Urgent?" she said. "You flatter yourself, Aidan."

"All right, pressing. A pressing need to see me."

"Important. Maybe, just maybe, I used the word *important*."

"Fine," he said, teeth gritted. "Important!"

"Wow, would you listen to that." Their heads snapped simultaneously toward Tanya. "Sorry. I've just always wondered what it would take for someone to get on Isabel's last nerve—and so quickly." In reply Aidan pulled the cap from his head, Isabel rolling her eyes. Apparently, deep-rooted Southern manners had survived Aidan Royce.

"This is Tanya Mariano and Mary Louise . . . Mary Louise . . ."

"Bland," she prompted.

"Bland . . . of course. They work with me; I work with them."

"Ladies, nice to meet you. Sorry, again, about the traffic jam. My fault."

They offered mouth-gaping greetings, Tanya continuing with unfiltered thoughts, "Gosh, that tattoo does make a statement, especially in person."

"Isabel gets the credit," he said, glancing at her. "Just one of a thousand incredible things that happened in Vegas . . . that summer." She listened to Aidan make small talk, standing there as if he popped into her office every evening at five.

"Funny, that's kind of the way Isabel told it."

"She told you . . ."

"Everything," Tanya assured him. Isabel felt her face blush, recalling the level of detail she'd shared with Tanya. His face showed a sudden look of surprise, Isabel guessing he was trying to summon the obscure memory.

"To be honest, if you add it all up, I'm not even sure the tattoo makes the list."

"You can say that again." Feeling like a footnote, Isabel arranged a pile of papers bound for the shredder. "Like he said, it was a year full of shockers."

"Isabel, I—"

She looked up, seeing a hard swallow bob through his throat. Her eyes locked on the tattoo, the thick line of his neck, and the smoothness of his skin and something inside her softened. She looked away, her glance bouncing from wall to wall. "Aidan," she said, focusing on her desktop, "what, for the love of God, are you doing here?"

"I told you, my mother called and said that you needed me. I just—"

"Stop saying it like that," she said, eyeballing him, any waver of indifference halted. "It wasn't like I called your mother, hysterical, desperate to see you!"

"Okay—well, you did call."

"Yes, I suppose."

"And you said that you needed me?"

"I said I needed your help."

"So here I am," he snapped. "Do you think this was easy, Isabel? Do you have any idea what it took for me to come here?"

"Why? Am I interrupting the wild life and times of Aidan Royce? Though I appreciate the risk, wasn't crossing state lines a condition of bail?"

"That was last time," he shot back, narrow-eyed glares passing between them. "Seriously, Isabel, whatever's happened between us, did you think that if you ever called I wouldn't come?"

Her lips pursed tight, eyes welling. "In a million years," she said, arms wrapped in a straightjacket grip, "I never thought I'd call."

"I see," he said, a deeper bob riding his throat. A taut thread of silence wove through the room. It was like barbed wire. The phone rang, granting a reprieve, and Isabel snatched it up. As she listened, her gaze tangled with Aidan's. It was the draw of a magnet, the pull of the tide, or maybe something stronger, like their past. As the sentences sunk in, Isabel's heart thundered, no longer startled by Aidan's impromptu presence but with absolute fear.

"Isabel? What's wrong?" She shook her head, holding up a hand.

"When?" she demanded. "Why didn't he— Yes, of course, I'm on my way. I'm not sure how long." Cradling the phone with her shoulder, she reached for her purse and rummaged for a set of keys. "Rush-hour traffic . . . I don't know." Aidan grabbed the purse and instantly produced the Mass General key ring that held them. "I'll be there as quick as I can. Tell . . . tell him I'm coming." Isabel hung up the phone—twice—fumbling frantically with the receiver. While grabbing the keys and running was not only appropriate but necessary she looked to Aidan, plainly telling him what she needed, "It's my father. I have to get to him."

CHAPTER TWENTY-SEVEN

Boston

WHETHER IT WAS TIMING OR FATE OR THE SITUATION HE'D set in motion, Aidan didn't question it. Isabel truly needed him, and he was determined to move heaven and earth to help. Her instinct was to drive, but Aidan held tight to the keys, countering. "I can get you there faster," he said, dialing Henry. But his plane was sidelined for routine maintenance and unavailable. It was unacceptable. Superstardom had its advantages, and Aidan didn't hesitate. He called Kai, telling him to find alternate transportation—pronto. By the time they arrived at the airport a small private plane was waiting. Aidan was relieved when Isabel didn't argue, doubly so when she didn't object to him boarding with her. In an instant circumstances had changed, even from their days in Catswallow when she had the answer to everything. For the first time, Aidan was in control, Isabel willing to depend on him for something. Something as important as this.

The small twin-engine charter was modest, the rumble of engines keeping conversation to a minimum. She conveyed a few details during the bumpy flight, filling in the years he had missed. Isabel reconciled with Eric Lang years ago, telling Aidan about her relationship with him and Patrick Bourne. "I was so stupid . . . so wrong."

"You were a kid," he insisted, "you didn't understand. Certainly, your mother was no help."

Still, she couldn't completely shake the shame on her face. "Patrick is amazing, kind, funny . . ." And through the shame she smiled. "They turned out to be the two most capable parents a person could ask for."

"I'll be damned, two competent, present parents. There really is such a thing."

"There really is. Right under my nose the entire time. And when I think of how much of it I wasted."

"But you did find it, Isabel. I'm glad you did," he said. "Even if I'm a little envious." But he wasn't sure she heard, having turned toward the window. Slowly, she looked back.

"Boston, that's where I went when I left Las Vegas . . . that night."

She couldn't hear the hum from his throat or thought in his head: *I know what night, Isabel, like I could ever forget.* She went on to say that they'd been lucky. Medication had kept her father's disease at bay. She talked about how lupus could be unpredictable, difficult to manage. She credited a terrific team from Mass General for overseeing Eric's care, Aidan listening and absorbing until she got around to Nate Potter.

"He's your father's doctor?" he asked, hoping that maybe he had it all wrong.

"Yes, and . . ."

"And something more?" She nodded; he breathed.

"Before all this, everything at the radio station, life had its challenges, but overall it was pretty perfect. Nate had just asked me to come live with him in Boston."

And for a moment, breathing was pointless. "I see."

Isabel's fingers wove through her hair as she spoke, explaining that Patrick had been trying to reach Isabel all day. In the ruckus of the radio station crisis, with Tanya and Mary Louise on the verge of joblessness, his messages were lost in the shuffle. There was guilt in her voice, though it didn't match the wave of bad karma Aidan was feeling. If she knew he was responsible for the radio station chaos—well, he suspected Aidan Royce would be freefalling from about ten thousand feet. At the moment he appeared little more than his hype, nothing but a spoiled self-absorbed rock star. No better, slightly worse, than the teenage boy Isabel had so often directed and corrected. He looked past her into blank blueness. Regardless of Nate Potter, Aidan was determined to prove otherwise.

As the plane neared Logan, Isabel conveyed the brunt of her conversation with Patrick. The disease had flared radically and Eric was admitted to the ICU of Mass General last night. Upon landing in Boston, Aidan didn't burden her with any more questions. Instead, he took charge of the situation and made certain that a car was waiting. Isabel said nothing as they walked through the crowded hospital, stares and comments following. *"Hey, aren't you . . ."* exclaimed the first fan, a woman who followed Aidan and Isabel around the revolving door. *"Oh my God, it can't be . . ."* said another, trailing them as the man she was with was wheeled in the opposite direction. Aidan flipped up the collar of his jacket, sticking close to Isabel, yanking the ball cap low. From behind dark sunglasses he kept them moving. As they boarded the elevator, two women pirouetted off in unison. *"You're . . . you're . . ."* one stammered, pointing at the tattoo—a permanent calling card.

"You know, I'm not," he said. "And for the life of me, I can't figure why people keep asking." Aidan rammed his fist against the elevator buttons. Never did he wish more to be no one. He recanted as the floor clicked by. Being someone got them to Mass General in record time.

He thought Isabel, rightfully distracted, was oblivious. But before the elevator doors opened, she said, "Sorry, I should have picked a less conspicuous spot."

"Who knew?"

"I did," she said, moving quickly down the corridor.

At the hall's end, they had to be buzzed inside. Moving toward the ICU desk, Aidan was relieved to find it relatively empty. Isabel hung a sharp right as a tall bearded man emerged from a room. Patrick Bourne appeared as Aidan might have imagined: the type who didn't ruffle easily. Yet, in this instance, he seemed ruffled all the same.

"Isabel, thank God," he said, rushing toward her. She fell into his arms—or he into hers. Aidan lingered behind, unsure if he belonged. "I'm so glad you're here," Patrick said, a quake in his voice. "He's going to be furious with me for calling you, but it was the right thing to do."

"How is he?" she asked, eyes flicking toward the door. "Never mind, I'll just go see for myself." She smiled. "Don't worry; I'll take the hit for coming." But before there was forward motion, Patrick had his hand firm on her arm.

"Isabel, wait." There was universal caution in his voice, and she pivoted sharply as Aidan drew closer. "I didn't tell you everything on the phone. In case you were driving, I wanted you to have a clear head. Eric is significantly more ill than I let on."

"What? How . . . how sick?"

"Things haven't been good for the last few weeks. I argued; Nate argued. We insisted he tell you, but he refused. You knew this was a possibility, that eventually the meds could stop working or the lupus could spiral out of control. Unfortunately, both things seem to be happening at once. I . . . I'm sorry."

Isabel's head cocked. "You're sorry. Sorry you didn't tell me? Or sorry there's nothing anyone can do?"

"Both," he said, folding her into an embrace. Aidan watched what Isabel couldn't see, the morose pain on Patrick Bourne's face. His eyes closed tight, his lanky body cocooning hers. It seemed meditative, a gathering of strength. He breathed deep before letting go, delivering the rest. "The past two days have been a domino effect. It began with a terrific headache. Last night there was paralysis, which brought us here, and now there's some loss of vision. They're doing what they can, but the outcome doesn't look good."

"No!" She retreated fast, backing into Aidan. Doubt vanished. This was exactly where he belonged. Instinctively, his hands clasped her shoulders. Patrick's eyes brushed over his, an unaffected glance telling him he was no one. Aidan's hands gripped tighter. "You said he was in the hospital. You didn't . . . You didn't say he might die!"

"I thought it best to relay the worst of it once you were here. There was no point in—"

"Where's Nate?" she demanded, and Aidan nearly let go. "He would have told me if it was really that bad. He would have . . ." She paused, hands wringing together. "No, he wouldn't have."

"Over the years, your father and I talked about what he wanted or, more to the point, didn't want if we found ourselves in this moment. He'd say, 'I'm a lucky man, Patrick. If I'm really lucky I'll die of old age. If not, I'd like to get hit by a line drive at Fenway or struck by lightning—something quick. But if it doesn't go that way . . .'" Patrick took another deep breath, this one shaky on the exhale. "He said if it came down to this, exactly this, he didn't want to linger. He didn't want to suffer. I've been talking to doctors nonstop; Nate included." Aidan looked toward the glassed room, getting a glimpse of the man in the newspaper photo. "Right now, the only thing we can do is honor his wishes."

With Aidan behind her, Isabel placed her hands in Patrick's. "This is impossible! I saw him only a few weeks ago. He looked tired but okay. We had a great time, the four of us . . . your birthday dinner." Aidan watched her hands lock tighter with Patrick's. "You insisted on cooking yourself because you had a new recipe. You said you were dying to try it, butterflied prawns in oyster sauce . . ." The ramble stopped, her hands breaking away. "You cooked because he was too ill to leave the brownstone!"

"More than anything, he wanted to spare you from this. He kept insisting that it was a bad flare and that it would subside." Aidan could feel her body tremble beneath his hands. He wanted to gather her tight in his arms, but he didn't dare move.

She was quiet, a groan of realization seeping from her throat. "You're sure?" she said. "Nate . . . he's sure? I know you, Patrick. You're so good at taking care of him. There must be something you can do," she pleaded. "You love him. You don't want him to die."

Aidan was amazed by what he was witnessing. The bond Isabel shared with these two men. The miraculous recovery of a relationship with a father whose letters she'd burned. "Isabel, I'm so sorry," he said, his mouth pressing into the top of her head. On his words, Patrick Bourne's fraught face met with his, as if seeing Aidan for the first time.

"I . . . I want . . . I need to go in. Is he conscious?"

"In and out. They have him sedated."

"Is he in a lot of pain?"

"No, he's comfortable. Nate's seen to that. I've made sure of it."

Barely a body width separated Aidan from Isabel. She inched back, pressing tight to him. Aidan would have given anything to hang on, anything to change her immediate future. She broke free, marching to the door of Eric's room, turning back around.

"How long until . . . ?"

"We don't know."

Isabel pushed her posture tight, a nod of solidarity passing between the two. Then she disappeared inside. Aidan watched as Patrick's hands scrubbed over his bearded face, rubbing around the back of his neck. Rumpled dress clothes cloaked his tall frame. A sure sign that he'd spent the night in them. On the ring finger of his left hand was a white-gold band. You couldn't miss it. That and the sober look anchored to his face. With Isabel gone, Aidan wasn't sure how to proceed. He started to say something. But the moment was too personal, his presence too complicated. He headed for a single chair set in a dim corner of the waiting room.

"What the hell are you doing here?"

He spun back around. Patrick's hand was still crooked around his neck, his voice as sharp as his glare. They'd spoken once, years ago. Aidan had called the brownstone, Patrick answered. In a sharp exchange he told Aidan that he was speaking as Isabel's legal representative, and that Aidan could go to hell. He supposed it made formal introductions a moot point. "It's, um, it's a long story. I . . . Let's just say I thought Isabel needed me. Thankfully, I was there when she really did."

Patrick's face turned more serious than it had in the minutes before. And Aidan was surprised that this was possible. "I don't understand. I can't imagine any reason Isabel would want you here. Have you been in contact with her?"

"Not before five o'clock today. I came to see her about something—something that doesn't matter compared to this. I just happened to be at the radio station when you called."

"You just happened . . ." he said, a hand sweeping past. His tone was decisive, in charge. "And she asked you to come with her?"

"I brought her here," he said, avoiding a direct reply. "I was able to get us a quick flight up, a fast ride to the hospital. I wanted to help, to make sure she's all right."

Patrick took a step in his direction, giving Aidan the distinct impression he was about to receive a hard right cross to his jaw. But instead of connecting to his face, Patrick's fists drew to his waist. "You want to help? Make sure she's all right?" he asked, incredulous. "Seven years later, and you want to what? Make sudden amends for being a complete ass?"

"Excuse me, but how was I—"

"Thanks, but Isabel's done fine without you. She'll get through this . . . Nate," he emphasized, "will get her through this. She doesn't need you."

"Just the same, I'd rather let Isabel make that call."

"You devastated her once." Sure that Patrick was referring to his and Isabel's wedding night, Aidan looked away. He could only imagine what it took for her to confide something so awful, not only to her father but to Patrick, two men she'd disavowed before that night. "You won't hurt her again," Patrick said. "Especially in the middle of this!"

"This isn't the time or place. I get that," Aidan said, an ugly glare passing between them. "Isabel and I . . . Look, I've made plenty of mistakes when it comes to us." He pulled the ball cap from his head. It was a symbolic effort, as if opening himself up to any argument Patrick Bourne wanted to make. "I'm incredibly sorry for what's happening to Isabel's father, to both of you. But you don't understand what's happening here, so let me be blunt: I love Isabel. I've been in love with her since we were kids back in Catswallow. I've spent years honoring Isabel's wishes. But I can't do it anymore. I . . . I had to take a chance—long shot that it is. She needs to know that. The divorce was a mistake."

Patrick sneered, backing up a step. "Are you for real? What's the matter, did you run over all the women in the fast lane? Maybe you're having a quarter-life crisis, a sudden urge to improve your image? Forget it—hire a better publicist. You're not doing this. When that man in there dies, which is almost a certainty, Isabel becomes my responsibility," he said, pounding a thumb to his chest. "And I promise you, on Eric Lang's last breath and mine, I won't allow you the opportunity to make this worse. Do you get what I'm saying?"

"I hear you. I swear, nothing could be further from my mind. Our timing, it's always been an issue—never, exactly, perfect. But I'm glad I showed up when I did. Just let me be here for her, let me help. Let me prove to you that I have no intention of hurting Isabel."

A fierce look softened as if he might grant Aidan an inch of trust. Then it vanished. "Get out. Take your ego, and your money, and your fame and get the hell out of her life before there are two dead men on this floor. She doesn't want anything to do with you!" He turned, stalking toward Eric's room.

Looking past Patrick's frame, Aidan saw that there was every chance he was right. A chunk of his soul rattled and cracked, watching Isabel find comfort in Nate Potter's arms. Maybe it was where she belonged. Maybe he wasn't anything more than Patrick saw, a self-absorbed ass who had fact and fantasy so confused he couldn't grasp basic reality: Isabel didn't want him on their wedding night. She didn't want him now. Humiliated, he stood in the empty waiting room as Patrick turned back, taking a last pass at him. "Believe me, she got your message seven years ago." It was all Aidan could do to move his eyes from Isabel and Nate and onto Patrick. "Hear hers and go back to wherever you came from."

From nowhere or from deep inside, Aidan wasn't sure which, he asked, "What message?"

Patrick barreled back around, storming across the waiting area. He came at Aidan, shoving him hard into the wall. "You fucking prick. You're right. Your timing is incredible. Tell me something, is it fate or do you make it a point to be a party to the worst moments of Isabel's life: her father's death, Rick Stanton nearly raping her, and the one where you so eloquently conveyed that she meant nothing to you. Lucky me, I got to deliver your heartfelt kiss-off. I'll never forget the look on her face. Isabel stood there, her own divorce papers in hand, signed for the sole purpose of keeping your sorry ass out of jail." His head shook, sneering. "You couldn't even allow her a moment of dignity. You had to plow ahead on your own, wanting out of the marriage so instantly, so badly!"

For a moment it didn't register. Aidan was divorced from Isabel. It was a fact he did not dispute. But as Patrick let go, backing off, the wording rang in his ears. "What the fuck do you mean, *I wanted out . . . ?*"

Hit him. Aidan was sure that Patrick's intent was to hit him. But as he reared back, taking aim at the forked tongue of the snake, Isabel rushed from her father's room. "Patrick!" she called as a swarm of medical personnel thundered past, oblivious to Aidan Royce.

CHAPTER TWENTY-EIGHT

ERIC LANG DIED QUICKLY, AND HIS DAUGHTER TOLD HERSELF TO be grateful. He didn't linger or waste away for months like many victims of lupus. He died of a sudden stroke. The massive blood clot that killed him was the more merciful of many plausible scenarios. While Isabel and Patrick did not get their wish, Eric got his. It was quick and painless.

Privately, she'd considered this day, thinking it would be reflective. Something dignified, as that is what Eric would have wanted—maybe the Sox game playing in the background at a gathering in his honor. But with every ring of the phone the vision lost traction. It wasn't a complete surprise when her mother called saying she wanted to attend the funeral. The two were high school sweethearts. She was married to the man for a dozen years. They shared a child. She'd never stopped loving Eric Lang. The ferocity with which she pushed him away proved it. Indifference, not hate, was the opposite of love, and it was one emotion Carrie never could claim. Gently, Isabel approached Patrick, asking how he would feel if her mother was there. Standing in his and Eric's bedroom, his generous nature never faltered. "Your mother couldn't make peace with it during his life. Let her come and make peace with it now. Your father would be glad for that." Then he handed Isabel a blue suit and gold speckled tie, "This one, I think." But the request took a turn for the surreal when Carrie told Isabel that she would need two hotel rooms. The entire Stanton clan, including Rick, Strobe, Trey, and Jack was piling in a very customized Stanton Motors van and driving north. It made logistical sense. Rick couldn't care for Jack alone; his wife couldn't manage him and his wheelchair, not in a big city, not without help. Resigned to it, Isabel made a reservation at a hotel with a beautiful waterfront view.

After speaking with Mary Louise, surreal took a turn for the bizarre. Coming out of her father's hospital room, Isabel suspected she'd endured some sort of mental break. The waiting room was vacant, Aidan gone. She'd read how the mind could go to astonishing lengths to protect itself from pain: men lost at sea for weeks, satisfied by repeating favorite recipes aloud, able to smell the food. Traumatized children retreating to a world of fantasy, immersing themselves in make-believe. Maybe that happened to her. Maybe in the midst of a horrific moment, Isabel's mind projected a person whose presence had, once, so thoroughly protected her. She was quick to accept the theory, especially when Patrick never mentioned his name. But Mary Louise set things straight: Aidan Royce's presence wasn't a figment of her imagination. If he was, then they'd all been sucked through the same matinee idol portal.

On the morning of the funeral, as she waited for Patrick, Isabel found she wasn't the only one wondering what had become of Aidan Royce. Flipping past a TV channel dedicated to celebrity gossip, a perky blond anchor—perky hair, perky breasts, perky gleam— reported from California. Apparently, Aidan Royce was MIA there too. Rumor had it that even C-Note Music couldn't get in touch, anxious to re-sign their biggest icon. Sources reported that he and his attorney fiancée were entertaining options as they vacationed on a private island somewhere in the South Pacific. The anchor went on to say that the DUI and assault charges had been dropped. It was the second time, to Isabel's knowledge, that charges against Aidan had come and gone without incident. As Patrick came downstairs, Isabel rushed to turn the television off. He'd never been a fan.

"Isabel, are you ready?" His image was striking, never a hair out of place, the beard always trimmed to a scholarly look. He looked particularly dignified this day in a black suit and silver tie. He was calm, centered, and flawless, the essence of Patrick Bourne. And if Isabel had to endure this day, she knew it was a blessing to have him by her side.

"Ready as ever," she said, pulling a sweater on over a dark blue dress. Like many wardrobe choices, Patrick helped her pick it out. In the midst of their common misery, the two had taken refuge in the mall in Boston's Prudential Center. For a short while they roamed from store to store, the public place offering half-off sales and a sense of normal. Everything was fine until Isabel tried on the dress, a wraparound style that flattered her. She asked Patrick what he thought.

"It's lovely. Your father will . . . Would," he corrected. "Eric would have thought you look lovely . . ." He turned and rushed out of the store. Isabel found him a short time later, visibly shaken, his vibrant brown eyes edged in red. He stared into a store window overrun with Red Sox paraphernalia. Patrick, who owned season tickets, didn't give a damn about the Red Sox.

The church service was beautiful and without incident. Carrie arrived just before it began, relegated to a rear pew. It wasn't a marker of her importance but because that's where the narrow aisle dictated she and Rick sit. Trey avoided eye contact while Strobe offered a sympathetic smile. They corralled Jack, keeping him quiet during the service. The small church was crowded. Episcopalian, Isabel thought. Patrick attended there regularly; her father was never much for God. Staring at the casket, Isabel prayed he was wrong about that.

Aside from her mother, the church was filled with Eric's

co-workers, professors, and students from Boston University. Patrick also had ample supporters, both friends and colleagues. Nate sat next to Isabel with Tanya and Mary Louise seated behind them. There was a smattering of relatives, including Eric's sister, who Isabel had not seen in years. Patrick leaned over and asked if that was Denise. While the two had never met, he recognized her from photographs. Isabel nodded, appalled by her pious presence. Closing her eyes as organ music grinded, Isabel thought how truly ashamed she was to be related to her. Nate held tight to her hand— or she to his—as they made their way to the gravesite.

This part was a private gathering, even Carrie saying she would see them afterward. With so many people in the church Isabel was glad for the tiny group. There was the real possibility that Patrick's stoic nature would be permission for hers to come undone. She managed to hold it together, even as they said their final goodbyes. Mercifully, it was brief, as she could not imagine her father wanting anyone lingering for the sake of tradition. "Doing okay?" Nate asked, helping her into the waiting limo. "As long as you're here," she said. But as she answered, Isabel's eyes skimmed the cemetery's edge, finding nothing but the dead.

Patrick made arrangements for a gathering at the Back Bay Bistro, his choice as eclectic as it was intentional. The restaurant was the perfect complement to himself and Eric, an informal ambiance with an upscale wine list—a TV at the bar, which could be seen, if seated just so, from the dining room. Fate was kind enough to color the moment, the Red Sox playing an odd day game. An hour in and Isabel lost Patrick to the swell of well-meaning guests. Nate had to stop by the hospital, he'd rejoin them shortly. Isabel said goodbye to Tanya and Mary Louise, who needed to get back to Providence. They'd brought a suitcase of belongings, Mary Louise saying that she'd taken Rico home for the time being. Isabel was appreciative but unable to envision Mary Louise negotiating a litter box. They didn't mention the radio station, though Isabel knew they were dying to ask about Aidan. It wouldn't have mattered if they had. She had nothing to say, other than it was another episode of unpredictable behavior from one of the world's biggest artists.

And that's how Isabel was starting to think of him. Not as her best friend from Catswallow or momentary husband or even someone there to protect her from the unthinkable, but someone bigger than life who'd wandered into an all too real situation. Aidan managed to get her to Mass General before Eric died, and perhaps that was all he was meant to do. He owed her nothing—including a one-night-only show. If that wasn't clear via Aidan's sudden appearance and even more abrupt departure, Anne Fielding had crystallized things. After her visit, when no one was looking, Isabel googled them, finding dozens of images that illustrated the relationship Anne described. Isabel saw the glamorous couple at red-carpet events, moving on to candid photos depicting more private moments. She'd clicked it closed, feeling like a pathetic voyeur. Cursing misty eyes and a wedge in her throat, she'd blamed herself for breaking the rules of indifference.

Standing alone in the crowded restaurant, there was no choice but to move on to the other side of her family. Carrie had kept a polite distance from Patrick, which also meant that Isabel had barely spoken to her mother. Trey and Strobe lingered near Rick, Carrie meeting her halfway.

"Isabel," she said, hugging her daughter tight. "How are you doing?"

"I'm okay. Patrick's been a tremendous help." She didn't think before she said it, the statement being a natural response. "Nate's been great too," she quickly added. "I'll introduce you as soon as he gets back."

"I'd like that. You've been talking about him for what, a year now?"

"He was Dad's doctor before . . . And we were friends before anything . . ." She fidgeted, tugging at the dress, arms folding and unfolding. "We've been dating for about eight months."

"Oh, that is a while. Do you think he's the one, that the two of you . . ."

"Things are serious. Nate, he's asked me to move in with him."

Carrie nodded. "That's a big step. And are you?" Isabel replied with a queer look, considering the question rhetorical. "Well, I look forward to getting to know him." She glanced around a room full of strangers. "How is Patrick doing?"

"He's devastated. This is difficult for him. It will be for a very long time."

"Yes it will. From experience, I know how hard it is to lose your father. I'm very sorry this happened to him. Isabel, we've managed to fix so much between us. I'm grateful for that. And now . . . well, with your father being gone, I want you to know that I'm here for you, one hundred percent."

She was grateful too, though looking toward Carrie's entourage Isabel was still unsure how to factor in a certain percentage. She guessed it was the kind of thing you learned to live with. Rick offered a curt nod as Trey made an incidental offer of condolences. He was the image of his father, towering over Isabel. She took a step back. Strobe bridged the gap, hugging her tight. "I'm so sorry, Bella." His boyish build hadn't changed, though every time she saw him there was less blond hair on his head. Jack shot out from the back of a booth, scattering crayons.

"Isabel!" he said, barreling toward her. There was comfort in his small embrace, his inability to grasp the situation. Isabel glanced around at the loosely related group and the boy who wove the bond. Jack was adorable, more an image of their maternal grandfather, and she was thankful for that. "Are you going to come sightseeing with us? Daddy says he'll get me a real musket. Maybe we can go today if we get out of here in time. That's what Daddy said!"

Daddy. Isabel looked toward Rick, reminded of what she and Jack didn't share. *You son of a bitch, you've parlayed my father's funeral into a sightseeing trip.*

He read her mind. "He's only six, Bella. Can't expect to drag the boy on a road trip like this and not offer him something fun in return."

"No, I guess you can't." In the same instant, Jack gave Rick's comment credibility by knocking over a glass of soda. Half spilled onto the floor while the other half dripped down his dress clothes. A waitress swooped in, sopping up the mess as Carrie headed to the restroom with Jack. She offered a wary glance back, leaving the mismatched group behind. Isabel breathed deep, decidedly alone with the wheelchair-bound Rick and Trey, who stood with the presence of a pit bull. Displaying a true Stanton trait, he guzzled the last of what was surely his fourth or fifth beer.

"So that's him?" Trey slurred. He swung his empty beer mug in Patrick's direction. "That's your daddy's, um . . ."

"Yes, that's Patrick," Isabel said, wondering why she bothered answering.

Trey looked on, staring. "Geez, looks like a regular fellow to me. You'd never guess . . ."

"Guess what?" she snapped. "Guess that across the room from you stands the most intelligent, caring, well-respected man I've ever met?"

"Take it easy, Bella," Rick said, a hand thrusting at her. She instantly skirted back. "Trey didn't mean anything by that. You've got to remember, you live in a much more liberal part of the country. Folks in our neck of the woods . . . well, it's not to say his kind don't exist, but they're not as *integrated.* You should understand that."

His dominant tone was too much and everything else that occurred in Catswallow barreled back. Rick was still an imposing man, even from a permanent sitting position. Isabel stared at his paralyzed body as flashes of what, before the shooting, it had tried to do to her. Even for Jack's sake, civility was elusive. Currently, air was elusive, Isabel having trouble moving any in or out, her own legs feeling unsteady. Isabel could hear Rick's voice, hot and thick in her ear. But it wasn't him. It was Trey, loud and angry, his voice matching his father's—an evil surly pitch.

"I can't believe it. What the fuck is that bastard doing here?"

From behind wire-rimmed glasses, Strobe's milky blue eyes peeled wide. Rick strained his neck, peering into his waist-high point of view. Halfway back from the restroom, Carrie staggered to a halt, holding on to Jack as if he were holding her up. A hand rose to her mouth as she looked past her daughter's head. Isabel turned toward the maze of mourners. It was like lightning cutting into earth as Aidan made his way through the crowd. There was still a shock factor, but not quite as stunning as the first. The ball cap was gone, Aidan wearing a conservative but well-fitted suit. Even so, the rock star in him oozed out. No tie—just like the gala. But the focus tipped like a teeter-totter as Rick came into Aidan's line of vision. Any trouble reading him at the radio station was corrected, Isabel recognizing the livid look on his face. She rushed toward him.

"Let's go outside."

"What the fuck is that son of a bitch doing here?"

"Funny, they said the same thing about you. Aidan, please. I can't have a scene here. Don't do this. Please come outside with me." Isabel looked across the crowded room, relieved that Patrick was not in sight. Regardless of any wheelchair, Aidan was intent on finishing what he started back in Catswallow. Her hands pressed against his chest, shoving him in the opposite direction. It was like pushing against a locomotive. His glare shifted between Rick and Isabel, seeing the rest of the room.

"Fine," he hissed, retreating.

CHAPTER TWENTY-NINE

THERE WAS A SIDE DECK TO THE RESTAURANT. NORMALLY, IT would be packed. But it had grown cooler, a typical late-summer Boston day. "Over here," Isabel said, coaxing him from the street where she assumed the stares and interruptions would only increase. Isabel turned, speechless. Her arms jerked through the air, slapping against the fabric of her dress, stinging at her thighs. "I don't know where to start."

"Start with what's most important. How are you? How was the funeral? I'm sorry, Isabel, so sorry about your father."

Her head shook with questions, or maybe frustration. Either way, it was a hallmark reaction to Aidan that she was no longer used to. "I might buy that if you hadn't disappeared at the hospital."

"I wanted to give you some time. I didn't want to make things worse, not in that moment. My being there upset Patrick. We talked while you were in with your father. Or I should say he talked. Circumstances aren't . . ." He hesitated, his eyes glossing over her. "Something demanded my immediate attention and I had to fly back to L.A."

Fingertips pressed to her forehead, Isabel blinked, bringing the present-day Aidan into focus. "Emergency fan club meeting?" His mouth opened, though he didn't offer any further explanation. He was oddly aloof, this being the man who'd dismissed her for another life. "Aidan," she said, hands curling into fists. "What, for the love of God, are you doing here? I don't get it. You blatantly, and not so nicely, excused yourself from my life a long time ago. And now, in the middle of this, you want to what, resurrect a friendship?"

There was misplaced laughter, Aidan's hand rubbing over his square jaw. "Trust me; friendship is the furthest thing from my mind. If you would just—"

"Seriously," she said, peering toward the restaurant. "This is bold even for you. If you felt that bad, you could have just sent the world's largest floral arrangement. I certainly can't have you and my mother and Rick Stanton in the same room. The police dropped the charges years ago. But Rick and Trey, they believe that you're responsible for—"

"Well, you and I know that I'm not." The two of them traded the confounded look anchored to that night, Isabel almost telling him what Strobe had alluded to. But Aidan moved on to other things. "Besides, I could give a shit what either of them thinks. More to the point, Isabel, would you mind telling me what Stanton is doing here? Don't tell me you've made peace with what happened, because God knows I haven't."

There was that timbre to his voice, the one that sent her reeling back to their wedding night. She turned, walking to the other side of the deck. *Don't do it! Don't trip on something so out of sync with the here and now! He has a life. More important, you have a life, and it has nothing to do with him.* Isabel turned back, grasping Aidan's anger. It was nothing more than pride, an old wound. The boy who came to her defense and came away feeling he didn't do everything he should have. Some other person was walking around with the knowledge and pleasure of having shot Rick

Stanton. "No, Aidan. I haven't forgotten and I haven't forgiven him. But there is Jack to think about. He didn't ask for any of this."

"Your half-brother. He's what, about six?"

"Six, last winter. And if I can have any influence on his life, counteract Rick and his good-ol'-boy thinking, I'm willing. Jack is a great kid, despite his paternal DNA."

"I don't know how you do it, face Stanton." His hands slipped into his pockets, his focus dropping onto mildew-covered floorboards.

"Strobe is a lot of help. He's not like his father."

"Still, I don't know how . . ." Aidan's voice trailed away, Isabel seeing the teenage boy who was never as confident as his audience imagined, and this tugged at her heart. "Yes I do. Isabel the capable," he said as if this should be her tattoo. "You'll do whatever is necessary to keep someone you love on the right track."

"Maybe . . . something like that," Isabel said, knowing what she was prepared to do to keep him on the right track. "But you're right. Anytime I visit them, it doesn't bring back a lot of pleasant memories."

"Me included?"

The answer to that was too complex and she was grateful when a voice interrupted, grateful until she turned and saw Trey.

"Interesting how this worked out."

"How what worked out?"

"Roycroft being here," he said, studying Aidan. "If you think I've gone a day without considering what you did. And here you are, in plain sight, without one bodyguard or handler to see to Aidan *Royce's* safety."

"I can take care of myself."

Years had passed, but clearly Isabel didn't believe it, taking a bold step in front of him. "Go back inside, Trey. You're drunk."

"Royce," he snorted, ignoring Isabel. "Like some uptown vehicle, shiny and worth a million bucks."

"More like a hundred million," Aidan offered. "But who's counting."

Trey narrowed his eyes. "You don't deserve a dime of it. You're nothing but trailer trash from Catswallow. The only thing you deserve is a seven-by-ten cell, maybe a boyfriend not near as polished as the one inside." Isabel lunged, Aidan pulling her back. "Aw, my apologies, Bella. I ain't got no beef with him," he said, jerking a shoulder toward the restaurant. "Long as he keeps his hands to himself."

"You stupid ignorant ass! You're disgusting, Trey! Get out!"

"Not yet. We have unfinished business. Roycroft gets away with attempted murder, wins a lottery ticket life while my daddy gets to spend his in a wheelchair. There's got to be some justice. And here you are," he said, a sour look spilling over Aidan. "'Course, you're probably right at home, being morals got no place in your world. Rumor has it you lead your own depraved life."

"Whatever my life," Aidan said, "I definitely prefer it to the hate and ignorance in yours."

He sneered, a dumb grin crossing his lips. "Did you think it wouldn't catch up with you?" Trey circled around, and as he did Aidan turned too, forcing Isabel behind him.

"What is it you want, Trey?"

He raked a hand over the stubble on his chin, a beard that seemed to sprout hourly. "That's a great question. I wasn't anticipating an opportunity. Not today. But then I thought on the unique circumstance. And, well, it's a good thing I'm always prepared." He placed his hands on his hips, pushing his jacket back to reveal the gun he carried. Isabel was startled but not surprised. For Stanton men, wearing a firearm was like wearing Fruit of the Looms— you wouldn't leave home without them. Isabel scrambled to get back in front of Aidan. But now she was standing behind the locomotive, and it wasn't budging. Aidan's hands locked around her wrists, holding her there. His voice was calm, incredibly steady.

"Isabel, I'll let go if you promise me you'll go inside."

"I will not either!"

He gripped tighter, mumbling, "Thick as ever . . ."

She peered over Aidan's shoulder. "What are you going to do, Trey? Shoot Aidan Royce on the deck of the Back Bay Bistro? The spot may be private, but I'd make a pretty good witness."

"Could always shoot you both and disappear," he said as if the deck were a deer stand and they were venison stew. "I could be out of here in a heartbeat. It'd go unsolved, just like my daddy's shooting." He pulled the gun from his waistband, but didn't point it at them, examining the small silver revolver. "It would be fitting. You'd go down in your glory, in your prime. Hell, I'd be doing you a favor. There's nothing sadder than an aging rock star. Forever young, like the ones before you: Hendrix, Morrison, Jackson . . ."

"They died of drug overdoses."

Trey pointed the gun at him. "Okay, Lennon then."

For one wild second Isabel believed he was going to shoot. She jerked her arms, but Aidan's grip had turned to handcuffs. Otherwise, he was amazingly sedate, so different from the teenager that pummeled Rick. "You're not going to shoot me, Trey. You're too much of a coward. If that's what you wanted, you could have hunted me down years ago. You're nothing but a lot of bullshit—just like your daddy. Unless, of course, the prey happens to be smaller . . . weaker."

"Aidan, shut up," she hissed from behind.

"Then you might take advantage to prove your manhood. Now put the gun away, Trey, and go sober up."

"Yes, put the gun away," Carrie said, coming up behind Trey. "Are you insane? Would you like to spend the rest of your life in a Massachusetts prison?"

He didn't respond; it was a standoff of wills. "You ready to let him walk away, Carrie, after what he did? I can't believe that. Because of him," he said, wiggling the gun at Aidan, "my daddy will never walk again and you get to spend your life with a cripple. The police refused to bring him to justice. You don't want even a little revenge? Maybe I can just aim good enough to return the favor. I might be willing to do that kind of time."

Isabel squirmed from Aidan's grip, pivoting in front of him. "Don't you dare!"

Aidan shoved her aside as Carrie yelled, "Isabel, don't!" She looked toward Trey. "Put the gun away!" But Isabel could see it in his eyes; he wasn't about to take direction from a woman, particularly his stepmother. She was only agitating him, the point proven as she took a step forward and he cocked the trigger. "For God's sake, Trey, he didn't do it! Aidan didn't shoot Rick—I did."

Three gaping stares volleyed in Carrie's direction. "What . . . what the hell are you talking about?" he asked, his aim wavering. "We all know who shot him!"

"No," she insisted. "You don't. I know . . . your father knows."

"My father knows you shot him?"

"Yes, he does. He's well aware." She glanced at Aidan's and Isabel's slack-jawed faces. "It's, um, it's complicated, and I think it's best if you heard the whole story from Rick. Strobe was just getting him into the van. Go and help, unless, of course, it's your intention to shoot me."

As real as Trey's threat was toward Aidan, no one believed he would shoot his stepmother. It seemed particularly unlikely after informing them that Rick had known of her culpability since the night in question. Carrie Stanton didn't physically disarm him, but she raised enough doubt to make Trey put the gun away. Isabel exhaled, realizing that Aidan's arm was tight around her. She pushed it away, the two of them trading a bewildered gaze.

Trey exited to the parking garage, Carrie telling him to go ahead without her. She'd take a cab back to the hotel. Then she looked between Aidan and Isabel, motioning to a bench. "You'd better sit."

CHAPTER THIRTY

N EITHER AIDAN NOR ISABEL SAID A WORD DURING CARRIE'S explanation, Isabel erasing the laundry list of scenarios she'd accumulated. The most satisfying centered on a victim payback theory. Surely other women had suffered what Rick promised Isabel that night. She'd imagined one of them stumbling upon the already beaten predator. She understood how the chance at revenge would be too tempting. But Isabel never could conjure up a premise as to how one of them showed up on cue. Of course, her most realistic conclusion involved Strobe. Maybe a bloodied and beaten Rick called his lesser son after first calling Trey who was either A) in bed with the woman of the week, after wooing her with the vehicle of the month, or B) on a shooting range, honing his manhood and aim. Perhaps Strobe rushed to his father's aid, but after seeing his injured imperious father, he chose retribution over medical assistance. It would have been poetic justice, the physically frail Strobe deciding to take his father's testosterone level down a notch.

As it turned out, it was none of those things, Isabel never suspecting Rick's wife and caregiver. It took Carrie a while to explain it. Chances were she didn't come to her ex-husband's funeral expecting to confess to the current one's shooting. But as Carrie pointed out, they'd all moved on, and the time had come for her to do the same. She never used the word *lie*, but an *agreed-upon omission of facts*. She'd been called in to work, just as Rick told Isabel when she arrived at the trailer. Two hours into the emergency shift, Carrie decided to go home. Apparently, morning sickness could occur anytime of day or night. She was flabbergasted to find the trailer torn apart, Rick lying on the floor, a tooth nearby, bleeding. He was semiconscious, not completely out of it but not coherent enough to lie. "In a two-minute span I considered everything from a random intruder to a political rival with an ax to grind." From there Carrie asked a woozy Rick to tell her which one it was. He shook his head, sputtering, "Roycroft . . . Aidan Roycroft, he was all over Bella." To Carrie, this was plausible, making it easy to head down the same path that the Catswallow police would. "Rick, he was the hero. What other explanation could there be?" Then solemnly she said, "I'm sorry Aidan, but you've no idea how badly I wanted to believe that." A guilty gaze washed over her face, and she went on to admit that her initial conclusion didn't add up. "As I knelt beside him, I realized Rick smelled like every drunk I'd ever x-rayed at two a.m., reeking of blood and booze. I'd seen him that drunk once or twice. I knew he could be . . . aggressive. Then," she said softly, "I saw the greater physical evidence of what had happened. His, um, his belt was unbuckled, his pants unzipped, and I knew. I knew because of what I saw; I knew because you tried to tell me as much before the gala. There were faint sirens coming; they were nothing compared to the one in my head. I picked up the gun. I told Rick to focus, to look at me. He did, and I pointed it in his face. I said, 'Tell me what you did to Isabel or I swear I'll shoot you dead regardless.' He grabbed my wrist. He wasn't as out of it as I'd assumed. He cautioned me to think it through—Rick said we had a promising future, a baby on the way. Did I really want to put a bullet in him over one, *attempted*, regrettable act? We struggled for the gun. I won. While shooting him was a fine idea, I did hesitate. I did consider the whole circumstance. I would still be pregnant with his child and certainly not in his will. I'd have a teenage daughter, a baby on the way, and a single wide full of broken furniture—just like we spoke about that night, Isabel." Nodding, she recalled the vivid scene. "The sirens were getting closer. I had seconds to make a lifelong choice. I struck a deal with myself. I'd make Rick pay and I'd make sure it never happened again. I'd been abandoned by one man. I wasn't interested in a repeat performance. So in the end, I chose an altered state of promise. I'd seen enough bullet wounds. I had a good idea about the angle. Enough to make my point, not quite enough to kill him."

Exchanging a round of stunned looks, Isabel murmured, "You shot him?"

"I did," Carrie said, as if she'd done no more than slap his face. "Rick passed out. I left seconds before the ambulance arrived. I went out the back way and returned to the hospital before anyone missed me. The back way," she repeated, reminding them that the back way would have taken her past the farmhouse. "I stopped when I saw Aidan's truck. I knew the two of you were together." As Carrie spoke, the scene inside was repainted, giant images of two young lovers shadowing the old farmhouse walls. Isabel felt Aidan's glance. His hands were knotted, curled into two white-knuckled fists. Carrie cleared her throat for all of them, moving on. "When Rick regained consciousness, I made sure mine was the first face he saw. I laid it out for him. I told Rick to think it through. He was lucky not to be handcuffed to the bed and he was luckier still to be breathing." She looked squarely at her daughter. "He never recanted. He never once said, 'Carrie, you're wrong. I didn't try to rape your daughter.' In my life," she said, glancing at the door of the Back Bay Bistro, "I've lived with things I didn't want to know. This was, by far, the worst," she said, her chin tipping high.

Questions ricocheted through Isabel's brain. She tried to put them in order, get them out of her mouth. Aidan asked the first one, wanting to know at what point Rick and Carrie decided to hang him for the crime.

"That, in large part, is why I'm sharing this. When I saw you today, Aidan, I knew it was time." She looked at Isabel. "Maybe it was your father whispering in my ear, '*Here's your chance, Carrie . . . make it right.*' But consider things from my point of view, Aidan. What was going on inside that farmhouse, it only reinforced my conclusions. I wasn't about to let Isabel become an Aidan Roycroft casualty. I think we all recall how you went through girls faster than guitar picks." And Isabel watched the clenched fists unfurl, his arms folding tight against his chest. "Friends? Fine. But Isabel wasn't going to become *one of them*. Not if I could help it." Isabel's jaw slacked, amazed by their mutual unspoken objective. "I lived through those very feelings, inconsolable hurt and rejection. Back then, Aidan, she was so completely in love with you."

"Mom . . ." Isabel gasped, the rush of embarrassment no less had Carrie announced it when Aidan came through the door on the night of the gala.

Isabel felt him bristle at her side, Aidan clarifying, "Back then."

"As soon as the police learned you were responsible for the beating, they concluded that you shot Rick too. We never corrected their conclusion. It was that simple.

"For a while, I let it ride. I nearly convinced myself that Aidan had shot Rick and it was all . . . meant to be. But then Rick started talking about bringing Aidan to justice as if he did pull the trigger. I took a long look at the charge, knowing I was responsible. By then you were out of Isabel's life, and I wished you no further ill will. I was prepared to come forward. I'd gone to Rick's rehab to tell him that. I found two men with him. One was definitely a lawyer; he did most of the talking. I listened at the door. The other seemed like a slick businessman on a mission; he said that they were there representing *Aidan Royce's* interests. It was the first time I'd heard your new name, the life that had fallen squarely in your lap. In exchange for a retraction, a hefty donation would be made to Rick's campaign for state senator. Rick was trying to adjust, figure out his life, we all were. Knowing full well that you hadn't shot him, he was willing to use his influence to see that the charges were dropped. He took the cash, ready to throw himself into a renewed campaign. It didn't sound like an awful solution to me. Rick was satisfied with the outcome—"

"And your guilt was absolved," Aidan said.

"Trust me. You have no idea about my guilt." She stared for a moment, Isabel stunned by her precarious choices. "And that part did manage to work out fine. Surely you can't disagree. You and Isabel went your separate ways, and things turned out exactly as they should."

"Exactly as they should," he repeated.

"Not to sound stalkerish, but it's hard to miss your life, Aidan. I've seen the magazine covers, heard the stories. Seems you moved on from a town to a planet. I was right to protect my daughter. Isabel, she has a wonderful life. In fact, she was just telling me how serious things are between her and Nate—"

"Mom!"

There was restless movement from Aidan. Isabel was unable to detect a lazy shift of indifference to her love life or if it was a reaction to the fact that she had one. "I'm only saying that you have a very full life. I'm not proud of what I did to you, Aidan. You came to Isabel's rescue that night. Rick was drunk, he did a very foolish thing," she said, downplaying her husband's role of predator. "I'm grateful it didn't end worse. Please try to understand . . ."

Standing, striding to the opposite side of the deck, Aidan stared at a snaky tributary of the Charles River, Isabel suspecting he didn't.

CHAPTER THIRTY-ONE

CARRIE LEFT, SAYING SHE WANTED TO OFFER HER CONDOLENCES to Patrick. The gesture stunned Isabel, her mother never having referred to Patrick as anything but "that man." *Patrick*. So sidetracked by Carrie's bombshell, Isabel had all but abandoned him. She needed to get back inside. But her body had other ideas, lingering near Aidan who finally withdrew from his contemplative gaze. His arms dragged through the air meeting with the rich fabric of his suit. "Do you think the son of a bitch would have shot me?"

She almost laughed. It was such an Aidan response. Take the flames of disaster and reduce them to a firecracker. Despite everything, she missed that. "Seriously, Aidan, what makes you think bullets don't bounce off you?"

He did laugh, moving toward her. But the air quieted as their gaze wove as tight as the winding Charles. "Isabel—"

She stepped back, dodging him and an unexpected wallop of emotion. "Aidan, I have to—" But she couldn't remember where the thought was going, where she was going. *People are waiting . . . Patrick is waiting.* Blindsided, her mind followed her body, letting in the touch hunger he'd so completely satisfied on their wedding night. She wanted to wade further in, but rightfully so, gravity anchored wistful memories. Nate was also waiting. She'd have a fine time coming clean about Aidan Royce in the middle of this. "I have to go," she said, turning toward the restaurant.

"Don't." There was invitation in his voice, his hand on her arm.

Her eyes closed, unable to stop the thought. *Pull me closer.*

He didn't.

She opened them, seeing the snake nearly lunge with the tremendous bob that wove through his throat. He let go, his hand almost repelling. "Isabel, there's something we need to talk about." But his tone had changed, more wary than warm. "It's, um . . . it's complicated. I don't know that here is the right place." Aidan looked anxiously toward the bistro. While his outward appearance hadn't changed, there was maturity he lacked last time they were alone together.

For Isabel, old feelings unearthed. The ones she abandoned long ago. It was all the things she wanted to say that night in Vegas but couldn't. The words seemed absurdly fresh in her head. She felt like a fraud finding them there, a fist pressing to her mouth, keeping them at bay. It was just the raw emotions of the day. Weren't funerals a time to reminisce? The place to put a shiny coat of happy on the past, making you forget bad outcomes. Aidan's phone rang. She tucked a piece of hair back, grappling for calm, steadying her balance. "Aren't you going to get that?" she said, her glance cutting to the river.

He looked at the caller ID. "It's just Anne, just my—"

"Fiancée."

"I was going to say *attorney.*"

Even so, indifference met with surer ground. Aidan and Isabel, they were a Wikipedia footnote, paragraph ten, page two. They were barely worth a mention in the highly touted life of Aidan

Royce. Isabel shrugged at his surprised look. "Like my mother said, you're hardly a mystery. Even for someone who isn't following you on Twitter. Your fiancée," she said, reiterating his life, the one where she didn't belong. "I'm surprised she's not here. When we met, she seemed so very adamant about her commitment."

"Wait. You met Anne? Anne Fielding?" he said, the bridge of his annoyingly perfect nose crinkling.

"No, Anne Hathaway," she replied, retreating to the mocking banter of their youth. "But I understand your confusion. I suppose there's every chance you dated her too." He didn't respond in kind, as if he'd forgotten how. It stung more than the idea of an Anne Anybody.

"When was she here?"

"Who? Anne Hathaway?"

"Anne Fielding," he said, irritation coloring his voice.

"She showed up in Providence about a week, maybe ten days ago."

"What did she want?"

"Nothing that was a terrific shock. She came to inform us that your wildly busy calendar prevented you from helping out. You know, before your mother got to you. Of course, there was your grand donation to Grassroots Kids. My thank-you note is in the mail."

"My donation."

"Yes, your six-figure, tax-deductible, '*I don't want to look like a complete ass*' contribution. Not to sound ungrateful, Aidan, but I got the distinct impression I was being bought off."

He shook his head, muttering, "I knew that's exactly what you'd think!"

A group of Eric's colleagues approached and Isabel grasped at the safe exit. Calm and forward motion remained her best ally.

"Look," she said over her shoulder, "whatever your issue, it's not my priority. Not today. It would be better if you left."

"Isabel, if you'd just listen. I swear, you are still the most stubborn woman—"

"She asked you to leave." Through the swell of well-meaning guests Nate emerged. "Aidan Royce, correct?"

"Yeah," he snapped, "you a fan?"

"No, not really." While Isabel busied herself with condolences, an ear remained tuned in to Nate and Aidan's conversation. She assumed Nate's understated reaction was no more than celebrity recognition. Even so, he lacked shock value, as if perhaps Aidan Royce's presence was expected. "I'm Nate Potter. I was Eric's doctor. I'm . . ."

"I know who you are," Aidan said.

"Glad to hear it. I see rumor is right. Aidan Royce has crashed a funeral. But Isabel made it clear that you're an unwelcome guest. Do the right thing and respect her wishes."

"Isabel," Aidan said. "Please, this is important."

"More important than her father's funeral? I doubt that." Nate took a step in Aidan's direction. "Or does your image meet expectation, your egocentric mind unable to see any alternative to getting your own way? Stay and prove me right."

Keeping her focus on the group, Isabel couldn't help but feel Aidan's on her. "You're right about that much, Doc. I am hell-bent on getting what I want. But, as usual, the timing is all wrong." As he backed away, she glanced over, catching the icy look he pasted on Nate. "I'm very sorry about your father, Isabel. I'm sorry I never got the chance to meet him." He left, Isabel damming off the tiny holes in her heart that defied indifference.

She was glad he was gone. Glad he was no longer there to disrupt the modicum of comfort that this gathering offered. The small group departed, leaving Nate and Isabel on the deck. "Are you all right?" His fingertips rose toward her face, but he didn't make contact. "I'm not a violent man, but it would have given me great pleasure to have tossed him out on his solid-gold ass."

Her gaze panned to the exit. There was the roar of an engine, the over-the-limit speed of a sleek sports car whizzing past. "Platinum," she said, finding comfort in the rhythm of youthful banter, more so than any mourner's words. "I think when you're in Aidan's league it's platinum."

"Whatever. He shouldn't have come here. He shouldn't have upset you, today of all days." His gentle face was troubled, though his expression had turned dubious. "Isabel, I have to tell you something." Her attention turned to Nate, where it belonged. "You should know. I'm aware of your history with him . . . with Aidan."

"You are? But how? I never . . ."

"Before you and I . . . Well, your father confided in me. This," he said, motioning between Isabel and the empty air that led to the street, "bothered him greatly. Talking about it alleviated stress, which wasn't good for him."

"I can understand that. Other than sports," she said, "it was the one thing he and Patrick disagreed about. He would not have been an empathetic ear, not about Aidan."

"That's putting it mildly. Patrick would do anything to keep him from hurting you." With his hands in his pockets, Nate shrugged. "But your father felt differently, more like it was unfinished business."

And Isabel sighed, wondering which side she might have shared, had she shared anything at all. "My father was idealistic about love. He had to be; it cost him so much." Isabel poked at the deck with the toe of her shoe. "As for Aidan . . ." She looked into his expectant brown eyes. "I'm sorry I didn't tell you about him."

"Because there's nothing to tell or because there was so much left unsaid? When I first heard the story, it wasn't really my business. Now," he said, his fingertips laying claim, brushing her cheek, "before you and I go any further, I think I have a right to know."

Isabel looked toward a dimming Boylston Street. It was filled with nothing but pedestrian traffic. "It looks like everyone is leaving. Could we go somewhere, get a cup of coffee?" He nodded, Isabel pulling her sweater tight, deflecting a late-summer breeze that had turned bitter. While Nate retrieved the car, Isabel told Patrick she was leaving. She found him at the bar. Finding Carrie seated beside him, she shuffled to a halt. Each was drinking a black and tan, her father's old standby, the Red Sox game lighting the background. It was the only part that made sense. "Mom? What are you doing?"

She turned, brushing a tear. "Making peace with the past, I think." Patrick nodded as if to say any exchange had been amicable. Carrie's gaze surveyed the thinning room. "Is he . . ."

"He's gone," she said quickly. "Nate's getting the car. Patrick, I'll see you at home." He leaned over, hugging her tight. As he did, Isabel saw her mother breathe deep, living with what was.

"Let me walk you to the door." She rose from the bar stool, her hand brushing lightly over Patrick's arm. "I'm glad we spoke. It's taken a very long time to understand that Eric did love me."

"Of course he did," Patrick said, nodding.

"But he belonged with you."

While Isabel didn't think Carrie and Patrick would ever share another conversation, they'd shared a moment of respect, and perhaps that was enough. Thinking how it would have pleased Eric, her mother was mid-thought by the time she caught up.

"What I did that night, back in Catswallow, I understand that it was an extreme choice. But it was the only one I could make."

"I could see where you felt cornered, even vengeful," Isabel said, knowing she'd entertained the same word. "But it's hard to believe . . . Well, that my own mother—"

"Shot him?"

"Frankly, yes. I never realized you could be so . . . deliberate."

"Back then I lived with so much anger. Rick was the physical target. I definitely wanted him to pay. But it was also longstanding rage; other things that made me pull that trigger. Things," she said, glancing between Patrick and the empty bar stool next to him. "Things I do regret now."

"What sort of things?" Isabel said, her gaze following Carrie's.

"Nothing specific," she said quickly. "Just perspective that only time could deliver. Maybe I just wish I'd been less . . . Well, more empathetic about your father and Patrick. You and Eric could have had so much more time together."

"Yes, but so many things would have had to play out differently for that to happen. For one, if we'd never moved so far away, to somewhere like Cats—" A few paces from the door, Isabel stopped, grasping her mother's hand. Carrie turned, Isabel seeing how she stood on a path of deliberate and vengeful. It was a path that a thirteen-year-old girl might never have questioned.

"You know, honey, I'd best call a cab. Trey and Strobe can only handle Rick and your brother for so long."

"Mom?" Isabel said, plugging fresh facts into an old story. "Tell me we left New Jersey because of your job. Tell me it was only because of what you said, 'A great opportunity . . . A new start.' It was coincidence, right? That we ended up in ultraconservative Catswallow. Tell me," she said, her voice quaking, "it wasn't on purpose, a way to get back at Dad."

She tucked her own hair, the same way Isabel did when she was feeling nervous and unsure. Carrie's watery gaze wove erratically around the room. While visually she avoided her daughter, she was unable to elude the prodding ghost of Eric Lang. "Isabel, you were so young . . . impressionable," she said in a hoarse whisper. "Eric was my whole life. And I'd lost him—for good. It wasn't as if he left me for another woman; there was no hope of ever putting our family back together."

Isabel let go of her mother's arm. "It was intentional. It was never about your job or a fresh start. It wasn't even out of devastation. Taking me away was nothing more than revenge—even if we had to live in a trailer to do it! Say it! Admit it! You owe me . . . you owe Dad that much!"

"Yes," she said, arms wrapping tight around herself. "I admit there were motives that I regret now. People make all kinds of mistakes, Isabel. Some are made out of love, the kind that amount to an unexpected embarrassing moment," she said, her chin cocking at Patrick. "Others, well, they can be more calculated."

"Is that your excuse?"

"It took a long time for me to accept reality. Maybe it even took Rick's shooting, but eventually I realized what I'd done. Taking you away from Eric was wrong. Why do you think I was so okay with things when you ran from Aidan to your father?"

"I don't know," she said, a swell of anger rushing her. "Because underneath your blanket of security you knew it was absurd to force your daughter to live with the man who nearly raped her!"

"I didn't have a crystal ball into the future, Isabel. I couldn't have known your time with Eric would be cut so short." There were seconds of silence, longer than a clock might dictate. The only sound was the clinking of glasses being cleared away, voices rising and fading with a promising fly ball that ended in an out. "I can understand your anger, even shock. Just give it some time. Let's talk about this tomorrow, maybe over breakfast. Just the two of us."

"Isabel?" Nate's voice came from behind, holding open the restaurant door.

She didn't make the introduction promised earlier. She didn't even consider it. But as Nate held the exit open, Isabel offered a pitying glance back. In the eerie light of the Back Bay Bistro stood a woman, a stranger, cloaked in deliberate and vengeful. "I can't do that. I'll be busy, having breakfast with the only parent I have left."

THE SUGGESTED COFFEE TURNED INTO A BOTTLE OF WINE. EVEN SO, it was hardly a smooth segue into conversation about Aidan. Although Isabel was certain she didn't want to talk about Carrie. They began with the things Patrick had shared, Isabel reluctantly exploring Eric's feelings on the subject. "He understood what happened with Aidan as well as Patrick and I. But my father, I think because of his life experiences, was adamant about doing everything within reason to find what truly makes you happy, because . . . Well, because life," she said, toasting her wineglass, "is shorter than you think."

"And do you think Aidan Royce would make you happy?"

Isabel forced the wine down her throat, perceiving it as the most complicated question she'd ever heard. "The memories, most of them, make me happy." She turned the thought back on him. "I, um . . . I spoke with Jenny—on the phone."

He nodded, sipping from his glass. "She mentioned that."

"She's very nice. Not that I expected less. I suppose it's natural, first loves never completely fading . . . and all that nonsense. Doesn't it allow a place for the memories?" Isabel asked, tacking logic to nonsense.

"If that's all it is," he said. "Just memories."

"I think you can snag on one momentarily." Isabel reached for his hand. "But the past is still the past, Nate. I understand the difference."

A short time later, the black Audi pulled to the curb of the brownstone. It was a quiet ride until Nate's phone rang. They sat in the car as he took the call, Isabel absorbing the brownstone entry. It was as pristine as the night she'd arrived in Boston. All day she'd looked forward to escaping to its safe sanctuary. The cheery bedroom with rosebud wallpaper was home from the night she left Las Vegas until she moved to Providence years later. She'd abandoned a place that was all light and energy—one with unspeakable affect—for a place that represented peace and destiny. Neither had lived up to expectation. Catswallow, Las Vegas, Boston, Providence, or that rose-covered room, Isabel guessed she was too old to run away anymore.

"Isabel?" Nate said, opening his door. She didn't realize the call had ended. He came around the other side, opening hers. "Hang in there, day's almost over." The air was cooler now, a salty sea breeze rolling in from the not-so-distant shore. It mirrored an August night from seven years before. But as Nate walked her to the door, she was distracted by two howling cats that weren't there then, the sound of an engine revving and falling silent.

The wine and day insisted she lean. He pulled her closer. As he did, her hand brushed over the door. "It's just a workout walk from your apartment to here. Patrick will like that. I'll like that."

"Meaning what, exactly?"

"Meaning I'll be nearby after I move in with you."

"So is that a yes?"

"Nate, it's been a yes since you asked. You know that."

"Do I? You haven't answered, not in so many words. And now that the past has made its presence known, I have to wonder if he's the reason."

"Aidan? I thought we were done with that. Don't be ridiculous. I—" She hesitated, realizing that she hadn't answered him, not in so many words. But there were reasons for that. "It's been one distraction after another. All of them unpredictable. But if we're talking about Aidan, he's probably on his private jet halfway back to California, or God knows where, by now. I told you, he's a natural unavoidable memory. That's all." Her brow furrowed a tad tighter than his. "Nate, please, I can't do doubt this second. Not after today." She unlocked the door.

"Okay. No doubts." On the stoop, with his arms around her, he kissed her. It was a soft kiss that channeled naturally, from comfort to claim. The kisses grew needier, anxious. They filled the emptiness, Isabel gratefully sinking into them. She wanted Nate to be that man, the one who would console when that hardy well of calm hit bottom. The open door created a fluid path, and they turned in waltz-like fashion into the lighted foyer. An evening breeze fanned the urgency, framing their image like a picture. Nate pushed the heavy door shut. As he did, there was a roar from the Beacon Hill neighborhood, tires screeching like a drag race. Isabel listened to a sound that consumed everything. She glanced down, watching Nate's hands undo the bow, the fabric loosen as the dress fell open. His hand cupped her chin, tilting it upward to meet his steady gaze. "No doubts, I swear. Not for either of us. Not as long as moving in with me isn't code for running away from him."

CHAPTER THIRTY-TWO

IT WAS A ROUGH FLIGHT FOR AIDAN, THOROUGHLY EXACERBATING for Henry. From Boston to New York his famous employer ran a gamut of emotions, surely making Henry think Aidan Royce was either high or certifiably insane. He was besieged, if not possessed: hostile, brooding, sullen, contemplative, distraught, snarky, and, lastly, apologetic. The always-at-his-service attendant was without a remedy for his rock star boss, not that Aidan expected one. There was nothing money nor power nor celebrity could do, no quick fix, not even the kind found at the bottom of a bottle. Midflight he nearly gave in, knowing there was the full bar his entourage enjoyed. He sneered. There wasn't enough fucking liquor on the planet. Not for this. The risk was a choice. The consequences unavoidable, Aidan absorbing Isabel and Nate and passion poised at the threshold of a Beacon Hill brownstone. His gut had turned inside out, taking in the heated display, their married steps spinning into the bright light of the foyer. As Aidan leapt from the car, the brownstone door closed, shutting him out. He'd dared himself to go after her. But imagining Isabel's pitiable glare, Nate berating him again before taking the woman he loved to bed,

Aidan retreated. The opportunity to make an even bigger ass of himself had no appeal. Nothing had gone as planned. By the end of the flight, his mood had turned sullen, offering the contrite emotion to Henry as he exited.

"Don't give it another thought, Mr. Royce. I do hope whatever it is you're able to work through it."

Having knotted enough rope to either hang himself or hang on—Aidan was undecided which—he said, "At the very least, I'm going to get some answers, right the situation that's my responsibility. As for anything else . . . Well, I don't suppose this thing can fly me to another dimension?" There was only a sympathetic smile as Aidan deplaned, darting into a waiting limo.

"YOUR CALL WAS SUCH A SURPRISE," ANNE SAID, OPENING THE DOOR. "I thought you were in Monterey with your mother." Aidan's eyes skimmed over sexy lingerie that didn't translate into an evening alone with a book, which is what she'd told him on the phone. "You look upset, Aidan. What's wrong?" He circled the apartment, surveying her vintage Fabergé glass and the lifestyle that he'd vainly tried to mesh with his. "I know you don't, not usually, but do you want a drink?"

"You've no idea. But no, just club soda."

"Coming up," she said, making her way to the bar.

The entire room flickered, Aidan double-checking the skyline for a blackout. "Reading by candlelight, Anne?"

"What?" she said, filling a glass. "Oh, well, you sounded so tense on the phone. I know how candlelight soothes your mood. Here, why don't we sit?" He did, sipping fizzy water, thankful he'd beat the demon. Never in his life did he need a clearer head. "Are you going to tell me what's going on?"

"I just came from a funeral."

"I'm sorry. I had no idea. Who died?"

"Isabel Lang's father." Her willowy frame pulled tight and locked. It acknowledged her deception without Aidan ever making the accusation. "Why did you go there, Anne? Why didn't you tell me Isabel called, that she wanted to talk to me?"

"Aidan," she said, rising and circling the apartment herself. "I know what it looks like, but just hear me out. Fitz came to me—"

"Ah, now we're getting somewhere." As he surmised, it didn't take long for Aidan's self-anointed keeper to turn up in the mix.

"Fitz came to me," she repeated, lawyerly spin kicking in. "He explained your history with this woman. The one you never bothered to mention to me." They traded a cool stare, Aidan still not filling in any blanks. "Fine, have it your way. As your attorney, it's my job to make sure no one takes advantage of you. Asking for something from Aidan Royce isn't like asking your average ex if he could spare an afternoon and help move a mattress. Your celebrity is worth hundreds of millions of dollars. It keeps thousands of people employed. It has to be protected—even if I'm protecting it from you." He twisted around, Anne shrugging a delicate shoulder.

"Keep going; I'm listening."

"Isabel's inquiry was suspicious. How many times have strangers attempted to extort money or destroy your image? To us, the sudden emergence of a very real ex-wife was disconcerting. From my point of view, not only did I have the right, but I had a responsibility to act on your behalf."

Aidan nodded, maintaining his agenda. "Okay, let's say I buy that. Expand on *point of view*, because, let's be honest, Anne, yours includes more than a professional interest."

"Fair enough," she said, sitting next to him. "While Fitz was concerned by Isabel's query, he assumed it was all her idea. I, as you might guess, saw a clearer catalyst. I negotiated the purchase of that stupid radio station, Aidan. Your manic call from Kuala Lumpur, demanding I put in a mega bid on a radio station that wasn't even for sale. I thought it was rock star eccentricities. My mistake, apparently."

Culpability put him on the defensive. "It started out honest enough, as the means to an *end*—long overdue closure. No one was more surprised than me when it didn't go that way. Buying the radio station . . . It led me to a place I never expected."

"Or the place you'd hoped for all along?"

This time the silent acknowledgment was his. "I'm sorry, Anne. You're right. A place I never left."

An indignant glance cut across him. "I almost fell onto a nine-iron when Fitz told me where Isabel was employed. That her request was driven by a brazen demand to produce an unprecedented promotional event. Going with the odds that Isabel hadn't married two incredibly successful artists, it was almost a guarantee that she'd reach out to you. How about you explain that to me?"

"Was it my intention to generate an opportunity? Yes. Should I have told you? Clearly, sooner would have been wiser than later. But I'm not the only one who's been hiding information." For the first time since he'd arrived she appeared unsure, nervously drawing a breath. "It's your turn, Anne. Was it ever your intention to tell me about your trip to Providence?"

"To be honest . . . No."

"No?" he said, eyes peeling wide.

"No. Especially not after my conversation with Isabel, the one where I met her significant other. He's a very nice man, Aidan. A doctor . . . Nate Potter."

"Jesus, did you all have lunch together?"

"We met in passing, but their relationship was evident. I even heard them making plans for a romantic getaway." Aidan absorbed that bit of news, Anne jumping on the confirmation express that said Isabel was, indeed, in love with another man. She touched his shoulder, forcing his attention. "Aidan, listen to me, whatever feelings you think you harbor for this girl, whatever past you're trying to recapture, she's over it. Isabel assured me of that. Regardless of how much I was hurt by your actions, I had no desire to do the same to you." Aidan moved from the sofa, taking refuge at a window, a suggestive skyline glowing. She followed. "But I see that my effort to protect you was in vain." She sighed, shaking her head at the view. "Never let it be said that Aidan Royce doesn't work hard for what he sets his sights on. So tell me the rest. You went to her father's funeral and what? Did your plan work? Did your ex-wife fall helplessly into your arms?"

He snickered, finishing the club soda. "Shows what you know about Isabel. She doesn't do helpless."

Anne folded her arms, murmuring, "I see. Well then, my apologies up front for the reality check. But your presence here suggests she also didn't come to you for comfort." And what was left of Aidan's heart picked up pace, his eyes narrowing at the fact. Acrid images of Nate and Isabel popped as a soothing voice offered an alternate end to the evening. "Aidan, I can make this better . . . you know I can," she said, touching his arm. "We're good together. You can't deny that." In reply there was only the pitchy squeal of skin on glass, Anne prying the crystal glass from his hand, putting it aside. "We've gotten off track. That's all this is. But maybe it's what we needed, some hard closure, something to give us perspective. We belong together. *We* make sense." Aidan looked at her, his whole body tightened. His hands wove through his hair, squeezing his head hard, hoping he might crack it open. "Why not give us this one night? Who knows how things could change by morning."

Anne's arms moved around his shoulders. The scent of expensive perfume and distraction filled his nose, invading his head. Maybe Isabel did love him once. Carrie admitted it, even if Isabel never had. *"At the time, she was so completely in love with you."* But he felt it too, or at least he thought he had, outside the restaurant, wanting desperately to pull her into his arms. He didn't, too haunted, too unsure about the aftermath of what he'd done to her in Vegas. Anne's body pressed against his. It demanded his attention, silky fabric accentuating her willingness to console. Her hands made a rapid advance, caressing every part of him, fingers nimbly working the buttons on his shirt. "Aidan, be reasonable. Look how your life has changed. You were both so young. Isabel never loved you." But that wasn't true, another counselor alluding to different testimony. *"Isabel stood there, divorce papers in hand for the sole purpose of keeping your sorry ass out of jail."* It suggested something other than the scene that had played out in a Vegas hotel room. Aidan breathed deeply, eyes closed. Why would Patrick Bourne, a man who clearly despised him, make such a claim? On the other hand, what did it matter? What difference did old circumstance make if Isabel was in love with Nate Potter? *It's too late. I waited too long.* Anne enabled the thought, whispering well-placed words of encouragement. Pouty lips grazed over his neck, edging toward his mouth. She kissed him. He was desperate for the pain to go away. She kissed him again, Aidan's arms reaching. But he felt more mannequin than man as she unbuckled his belt. "Aidan, I promise, I'll have you somewhere else in no time. And you'll realize you don't love her either."

And in all the confusion, for every unanswered question, throughout the chaos that was his life, this was the one thing Aidan did know. Instead of responding, he pushed away, Anne nearly stumbling on the empty air she now embraced. "I came here for two things," he said, buttoning his shirt, buckling his belt. "You've explained one—more or less. As for the other, I want you to call Kai and arrange a one-night-only show in Providence, the biggest venue they have. Pull out every stop, do whatever you have to make it happen as quickly as possible. If you can't or won't do that, just tell me. Kai doesn't need *you* to follow through."

"Wait . . . what are you talking about? You're going to go through with this ruse? Why? What for?"

"Because I caused Isabel a huge problem at *104.7—The Raging Fever FM for Hot Sound*. If nothing else, I will fix that before walking away." Aidan started for the door. "And if you have any ideas about sharing this information with Fitz, I suggest you think long and hard. Especially if you covet your position as my attorney. With the contract I'm about to sign, it's something you might want to consider."

CHAPTER THIRTY-THREE

Boston

H E'D DRESSED WITH THE INTENTION OF BLENDING IN, A SPORT jacket and jeans. As he waited, it didn't help much. A full docket of patients came and went, Aidan doing his best to stay neutral to stares and bold whispers. Tomorrow the shocking headlines would surface: *Aidan Royce Seeks Boston Specialist.* Yet, no media source would know his real reason for reaching out to the best of the best. He flipped through magazines and checked in with Kai who was executing a detailed to-do list. Aidan's no-appointment non-patient status increased the wait, Nate Potter making it clear where the rich and famous ranked on his schedule. Two hours in and the receptionist, who'd steadily worked the gossip on her phone tree, said Dr. Potter would see him.

"I appreciate you taking the time." Aidan sat tentatively, looking around an office that showed off pleasant green views of a Mass General courtyard. As Nate made his way around the desk, Aidan couldn't help but think how many times Eric Lang had been there. More to the point, he wondered when his daughter had fallen in love with the man seated across from him.

"I wouldn't thank me yet. Depending on what you want, security is one phone call away."

"I'm not here to cause a problem. I came to ask if you'd be the go-between." Nate's face turned quizzical, his hand tapping a folder against the desk. "It will make things easier. Isabel will get a phone call today from Kai Stoughton, he works for me. I'm going to do the promotional concert. Isabel . . . well, she can be stubborn. I want you to tell her to go with it. There aren't any strings attached. It will solve her ratings crisis and the proceeds will go a long way to benefitting Grassroots Kids."

"Why?"

"Because she asked, because there's no legitimate reason to turn her down."

"No, why do you want me to be the go-between? Why don't you tell her yourself?"

Aidan was unprepared for the question. "Because I want to do the right thing before getting out of her life for good. I've, um . . . I've amended my hell-bent ways to get what I want."

"Since when?"

"Since I got the graphic visual on what Isabel wants, her feelings for you."

There was a slight shake to Nate's head. "And how did that come about?"

"You were together, after the funeral, in the doorway of the brownstone."

His dark eyes widened. "Are you having her followed? Are there Polaroids I should know about?"

"What? No! Of course not. I knew where Eric lived. Years of a repetitive return address label. Ask Isabel. I wasn't thinking straight when I left the restaurant. I went to the brownstone to tell her what I just told you, that I'll do the concert, and thinking maybe . . . Well, it doesn't matter what else I was thinking." Nate only stared, prodding more explanation. "I got where it was going before the two of you went inside."

"I see," Nate said, leaning back. "I suppose it was obvious enough, not the kind of moment even you'd interrupt."

"Yeah, huge as my ego may be, we're good. If you have Polaroids, I don't need to see them." He stayed on task by focusing on the benign objects scattered across Nate's desk. Aidan used them to blur intimate visions: paperweight, prescription pad, lots of papers, a note in bright red pen: *Jenny Called* . . . "Beyond that, I can see that you're a good person. That you'll take care of Isabel, you won't do anything to hurt her—ever." It wasn't a statement, more of a demand for reassurance. "Isabel, she's smart and she's capable, she doesn't deserve anything less in return." Having said his piece, he should have left. But Nate's physician serenity got in the way, trustworthiness a lure. "Mostly, I can't tell her because it would kill me to see her again, knowing I'll never be that guy . . . that I'm not you."

The folder slipped from Nate's hand, catching it with his other. He shifted in his chair, pressing forward. "Aidan Royce wants to be me? Even with my respectable position and comfortable life, it's not yours. Trading places doesn't seem like a must-have for a guy like you."

"I'd be the fucking dogcatcher—a very happy single-wide resident of Catswallow, Alabama—if that's the guy Isabel was in love with." And through his considerable pain, Aidan smiled. "Rock stars don't get many fantasies. Downside of the trade. That one will always be mine. Success, money, fame . . . the endlessly spinning crap that goes with it. Isabel is the only thing I ever really wanted. That hasn't changed since I was a kid," he confessed. "For a while, I convinced myself it could happen. If I could just make her see that any divorce was a mistake. That given the right *circumstance*, the timing would be perfect." He rose from the chair. "It was an egotistical arrogant assumption. So if you could tell her . . . about the concert." Aidan was to the door, one step away from the beginning of the end.

"Wait." He turned, Nate stood behind his desk, the folder in a choke hold. "You should know, the same night you saw us at the brownstone, Isabel told me she'd move to Boston, come live with me."

Okay, maybe I missed the sadistic streak. Aidan gulped hard, fists clenching. "Congratulations."

"And here's what you missed after the door closed." He tossed the folder onto the desk, loose papers fluttering. "I made the enlightening error of suggesting that moving in with me was code for running away from you." A breath fell from Aidan, listening harder. "Isabel insisted it was absurd. Halfway up the stairs, on the way to her bedroom, she insisted that she needed to think about it. That was a week ago. I haven't heard from her since. As much as I wish otherwise, I'm not that guy." He sat, busying himself with the papers on his desk, glancing back. "But I think there's every chance you are. Talk to Isabel."

Aidan moved forward, his fingers digging into the back of a leather chair. "I can't. Every time I get within twenty feet of her it blows up in my face."

"Not my problem," he said, reaching for the largest stack. Nate looked up, perplexed. "Jesus Christ, you're Aidan Royce. How is confidence an issue?" Aidan didn't reply, Nate pushing back in his chair. "Well, don't look at me. I'm sure as hell not brokering an audience with your ex-wife."

My ex-wife . . . That's where he needed to start. Aidan needed an audience with the one person less willing to see him than

Isabel. "Fair enough. But would you broker one with Patrick Bourne?"

❧❧

"I SUPPOSE KEEPING BUSY, GETTING BACK TO WORK HELPS . . . SOME." He struggled for small talk, the setting riddled with awkwardness. "I admit; I was surprised you agreed to see me."

"Not half as fucking surprised as me." Patrick didn't indicate that Aidan should sit, the two standing at opposing angles in an office far more intimidating than Nate's.

"I understand that you have a great deal of respect for Nate Potter, so I appreciate . . ."

Patrick's tall frame leaned against a bookcase, the sleeves of his dress shirt rolled up. His face was drained of color, every indication being that Aidan Royce was aggravating an already cumbersome workday. "While my respect for Dr. Potter is tremendous, not even he could convince me to talk to you. He asked that I do it for Eric. I can't imagine he would say such a thing without a hell of a reason. Now, what do you want?"

To answer directly seemed like the long way around, and Aidan decided to go with his gut. Of course, there was every chance his gut would lead to the punch in the face he'd narrowly avoided during their last encounter, but he could think of no other way. "I need a lawyer."

There was a snort of laughter, Patrick turning toward a credenza. With a room-rattling thud a giant phonebook landed on top of his desk. "Try the Yellow Pages. I don't do entertainment law, and my involvement with scum generally results in deportation. Of course, if you'd like, I'd be glad to expedite the paperwork on that front."

While Aidan was chary of Patrick's state of mind, he was determined to stand his ground. "I may not be able to prove much to you, but I don't think my citizenship is in question. I asked for a meeting so you could clarify something." Aidan produced a blue-backed document, dropping it atop the phonebook.

Patrick glanced at it. "You need me to clarify the document legally nullifying your marriage to Isabel? Catch up, Aidan, that's old news."

"No, I got that part seven years ago, C-Note lawyers assured me our divorce was ironclad and well executed. I want you to clarify a more recent statement. The one you made in the hospital ICU. You said, *I* wanted out of the marriage. Look closer, Patrick. That petition was generated via Isabel's attorney, which was you. She divorced me. Not what you indicated, not the other way around."

"What the hell are you talking about?" Patrick snatched up a pair of reading glasses and the document. He flipped through, scanning furiously. "Where did you get this?"

"From the safe where it's been since it arrived in California—from Boston. I couldn't ask you to explain at the hospital. But I'm asking now. I assumed you wouldn't take my word, so I personally flew back to L.A. to retrieve it," he said, pointing. "Now that we're both caught up, would you explain how *I* wanted to end the marriage?"

He snapped off the glasses, his stare bearing down on Aidan. "I did generate this . . . Isabel signed it—but only to keep you from going to jail!"

"Okay, explain that part first," Aidan said, waiting anxiously.

Patrick looked up from the papers he held. "According to Fitz Landrey, the last thing your rocket to fame required was a teenage bride. He was prepared to abandon everything he'd promised if you and Isabel remained married. He wanted any liability she represented gone. He also held a significant trump card, enough that she wouldn't consider any other option. In addition to Isabel being responsible for your noncareer, Fitz also assured her that you'd go to jail for Rick Stanton's shooting. Even I had to admit, he had her from every angle. I was prepared to do whatever she wanted, but any courtroom trial would not have ended in your favor. She knew that." They traded a stunned look, Patrick shaking his head. "But here's the thing, I never filed this petition because . . . Wait," he said, crossing the room to a wooden filing cabinet. Moments later he returned, plunking down a similar set of blue-backed papers. "These arrived the morning, almost to the moment, Isabel signed those. After your curt dismissal, considering what she was willing to do to save your ass . . . Well, it was clear that you'd made your choice, and certainly not for the same reasons she'd made hers. I was appalled by your heartlessness. When I spoke with your attorney—"

"When you spoke with my what?"

"Your attorney," Patrick said, his voice growing as quizzical as Aidan's. "We had an in-depth conversation on the matter, and he assured me of your wishes. At that point, there was really nothing for Isabel to do except sign and salvage a moment of dignity." Aidan picked up the documents, carefully, without the advantage of Patrick's legal eye examining them. "Those are copies. Isabel has the originals. As you see, the letter . . . it's extremely personal. Telling her you'd decided she was right, that a marriage could only work if two people were in love. You said your wedding night proved as much. Only a conversation you would know about, Aidan."

"Only a conversation I would know about unless, in a moment of despair, I confided it to someone else. Someone who had nothing to lose and everything to gain." Aidan stared at his signature, which he did identify but couldn't explain. That didn't matter, as his ability to speak was stunted.

"I'll be a son of a bitch," Patrick said.

Aidan could barely make his eyes move, forcing them from the papers onto him. "What?"

"I make a living, even life and death judgments, by reading peoples' body language, their raw reactions to situations. And I'd almost swear you've never seen those documents before."

"Well," Aidan said, swallowing hard, calculating what fame and money had cost him. "I'd say you're damn good at your job, because I haven't."

CHAPTER THIRTY-FOUR

ISABEL ONCE BOUGHT A TICKET TO AN AIDAN ROYCE CONCERT. IT was her last year in college. He was playing a sold-out performance in Connecticut. It was as near to Boston as he'd ever come. It was a good seat, eighth row center. She'd bought the ticket online, paying a small fortune, money she didn't have at the time. Isabel had lied to Eric and Patrick about where she was going. She lied to herself thinking she'd go through with it. Maybe it was lingering curiosity, wondering if the past would make her stand out in the present. After fighting miles of backed-up traffic, car windows soaped with *Aidan Royce Rocks!* she watched hordes of fans stream toward the arena. Almost everyone was clad in T-shirts advertising the Royce brand. Isabel sat in a twenty-dollar-an-hour parking lot, stunned and awed. Aside from being married to Aidan Royce for less time than it took for his first record to turn gold, she was no different than the thousands of others who'd paid the price of admission. It was humiliating and sobering. She never got out of the car. Afterward, Isabel pacified herself with the idea of Aidan looking into that packed audience and seeing one empty seat. Maybe he'd wondered who passed on the opportunity to share the same breathing space. *I did, Aidan, because I still refused to be one of them.*

Tonight she would sit, marginally willing, basically required, mezzanine level in the giant outdoor venue. It was a private box with a bird's-eye view of the stage, Isabel still trying to grasp the unlikely turn of events. She'd hung up on two phone calls from Kai Stoughton, a man who claimed to work for the Royce brand. It had to be an on-air prank, compliments of Providence Power. Making *104.7—The Raging Fever FM* direct competition also made it a prime target for rock radio's adolescent humor. Eventually Mr. Stoughton gave up on Isabel, going directly to Rudy Shaw, who took the call and verified the facts: Aidan Royce was, indeed, prepared to do a one-night-only performance to promote the station format change. She'd asked. He answered, but the result wasn't sitting well, particularly after tickets for the private box seats arrived. Her reaction was staid, mumbling under the delighted squeals of Tanya and Mary Louise: "Great, now I can owe you for the rest of my life." Regardless of what the concert would fix, that was how she felt. Adding to the annoyance, spread out before her, was the reality of a packed football stadium. No indoor venue could accommodate, emphasizing the draw of Aidan Royce. The show had sold out in minutes, prompting a wild demand from what seemed like an endless well of fans. With *104.7* holding a large number of giveaway tickets, ratings were launched into the stratosphere. Mission accomplished. She huffed, sinking into her seat. Admittedly, it was impressive. Aidan's people ran things with the precision of a small military undertaking. Isabel tried to make peace with gratitude. Aidan was doing a good thing, and she had no business feeling slighted. But in his grand effort to help, it was also clear that he was avoiding contact with her. In the days leading up to the concert they'd heard plenty from his entourage, but Isabel hadn't heard a word from Aidan.

Of course, perhaps avoidance, not to mention guilt, was just on her mind. She'd left Nate a message, telling him about the concert and apologizing for her hesitance. They hadn't spoken since he'd made his point about running away. It wasn't fair, not to him, and she needed to permanently put away the past. Tonight, Isabel had hoped to do that. But in her purse was his reply to her ambivalence. It was a note that ended the need for any further speculation about a future with Nate.

Isabel,

Sometimes, the rational, levelheaded choice has little to do with the truth. No worries, as our situation has prompted me to make a decision of my own. You know how it is, how first loves never completely fade and all that nonsense. Despite what we shared, I need to know if the past can be repaired—I hope you'll do the same. I think it's where we both belong. Under the heading of Happiness, it's an important lesson I learned from your father.

Take care,
Nate

There was commotion from the private box entrance and Isabel turned, thinking he might have had a change of heart. Upon seeing Tanya, her guilt intensified. Nate had been the easy answer, and he deserved so much more. Perhaps enduring the evening alone was karma's well-deserved punishment.

"Sorry," Tanya said, squeezing past Joe's casted leg and Mary Louise, who sat to Isabel's left. "The boys got into a wicked wrestling match, and Lucy had a sticky mess of something in her hair— I'm not sure if it was glue or gum. Anyway, here I am!" As Tanya plopped down, Isabel smiled. No one would guess she was the mother of three, wearing non-mom jeans and a fringe-trimmed blouse. Having struggled without Patrick's fashion input (though rock concert attire was decidedly out of his element), Isabel was glad to have gone on instinct, choosing a bold-print dress and fishnets. If she was going to feel out of place, she didn't want to look it.

With Tanya settled in her seat, Isabel turned her attention to the crowd. The sight was intimidating and bizarre. The adulation people were willing to bestow on one man. She was definitely in the minority, the only person who'd ever wished Aidan a case of laryngitis. *"Five o'clock on a Sunday, would you quit with the music so I can finish my calc homework—and you can copy it!"* She'd also bet that she was only body present who'd have the nerve to remind Aidan that, despite the crowd, the world did not revolve around him. Isabel leaned forward, pressing against a tide of adoration. Of course, there was the iced tea, honey, and grapefruit juice mixture, its secret ingredient still a secret. She'd almost forgotten that. Not a person in his entourage would be able to re-create it, not even Aidan. She'd come up with it after he performed at the West Alabama State Fair in Tuscaloosa, before an evening gig at a popular Talladega bar. He was exhausted, fighting a cold, unsure if he could go through with the second show. He also couldn't afford to cancel. Between the two venues he'd have enough cash for the rent and electric bill. Aidan and his mother were on the verge of eviction, already sitting in the dark with Stella decidedly between jobs. At a loss for a real remedy, Isabel mixed the liquids with a glop of honey and poured it over a ton of ice. At the last second, unbeknownst to Aidan, who lay prone on the sofa, she'd spied something that ensured a burst of energy. Impulsively, she dumped it in. To her amazement, it worked—a clever potion enhanced by the power of suggestion. He performed beautifully.

It became a tease between them, Isabel unwilling to share the secret ingredient that fortified the concoction he came to rely on.

She looked on, drawn to the recollection, distracted by frenzied fans. Anticipation nearly crushed the arena as they sat through two opening acts. Finally, teaser music pumped in, Isabel pushing back in her seat as if she was about to embark on a death-defying amusement park ride. It surrounded her, expectation married to the idea of things coming completely unhinged. For the crowd it was a concert. For Isabel it was an apt description of any past she and Aidan shared. A cannon-like bang grabbed their collective attention, signaling the start. The thrum of music intensified as the opening chords to one of Aidan's most popular songs grew louder. There was a fantastic flash of fire, an explosion really, as a black curtain dropped. He was there. From the volume of ear-piercing screams everyone saw Aidan Royce—rock god. Isabel felt like the calm in the room, seeing only Aidan Roycroft—at work. The noise was stunning. It definitely wasn't where she'd want to clock in every day. It was frantic and unnerving. Whether five hundred or fifty thousand people were anticipating his every move, she never could fathom how he wasn't scared to death. Isabel made a conscious choice to focus on his guitar. It was a neutral object, avoiding Aidan's face, his body clad in dark jeans, a vintage-looking T-shirt, and cowboy boots. Surely, they were genuine snakeskin, the best that money could buy. Her concentrated stare lasted only seconds before ticking to his hands, the way he moved them. Isabel had inadvertently studied it for years, familiar as her own reflection. She was comfortable with it. Unsettling as the scene was, a smile curved around her lips. Her mood shifted, along with her body, inching forward, letting the atmosphere sink in. She remained on the edge of her seat, not quite willing to stand with the masses.

After repeating the intro a few times, Aidan cavorted with the band, whipping an ocean-deep crowd into irreversible ecstasy. She recognized the tactic. Aidan wanted them in the palm of his hand before he began, in case he screwed up or forgot the words. He never would, but that's how you became the staggering talent that was Aidan Royce. He tempted them for a moment longer, saying there wasn't anywhere he'd rather be, thrilled to be the headliner for *104.7*'s switch-to-rock coup. Isabel almost believed him. From the roar of the crowd, they certainly did. He asked how everyone in New England was doing tonight. *Well, I expect they're high as a kite. Not only is Aidan Royce standing in front of them, he insists this rare venue is where he wants to be!* Her brow crinkled at that, but there was too much noise and excitement to think it through. As Aidan took his place at the center mic, his voice hit her ears and any misguided notion of enjoyment faded. Hearing him through a sound system was one thing, live landed Isabel somewhere else. He began with a signature song, "One Guitar." She'd listened to it since the radio station switch, but Isabel hadn't heard the words. It was a song about a kid from nowhere with a destiny he couldn't place. Randomly, the guy in the song picked up a guitar, finding his future. She was with Aidan when he bought his first guitar at a yard sale in Catswallow. They went straight to the farmhouse with it. It was like watching a great painter being handed his first brush. He just knew what to do with it. Isabel smiled at the yesteryear thought. Even in Aidan Royce's mega world, they were the only two people who shared the memory.

The song built and climaxed, Aidan crooning to the crowd he'd captivated. The clamorous screams didn't subside, not a decibel, as he drifted into something with a harder rock edge. He always preferred the loud stuff, but she suspected he saw the wisdom in the ballads. It was an effective tease, making the women in the audience wait four numbers in to hear an Aidan Royce love song. He introduced it, asking, "Do you want to hear something real pretty?" He used to ask Isabel the same thing. She'd shrug and say, "In a minute." This, adherent screams, was probably the response he had in mind. The wispy ballad was from his most recent CD, so it struck her as odd when she heard something familiar. Isabel applied the lyrics to different women, thinking of Miss October, Fiona Free, and Anne Fielding. But she couldn't get any of them to fit inside the words. Whoever his muse, the affect was compelling. The song was overrun with regret, every woman in the crowd poised to help him get over it. On his last pass through the chorus, she wondered how he could tell the difference: women drawn to his image versus the one who was drawn to him. It was a problem, she supposed, that went all the way back to Catswallow. He put down the guitar, the band backing him up on the next song. His focus was on the audience, his gaze tipping in her direction. Isabel felt her face grow red, embarrassed by the lure. Aidan didn't know where she was sitting, nor did he care. The fishnets snagged on the fabric of her seat, reminding her that Aidan had his place and she had hers.

Halfway through, she managed to find her own rhythm, content to watch him work. His charisma and talent drove the show, but it was Aidan's command that kept things mesmerizing. Numerous fans cried out, "We love you, Aidan!" He replied, very much like he meant it, "I love you guys too!" Isabel was amused. It was the only way she'd never loved Aidan. At one point, he whipped out a cell phone, snapping pictures from his point of view. The crowd went crazy for it, but Isabel was struck by the irony. They were watching something so singular while his photos—from Beijing to Boston—had to capture the same repeated blur. Wiping sweat from his effort, Aidan tossed a towel to a vocal cluster of fans. That turned a little ugly, women tearing at the prospect of taking sweaty DNA home. Isabel wriggled her nose, recalling his stinky gym bag, vapor-like and repugnant. While she wouldn't fight a single one of them for any physical memento, what she did find herself hopelessly deprived of was being with Aidan.

As he continued to perform, she was confronted by an odd memory. Driving to Sandy Springs to buy an amplifier, they got lost. Actually, Isabel got them lost. She was so frustrated with the back roads and the map she wanted to cry, maybe she did. She was sure they would run out of gas and be stranded in the middle of nowhere. It was a hundred degrees and she was dying of thirst, aside from having a pounding PMS headache. Stubbornly determined, she hadn't mentioned a word of it to Aidan. He pulled over, insisting she give him the map. In less than ten minutes he delivered them from nowhere to a gas station. It was nothing short of a miracle in her opinion. Silently, Aidan got out of the truck and stalked inside. She thought he was really mad. A few minutes later, he came out with foolproof directions, a can of soda, and a candy bar. In the bottom of the bag was a box of Midol. He never said a word. He just got back in the truck and started driving. Proving, Isabel supposed, that she needed Aidan as much as he did her.

With her focus on the memory, Isabel stared at her folded hands. She was impressed with the man performing onstage. Who wouldn't be? But that wasn't whom she'd missed all those years, it was Aidan Roycroft, whose it factor included a Mountain Dew, a Hershey bar, and a box of menstrual pain reliever. As the lack of indifference finally made room, Isabel pushed farther back into her seat. No other man, no matter how affable or pragmatically perfect, ever had a chance.

CHAPTER THIRTY-FIVE

AIDAN LAUNCHED INTO HIS LAST NUMBER, GIVING ONE FINAL wave before jogging off stage with as much gusto as he appeared nearly two hours before. He was gone. From her vantage point, Isabel saw a flash of blond hair disappear into a shroud of black curtains and metal catwalks. A last glimpse was poignant as Fitz's forewarning came to fruition. Aidan handed off the guitar to a roadie who, in turn, handed him a water bottle. It was time to let it go—for good. In that effort, she stood. Mary Louise leaned over.

"Isabel, what are you doing?"

"Show's over. We should go."

"Isn't there an encore?"

"Does it matter? If we go now, we can beat the rush," she said, desperate for an exit.

"For heaven's sake, sit down," Mary Louise instructed, tugging at the hem of her dress.

She obeyed. One tended not to mess with Mary Louise on a direct order. Except for the cliché lighters, the stadium remained dark. She'd also attended enough 98.6—*The Normal FM* concerts to know that even '80s mothball talent prepared an encore. She resigned herself to facing Aidan one more time, the crowd breaking into a spontaneous chant of, "Ai-dan, Ai-dan . . ." A few moments later he accommodated them, walking back on stage with an acoustic guitar. While fan enthusiasm hadn't waned, Isabel could see that Aidan's energy level had dipped. That or something had decidedly changed in those few minutes he'd disappeared off stage. She could see it, even from the distance. His clothes had changed too, from a T-shirt to a collared one, though, naturally, the tails hung out. Tilting her head, she gave in to the familiar sight, absorbing him one last time. A stool had been placed center stage. She hadn't noticed.

Settling onto it, Aidan thanked the crowd once more for coming out. She found herself smiling at his deep-rooted manners. Clearing his throat, Aidan hesitated. Isabel's heart skipped a beat because it appeared that he'd stumbled. There was an urge to rush from her seat and help him out. Maybe he'd forgotten the words or what song he was going to sing. While she couldn't help with that, she might reassure him that things would be okay, that they'd love him regardless. Squeezing her eyes shut, Isabel sensed that along with a fresh Aidan-less start, some behavior-modification therapy might be in order.

He sighed, everyone noticing his angst. It was an unnerving juxtaposition, the crowd more silent than him. He adjusted the microphone, rubbing his palms on his pants—like he was nervous. "Normally, I do two numbers in the encore, but tonight I'm only going to do one." There was a collective moan of disappointment. "When I explain, you'll understand. The rest of my life is riding on this one song. But, um, first we need to finish up some business. Not only was this a successful launch for *104.7,* but we also raised a lot of money for a great cause. I want to let everyone know that the proceeds from tonight's show are being donated to Grassroots

Kids. They're a charitable organization that does a whole lot of good."

"Did he just say . . . ?" Isabel said as thunderous applause responded to his benevolence. Her head whipped left and right, looking to Mary Louise and Tanya.

"That's what he said," Mary Louise replied, her gaze scanning the crowd, doing the math.

"In fact, I'll be picking up the tab for this entire evening." Aidan turned to a tall man at the edge of the stage. "Kai?" Isabel's eyes widened, realizing there actually was a Kai. Aidan looked back at the crowd. "Kai has made sure that everyone leaves with something. Um, what did we bring?" He leaned toward him, unable to hear the un-miked man. Isabel was sure Aidan hadn't a clue. Complex lyrics, foreign languages, and columns of numbers— do not ask him to remember what you wanted from the Piggly Wiggly. "Oh, T-shirts and CDs. Got it," he said. "I wanted tonight to be memorable for everyone, because it's such a special date for me."

Game over. Isabel tensed, uninterested in any other magnanimous gesture on Aidan Royce's part. She knew exactly what date it was, although he'd long since forgotten. She braced for his announcement, her imagination cliff-diving. *"Tonight, I'd like to publically claim the love of my life, the woman who spends every waking moment tending to my happiness, Anne Fielding . . ."* "That's it, I'm done," Isabel said, standing. "If that's his plan, I'll kill him. I don't care who he is. I've had enough Aidan Royce hoopla for one lifetime, and I'm seriously going to kill him."

"This is kind of personal," Aidan continued, Isabel realizing she was trapped by Joe's casted leg. "But if you could bear with me. Seven years ago tonight, every dream I ever had came true. That's not something too many men get to claim. I'm very lucky, blessed, whichever you believe. Probably a lot of both. Tonight marks the anniversary of my debut performance at Caesars Palace." On his cue, the crowd whipped into congratulatory rapture.

Blindsided by his recollection, Isabel was motionless. *That's what he recalls happening on this date?* "Indulgent, lazy, self-centered . . . jerk!" she said, grabbing her purse, thinking she'd climb over the seat. "I'm going home!" Before she could turn, hoisting herself over, a spotlight landed on her. In the darkened arena Aidan and Isabel were face-to-face. He stared. The same way he did years ago in his pickup truck, holding tight to her wrist, the same way he did on the dance floor at the gala. The same way he did in the moment she left him.

"If you can believe it," he said, still staring, "something even more important happened that day. As dreams of fame and fortune go, this topped everything. I've always known that." Then, in a softer voice: "And I'm a fool because I should have never given up." Even from her vantage point, Isabel could see the gulp roll through his throat. "It's my great privilege this evening to introduce my wife, Isabel Royce." He gestured to the box. Isabel responded by sinking to her seat.

"What's he talking about?" she hissed to Mary Louise. "We're divorced!" From her right, Tanya nudged her. It was like being on a palace balcony, Isabel offering a deer-in-headlights wave to the subjects, a thoroughly baffled look at Aidan. In return, he smiled at her clear confusion.

"My wife . . ."

Why is he calling me that?

There was a mixed reaction, lots of gasps, some applause, and the disappointed groans of female fans. "She's done me the tremendous honor of making a rare appearance at one of my shows. Seven years ago, she agreed to marry me. At the time, my life was more trouble than promise. We were just two scared kids who had nothing but each other. Really, it was all I needed. We were married in true Vegas fashion." Hoots and hollers echoed, his glance dropping to the stage floor. Sharing this was making the performer uncomfortable. He pushed on. "While most women would have been satisfied with a ring . . ." His long fingers fluttered over the snake. "*This* was Isabel's idea of a permanent bond." It drew a wave of subtle laughter, Isabel included. "Do you remember how the story went?" he said, speaking only to Isabel in a crowd of thousands. "As long as I had it, I'd never be without you. Turns out, it wasn't a story, it was the absolute truth. Lately though," he said, turning back to his public narrative, "circumstance, some serious, some calculated, has prevented me from getting my wife's attention. So tonight I resorted to an old performer's trick, a captive audience. I planned this moment, Isabel, knowing you'd be here. Regardless of anything you may believe, I meant what I said on our wedding night, in the moment I said it. I love you. I always have."

This time Tanya elbowed her, Isabel catching a victorious nod as theory became fact. She pulled in a low breath, her hands making a motion of surrender, flopping onto her lap. "So, I'd like to do two things. First, I'd like to wish my wife a happy anniversary." The applause was warmer this time. "Secondly, I'd like to do a song I've never played in public. In fact, I originally wrote it in Spanish. Though tonight, I'd like to do the retitled English version. I hope Isabel remembers it." She nodded, hearing in her head a melody for which the music was powerful, though its story a mystery. "Isabel has always been the muse for this and for me, a piece of music and a man I've been fine-tuning half my life." Strumming the guitar, before gliding into a sweet verse that only Aidan could have written, he looked up, his voice pinching ever so slightly, "This is called 'Isabel's Rhapsody.'"

The light over her dimmed and Aidan was left in the spotlight, as it should be. His voice echoed through a silent arena as hands swayed in unison. Isabel sat through the entire song, hands pressed to her cheeks. She knew the music and she finally understood the verses. The ones he sang to her in Spanish on gray rainy days and during searing August summers. He'd sung them sitting on the front porch of the farmhouse, and from the front seat of his truck on their way to some two-bit gig. It was a brilliant piece of music that complemented the story of them—a story Isabel knew by heart. Afterward, he thanked the crowd for indulging him. Aidan left the stage, but not before blowing a kiss over his shoulder in her direction. The houselights came on and she was met, once again, by thousands of probing eyes. Strangers called her name. She looked between Tanya and Mary Louise, the calm inside her decidedly rattled. "What . . . what just happened?"

"I think your husband just delivered a very public message to his rather stubborn wife," Mary Louise said, smiling.

"But it doesn't make . . ." she stumbled, looking toward Tanya who was busy wiping tears. "We're not . . ."

Two burly men, wearing earpieces and carrying walkie-talkies stepped into the private box. "Mrs. Royce, Mr. Royce has asked us to escort you to the car. Would you come with us, please? And we're sorry, but you'll have to hurry."

"I'm not . . . What do you mean, *come with you*?" She turned. "Mary Louise?"

"Go with them, Isabel."

"Look, I have no idea how to explain that, but I'm telling you, we're divorced."

"Either way, does it matter?" Tanya said, fishing fresh Kleenex from her purse. "Take it from me, marriages come and go. What just happened on that stage is beyond marriage."

Looking to Mary Louise for backup, she offered aberrant spontaneity. "What more do you want him to do, skywrite it?"

"Really, Isabel, give him an inch. Whatever the past, I think he's earned it."

"Mrs. Royce, please, we need to go. It's a very small window."

Damning pride, she turned toward the name and request.

CHAPTER THIRTY-SIX

PEOPLE WHO WORKED FOR AIDAN ROYCE DID SO WITH ENTHU-siasm and without foul-ups. He'd always been grateful for this, but never more so than tonight, as his plans required a Herculean effort of timing and coordination. Things moved quickly after the concert, Aidan boarding his plane, alone, bound for Teterboro Airport in New Jersey. Easily negotiated, it was an excellent alternative to busy New York airports. From there he was whisked into a waiting limo headed to Manhattan. During the flight he'd showered and changed, looking more like a rock star ready to party than a husband in search of a home life. But there was unfinished business, and he was intent on seeing it through. His first stop was Anne's apartment. She was waiting, the doorman and driver ushering her into the cavern of the limousine.

"Aidan," she said, settling in across from him. "You were the last person I expected to hear from tonight. The concert, didn't it go well?"

"The concert went fine. It always goes fine. It's my job."

"Maybe so, but it does take a tad more finesse than, say, night manager at the Holiday Inn." They traded small smiles. "I wasn't referring to the concert, not completely."

"Oh, you mean my reason for the show." He shrugged. "I told you, I caused Isabel a huge problem. I wanted to rectify that. Kai tells me you were helpful in arranging things. I wanted to thank you—personally. Apparently, you were discreet too; I haven't heard a word from Fitz."

Her head bobbed in a conciliatory gesture. "I wanted to prove that I'm on your side. So tell me," she said, offering a nonchalant shrug. "Did you see Isabel before the show, or after maybe?"

"Honestly," he said, sipping from a water bottle. "I didn't. You know how a gig like that goes, not exactly a one-on-one atmosphere."

"True. And here you are." A hand reached across, grazing his. "I realize you're still angry about my trip to Providence. But if we could just talk things through."

"Don't give it another thought, Anne. I'm over it." She relaxed, sinking into the plush seat. "Let's move on. We'll circle back around to us in a bit," he said, smiling warmly. "Right now, I'd like to conclude my business with C-Note. Do you have the new contracts with you?"

"Absolutely, just like you asked," she said, holding up a bulging black satchel. "You're going to be amazed by their proposal for expanding your image to the big screen. Maybe we could have a late supper, discuss the details. I know you had some questions. You can unwind, we can reconnect."

"Not necessary. I'm ready to sign. In fact," he said, as the car rolled to the curb, "we're picking up Fitz right now."

"Fitz?" she said. "You didn't say anything about Fitz."

"Yes, well, you know he's been in Europe. But he's back, landed a couple of hours ago. Since we're all here, I thought we'd take care of this."

"If that's what you want. But why—"

The car door opened. Outside was a stretch of Manhattan real estate that housed posh hotels. Currently curbside stood Fitz Landrey, the doorman and driver nearly colliding in an effort to assist him.

"Aidan, what the fuck are you doing here?" he groused. "I get off a fucking plane from Paris and get a crazy call from Kai. He informs me you're in New York and that you need to see me right away. You're supposed to be in L.A. retouching the last tracks for your new CD." As Fitz settled into his seat, Anne's presence registered and his expression shifted from irritated to suspicious. "What's going on?"

"Glad you could join us," Aidan said, as the car started moving. "How was your trip?"

"My trip? My trip was a waste of time. European talent won't sell in an American music market. Forget that. I want to know what we're all doing here."

"My C-Note contract," he explained. "It expires at midnight— or did you forget?"

"Of course I didn't forget. But your current contract includes an automatic grace period. I assumed we'd take care of it tomorrow, when I was back in L.A."

"Fitz, don't be so cranky," Anne coaxed. "Aidan's here to resign. What difference does the location make?" She produced the thick contract, turning up the dim lights of the limo. "We can take care of it right now."

"Like Anne said, I'm ready to sign. I thought you'd be pleased. It's the perfect opportunity since it's paramount that I have my attorney present—somebody solely dedicated to my interests. Would you believe," he said, speaking to Anne, "last time I did this there wasn't a single person in the room representing me. Stacks and stacks of contracts, a sea of C-Note attorneys, and an overwhelmed nineteen-year-old kid."

"Seriously?" Her gaze jerked to Fitz, who was quick to reply.

"And was there anything in our agreement that didn't make you filthy rich and incredibly successful?"

"Well, you've got me there."

"Aidan, I don't know what kind of high-octane, rock star trip you're on, but don't pull this bullshit with me!"

"Fitz, let's try to focus," Anne said, negotiating the tension. "Aidan's just a little hyped up from the concert he did tonight."

"You did a concert tonight? Where? Why didn't I know about this?"

A puzzled look drew over Aidan's face. "Didn't you get my memo?"

"No. But, clearly, you missed mine. It's the one reminding you that Aidan Royce isn't a person. It's a conglomerate to which you, my overly talented friend, are merely the largest piece of many moving parts! You don't own exclusive rights. Now, if Anne's presence were a concern, I've no doubt she would have dropped everything and flown out to the coast."

"That would be great if it wasn't for one thing."

"What's that?" Fitz said, loosening his tie.

"She's not my attorney." The car petered to a halt, pulling up to another hotel, more posh than the last. The door opened and a man carrying a valise slipped inside.

"Aidan," he said, sitting next to him, shaking his hand. Impeccably dressed, an aura of solid command surrounded him. "How did everything go?"

"Fine, I think. I'll let you know later, she was a little, um . . . stunned."

"Who was stunned? Who the hell are you and would somebody please tell me what the fuck is going on?"

"Being left in the dark is a bitch, isn't it, Fitz?"

"I'm Aidan's attorney."

"You're his . . . Aidan?" Anne said, her eyes flicking fast between them. "I don't understand. *I'm* your attorney."

His counsel held up a hand, as if advising his client to let him handle things. "Going forward, I'll be representing Mr. Royce, including his new recording contract."

"Fitz?" she said, panic coloring her voice.

Fitz's narrow-eyed gaze never deviated from the attorney. "Aidan's choice of representation is up to him. There's nothing I can do about that—as long as he's willing to sign."

"I am," Aidan said, focusing on Anne. "Whatever your reasons, whatever your logic . . . whatever you thought you were going to gain, I trusted you. You broke that trust on every level." As he spoke, Fitz reached over, removing the fat stack of contracts from her hands.

"I'm guessing your new attorney is familiar with these?"

"Actually," the man said, taking out a pair of glasses from his breast pocket, "I'm not. But I'm very familiar with these." From a sleek leather valise he produced a similar set of documents. "Everything's in order. I'm assuming you'd still like him to be a witness."

"Absolutely," Aidan said, accepting a pen. "I think it's more than fitting that Fitz Landrey watch me sign my new contract with Sony." With a rainbow of pages flagged, Aidan began the tedious process of signing his name, over and over.

"What the fuck! You ungrateful bastard. After everything I've done for you!"

Aidan stopped signing. "Don't you mean after everything you've done *to* me?"

"What are you talking about? I made you the most successful artist of your generation. Why the hell are you so pissed off?"

"Seems you're missing a piece of information; I believe we skipped the introductions. Fitz Landrey, meet Patrick Bourne."

"Patrick . . ." His mouth pursed, color draining. "I don't fucking believe this."

"Believe it," Aidan said, resuming his signature, Patrick observing.

"Do you know him?" Anne asked.

Patrick intervened. "We've never met, but I'm sure my name is familiar. Most recently, I was a special prosecutor for the United States government, Department of Immigration. More relevant to Mr. Landrey, I once represented Isabel Lang during her petition for divorce from Aidan—the one he blackmailed her into."

"The one that you what?" Anne said, incredulous.

"That's hardly the half of it, Ms. Fielding. Thanks to Mr. Landrey's effort, it was also erroneously filed on her behalf." From the same valise, he produced the decree, Fitz Landrey not offering so much as a tick.

"Imaginative conjecture, counselor, but how could you ever prove it?"

"I'm glad you asked, because the fact is I can. Seven years ago, there was a disturbing break-in at my home, the place left in ruins—particularly the study. The police, myself, my husband—we all attributed it to either homophobic vandalism or the dangers of my job. Sadly, both were plausible. It never occurred to anyone that a benign, albeit signed, petition for divorce was the real catalyst." Fitz Landrey shifted slightly, an unaffected gaze trained on Patrick. "In addition to my legal expertise, my job requires an innate ability to retain faces and names. Sometimes the safety of a country depends upon it; sometimes it's a more personal issue, like naming the messenger who turned up at my door not long before that break-in. Vince Ederly. Mean anything to you?"

Fitz's mouth bent to a frown, shaking his head. "Never heard of him."

"Really? Because the IRS has. Luckily, my position also affords me access to a wide spectrum of information, including tax records. C-Note Music reported paying a hefty bonus to Mr. Ederly seven years ago—particularly odd since he has no known musical talents. His job was listed as *staff.* From there, a thorough background check revealed a most colorful past." He reached for one more folder, a mug shot paper-clipped to the outside. "This is a condensed history of Mr. Ederly's background," he said, handing it to Fitz. "It includes a petty-larceny career before he came to work for you. Apparently, breaking and entering was high on his skill set."

"So he worked for C-Note, lots of people do. The music industry attracts all types; that's a well-known fact. Your paper trail won't lead directly to me."

"Interesting, when we chatted, Mr. Ederly wasn't quite of that opinion." Patrick smiled, raising a brow. "Suffice it to say a petty thief who picks a good lock didn't last one round in my interrogation room. In fact, he was rather quick to recall witnessing Ms. Lang holding that very document," he said pointing. "Upon reporting his suspicions, he was contracted, by you, to find out more. And what an incredible jackpot he hit—not just a prepared divorce petition, but one bearing Isabel's signature. More than you could have hoped for, I suspect."

"Fascinating, Mr. Bourne. A documented two-bit thief's word against mine. Should make for titillating headlines, certainly incite a ravenous media frenzy." There was no fluster in his voice, turning to Aidan. "I assume you're ready to go public with this? You're ready to have the media probe into every part of your past. Revisit your life and Isabel's going all the way back to Catswallow, your arrest . . . the attempted rape by Rick Stanton. I'd imagine she'd love fielding those questions. It will come out, Aidan, every bit of it. The press will eat her alive." There was a swelling pause. He snickered. "I didn't think so."

"Well," Aidan said quietly, "maybe not *that* scandal. But I might be willing to endure this one." On his cue, Patrick handed the divorce decree that Aidan had signed, the one Vince Ederly delivered to Isabel. "Explain this to me. In exchange for the truth, I might reconsider your future. How the fuck did you get me to sign this?"

Fitz took the second document in hand and put on his own reading glasses. "I have no idea what you're talking about. I've never seen this in my life."

Aidan lurched forward, Patrick grabbing his arm. "He's not worth it, Aidan. Let the authorities deal with him. He's easily looking at charges of forgery, conspiracy, tampering with public records. It might involve you, but I should think the direct threat of jail would concern him more."

Aidan shook his head. "Just tell me how? Even at my worst, I was never that high."

Anne picked up the two documents, offering her opinion. "Having been lured in myself, I can tell you that Fitz is a master manipulator. Orchestrating a situation that included no representation would have put a younger Aidan at a serious disadvantage. But what I can't fathom," she said, turning to Fitz, who stared out a rain-streaked window, "is why? Why would you engineer such a thing?"

"Because it was the only way he could keep Isabel from me and me from Isabel. And according to Fitz's theory, our marriage was the only thing keeping Aidan Royce from becoming a conglomerate worth millions."

Fitz looked back, his voice dull and even. "I know my business, Aidan. It was no theory. It was always a fact, like it or not."

Anne, who continued to study the documents, glanced up at Patrick. "Wait. If neither one of them consented, then these decrees are invalid. I don't care if Lady Justice herself filed them."

"Totally bogus legal maneuvering," Patrick said. "Clearly

fraudulent, definitely criminal. Charges I'll be pursuing as soon as Aidan gives me the go-ahead."

Three glares trained on Fitz as the car arrived at its final destination. Aidan opened the door of the limo and stepped out, Fitz following. "Aidan, wait, I want to know what your intentions are! Don't be impulsive. I can explain."

Aidan spun around, facing him. "Damn right you're going to explain. But not to me."

CHAPTER THIRTY-SEVEN

A HARSH WIND RIPPLED THROUGH AS THUNDER RUMBLED. FITZ looked around, adjusting to the destination. "What are we doing at an airport? Never mind. Aidan, if you would give me two fucking minutes . . ."

His words petered out as the stairway to a small jet dropped; it sat nose-to-nose with a much grander version. Two men with a bodyguard vibe headed down, in between them was Isabel. The burlier of the two waited at the bottom, offering her a hand. Seeing Aidan, her perplexed expression burst into a wide smile. He took a few steps in her direction. Isabel rushed the distance. For a moment he just held on, forgetting Fitz and Anne and everything around him. For the first time since a crazy night in Vegas, Aidan held still as the center of his gravity locked into place. "You're here. I know you are, but just say it. I need to hear you say it."

Leaning back, her fingertips fluttered over his cheek. "I'm here."

He turned a steely glare onto Fitz. "You're going to explain it to her—all of it." As Fitz and Isabel exchanged a curt glance, Anne emerged from the limo.

Isabel looked between them, breaking from Aidan's hold. "Anne."

"Isabel, listen to me," Aidan said as her glance jutted from Anne to Fitz and, finally, onto Aidan. "Whatever she led you to believe . . ."

"She said she'd just come from California. That despite what happened at that nightclub, your arrest, the two of you were working things out."

"Anne?" he said, turning toward her. "Would you like a chance to clarify?"

Inching forward, she pursed finely painted lips, her tall frame pulling tight. "Well, perhaps my interpretation was more desirous than . . ." Her words faded, taking in his persistent stare. She sighed, forcing a culpable smile. "When I saw Aidan in California, he said he wanted time to think." She cleared her throat, looking between Aidan and Isabel. "I suspect he was looking for a gentlemanly way out. The truth of the matter . . . well, the truth is he's never been in love with anyone but you."

"For that much, I am sorry, Anne."

She sniffed the air, chin tipped high. "You only beat me to the punch. You were right, Aidan. Your life and mine, they would have never quite . . . *jelled*. Now, if it's all the same to you, I've had enough revelation and reunion for one night." Glancing at the limo, she started walking toward the airport terminal. "I do wonder what time the car rental counter closes."

In the distance lightning flashed, Aidan turning his attention to Fitz. "Now you. And move it along, the next bolt probably has your name on it."

A growl sputtered from Fitz as he retreated a few steps. "I don't have to stand here and take this. You made yourself clear; I have no obligation to you."

"Well, I do." A gasp pulsed from Isabel as Patrick emerged

from the car. "It would give me great pleasure to tell Isabel the truth."

"Patrick!" she said. "What are you doing here?"

He stepped to the center of things, hesitating. His fingertips reached toward her. "I'm sorry. These past few weeks have been . . . It seems like so long since I've seen . . . your face," he said as her hand clasped his. "I've decided to take a leave of absence." He smiled at her puzzled expression. "So much has happened. I thought it was the right time to explore new opportunities. In addition to some nonprofit work, I'm going to be handling Aidan's business affairs."

"You're working for Aidan? How did that happen? You—" She stopped, her green eyes flicking between the two men. "Patrick, you're, um, you're not exactly an Aidan Royce fan."

"He's growing on me," he said. "I'll share the details later, there's something more urgent right now. Isabel, the petition that was served to you on Aidan's behalf was a fraud—"

"A fraud?"

"Everything, Isabel, including the letter from him. It was all cleverly manufactured to make sure you were under the impression that Aidan wanted to end the marriage. And the divorce complaint I drew up—the one you signed—it was delivered to him, unbeknownst to me."

"But how? You never filed it."

"No, I didn't. Nonetheless, circumstance was crafted to hand both of you a very unfair reality. As for my part, I'm not blameless. My influence, some of my decisions, only facilitated things. Isabel, I can't tell you how sorry I am. Had we both listened to your father . . ."

"Patrick, you couldn't have known."

"Still, Eric was a wise man. I'd give anything for him to know how right he was, how sorry I am."

With her thumb to his cheek, she caught the tear at the edge of his eye, hugging him tight. "He knows, Patrick. He loved you so much. I'm sure he knows." He backed up, reclaiming the quiet poise with which he was most comfortable.

"Of course, both decrees are null and void. It will take some legal maneuvering to have them overturned, but I'm confident I can get the job done."

"Null and void?" she said, looking between Aidan and Patrick. "What does that mean?"

"It's exactly what I wished you at the concert," Aidan said. "In fact, to celebrate, I bought you a sheep farm in Ireland." His smile widened as her confusion deepened. "Seventh wedding anniversaries . . . Wool? Come on, Isabel, it is the traditional gift."

"What Aidan is trying to tell you," Patrick said, "is that the two of you are as married today as you were back in Vegas."

Isabel grasped Aidan's arm. "To me? You're still, all this time, married to me?"

"Nah," he said, beaming. "You're married to me." Isabel stood tight to his side. She wasn't moving, not outwardly, but Aidan sensed a fine tremble. Enough explanation on a windy tarmac, he just wanted to get them out of there. "Patrick, thank you for being here, I couldn't have done this without you."

He reached out, shaking his hand. "Yes, you could have. You're a good man, Aidan. You would have found a way." He kissed Isabel's cheek before moving toward the car.

"Patrick, wait!" He turned. "When will I see you again? Without my father, I don't know how things . . ."

"Isabel, don't you realize?" Eyes glistening, he smiled at her. "Eric brought immeasurable happiness to my life, not the least of which was a part-time daughter. When he died, he left me the greatest gift possible, because now I am a full-time father."

"You are," she said, hugging him. "You absolutely are. I . . . we'll come to Boston—soon."

"Or you could come out to the coast," Aidan offered.

He stopped at the car door. "I might do that," he said, pulling in a heavy breath, admiring them. "This would have made Eric so very happy."

The car sped away, leaving Aidan with Isabel, Fitz looking on. "Come on, we have somewhere to be."

"That isn't your plane?" Isabel said, as Aidan led her toward the larger of the two jets.

"That thing?" he said as thunder rumbled and rain fell. "Are you kidding? No, just a loaner. I would have sent you in mine, but I needed to beat you here."

"Wait a damn minute," Fitz yelled. "Have you forgotten that C-Note owns the rights to every song on that new CD? Go with Sony, and it will be worthless. I'll bury it. It's nothing without me."

"Maybe so. But I'd say it's worth even less without me. And just so you know, it wasn't even my A-game. I saved the best stuff for the competition. Patrick will handle the legal recourse, but that payback, my overzealous record-producing friend, is strictly compliments of me."

"Go ahead, Aidan, see what retaliation gets you. Had the two of you stayed together your career wouldn't have been anything close to this," he said, gesturing toward the jet. "Right or wrong, *circumstance* guaranteed the phenomenal success you are. You can't take that away from me."

"Maybe not, but you didn't hesitate to take her away from me!"

"Fine, you're so high on the truth. Now that any counsel is out of earshot and this will never be more than hearsay, you're damn right I orchestrated circumstance. How difficult do you think it was to get an exhausted, emotionally overwrought kid to sign his name to a stack of legal documents, a couple hundred *feel-the-love* letters thrown in to ensure hand-cramping repetition? Add to that some very personal information you confided on a bleary-eyed trip from Las Vegas to L.A., and I had the perfect storm. Isabel was the bigger problem. If only from my brief encounter, I could gauge her *hardiness*—she wouldn't have stayed away. But I could also see she was a prideful young woman. She would not take kindly to any rejection from you, and I used it to my advantage. I used it to yours, Aidan. Had I spelled it out back in Vegas, told you to choose being a rock icon, millions of dollars and millions of women . . ." Fitz looked at Isabel. "Just keeping it real, Mrs. Royce. You should know; they weren't seven lonely years." Rain fell harder, Isabel's gaze dropping to the wet tarmac. "Honestly, Aidan, which one would you have chosen?"

Aidan took a foreboding step in Fitz's direction. "Had I been given a choice—by either of you," he said, glancing at Isabel. "There's no doubt which I would have chosen. When I married Isabel, I told her I wanted her more than I wanted this career or a life in the spotlight. She knows that. My answer is no different today." He turned, grasping Isabel's hand as they pushed through a curtain of rain toward the plane.

Fitz called after him, "We'll see how far you get without me. Your career is as good as over. I don't care who you signed with! Enjoy it Aidan, your nosedive to the discount rack, playing second-rate concert halls, being yesterday's news. That's all this will get you—that and your Catswallow trailer park bride." An old temper surged through Aidan, moving angrily at him.

"Aidan, don't!" she shouted.

Grabbing a shoulder, Aidan spun him about, landing a solid punch to his jaw, knocking the record-producing mogul onto the pavement. "Get it straight," he said, jerking his lapel. "She's from New Jersey."

Aidan shook the sting from his hand, returning to Isabel's side. "Are you all right?"

"Yeah. It's been a long time since I took a swing like that."

"I remember the last one," she said, running her hand over his.

"He had it coming." Aidan looked back at Fitz, who moved hurriedly toward the airport. "Forget him. Let's just get on the plane and go. We have a lot to talk about—including what the heck I'm going to do with a 30,000-watt radio station in Providence, Rhode Island." He tugged at her hand. Gusts of wind and stinging rain prodded, but none of Isabel budged.

"What did you say?"

Aidan stopped at the base of the steps. "Oh, that's right. You don't know." He smiled at what now seemed like an absurd confession. "*104.7—The Raging Fever FM for Hot Sound* . . . I, um, I kind of own it. In fact, I just put on a concert to promote my own radio station. That'll be a nasty fine from the FCC, but it was worth anything to—"

"You? You were behind the buyout, the format change, everything?"

"Guess I was, Isabel," he said, flipping up the collar on his jacket, rubbing her wet arms. "Could we talk about this on the plane, where it's drier? Come on, you're soaked."

She took a step back. "I'm not going anywhere with you."

CHAPTER THIRTY-EIGHT

I SABEL HAD KNOWN HIM HALF HER LIFE. AND IN THAT TIME, THERE were days she found fault with Aidan, moments where slapping him upside the head seemed like the only action that would get through. Until five minutes ago, she'd blamed him for behavior that made his wedding-night confession seem like a slick-salesman pitch. But there, on the tarmac of Teterboro Airport, realizing what he'd done, that he'd done it for the sole purpose of satisfying his own self-serving agenda . . . Well, Isabel could not recall being angrier with him.

"Let me get this straight," she queried, heavier rain falling around them. "You bought 98.6—*The Normal FM* to make tonight happen, just to make this grandiose reentry into my life?"

"No. Not exactly. It didn't start out that way. But eventually . . . yes. I had to find a way to make contact, Isabel. I couldn't just show up at your door. I had to be invited." Aidan looked toward a fierce rumble of thunder. "Now, can we go? I hate like hell to think we went through this just to get struck by lightning." A wall of rain dropped between them, Isabel not budging. "Okay, so I knew it was a risk. I knew that you'd probably be a little irritated when you found out."

"A little irritated?" she said, hands drawing to her hips.

"Isabel, try to look at the bottom line. Changing the station format is a great idea. If my less than up-front approach caused any collateral damage, I'm sorry about that—I really am." While he offered the contrite explanation, she also sensed satisfaction, more or less blind to the havoc he'd caused. Typical Aidan.

"Are you kidding me!" she yelled. "Do you have any idea what you put everyone through—not to mention firing four perfectly good DJs!"

"I gave them each two years' severance pay and used C-Note connections to find them similar employment elsewhere. I thought that was fair."

"Fair? Sure, because people love being yanked from their jobs and having their lives thrown into turmoil for no other reason than to facilitate your *miscreant* plans! And did you even consider the chaos it caused the rest of us?" A vague expression said the concept was foreign, Isabel wondering how far the eccentricities went. "Oh my God, did you burn down Grassroots Kids too, our building?" With Aidan, you could never be completely sure.

"What? No, I didn't burn it down," he insisted, shaking his blond locks as rain flew off in every direction. "I read about Grassroots Kids in the newspaper, the story in the *Boston Globe*."

"You read a newspaper?"

There was a deadpan glare. "Must have been a weak moment!" She replied to his narrow-eyed look with one of her own. "For your information, I generally do my homework before making any investment—review the company portfolio, research financial statements, run a thorough margin analysis on returns—you know, the basics." Her head bobbed back, but she offered no rebuttal. "Now, can we go, before the weather gets worse and we can't get off the ground?"

"Aidan, people were terrified of losing their jobs, their insurance. Most of us don't have bank accounts the size of Mt. Rushmore!"

"Isabel, I understand you're upset. But I think you're overreacting. Maybe my motives were unorthodox, but I promise you, this will be a good thing."

Rain beat down as a chilly wind slapped around them. As far as Isabel was concerned, it couldn't slap him hard enough. "You just don't get it! Tanya and Mary Louise, they're real people with problems that to you, I'm sure, are insignificant. What you did, it absolutely turned their lives upside down. Did you know that Tanya has three kids she's practically raising alone? Do you know her child-support checks bounce on a regular basis?" His brow creased and he opened his mouth to speak, but she wouldn't let him make excuses. "Two of her kids have chronic illnesses. Imagine how she felt thinking her job was in real jeopardy. And then there's Mary Louise."

"Yeah, she seemed nice when I met her in your off—"

She refused to let him charm his way out of it. "Maybe Joe Bland falling off the roof and losing his job wasn't exactly your fault. And maybe he and Mary Louise could survive on recyclables . . ." His expression shifted, looking at Isabel as if she'd come a little unglued. "But he desperately needs his medical insurance. Add to that the huge fight Tanya and Mary Louise had when we couldn't find anybody to do the show. Good times, Aidan! Sharing the sordid details on a dirty linoleum floor, not having a clue if you'd help or laugh in my face—thinking you only showed up because your mother made you!" She slapped a hand to her soggy forehead, turning in a tight circle. "I'm an idiot! I've been punk'd by Aidan Royce!" The circle stopped, fists planted firmly on her hips. "I am *so* not getting on that plane with you! You self-centered, indulgent—jerk!" Isabel stormed across the tarmac doubting a speck of what she said would sink in.

Twenty feet into her retreat, an arm encircled her, whirling her around. "You forgot lazy!" In one fluid motion he hoisted her over his shoulder. Plowing through the rain, up the stairway of the plane, she kicked, pelting him with more choice words. "Close the door," he ordered. After the man on board secured it, Aidan put her down with a defiant thud. "You're not going anywhere without me."

Isabel stumbled back, her mouth gaping, out of fresh cuss words. With hair matted like a wet sheepdog, Isabel shook water from all of her, curtly folding and unfolding her arms. Her soaked heels squeaked as she shifted, imagining how she looked, mascara puddled into two black smears. She glanced down to see that it was all nicely complemented by a raunchy run in the black fishnets. One guess as to how that translated. The dress, plastered to her body, made an unattractive sucking sound as she peeled it away.

"This," Aidan said triumphantly, "is my wife, Isabel."

The man never flinched. "She's perfectly lovely, Mr. Royce."

"Ha!" Isabel snorted. "You must be the one they hired to understand him."

"Don't be rude, Isabel," Aidan said, removing his wet jacket, unbuttoning his shirt, handing it to him.

Oh, he would have to do that. She looked away.

"This is Henry Wilke. He takes care of everything in-flight. He's very reliable."

"Thank you, Mr. Royce," he said, apparently blind to the bizarre scene. "Can I get you something besides a dry shirt? Perhaps some hot tea and a towel for Mrs. Royce?"

His ability to keep a straight face was impressive, as if she was exactly what he anticipated regarding Aidan's wife. "Isabel," she insisted, though she didn't say Lang. "And a towel would be super."

"Very good, something else for you, sir? I made a fresh batch of iced tea with grapefruit juice and honey."

"You still drink that?"

"Yes, but it's not the stuff you used to make. Helps my throat, but that's about it."

"Wait," she said to a retreating Henry. "Red Bull."

"Pardon me?"

"Do you have a can of Red Bull on board? That's what it's missing."

"Red Bull?" Aidan said. "That's it?" She shrugged.

"I'm not sure we have Red Bull, but I believe we have some Rockstar on board."

Isabel rolled her eyes. "Of course you do. That'll work."

"Very good. I'll take care of it."

She sloshed into the cabin interior, looking around so she wouldn't have to look at a bare-chested Aidan. Isabel felt the engines rumble, or maybe it was her libido chiming in as she stole a glance. She couldn't speak for the polish, but they'd certainly applied the buff. And Isabel found herself wishing she'd kept up with her Y membership. "What's your plan, Aidan, to hold me hostage on your Learjet?" She paced the opulent interior. He was right, the plane she arrived on was nothing compared to this. It was a luxury hotel with wings.

"It's a Gulfstream," he said, buttoning the shirt Henry brought as she took the towel. After handing her another of Aidan's shirts and a pair of sweatpants, Henry placed a drink on the table, disappearing again. "And building them keeps thousands of people employed." She hummed at his feeble attempt to acknowledge the support of working-class people. "You're right. I'm sorry. I didn't think about any of those things. I didn't care about the radio station, though it will benefit from the new format. And even you have to admit using the proceeds for Grassroots Kids is a good idea."

"It's not the point." Holding on to the towel, Isabel dropped the dry clothing on a chair. She wasn't about to change in front of him, even if he was her husband. "You didn't have to go to such extremes, Aidan. You could have just called."

"No, I couldn't have. The radio station, the concert . . . well, if I made that much happen, I thought maybe things would . . ." He shrugged, firing up that innocent grin, the one he crafted all those years ago. "Fall into place."

Statistically, she supposed swooning at his feet was the appropriate reaction. *Right away.* "Well, you did a bang-up job." He took a step toward her. Just as fast, Isabel stepped back. In return for his effort all he received was the same critical glare she'd offer when he screwed up back in Catswallow. "Why now, after all this time?"

"When I saw the story in the *Boston Globe*, the effect wasn't . . . It wasn't the way a person should react. Not if it's over, not if it no longer matters."

While she couldn't grasp his grandiose scheme, she did understand that. "Because the opposite of love is indifference."

"Indifference has never been an option when it comes to you. Not in Catswallow, not in L.A., not halfway around the world." He looked hard at her. "Isabel, I need to know something. Something that goes way beyond radio station buyouts and big concerts. It's something that only became a possibility after Patrick explained the position Fitz put you in. In Las Vegas, on our wedding night . . ." His words stopped, the wrecked expression on his face finishing the thought.

"Aidan—"

He held up a hand. "Let me get this out. It's been stuck in my head for seven years. After what happened in Catswallow, what Rick Stanton almost did to you . . ." Isabel looked away, still rattled by the memory. "The way you reacted in Las Vegas, it scared the hell out of me. I thought that what happened between us in that hotel room, in bed . . . I honestly believed it was one step worse than what went down with Stanton."

Her head jerked back, her mouth gaping. She'd never put the two things together. Why would she? Unbeknownst to Aidan, it was the most incredible moment of her life. Of course he couldn't fix it with a phone call. No wonder he'd stayed away. All the way back to her protest over going to the Catswallow gala, Aidan had taken Isabel at her word. And for all his antics, including the radio station buyout, her deception—what she did in that Vegas hotel room—suddenly seemed far crueler.

"Given the way you left Vegas, obviously happiness wasn't something you were going to find being with me. And there was a hell of a reminder every day—big as a tattoo," he said, a hand running around his neck. "When the divorce papers arrived from you, what more proof did I need? Over time, I realized . . ."

"Realized what?"

"Realized that without you my destiny was fame and fortune and misery. But mostly misery. When Patrick told me what you did to keep me out of jail, to secure all this," he said, his arms spreading wide before him, "I suspected our wedding night wasn't what it appeared."

"Fitz, he, um, he didn't give me any choice. I couldn't let you go to jail. And after I left Vegas everything started to change, just like he said it would. I saw your picture everywhere, with other women—glamorous actresses, royalty, Southern debutants . . . whatever," she whispered, going down a list that went all the way back to Catswallow.

"One sentence, Isabel. That's all it would have taken and none of those things would have ever happened. We would have celebrated the six anniversaries before this one."

"From where, Aidan? The visitors center at the Bullock Correctional Facility? Not if I had anything to say about it."

He rejected her reasoning, angrier than she was on the tarmac. "You should have told me! I had a right to know!"

"I'm . . . I'm sorry. After you went to California, after the divorce . . ." But her words were lame and years too late. "And it wasn't just what Fitz threatened. Or even the idea of other women." Staid blue eyes darted from the floor to her, waiting for Isabel to explain why she never came after him. "What Fitz did, it only meant I didn't have to face my fears. Think about it, I could barely handle the idea of *us* inside the confines of an old farmhouse. What he did was cruel and totally over the line. But he wasn't completely wrong. I wasn't ready for the reality of being Aidan Royce—or even Aidan Roycroft's wife. I was too afraid of all of it," she said, confessing the fragile thought. "I'm still afraid of it. You only have to look as far as where I work to see the proof. A radio station that had all but banned you! Do you have any idea how hard it is to get away from Aidan Royce?"

"Actually, I do. Someday, I'll tell you how the son of a bitch nearly killed me." And in his face she saw something that assured her it had cost more than it was worth. "Seems our mutual misconceptions go both ways." He picked up the drink, downing it like it was ninety proof. "Care to guess what your wedding-night performance cost me in therapy?"

It drew a bug-eyed stare. "But that's not what happened."

"For years I told myself that letting you go was the right thing. Knowing that you were safe, that you'd made some kind of peace with your father was my only consolation." Aidan sat on the sofa, Isabel sitting in the leather chair across from him. An old ease sat down with them. "But the second I walked into your office, every doubt, every question, even the ones I had no answer for went away."

Henry returned, informing them that they were prepared for takeoff. The dampness of her clothes had turned to a chill and Isabel wrapped her arms tight. Aidan got up and retrieved a blanket, attempting to drape it around her. She flinched. It was as unexpected to him as it was to her. Being in a room with Aidan and physical contact, they were such different things. He handed it to her, despondently turning away. Maybe it was sensory overload. She couldn't take anything else in. "It can't be that simple, Aidan. We're not the same people we were in Catswallow. Even then, I was never *one of them* . . . your girlfriend."

"Actually, Isabel, I think that's the reason it's lasted," he said as the cabin lights dimmed. "In case you never noticed, my track record with girlfriends pretty much sucks." There was a hum of agreement as she wrapped the blanket tight. "And maybe you never have been my girlfriend, but you're the only woman I've ever really wanted to be my wife."

The frown curved upward, Isabel spinning in the chair to face the window. The plane rose against a black sky, rain trickling across the glass. She could feel Aidan's eyes on her. As the lightning flashed she saw his reflection in the pane. His grim face was more ominous than the storm. She turned and he leaned forward, elbows resting on his knees, fingers locked together.

"I meant what I said to Fitz. If I had to choose, I'd choose you. I told you that on our wedding night." He was quiet, the moment drifting to one of those endless pauses she hated. He put a fine point on things by pulling a thin gold band from his pocket, placing it on the table between them. The sight of it drew a shaky breath from Isabel, and she watched it seep solidly into him. "Once we get where we're going, I don't need to leave again. Sony doesn't have that contract yet. One phone call to Patrick and I'll happily retire, take up fly fishing, maybe woodworking." Isabel inched back, her head cocking. "Okay, so I'll have to work on a hobby list. But my point is the same as it was back in Vegas. I'll do whatever it takes to keep us together." He hesitated, all of him so serious she didn't dare interrupt. "But here's the thing. When you factor out the smoke and mirrors, it seems to me that I'm the one who's known exactly what he's wanted—how much and for how long. You, on the other hand, have made a spectator sport out of running away from me. You have to believe in us, Isabel, as much as I do or it's never going to work. It *is* that simple." He got up and disappeared through a galley into another room.

CHAPTER THIRTY-NINE

OKAY, SO WHEN DID HE BECOME SUCH A WELL-ROUNDED, insightful individual? Curling tight in the chair, Isabel pulled the blanket to her chin, staring at the ring. She should grab it, because if this were a merry-go-round, it would be brass. But things were always easier to handle when Aidan was romantically out of her reach. She didn't touch it. It had the luster of a dream; it wasn't supposed to come to life. How could he ever live up to it? How could she? Nuzzling into the blanket she closed her eyes, trying to imagine what might happen if she let go of gravity.

Minutes passed as the plane bumped and shimmied, Isabel sensing that gravity had become a pertinent issue. The turbulence swelled, leaving her to wonder if a Gulfstream was as safe as a Learjet. Did Aidan do the research, or did the plane just catch his eye? They bounced around more like high seas than rough air. The lightning seemed remarkably close. Isabel looked behind her; Henry wasn't anywhere. Maybe he'd gone for the parachutes. Ignoring standard safety rules, Isabel unbuckled the seat belt and stood, the next bump putting her right back in the chair. She stood again with a single thought in mind: *If they were going down, if this was it,*

Aidan wasn't getting the last word. But as Isabel shuffled forward, negotiating the unsteady cabin, the ring caught her eye. It moved in the wake of the turbulence, vibrating fast to the table's edge. Instinctively, she dropped to her knees and caught the ring, her hand closing tight around it. Her fist turned palm up, her fingers slowly unfurling. The token band of metal, it wasn't even a Cracker Jack prize in Aidan's wild world—yet he'd hung on to it as if it were his greatest treasure. Her fingertips brushed over it, realizing what it meant to him. Clear enough. But what did the ring mean to her?

Sure she was angry with Aidan; who wouldn't be after the stunt he'd pulled at the radio station? Although his motive wasn't nearly as indulgent as she'd initially assumed. A breath stuttered out; it all but crushed her to absorb the ingrained reasons Aidan had stayed away for so long. The plane shimmied harder. Isabel's fist closed around the ring, drawing it tight to her body where it would be safe. Now that she had it back, the thought of losing it was inconceivable. It belonged to her. *He belonged to her.* There had been a life and goals and another lover, all of it within her reach. In theory, in conversation, in fact, it was a noble ending. But none of it made her quite whole, because none of it included Aidan. Fighting the uneven air on which the moment balanced, Isabel stood steady and tucked the ring in her pocket.

Making her way through the galley, she found Henry engrossed in a romance novel. She recognized the title. He appeared oblivious to the rough ride. "Um, it has a good ending. When he wakes up from the coma, they live happily ever after."

He smiled and nodded. "Is there something I can get for you, Mrs.—Isabel?"

"No, I'm good," she said, gripping the cabinetry. They traded awkward glances. While Isabel felt compelled to offer some explanation for what she wanted, he didn't seem to be waiting for one. "Well, I just wanted to know . . ."

"Yes?" he said, closing the book.

Her hand brushed over her pocket. "Aidan. He's in there?"

He smiled again. "You know, the pilots might like that cup of tea. I'll be in the forward cabin for the rest of the flight." He unbuckled his seat belt and disappeared into the front section of the plane.

On her left was a bathroom. Isabel made a cursory stop, checking the damage. It wasn't so bad. The mascara hadn't smeared. It was just gone. In fact, most of her makeup had washed away as wavy damp hair fell around her shoulders. Fingertips rose to her reflection. Misty green eyes, a nose that denoted character, and a resemblance she'd have forever. Happy with the image, it was certainly more confident than years ago. Maybe, all along, this was what Aidan saw.

Opening the door, she was surprised to find a bedroom. Sitting in the middle of the bed was Aidan, plucking at a guitar. He'd changed out of the suit pants, wearing a worn pair of jeans. That much was a familiar sight. A television flickered from behind her, the sound muted. Aside from the shuddering, she could forget they were on an airplane. But what she couldn't overlook, what she didn't want to forget was the fantastic flutter in her belly. Only Aidan could coax such an acute vulnerability to the surface.

"Turbulence bothering you?" he asked, looking up.

"How'd you know?"

"I know you. It's beyond your control."

"Aidan—" She hesitated. "The turbulence isn't the only thing throwing me off balance."

He put the guitar aside, folding his arms. "If you mean us, I can't help that, Isabel. I don't want to."

He wasn't going to make this easy. Why should he? After what she'd put him through back in Vegas, he had a right to some assurances. He had a right to be angrier than she was over any radio station buyout. "Aidan, I . . . On our wedding night, what I made you believe, it had nothing to do with anything that was in my head."

"Meaning?"

"Meaning . . ." She stopped, having trouble linking the intimate emotions with simple words. It was overwhelming. "Meaning it was incredible, that I never wanted anything more in my life." Silence was all she got in return, the same look she'd give him when demanding alternative behavior. "Meaning I've never felt that way—not with anyone." It was more than he wished to know, the fact diverting his glance as his own vulnerability surfaced. In the small space she took big steps, knees pressed to the bed. "Meaning I thought about what you said. I considered everything you did— why you did it."

"And?" he said, looking back at her.

"And I'd give anything for you to make me feel that way again." He didn't move. It was agony, perhaps a bit of payback, making her wait for a reply. He still didn't speak. Instead, he got out of the bed and circled her. Isabel didn't turn, Aidan standing behind her. His voice was soft. Isabel was certain that her heart was pounding decibels louder—an unspoken code she thought was long lost.

"You understand that this is an even playing field. That you won't be in control."

His hand touched her waist and her eyes closed tight. "I appreciate the control part, but I don't know about an even playing field." As much as she wanted this, a tiny piece of Isabel made itself known, not wanting to give in to those fragile feelings.

"I can't help that either." His hand pushed her hair over one shoulder. "I don't want to." For a moment there was nothing— nothing but Aidan, which in the past was too much. But a more mature instinct also seemed present. It made Isabel want more. He accommodated and she felt the dress's zipper slide. There was

cool recycled air, the wild warmth of Aidan's mouth making contact with her bare back. She drew a long shaky breath that he had
to feel. She knew he did, pulling her tight to him, almost holding
her up. "Your choice, Isabel. But if you turn, game over." She
considered the tight proximity, if she could get to the door before
he got to her. Of course, they were on an airplane. Where would
she go? Perhaps that was part of his plan. Her head tilted back,
eyes closed tight as his mouth met with her neck. The kisses were
soft and safe, a sharp contrast to his hands, which moved with
more obvious intent—across her stomach, over her breasts. If she
wanted this, she had to trust him. She stood straight, the less passionate motion causing Aidan's hands to drop. She hesitated. He
waited. Slowly, Isabel chose to turn, high heels bringing them as
close to even as they were going to get.

"I surrender," she said, a soft shrug to her shoulder.

He was done with boundaries, capturing her with a singular
kiss, Isabel's response a reflex. With his arms fast around her, there
was husky confession from Aidan, "Do you have any idea how
fucking great you kiss?" The abrupt assertion was warm and rattling, Isabel thinking, *Ditto,* but unable to find her voice. "I've
wanted to say that since I stole a Jolly Rancher right out of your
mouth." The long-overdue information caused her gaze to dip. It
passed by the open button on his jeans before settling on his bare
feet. "No," he said, "look at me." She obeyed. "Don't stop looking
at me." Her only response was the sharp bob to her throat. In any
other situation, disrobing from the damp dress would have proved
an awkward act. But Aidan unwrapped her like that prize piece
of candy, all of her crinkling with anticipation. It was a submissive
visual that heightened vulnerability, weakening any control. And
perhaps, she thought she even liked it. He kissed her again, Isabel's
fingers gathering fists full of the cotton shirt he wore. Aidan
reached up, undoing her grip. "No again." She blinked at his

insistent tone. "I don't want anything between us, Isabel. Nothing to hang on to but me." Quickly unbuttoning one more button, he dragged the shirt over his head and tossed it aside. For a moment she didn't know what to do with her hands. "And remember what I said." Her wandering gaze made up for the nervous flutter that her hands wanted to express. An edgy glance locked on his, recalling the instruction. Solid eye contact put her at ease, her hands finding their place, touching him. Aidan kissed her again, Isabel reaching hungrily for another. He didn't oblige, moving a half step back. Apparently, the rule regarding focus did not apply to him as Aidan's eyes moved decidedly down her body. She hung onto a thin veneer of control, allowing him to look. "When, um . . . when did you start wearing thigh-high fishnets and lacy black bras?" There was a fluster in his voice, telling Isabel that he was as affected as her.

"Tonight," she answered. "I guess I wanted to look the part."

"It's, um, beautiful," he gulped. His eyes jerked back to hers. "But you own the part—no special wardrobe required." From there a slow fire began to smolder, Aidan offering the kisses he'd withheld. She kissed him back, their mouths meeting a rhythm they'd only flirted with before. With perfect timing, he unhooked her bra as Isabel reached for the zipper on his jeans. She kicked off the heels, the two of them landing on the bed where almost nothing was between them but a pair of thigh-high fishnets.

"Do you want me to take the stock—"

"On," he insisted, his mouth and hands traveling south, peeling off her underwear, "just leave them fucking on." The combination of curse word and hard order pulsed through Isabel, letting the last bits of control fade. Small kisses rocked between stocking and skin as his hands, slightly more anxious, pushed her legs apart. His fingers found their way inside her. Isabel gasped at an onslaught of sensations, his mouth meeting with an even more sensitive spot. She'd never experienced such a stirring, everything she felt for him marrying with this one decadent act. Her body pressed harder toward him, wanting to lasso the feeling. It reached a pinnacle, his tongue moving with precise fiery strokes. It told her to let go, that perhaps walking around in such a state would prove counterproductive. At the second Aidan intended, it crushed around her, sending Isabel miles outside her comfort zone. She wanted to reach for him, unable to determine up from down, much less a moving target. Moments later, Aidan rose over her. A wider than usual grin was anchored to his face. "Good to know."

"What's that?" she asked, her voice ragged, her stomach rising and falling, breathless, the lone participant in an Aidan Royce marathon.

"It's clear that money and fame aren't going to hold your attention. I think I may have stumbled on something that will."

"A definite possibility," she said, giggling at his discovery. "If we weren't already married, I'd demand it in a prenup."

"Well, wouldn't the lawyers have had fun with that?"

With an unexpected burst of energy she caught him off guard, pushing against his shoulders, Aidan finding himself flat on the bed. It wasn't control but the desire to return the erotic spell—well, perhaps a little control. Lingering kisses made their way from the split of the snake's tongue, dipping past its painted coiled bottom and across Aidan's smooth chest. At first he seemed all for it, Isabel arriving to the point where even the edge of European-cut briefs would be challenged. But as she settled in at his waist, he stopped her, pulling Isabel back to him.

"Not this time," he said, though a wavering voice disagreed.

"Why not?"

"Because there's something else I'd rather you did for me. Something a little wicked." He hesitated before asking, "How do you feel about fantasies?"

"Fantasies?" she said, her own voice vacillating. "Um, sure. I don't know much about that sort of . . . *thing*, only bits of Mary Louise's phone conversations with Joe. Stuff you don't really want to hear but do . . ." The rambling stopped as her gaze flitted about, looking for battery-required paraphernalia, perhaps an out-of-place riding crop. Mary Louise, who wouldn't know a stallion from a mule, mentioned those a lot.

His own glance followed hers around the room, a mischievous smile settling on Isabel. She recognized the look. He'd thoroughly rattled her and he was enjoying it. Propping himself on an elbow, Aidan's expression darkened as his mood turned tawdry. She braced for impact, reminding herself that his experiences covered the gamut while hers covered . . . well, Rhode Island. "What I want," he said, his tone pure demand, his forehead bumping against hers, "more than anything, Isabel, is our wedding night."

"Our wed—" She broke contact, trepidation assuaged. "Is that where we're going, to Las Vegas?" Aidan's brow furrowed, as if he'd forgotten he was on a plane, destination unknown—at least to her.

"Vegas? No. I don't need that much of a visual. Believe me, this is definitely happening right here, right now." As if to prove his point, in one deft moment she was under him, the angle fitting like a puzzle piece. "Isabel, I want the moment Fitz Landrey stole from us. I want what should have been." And in his voice was the same sincerity she'd heard seven years before, almost to the moment. "Since that god-awful night, between the highs that came out of this lottery ticket life and the ones that came out of a bottle, there was that. This beautifully broken thing inside me, haunting me, no matter where I went—in the world or in my head. I've survived off the fantasy of fixing it. And now, here you are. Here we are and I, well, I was wondering if you'd—"

A sudden kiss ended his plea. His body pressed tight to hers, Isabel wanting nothing more than to deliver Aidan Royce's fantasy.

With his request came a wave of empowerment. She was the only person who could make that happen. Tracing his face with her fingertips, she whispered, "I'm in."

A gusty burst of passion took them from there. Aidan knew exactly what he wanted, making love to Isabel like this was, indeed, the first time. But the moment intensified as two adults broached an echelon that might have eluded two teenagers. In between the fervent moments, Isabel indulged in small things that even indifference never let her forget. There was the sharing of skin, Aidan's feet tangling with hers, a hand gliding over her hip. It was breathless and fearless and endless, everything slipping perfectly into place. Perfectly until a frustrated curse word slipped from Aidan's mouth. "What?" she gasped, a leg hooked hard around his.

"Nothing," he said, from the edge of his fantasy, which was about to come to fruition. But at the last second he stopped again. "I don't have a condom."

"You don't have a condom," she repeated, fingers digging harder into his shoulders. "You're kidding, right? You've had a condom in your wallet since I've known you!"

He squinted at her. "You'd be amazed how the lack of one will make you think twice. You're not on—"

She shook her head. "Plan B would be my usual go-to method . . ."

He offered a quizzical look. "I thought I was just upgraded to plan A?"

She laughed. "Plan B is emergency contraception. You buy it over the counter, at the pharmacy. You could . . . well, you could ask Henry if he has one."

"I'm not asking my flight attendant if he has a spare condom!" He groaned, his body hitting the mattress with a thud. "I don't believe this. After . . . Wait," he said, springing back up. "Why do we need one?"

"Your flight attendant? He seems so conscientious, helpful . . ."

He narrowed his eyes at the familiar lobbing of humor, clearly not amused. "Seriously, Isabel, think about it. As part of Sony's contract, I just had a complete physical. I'm in perfect health," he announced. "And I'm sure you . . ."

"Don't need to ask," she offered. "While that's good information, Aidan, aren't you skipping the obvious?"

"I don't think so," he said, sealing any gap between them, settling into a position as old as mankind. "Let's see. If you want to talk old-fashioned values and fidelity, we are married."

"You know, your public may never believe it, but the institution suits you." He kissed her softly, his body matching the same gentle ease as it made a natural progression.

"And if I recall," he said, breathing her in, "there was an agreement about waiting and comparing notes. I kept my end." He turned his head, offering a bird's-eye view of the snake. "You may have to make good on yours."

"Interesting spin," she said, gripping his body with a tad more aggression than he took with hers. "But I'm not sure I'm over the honeymoon phase yet." Nothing ever felt as perfect, Isabel gladly forfeiting the argument.

"Of course, sometimes these things don't happen overnight," he said, slipping into a seductive rhythm. It was like *feeling* Aidan sing. "But if it did, well, I don't think anything would make me happier."

Closing her eyes, she didn't want him to see the tears. They were hysterically happy tears, but she feared he'd draw the wrong conclusion. "I don't know if this theory works in reverse," she whispered. "But I want you to know, I love you, Aidan. I've always loved you."

CHAPTER FORTY

T HE ALTITUDE EVENTUALLY DROPPED AND THE LANDING GEAR locked. Isabel's hand trailed fluidly over his body, thinking that staying in that aerodynamic hollow of bliss had great appeal. Couldn't they just fly somewhere else? But she supposed, even if you owned the plane, you were expected to get off when it landed. Reluctantly, they slipped into their clothes. Isabel's hand brushed over the pocket of the dress. "Aidan?"

"Yeah," he said, zipping his pants, buttoning his shirt.

She held the ring out in the palm of her hand. "Would you . . ."

He smiled, picking it up. "You know," he said, sliding it onto her finger, sealing it with a kiss. "I must look pretty cheap. All these years and no engagement ring. We'll have to take care of that."

Admiring the sweet but simple band, she smiled back. "It's not a terrible idea. But I could say the same thing. I don't see any ring on your finger."

"I'd like that," he said more solemnly than one might expect from someone in his line of work.

Padding out to the main cabin, she'd pocketed her watch, asking Aidan what time it was. He looked at her as if she'd asked him to repeat a grocery list from memory. "You don't own a watch, do you?"

"I'm sure . . . somewhere."

"Just past four," Henry offered.

She looked out the window into a predawn morning, clueless as to where they were. "Aidan, are you going to tell me—"

"No," he said. "I'm not. So quit asking."

He took her hand, heading toward the exit. Aidan stopped to greet the pilots, thanking them for a safe flight. Isabel smiled, hearing the pride in Aidan's voice as he introduced her as his wife. They deplaned and in the shadowy distance Isabel could see a small parking lot of aircraft, a couple of hangars. It was lit, but there were no signs, nothing to indicate where they'd landed. As they walked she recognized the smell in the air; summer heat was in full swing.

"Um, this way," he said, taking a moment to get his bearings. He produced a set of keys, hitting the unlock button until an SUV responded, flashing its lights. "Here we are."

"Your car?"

"Ours," he said, opening the door for her. "Everything," he emphasized, "is ours."

They drove for a time, Isabel content to hold his hand, watching civilization thin until pavement turned to a little used country road. A massive gate bordered a once dusty drive; Aidan stopped, punching a code into a piece of technology that did look marginally out of place. "It's set to your birthday," he said, driving through. They drove past an orchard and a graveyard. A muddy spring day dawned on Isabel, the wave of construction vehicles she'd passed on her retreat. She'd driven there in search of safety and peace, standing on the farmhouse porch where she was sure the echo of guitar music was nothing more than a memory. "Aidan, were you here in early spring?"

"Yeah, I was," he said, the SUV's lights illuminating his plan. "Right after I got back from Asia, right after I decided to put everything I had into this." On the footprint of the old farmhouse was a stunning replica. "How did you know that?"

She looked between the house and him. "Just a feeling," she said, a quiver in her throat. The moon, she guessed, was on Aidan's payroll, as clouds parted and a path of light fell over the house. "Aidan, this is incredible."

"We couldn't save the farmhouse; it was too far gone. This house was built on its foundation. It became my project hope, hoping you'd come home to it."

"It's so big," she said, thinking two moons might do a better job of showcasing it.

"It's not that big," he insisted, his arms wrapping around from behind. "I tried to make it what you'd want. I really couldn't picture you rambling around a West Coast mansion—not full-time anyway." He paused, kissing her neck. "But if you don't like it, we can buy something else, anywhere you want."

"Maybe a vacation home in Maui too?" she teased, glancing over her shoulder.

"Isabel," he said, spinning her around to face him. "You can have anything you want for the rest of your life." There was wide playful grin. "It's an obscene amount of money. I was hoping you'd help me figure out what to do with it—coast-to-coast Grassroots Kids complexes maybe? Patrick will help with whatever you decide. Do whatever you like, because I have the only thing I want."

Gazing into his sure expression, a twinge of his incredible life sunk in. "Are you sure, Aidan? I'll be enough, or maybe even too much. It's worth asking yourself. Will I fit into your life, because—"

"Isabel," he said, both hands cupping her face.

She cut him off. "You know it's never been my nature to make things easy for you. I don't think that's changed."

"Isabel," he repeated. "I wouldn't want it any other way. You've always been my balance . . . my gravity. And to be honest, I think I do a pretty good job of being yours."

She took a deep breath. "This is going to take some getting used to. My life, my job at the radio station, even Grassroots Kids, none of it is anything like . . ." She stopped, the profound changes registering. "My whole life will be different . . . everything." Isabel held tight, appreciating how abandoned he must have felt in that Vegas hotel room. "Was it hard, Aidan, adjusting to everything without me? Because I can't imagine doing any of this without you; I wouldn't want to."

"The truth?" he asked, holding her even tighter. "I almost failed. But eventually it forced me to grow up. The more I had, the less I wanted it." Aidan inched back, smiling. "But we'll talk about adjustments later, tomorrow . . . in a week or so." The grin widened. "I promise, Isabel, the money, it's really not a bad problem to have. For now, why don't we just go inside?"

The door swung open and the rest of Aidan's hardcore fantasy came to life. As promised, it wasn't too much but comfortable and warm. She stepped into a great room with a huge cathedral ceiling, a stone fireplace soaring to its wood-beamed peak. There was a giddy flutter inside, picturing a massive Christmas tree on the far wall. On a table near the fireplace was a tiny framed photo. Picking it up, she ran her hand over the snapshot of them kissing in a Vegas photo booth.

"I found that in the pocket of my tux. I knew you took the others, our marriage license. I guess, over time, I read what I wanted into that."

"I guess you read right," she said, putting it back. Isabel took another look around the brand-new place that felt very much like home. Aidan followed, watching.

"I made sure there was enough furniture so we'd have

somewhere to sit, but I thought you might like to pick the rest out yourself. Girls like to do that kind of stuff, right?"

Her hand brushed over the stone of the fireplace, taking it all in before turning toward him. Time offered Isabel the fantastic favor of standing still. In the middle of the farmhouse she saw Aidan. His shirttails hung out, shaggy blond hair looking wind-blown, a chiseled smile anchored to his ridiculously handsome face. "Yeah," she said, giving up on blinking back tears. "Girls like that stuff." Her fingertips trailed over the back of a vintage leather sofa. "This is beautiful."

He read her mind. "It's out in the barn if you want to visit."

ALTHOUGH THERE WERE BLINDS, THE SUN POKED THROUGH THE bedroom window. Isabel rolled over in time to see a powerful laser-like beam of light across Aidan's face. He groaned softly in his sleep, turning his head away. He had to be tired. She certainly was. The sun crept up not long after they'd gone to bed. Everything in the bedroom was as comfortable as the rest of the house. But Isabel was too excited to be still. Slipping from beneath the covers, she took a thick cotton robe from the back of an overstuffed chair. It was like living with elves. Before leaving the bedroom she glanced back, admiring a sleeping Aidan. Even with the sun on his face he looked at peace. While elves made for an amusing visual, Isabel was relieved to find there wasn't anyone in the kitchen whipping up a gourmet breakfast—or lunch. She smiled, realizing she didn't have a clue about the time. Better yet, it didn't matter. After taking a daylight tour of their house, Isabel ambled outside. It was reminiscent of the old farmhouse, mirroring its easy low-country style, but she couldn't say the same for the grounds. Overgrown and unkempt for years before she and Aidan showed up, he must have employed every landscaper in the county, maybe the state. Captivated, she walked to the middle of the apple orchard, remembering how they fought worms and bugs for a few good ones. Come fall, there would be a bumper crop. Even the smallest touches were tended to, a new wrought-iron fence around the Kessler family plot, the ground perfectly manicured. Seeing Aidan come across the yard, she sensed a shift in family ownership, their roots firmly planted.

"Did you think I ran away?" she asked as he greeted her with a kiss.

"Nah, I just missed you." Hand in hand they roamed the grounds, admiring the deep green views and outbuildings that were now in perfect repair. As they walked, Isabel noted the tall stone-and-iron fencing, discreet and decorative as it was. She imagined it was a necessary evil. "Isabel, I was thinking, what you said about what I put everybody through at the radio station, Mary Louise and Tanya in particular."

"Maybe I was a little hard on you," she said, feeling rather forgiving today. "Like you said, the format change will be a positive thing."

"Yeah, but I want to make it up to them. I want to give it to them."

"The radio station? You want to give Mary Louise and Tanya the radio station? Aidan, you can't just—" She shut up, realizing he could. He could hand it over gift-wrapped if he wanted. "That's very generous. I'm sure they'd be thrilled."

"Good, so, they'll have the radio station. And you'll be working with Grassroots Kids and Patrick. And I'll be . . ." He shoved his hands in his back pockets, turning, surveying the acreage. "Farming. I can take up farming."

"Farming," she said, arms folded, following as he walked backward.

"Yeah, farming," he said, nodding hard. "I have to do *something*, Isabel."

"Fine by me. It would certainly take up your time. But that's a pretty tough life. Have you thought about it? Long hours, lots of manual labor." He shrugged, squinting toward miles of rolling pasture.

"I could do it . . . if I had to—be a farmer."

"Noble profession. But you do realize farming involves dirt, up at sunrise, back-breaking labor, zero time for anything lazy or indulgent?"

"Whatever it takes," he said, running a hand along brilliant hibiscus.

"I don't know, Aidan. Maybe you should think about it. Farming isn't for everyone. Why don't you postpone agriculture for a few years, pursue something more suited to your natural skill set?"

"You think?" He ran his hand around the snake, sighing. "Well, there is my portfolio, but that's more about growing investments than a steady job. Otherwise, I'm not sure I have many marketable skills. Not the kind that would get a second career off the ground."

"Hmm, that does sound like a problem. But if you're serious about a second career, you may have to start at the bottom." She bit down on a thumbnail as she walked, looking him over. "You know, Piggly Wiggly never could hang on to a night stock manager. Your math skills would be a plus, maybe even your Spanish, and you don't mind staying up late."

"Piggly Wiggly, wow. I hadn't thought about that. I'll swing by, pick up an application tomorrow. But if it doesn't pan out maybe . . . Never mind, it's a crazy idea."

"No, tell me. I want to hear it."

"Well, just as a backup plan, I did hear that Sony has an opening. They're, um, they're looking for a rock star. The hours suck, but it's no worse than night stock manager at Pigs. I bet it pays better too."

Isabel stopped in her tracks, playfully slapping his arm. "Aidan, that's genius! That's what you should do! I've heard you sing, you can carry a decent tune." She looked him up and down. "With a little work, you can probably pull off the image."

He tugged on her arms until she was in his. "Only if you're sure. Only if it's what we want."

"Aidan, it's who you are. I've known it since the day we brought that first guitar here. I'd never want to take that away."

"Okay then," he said, his focus on a pastoral stretch of land behind the house. "Instead of forty acres of corn, I was thinking we could use that land for something else."

"Something else?"

"That acreage, it's the perfect spot for a recording studio."

She leaned into him, laughing. "A recording studio?"

"Yeah, the ultimate work-from-home office. Come on," he said, pulling her by the hand. "I'll show you where."